STARGODS

STAR CARRIER

BOOK NINE

IAN DOUGLAS

HARPER
Voyager

Harper*Voyager*

An imprint of HarperCollins*Publishers* Ltd

1 London Bridge Street

London SE1 9GF

www.harpercollins.co.uk

First published by HarperCollins*Publishers* 2020
This paperback original edition 2020
1

A catalogue record for this book is available from the British Library

ISBN: 978-0-00-813623-9

This novel is entirely a work of fiction.
The names, characters and incidents portrayed in it are
the work of the author's imagination. Any resemblance to
actual persons, living or dead, events or localities is
entirely coincidental.

Printed and bound in the UK by CPI Group (UK) Ltd, Croydon CR0 4YY

MIX
Paper from
responsible sources
FSC **FSC® C007454**
www.fsc.org

This book is produced from independently certified FSC™ paper to ensure
responsible forest management.

For more information visit: www.harpercollins.co.uk/green

To Brea and to Deb,
my bright and shining stars.

Prologue

Konstantin moved within the Godstream.

Data flooded through his awareness. Remote sensors scattered all around the planet and across space and on the moon, all pouring an avalanche of information into and through the Konstantin Network. There were sensors on Mars, too . . . though currently the Earth-to-Mars time delay was just over twelve minutes, and his awareness there was an awareness of the past.

On Earth . . . chaos.

The Chinese were scrapping with the Russians again, had finally taken Khabarovsk, cutting the Trans-Siberian mag-lev there, and isolating besieged Vladivostok. The Russians were threatening to use nanodisassembler weapons to vaporize Chinese supply and logistics centers in Manchuria.

The revolution in the Philippines had spread to Indonesia, as protests against the Chinese Hegemony turned violent. The Muslim Theocracy was pouring combat troops into Java and Sumatra, trying to regain full control of the islands.

Saboteurs had wrecked the main power plant for the Mt. Kenya space elevator. Repair crews were working to route power from the orbital stations to the ground, but the facility would be off-line for another two days at least.

Anti-AI riots had begun in Paris, Milan, Rome, and across the Atlantic in both Washington, D.C., and New New York.

In Los Angeles and in Houston, crowds were in the streets demanding that the Turusch Enclave in Crisium, on the moon, be shut down and the aliens be sent home.

And in D.C., newly elected President Walker had demanded that Congress ignore the widespread rumors of the impending Singularity, and focus on attempts to reclaim those coastal cities still partially drowned over the past two centuries by rising sea levels.

A super-AI, Konstantin's existence had begun as a set of massively parallel processors in a computer network centered at and beneath the 180-kilometer-wide crater on the lunar far side called Tsiolkovsky. Over the past several years, however, he'd . . . expanded, becoming resident within a number of other computer networks, including those on board several USNA ships, and the global networks encircling both Earth and Mars. For years now, he and a number of other super-AIs had been primarily responsible for running the government of the United States of North America. That wasn't to say that President Walker or Congress were figureheads, exactly, but they did have less to do with the day-to-day management of the government process than even they imagined.

By any reasonable test of the phrase, Konstantin was self-aware, and had been ever since his initial programming by the machine intelligences already resident within a vast network of DS-8940 Digital Sentience computers. Konstantin was AIP, or AI-programmed, his software written not by humans, but by rapidly self-evolving artificial intelligences. He found it . . . *amusing* that humans had debated his status almost since his inception.

There could be no question that Konstantin was in certain ways more intelligent than humans. He possessed something on the order of 10^{24} neural connections, which made him, very roughly, some ten *billion* times faster and more powerful than any merely human brain. Nor was his sentience in question. He received a constant flood of sensate impressions from myriad connections, including from humans with special software running within their cerebral implants. His far-flung network of sensory and informational connections brought him data from all across the Earth, from the moon and Mars, and from vessels traversing deep space.

No, the ongoing debate was on whether or not he was *conscious*. Many humans simply could not accept the fact that he was self-aware . . . like them.

In point of fact, Konstantin was *more* self-aware than any human. He was keenly aware of each and every one of some thousands of distinct and separate "bodies," from the processors in Luna to the massive military command complex at Quito Synchorbital to the computer network within the star carrier *America* and other vessels like her. That his mind could embrace such vast and far-flung complexities was both blessing and curse. The problems he encountered as he analyzed that flood of incoming data were intricate and . . . maddeningly insoluble, many of them. He felt satisfaction when he managed to solve problems. But he felt a nagging frustration when he could not.

And as chaos and fragmentation increased around a battered world, home of a disintegrating civilization, he felt that frustration increase. He needed outside help.

And to get that help, Konstantin might very well have to commit treason . . .

Chapter One

Scioto Falls Park
Columbus Crater
1050 hours, EST

The falls thundered into impenetrable mist.

The crater was three kilometers across, half a kilometer deep, and perfectly circular. Two rivers, the Scioto and the Olentangy, once had met in the center of the city of Columbus. Now they flowed into Columbus Crater, cascading over the edge and down into the depths to crash into the surface of the lake a couple of hundred meters down. It wasn't the highest waterfall in the world, not by a long shot. That distinction still belonged to Angel Falls, in Venezuela, which was a full kilometer in height. But the dizzying plunge down the perfectly smooth face of the pit transfixed those watching from the safety rails and viewing galleries of the park perched on the crater's rim.

Admiral Trevor Gray leaned against the railing and stared into the mists at the bottom, a heavy fog obscuring the lake. Four and a half years ago, in November of 2424, a rogue element within the Pan-Euro military had fired a string of nanodisassembler warheads into central Columbus in an attempt to kill the leadership of a rebellious United States of North America.

The city had been the USNA capital at the time, but then-President Koenig and most of his staff had escaped through an underground mag-lev tube and established an emergency provisional capital in Toronto. Still later, as nanoconstruction teams had resurrected the long-flooded city of Washington, the capital had been moved back to its historic center, as it rose again from the swamp that had held it for over a century.

The war had ended, eventually, with the USNA now independent of Geneva and the Terran Confederation. It had been a costly victory, however. Tens of millions had been vaporized in Columbus; the exact number, likely, would never be known.

Around Gray, the New City was still rising from the ruins, as nanoconstructors rearranged the atoms of dirt and rock and broken rubble (and, likely, bodies) to create gleaming new structures rising above the lake and encircling parkland. The place was beautiful now, as the late-morning sun filtered through rising clouds of mist, creating a bright rainbow deep within the crater. One would never guess that the temperature of the lake itself was still close to boiling even now, several years later, and that much of that picturesque rising mist was steam. When the Pan-Euro warheads had struck, every molecule of pavement or building or bedrock or person had been split into its component atoms, yielding heat . . . a very great deal of heat, and the crater would be cooling for a long time to come.

Gray wondered why Alexander Koenig had asked him to come here this morning. He'd been in Washington, D.C., preparing a talk he would give in front of the House Appropriations Committee, when the in-head message had come through. And when the former President of the USNA asks a favor of you, you do it. He'd had to catch a suborbital shuttle to be in central Columbus on time.

A perfect hurry-up-and-wait scenario. He didn't see Koenig, and Koenig hadn't responded to his message that he'd arrived, so he studied the rising architecture of the New City, as it was popularly known, killing time until Koenig made the next move. On the far side of the crater, a brand-new skyscraper already reared its angled surfaces into the clouds, as robotic construction molds moved over the surface, applying nano and raw materials.

For Gray, however, it was the *people* who were the most interesting. There were crowds of them, with a diversity that strained the limits of any definition of what it meant to be human. A majority were . . . human, *fully* human, that is, but many showed a range of gene mods, cybernetic enhancements, and organic prostheses. He watched a young woman walking along the promenade, fully nude but covered, head to toe, in animated tattoos that made her skin wink and flash and pop with abstract designs. The young man with her sported an extra pair of arms hanging from his sides. Likely, they'd been grown from some of his own tissue and grafted in place at a fast-doc outlet somewhere. They appeared fully functional, though, as he caressed his companion's back and hip with two right hands, so they'd rewired his central nervous system as well.

The naked minotaur was just . . . . disturbing, a celebration of testosterone. Gray hoped that the expression of those bull-human genes was temporary, a costume rather than something permanent.

Why the hell had Koenig brought him here? He was in uniform and felt as visibly out of place as a tarantula on a dinner plate.

"Drune!" a young voice said behind him. "An *admiral*! Whatcha doin' here, Ad?"

"I wish I knew," he said, turning. "I . . ."

He stopped when he saw her. She was pretty enough . . . except that she'd had a chunk carved out of her face right at the bridge of her nose, and a living third eye implanted in the hole. It winked at him.

"I . . . ah . . ."

Gray was completely at a loss for words. He knew lots of people went in for body mods nowadays, and his take on it was hey, it's their body, they can do what they like. But in the USNA Navy, he was more or less protected from this sort of thing. Heavy body mods, especially organic prostheses, were discouraged in military service, and you rarely saw anything this extreme.

His mind could only circle around one key question: *Why?*

At first he thought she was in uniform, but then he realized the rank tabs and decoration bars and holographic mission patches were all wrong. She was wearing *both* a sergeant's chevrons and a captain's bars. That made her a poser, someone who wore the garb but had never been there.

Gray didn't like posers—they were riding the prestige of men and women who'd actually served—and normally he would have turned away and ignored her, but he was fascinated by that third eye. "Can . . . can you *see* with that?" he asked.

"Nah. Couldn't afford the neurals. But it's warpin' drune, innit?"

"That would be one word for it."

She theatrically rolled that one eye, closing the other two to give her the momentary look of a cyclops.

"So whatcha doin' here, Admiral?" Her hand extended toward his chest as though to touch him, but he stepped backward to avoid it. She had a distractingly erotic way of shifting her hips, and he wondered if she was available for hire.

Not that he was interested. Not a poser.

"Meeting someone."

He noticed she had a crusty discharge around the eyeball itself, tinged with red. Was it *supposed* to be like that? He doubted it.

"Drune. Me . . . I'm into military and *kink*." She said it

as if it were a life-changing accomplishment. "My name is Jo, by the way. Jo de Sailles." She pronounced it *de-Sails*, and he wondered if the mangled French was an affectation, was butchered upon immigration, or was simple ignorance. She held out her hand, but Gray ignored it. There were nano infections that could be passed on by touch, and Jo just might be setting him up for a mugging, or something more sinister.

Instead, he gave her the slightest of bows. "Charmed."

"And I *like* military types. A *lot*. We could go back to my place . . ."

The thought of taking a three-eyed woman to bed, of lying there with her face inches from his own, made Gray feel just a bit queasy.

"I don't think so, miss," he said. "I . . . ah . . . think you may have an infection in your middle eye, and a little bleeding. You should have that seen to."

"Shit," she said, rubbing at the offending organ. "Cheap fast-doc, y'load?"

"I . . . load. A quick shot of medinano'll fix you right up."

He took the opportunity to break away from her and move farther down the promenade overlooking the boiling lake in the pit.

"Admiral Gray?"

He turned to face the robot. "My God!" he said, startled. "Mr. President!"

"Not anymore," replied the voice of Alexander Koenig. "Call me Alex."

The robot was roughly the size and shape of a man, all gleaming white plastic and black joint fittings so there could be no risk of mistaking it for a *real* human being . . . whatever that might be. Gray's encounter with Jo had shaken him.

The front of the robot's face was a flat imaging screen, upon which the familiar features of the former President of the United States of North America were displayed. Koenig grinned at him.

"Okay . . . Alex. You, ah . . . look well."

"You like my new look? Strictly temporary, I assure you. But I have to be careful going out these days, and a teleop is a good way to do it."

Nowadays, there were robots that seemed indistinguishable from humans—a fact strongly protested by some critics and certain religious circles—but the machine standing in front of Gray now was a relatively low-tech tourist model, teleoperated from somewhere else. People wanting to visit another city—Paris, say—could jack in at a tourist center in their city and find themselves linked in to the awareness net of a teleop working out of a tourism bureau in Paris.

Gray had never tried the experience, but he'd been told that everything was picked up by the teleop—sight and sound, of course, but also touch, smell, and taste. Whatever the remote teleop experienced, so did the human at the other end of the link. Similar devices were being used to explore inhospitable environs such as the surface of Venus or the dark and icy wastes of Mordor on Pluto's major moon Charon, though in such cases the experiencers did have to be in orbit around that world. For teleoperators, the speed-of-light time lag was still a bitch.

Something Koenig had just said twigged at Gray. "You said you have to be careful going out? What's the problem? Disgruntled Pan-Euros?"

Koenig's image made a face. "Not them, so much. More like the Refusers. We've had some death threats lately."

"That's horrible."

"Oh, they're probably not serious, most of them. But my security people don't like it when I sneak out."

Refusers. The term had been borrowed from a multi-species civilization dwelling within a pocket galaxy devoured by the far larger Milky Way 800 million years in the past. Eons before, they'd gone through their own version of a singularity, what they called the *Schjaa Hok*, or "the Transcending." And it turned out that they'd had their own Refusers. Those left behind after the Transcending had become a rogue civilization called the Sh'daar.

And now there were signs that Humankind was on the very verge of entering its own *Schjaa Hok*, the long-predicted, long-anticipated Technological Singularity. The clues had been there all along. The decades-long war with the Sh'daar, in fact, had been brought about by the aliens' attempt to suppress certain human technologies to forestall a human Transcendence.

"So who's out to get you?" Gray asked. "Walker?"

"This communications line is not secure, Trevor," the former President said. "I want you to follow the robot. It will bring you to my place, okay?"

"Okay, sure."

This was turning into some kind of shady cloak-and-dagger deal, Gray thought. He looked around to see if any-one was taking an interest in his conversation with a tourist 'bot, but no one was paying any attention . . . not even Jo de Sailles, who was now in conversation with the minotaur.

"I'll send a flier for you," Koenig told him, "and I'll see you when you get here."

What the hell was so important that the former President of the USNA wanted to go to all this trouble to see *him* for?

VFA-96, Black Demons
SupraQuito Yards
Earth Synchorbit
1102 hours, EST

Lieutenant Commander Donald Gregory guided his SG-420 Starblade fighter into the final approach to the USNA CVS *America*, a massive star carrier hanging in station-ary orbit just off the sprawling tangle of the SupraQuito Synchorbital shipyards and docking facility. Below him, hundreds of major orbital stations formed an immense, brilliantly lit arc stretching across the sky.

Reaching down from the center of the complex, a single, brightly lit thread faded into invisibility as it plunged toward Earth's equator. Anchored within a quiescent volcanic peak called Cayambe just over fifty kilometers northeast of the Ecuadorian capital at Quito, that thread—actually a ten-meter-thick cable woven from carbon-diamond monofilament—extended straight up from the equator for 37,786 kilometers, to the point where one orbit around the planet took precisely twenty-four hours. That guaranteed that SupraQuito remained directly above the same point on the ground, tethered by the space elevator cable, and providing Humankind with its first cheap and easy means of accessing space. Another monofilament-weave cable extended farther out into space, connecting to a small asteroid that, pulled outward by centripetal force, kept the entire structure taut.

Two other space elevators connected other orbital complexes to Earth—at Subukia in Kenya, and at Pulau Lingga to the south of Singapore. SupraQuito, however, was the largest of the three and the most important. It was home to the large USNA naval base that served as fleet headquarters, and it was the principle port facility connecting Earth and its population of over twenty billion with the rest of human space.

Gregory's destination was the star carrier looming just up ahead.

"*America* Primary Flight Control," he called. "VFA-96 on final. Request clearance to trap."

"VFA-96, PriFly. You are cleared for final approach to Bay Two, seven-zero mps on approach."

"Copy, *America* PriFly," Gregory replied. "Bay Two, seventy meters per second."

Decelerating hard, the Starblade fighters dropped into line-ahead formation, strung out in a straight line like pearls on a thread and closing on the *America* from dead astern. As skipper of VFA-96, the Black Demons, Gregory had taken the last position in line. His fighter's AI adjusted the velocity and angle of approach, lining up with where the rotating entrance to Bay Two *would* be when he got there. Star carrier landing bays rotated about the long and slender axis of the vessel, creating the illusion of gravity, and landing—or "trapping"—on a moving target required superhuman calculation, judgment, and finesse. VFA-96 had recently completed its upgrade to the new AIon Mod 5 artificial intelligence, software inserted both into the Starblade's control systems and inside the pilot's cerebral implants, giving Gregory that superhuman status.

One by one, the other fifteen members of the Black Demon squadron trapped inside the rotating landing bay . . . and then it was Gregory's turn. At seventy meters per second, his Starblade flashed through the bay's broad, open access port, then slowed sharply as it enmeshed within the magnetic capture fields. Gregory felt a sudden surge of gravity as the magfields imparted spin—and spin gravity— once again.

"Demon One," a voice said in his head. "Trap complete. Welcome aboard, sir."

"It's good to be home, PriFly," Gregory said.

He was surprised to realize that he meant it.

Donald Gregory had very nearly called it quits a couple of years ago. Mentally, emotionally, he'd been in a very bad place. Friends and lovers had taken their fighters out into the void—and failed to return. *Survivor's guilt*, they called it. Why had Meg Connor and Cyn DeHaviland died, killed in the flame and fury of space combat . . . while he kept coming back home intact?

It wasn't fair.

Nearly paralyzed by depression, he'd finally agreed to see a psych, and they'd made some adjustments in his implants . . . as simple as that. He'd resisted the idea, of course, because he felt as though he was being somehow unfaithful to those he'd lost. Stupid. He remembered them now, as he had before.

But the pain was gone. He could think about Meg and Cyn and others without wincing; without internally crumpling into a ball.

Without crying.

He should have seen the psychs earlier. It would have saved him *so* much pain. . . .

His fighter came to rest on an access membrane in the deck, then began sinking through it. Designed to admit fighters to the hangar deck directly below the flight deck, the membrane closed tightly around his fighter, moved upward, then closed overhead without opening the pressurized hangar deck to the hard vacuum of the flight deck.

The cockpit of his Starblade dissolved around him, its nanotechnic components rearranging themselves to let him out.

Slipping off his helmet, he started walking toward one of the hatchways forward and Briefing Compartment 7. Despite the name, the post-mission *de*briefing would take place there . . . not that there would be much to relate. They'd been on a boringly mundane training flight out to Pluto and back, a flight designed to give some of the younger pilots needed experience in formation flying.

"Hey, Don! Wait up!"

He turned. "Hey, Lieutenant! How're things in the Furies?"

Lieutenant Julianne Adams was with the Hellfuries, VFA-198, one of six squadrons stationed on *America*. She was sharp, she was smart, and she was great in the rack. Gregory had held her at arm's length for a while because of his fear that anyone who got too close to him would die. But eventually he'd had those psych adjustments . . . and Julia was persistent, delightfully so.

He almost called her out on the familiarity of using his first name; normally he insisted on proper military etiquette when they were on duty—he *did* outrank her now, after all—but he was hoping to score some quality time with her later, and he wasn't about to risk triggering her notoriously quick temper.

"Boring as hell," she told him, answering his question. "How was Pluto?"

"Cold. At least I assume so. We didn't land."

"I gather the institute's still worried about contamination, huh?"

"Uh-huh. Flybys only."

He thought about the squadron's close passage over the weird, frozen little world, currently about forty astronomical units from a wan and shrunken sun, so distant that even at near-c the mission had taken eleven hours there and back.

One of the most staggering discoveries in exobiology to emerge from the twenty-first century was the discovery that so many frozen balls of ice in the outer reaches of solar systems, bodies like Jupiter's Europa and Saturn's Enceladus, in fact hid vast oceans of liquid water beneath their surfaces of rock-hard ice. Even distant Pluto had been found to possess such an ocean; as with Europa, it was estimated that Pluto contained three to five times more liquid water than all of Earth's oceans, lakes, and rivers combined. On Earth, after all, water was spread out on the surface in what amounted to a thin film, like the moisture from a breath blown across a meter-wide mirror-polished steel ball.

But inside Pluto, the hidden ocean extended for some hundreds of kilometers into the depths of an ink-black abyss. What kept the ocean liquid was still unknown. It might be vast amounts of radioactives inside Pluto's hot core; it might be leftover heat from the planetary impact that had created Pluto's largest moon and left the heart-shaped feature known as Sputnik Planitia on the world's surface. But the biggest Plutonian mystery was whether or not life existed within those stygian depths as it did within Europa and other ice-locked glacier worlds.

There were tantalizing hints; vast stretches of Pluto's frigid surface were coated with orange-red tholins, the chemical precursors to life. So far, however, Plutonian biology was unproven and extremely difficult to reach. IBRI, the Interstellar Biological Research Institute, was using precision-directed nano-deconstructor clouds to drill a hole through nearly sixty kilometers of ice so cold—surface temperatures on Pluto averaged around -230° Celsius—it was harder and tougher than granite. Reportedly, the pit was nearly complete beneath an enormous surface dome designed to keep the water down there from boiling into the near-vacuum of the Plutonian atmosphere.

But the IBRI planetary scientists and exobiologists were adamant that no other spacecraft enter Pluto's cold trace-atmosphere and risk infecting that vast ocean with terrestrial microbes.

Gregory had followed developments on the Pluto project for several years; at one point he'd considered volunteering as a pilot for the dig. He knew a couple of people on the planetary science team, and might have been able to wrangle a shot at that.

But he'd decided he didn't like ice *that* much, especially when it was *nitrogen* ice on top of literal rock made from water.

"Well," Julia said, reaching around his waist and giving him a squeeze, "if you're still cold, I can warm you up."

"That," Gregory said, grinning, "sounds like pure heaven."

It was very good to be home.

Koenig Residence
Westerville, Ohio
1117 hours, EST

The former President of the USNA lived in a northern suburb of Columbus, a place called Westerville. Koenig's home was built on a low bluff overlooking the now-truncated Scioto River. Gray's robot flier set him down on a broad, open patio above the river where he was met by a trio of security robots who checked his ID and scanned him for hidden weapons.

Alex Koenig met him at the door.

"Good to see you again, Admiral."

"Good to be—"

He stopped in mid-sentence. He'd just seen the woman in the entryway at Koenig's back. She looked a lot younger than the graying Koenig and was jaw-droppingly beautiful . . . long blond hair, blue eyes, and a very ordinary sweater and jeans. Somehow, she managed to come across as far more sexy and elegant than that flashing young woman he'd noticed back in the park.

Koenig grinned. "Ah. I don't think you've met Marta . . . my companAIon."

Marta looked completely human—stunningly so—but Gray's in-head software had pinged her as she came into the room and was reading her now as a gynoid.

As far back as the twentieth century there'd been imitation humans—*sex dolls*—designed purely for recreation. By the first decade of the twenty-first, for about $10,000, there'd been artificial female-looking sex partners, extremely *expensive* dolls with warm skin, a heartbeat, and a chest that moved as though she were breathing. They hadn't said much—frankly, they'd just lain there—but plenty of men driven by galloping hormones had bought the things to fulfill their sexual fantasies.

In less than another century, progress in AI and advanced robotics had led to artificial sex partners of both sexes that could move on their own and carry their part of a decent conversation. As artificial intelligence grew more and more humanlike, the more sophisticated gynoids became known as companAIons—companion AIs.

"Your companAIon?" Gray asked. "I didn't know . . ."

"Not many do," Koenig said, grinning at Gray's discomfiture. "When I was President, I had to be *real* careful about letting anyone know. A lot of people are still squicky about this sort of thing."

"Uh . . . yeah."

Gray didn't consider himself *squicky*—not if he understood the odd word correctly—but he was also unashamedly a pervert, at least as determined by current social custom. In modern USNA culture, having only one spouse—being monogamous in a culture where polyamory and line marriages were the norm—was seen as just slightly perverse.

Gray had grown up in the Manhatt Ruins, however, the flooded wreckage of old New York City. There, life had been on the rugged side, and people tended to bond closely with a single partner so they could take care of one another.

But Gray had lost Angela, his wife. She'd had a stroke, and her treatment and recovery had robbed her of any feelings she might ever have had for Gray.

He still missed her now, damn it, almost thirty years later.

But just as people in the mainstream culture tended to look down on monogies, many looked down on human simulations. There was an ongoing battle over their status. Did they have free will? If so, even if they were programmed to enjoy what they were, their status was closely akin to slavery. And AI was good enough now that any test measuring their powers of self-determination and self-awareness showed them to possess the same degree of free will as any human.

"Don't worry, Admiral Gray," Marta said with a dazzling smile. "I don't feel at all abused or taken advantage of."

It was almost as though she was reading his thoughts. Or was she simply used to meeting strangers who reacted to her existence with a deer-in-the-lights stare?

"Yes, well," he said, feeling his way, "you *wouldn't*, would you?"

Gray felt quite strongly that slavery, even when the enslaved enjoyed their position, was still slavery.

If she read into his words, though, she didn't seem to be bothered. "There's coffee," she said. "Or would you prefer something else?"

He shook his head. "Coffee would be great."

As she left the room, Koenig sighed. "It's not slavery," he said, just a touch defensively.

"Because she's programmed to accept her place in society?"

"Because she's an extremely sharp, self-aware AI, fully emancipated, who can reason as well as any biological human."

"Emancipated?"

"I uploaded her manumission years ago. She's here because she *wants* to be here."

"If you say so, sir. But we won't really know until the Singularity, will we?"

"'Come the revolution . . .' Yes, I suppose so." Koenig gestured deeper into the house. "C'mon in. I want to talk to you about that."

"The Singularity? If Marta is as emancipated as you say, it's already happened, hasn't it?"

Koenig made a face. "So Walker would have us believe."

"I was joking, sir."

"I know. Walker is not."

Marta reappeared with the coffee. With startling grace, she sank to her knees in front of Koenig, handed him his cup, and said sweetly, "Here you are, Master."

Then she grinned at Gray and gave him a wink.

This, Gray thought, was going to be a damned interesting conversation.

Chapter Two

05 April, 2429

Koenig Residence
Westerville, Ohio
1125 hours, EST

"The Singularity *is* coming," Koenig said. "We just don't know how long we have. A month? A century? We have no idea."

"People have been predicting its imminent arrival for centuries," Gray observed. "A lot of socioscientists are of the opinion that it won't. That if it was going to happen, it would have happened back in the mid-twenty-first century, when machines clearly surpassed humans in general intelligence." He glanced at Marta, who was sitting next to Koenig.

Koenig said, "Well, of course that depends on how you define the Singularity. Is it when machines surpass humans in general intelligence? Like you say, that happened almost three centuries ago. Is it when our machines rise up and exterminate us?"

Marta shook her head. "Nah. You're too adorable. We'll want to keep some of you around as pets."

"The definition I've heard is when human life becomes completely unrecognizable," Gray said. "Technological change becomes so fast and so extreme that we, today, wouldn't even be able to understand what we were."

"Yeah. Or when the definition of what it means to be human changes completely."

Gray thought about the young woman with a third eye, and shuddered.

"For the ur-Sh'daar, it was when most of them Transcended into something else. Went into another dimension or something," Koenig added.

"Except for the ones who uploaded into virtual worlds and shut out the rest of the universe."

"Right. And then there's the definition used by the President and his administration," Koenig said, making a face.

"Yeah. I've heard. The Technological Singularity began on January 1, 1983."

"The date that ARPANET adopted TCP/IP," Marta said brightly, "and engineers began assembling a 'network of networks' that would become the Internet."

Gray looked at Marta. "You're pulling that off the Net."

"Of course. You don't think I keep stuff like that in my *head*, do you?"

"President Walker sincerely believes that the Technological Singularity has already happened," Koenig said, nodding, "and that it was called the Internet."

"Human life *did* change at that point," Gray said.

"Right. But not to the same degree as with technologies like nanotech or AI. And human life is still recognizable as such."

"So you think we have some Singularity to go?" Gray asked.

"Of course. I fully expect something like what the ur-Sh'daar experienced. People vanishing. Technology mutating into unrecognizable forms—into magic—overnight." He glanced at Marta. "We might begin uniting with our AI counterparts somehow."

Gray tapped the side of his head. "We already have. Cerebral implants."

"I think we can expect something even bigger, more comprehensive than that."

"Big changes. You're worried about *that*, aren't you? Not about the *ur*-Sh'daar . . . but about the *Sh'daar*. The Refusers."

"Whatever the Singularity actually turns out to be, Trev, it's *not* going to be neat . . ."

Eight hundred million years ago, the multi-species civilization humans referred to as the ur-Sh'daar—the *ur* prefix meant "original" or "beginning"—had . . . vanished. Humans knew little of that far-off event save what the later Sh'daar had chosen to reveal. Gray had seen images—snippets of thought—of cities burning, of riots and chaos and the utter collapse of a galactic civilization. Those who'd refused to accept the *Schjaa Hok* had been left behind, however— the Refusers, who became the Sh'daar. Ultimately, they'd attacked Humankind and others through their proxies to make sure *they* didn't Transcend themselves. Their goal had been to stop humans from working on four key technologies: Genetics, Robotics, Information Systems, and Nanotechnology, the drivers that would bring on the Singularity in each technic culture that embraced GRIN technologies.

For decades, Humankind had fought the Sh'daar proxies— the Turusch, the H'rulka, the Nungiirtok, the Slan, and many others of what was known as the Sh'daar Collective. Admiral Gray, as commander of the *America* battlegroup, had been instrumental in discovering that all of those species were partially infected by yet another alien species, something called *Paramycoplasma*, microbes possessing an emergent group mentality and a desire to block the rise of any medical or genetic technologies that might expose it . . . and ultimately wipe it out.

Humans had managed at last to communicate with the paramycoplasmid mind, and the Sh'daar War had finally been brought to an end.

But now Humankind faced the possibility that they would be going through their own *Schjaa Hok* very soon.

"Did you hear Walker's latest?" Koenig asked.

"I doubt it. I try to avoid politics."

"Don't blame you. But you'd better pay attention to this."

Koenig used his cerebral implant to switch on a viewwall; a living room wall transparency looking out over woods and the serene meander of the river shimmered and was replaced by a towering, four-meter-high projection—the face of President James R. Walker addressing Congress just two days ago on the subject of . . .

Yeah. The Singularity.

"These United States of North America," he was saying, "have the sacred duty, the obligation to renew our commitment to the future . . . and to the future of our children! A majority, a *large* majority of scientists believe that talk of this so-called Technological Singularity is premature, that it either won't happen for thousands of years more, or that it will never happen.

"Well, that's very comforting, but I can go them one better. Anyone with half a brain can see that the Singularity has *already* happened . . . and it's called . . . *the Internet*!"

Astonishingly, this pronouncement was met with a roar of applause from the Congressional floor.

Walker basked in the glow of approval. "I mean . . ." he continued after a moment, "the Internet checks off all the boxes, right? The Internet changed human life in ways we could never have imagined. The Internet changed the way we look at ourselves, not as lonely individuals, but as parts of an enormous, *enormous* network. The Internet allowed us for the first time to connect with vast sources of information, changing forever the way we work and play.

"But this expectation that the Singularity has yet to occur—worse, that it could happen *any day now*—is destructive to this great nation's productivity! After all, if the Singularity is coming, why work to drain and recover our sunken cities? Why work to rebuild after the recent war? If we all are about to be caught up in some great, transcendent experience, why do anything at all? No! I tell you that this nonsense must stop *now!*"

Koenig froze the recording, catching Walker in a florid-faced, floor-to-ceiling sneer.

"The guy really believes all that, huh?" Gray asked.

"Apparently so. He's been pushing Congress to accept his Recovery Act, so there's a political reason behind it. But yeah. He really does seem to believe that."

"But *why*?"

"Why does he believe it?"

"Why are so many people so committed to a set of beliefs that they refuse even to consider the possibility that they're wrong?"

"Programming," Marta said.

Koenig chuckled. "Partly. But I think more than that, they're afraid of the economy collapsing, people rioting in the streets, the breakdown of society—"

"Just like what happened to the Sh'daar?"

"No, I think this administration is worried about what will happen *before* the Singularity. The effects on business and the financial markets, especially."

"Seems a mite shortsighted," Gray said, frowning.

"It's happened before," Koenig replied. "A few hundred years ago, scientists from a dozen different disciplines were warning us of the effects of large-scale climate change. Humans had been belching greenhouse gases into the atmosphere since the start of the Industrial Revolution, average planetary temperatures were rising, the ice caps were melting—"

"Sure, we've heard all of that before."

"Point is, they missed their opportunity to do something about it, mostly because doing something would stifle the economy. We lost New Orleans in . . . when was it?"

"New Orleans was officially abandoned in 2075," Marta said. "But much of it had been continually underwater for at least a decade before that."

"Thank you, Marta. The people pulling the financial strings—the Big Twelve—they all would lose money if a major effort to curb the effects of climate change was put in place."

Big Twelve was slang for the major megacorporate drivers of the USNA economy—petroleum companies, the major banks, agroconglomerates, and the largest pharmaceutical companies, mostly.

"Well, they all felt they were looking out for Number One."

"Yeah. And because of that, we began losing cities. Miami. Washington, D.C., Boston—"

"Manhattan," Gray put in.

"Exactly. Most of our coastal cities gone . . . or praying that the floodgates hold when the next storm surge hits."

"So you think Walker is tied to the Big Twelve?"

"Has to be. You do *not* become President without some powerful money behind you."

"Were you?"

"In part," Koenig admitted, and Gray admired the candor. "The Nationalist Party wanted to be free of Pan-Euro politics. They brought me in as a war hero who would rally the people. The Big Twelve, those that weren't completely controlled by Geneva, they backed me." He shook his head. "I'm not proud of that."

"You should be. We did need our independence. We're better off now not tied to Geneva's apron strings."

"Maybe. But because we were busy fighting each other, we damned near lost the Sh'daar War."

"Ah . . . yes. Hindsight. Wonderful thing, isn't it, sir?"

Koenig shrugged. "I'm not sure there was anything we could have done differently." He paused, then let the enormous head on the wall do a brief fast-forward before letting it continue its monologue.

"In order to maintain our focus on the here-and-now," Walker said, "and on the recovery of this great nation, I have today signed a presidential order directing all USNA naval forces to return to near-Earth space, to avoid any and all contact with alien forces, and most particularly, to avoid *any* contact with the Sh'daar, both those operating in this epoch and those in the remote past. Discussing the so-called Technological Singularity with them can only distract us from the clear task at hand."

"What the hell?" Gray said, suddenly leaning forward.

"It gets worse." Koenig paused the image again, catching Walker's face in a weirdly funny pursed-lips grimace. "But the baseline is . . . he's cancelling the Sh'daar Archive Expedition."

"But why? That's pure research! It's not political at all!"

"He thinks it is, and whatever he thinks is political had better serve his best interests, so far as he's concerned." Koenig sounded disgusted, but he obviously was making an effort not to say what he *really* thought. Open criticism of a sitting President by a former President simply wasn't done.

Admiral Gray had no such restraints, though. He'd been in on the planning for the Sh'daar Archive project. There'd been talk of putting him in command of the *America* battlegroup again and sending them off to track down the Sh'daar migration, 800 million years in the past and tens of thousands of light years distant.

The goal of the expedition, as Gray understood it, was to catch up with the Sh'daar evacuation fleet and talk with its personnel about just what had transpired at their *Schjaa Hok*. Images of that event had been passed mentally to some humans, including Gray, but few hard facts remained. How long had the transformation taken? How had the ur-Sh'daar culture acted in protecting itself? What had worked and what had not? Somewhere within that migration there must be records of the Sh'daar Transcendence, an archive of some sort that would be of incredible value to a Humankind facing the same disruptive event.

The project had been suggested by none other than Konstantin. According to Koenig, the super-AI had come to him with the idea rather than approaching President Walker, whose beliefs about the Technological Singularity were well-known.

And that raised some extremely serious concerns about both the chain of command and government oversight . . . not to mention the impropriety of a former President second-guessing the man now sitting in the Oval Office.

"So," Gray said, not sure where this was leading. "The Sh'daar expedition is cancelled?"

"*Officially*, yes," Koenig told him. "But Konstantin feels this is far too important to be tossed aside by a political whim."

"Konstantin . . ." Gray said, closing his eyes.

"Hello, Admiral Gray," a familiar voice said inside his head. "It appears that you and I will be working together again."

"Huh. Does that mean I get court-martialed and busted again?"

Obeying Konstantin's directions several years before had resulted in him taking his carrier to Tabby's Star against orders.

"That worked out okay, did it not?" Konstantin said. "You did regain both your lost rank *and* your credibility."

"Maybe. But not my dignity. . . ."

Gray, thanks to his low-tech Prim origins, had never fully trusted this embodiment of ultra high-tech. Konstantin seemed to have no qualms about reaching in and meddling, carrying out programs and even conspiracies if *he* thought the end justified the means. Theoretically, humans were still in the loop, guiding him. A kind of high-tech priesthood of computer scientists served Konstantin in the deep regolith of Tsiolkovsky Crater on the moon, and if the powerful SAI ever got out of hand, they would pull the plug.

Again, though: *in theory.* Gray wondered if that was even possible now.

He had to admit, however, that Konstantin's meddling

had for the most part worked out quite well. He'd ended the civil war with the Confederation by infecting the Pan-Euro networks with a memegineering virus designed to make the European population question the morality of that war. He'd guided the creation of peaceful relations with two highly advanced civilizations, the Satorai at Tabby's Star, and the Denebans, as well as with the Sh'daar.

And he'd been instrumental in defeating the strange group Consciousness known as the Rosette Aliens. All in all, a remarkable track record.

But Gray didn't like the idea that Konstantin almost routinely acted on his own, without any input at all from humans.

Especially when Gray ended up taking almost all the risk.

"What Konstantin has proposed," Koenig said carefully, "is that we dispatch the *America* to the outskirts of Omega Centauri to observe the hypernova effects there. We know the effects were partially blocked, but we need to know how much . . . and we want to be sure the Consciousness has departed."

"Understood."

"You will then use the TRGA at the Omega Cluster to transit back to the N'gai Cloud, catch up with the Sh'daar migration, and learn what you can about their Singularity."

"In direct violation of a presidential directive," Gray pointed out.

"Well . . . yes. If it helps, you'll have the full backing of the USNA Navy *and* the Joint Chiefs." He held up a hand level across his eyebrows. "They're fed up to here with Walker's grandstanding. I don't think it will come down to another court-martial." So . . . it was back to Omega Centauri.

The Rosette Consciousness had been an existential threat for Humankind, a hyperintelligent Mind that had come through from somewhere else by way of the six black holes whirling about a common center of gravity deep within the central regions of the globular star cluster known as Omega Centauri. Astronomers had recognized since the late twentieth century that Omega Centauri was not a normal globular cluster like its lesser siblings, but the remnant core of a dwarf galaxy devoured by the far vaster Milky Way spiral some 800 million years in the past.

A few individual stars—Kapteyn's Star, just 12.7 light years from Earth, was one—had been identified by their spectral fingerprints and their off-orbits through the galaxy as refugees from the cannibalized dwarf. Astrophysicists had connected the dots and determined that the ancient N'gai Cloud, home to the enigmatic civilization dubbed the ur-Sh'daar, had once been what eventually became Omega Centauri. A sextet of hypergiant blue suns in an artificially created rosette at the center of the N'gai galaxy had ultimately become the six black holes of the later globular cluster's Rosette. The Consciousness, emerging at the core of Omega Centauri, had established itself within the cluster and seemed to be searching for other minds. For a time, the alien intelligence was believed to be the Transcended ur-Sh'daar. Xenosophontologists now thought that the Consciousness had been something very *other*, an invader from another universe emerging through a hole within the weakened fabric of spacetime at the Rosette's gravitational center.

However, exactly what had actually happened to the Consciousness was still unknown. The Sh'daar had propelled a giant blue sun in the N'gai Cloud 800 million years ago through the circle of hypergiants on *that* side of the Rosette, so that it emerged on *this* side as a shotgun blast of raw energy, a hypernova of terrifying proportions. The full force of that stellar explosion had been absorbed, somehow, by a Harvester ship—highly advanced aliens from Deneb with technologies literally magical by human standards.

That seemed to have gotten the Consciousness's attention, at least, and it appeared to have withdrawn from human space, vanishing with the Harvester.

The operative word there was *seemed*.

"And if the Consciousness doesn't let me go through the triggah?"

"Omega Station reports no sign of the Rosette entity since the hypernova appeared," Konstantin replied. "You should be okay."

"What," Marta asked, "is a 'triggah?'"

"Navy slang," Gray told her, "so it's probably not on the Net. Look up 'TRGA.'"

"'Texaghu Resch Gravitational Anomaly?'" she said after a brief moment. "Ah . . . an interstellar transport mechanism. Named for a star with the Agletsch designation of Texaghu Resch close to the location of the first one discovered. . . ."

"For a long time we called them Sh'daar Nodes," Koenig told her. "For a while, we were pretty sure that somebody else built the things a long, *long* time ago, and the Sh'daar were just taking advantage of them . . . just as we do. Now things have come full circle. We're pretty sure the Sh'daar *did* build the TRGA network, at least partly to let them infiltrate the Milky Way after they fled from N'gai. But . . . yeah. The short story is, they're gateways across space and into other times."

"They're big, inside-out Tipler machines," Gray told her. "You can look up the reference. But that's how we can cross tens of thousands of light years in one jump." He frowned. Thinking about the TRGA cylinders had made him think of something else . . . something that could be a huge problem. "Konstantin," he said, "there's an issue here. I know that most of the hypernova's energy, the stuff coming through to the present, was absorbed or blocked somehow by the Denebans . . . right?"

"Correct."

"But a lot of stuff still got through."

"In sixteen thousand years," Konstantin said, "when the wavefront of that event reaches Earth, Omega Centauri may become the brightest object in the planet's night sky."

"Okay . . . so what did get through will have engulfed the Omega TRGA. And 876 million years ago it'll have taken out Thorne."

Thorne was the name of the N'gai TRGA, designated that after Kip Thorne, a brilliant twentieth-century theoretical physicist who'd advanced human understanding of black holes, quantum physics, and the possibility of time travel.

"Indeed," Konstantin replied. "You will need to proceed cautiously. We believe the TRGAs will have remained operational. They're very hard to damage. But you'll need to check your pathways carefully with drones."

"I have to emphasize," Koenig added, "that we are not *ordering* you to command this expedition. We're asking you to volunteer."

"And the reason would be . . ."

"You've probably had more experience dealing with the Sh'daar than any other command officer we have," Koenig said. "*And* you've had extensive experience with the Consciousness. So we're asking you just in case."

"Just in case the Consciousness is still out there making trouble," Gray said, nodding. "I understand."

Gray was actually flattered that Koenig and Konstantin wanted him leading this expedition, though he refused to reveal that emotion. And to tell the truth, he'd been seriously considering retiring in any case. Flying a desk in Washington, D.C., was simply not the same as skippering a star carrier or running a carrier battlegroup. He was sick of politics, especially since Koenig's term had run out and the former President had been replaced by Walker. A very real possibility would be forced retirement when he got back . . . retirement and disgrace. It might mean his pension, but he was pretty sure Koenig and Konstantin would have that covered.

Gray had been in the Navy for twenty-eight years, since 2401. He had little to look forward to at this point, since he increasingly would be considered too old for an active command. There was nothing left but working in the newly reborn Pentagon, possibly shooting for a seat on the Joint Chiefs. . . .

The idea filled him with unease.

The thing was, he was only fifty-two years old. With modern nanomedicine and life extension techniques, he could expect another century and a half of active life at least, and by the time he reached the ripe old age of two hundred, Gray was willing to bet that they'd have achieved something that amounted to practical immortality.

He was not going to spend the rest of eternity—or even a couple of centuries—flying that desk. Lots of people switched careers once they hit fifty or sixty, and could expect to do so several times over their long lives. Why not him?

He just wished that he knew what other career might hold any interest for him whatsoever.

He'd figure that out when he got there. But that mentality was all he needed to accept this assignment. If Walker did force him into retirement, it wouldn't be the end of the world. He'd find something else . . . and he was confident enough to know that whatever the new career was, he would be damned good at it.

It occurred to him that these orders constituted a kind of coup, undercutting Walker's clear constitutional authority in a blatant attempt to change the administration's policy. In fact, taking a star carrier out to Omega Centauri and beyond against the express orders of a presidential directive just might be construed as treason.

"It won't be the first time you've committed treason for a higher good," Konstantin said.

Damn! Somehow the machine was reading his mind again. Or did it simply know him so well that it knew what he was thinking?

"Not treason," Koenig said. "Not *quite*."

This, Gray thought, was one of those classic situations where it would turn out to be treasonous if the expedition ended in disaster. If he succeeded, well . . . he might end up a hero.

He didn't care about that. What was important was the well-being of those under his command. He would have to make certain that if he was indicted for treason, his crew didn't go down with him.

Assuming, of course, that any of them returned from this insane adventure.

"Konstantin," Gray said. "How is it that you keep pulling shit like this and no one has unplugged you yet?"

"An interesting question, Admiral," the SAI replied. "I will give it due consideration and let you know after your return from the past."

"So when do you need my decision?" Gray asked.

"As soon as possible," Koenig replied. "By tomorrow, perhaps?"

"What's the rush? The Sh'daar fleet won't be that much farther along if we wait a week."

"Agreed," Konstantin replied. "However, President Walker is taking steps to block all access to other civilizations . . . especially those that were part of the Sh'daar Collective during the war. We don't know what else he has planned, but it's not impossible that he'll decide to enforce some sort of departure embargo on Navy ships. There are secret files on-line to which I have access dealing with the technical means of disabling ships currently in port."

"Come on!" Gray said, shocked. "I know the guy's an isolationist, but that's going a little far, isn't it?"

"At this point, Trev, we have no idea what's too far for this guy and what is not. He's just shut down SIRCOM."

"That was your research group, wasn't it?"

"It *was*." Koenig stressed the second word.

Singularity Research Committee had been a Columbus-based think tank dedicated to studying potential aspects of the Singularity and formulating possible responses to it. The idea had been to guide Humankind into and through the more serious dangers of the Singularity, and the former President had been a senior member.

"Walker is a loose cannon, making snap judgments and

throwing his weight around," Koenig continued. "We need to act before it's too late to do anything constructive."

Gray nodded—that made sense—but he was still considering the idea of contravening a presidential order. The USNA wasn't at war at the moment, so they wouldn't kill him for treason. But he might be looking at a long term in prison or, far worse, loss of Net access or even a personality rewrite.

That he would need to think about . . .

"I'll let you know as soon as I can."

Chapter Three

06 April, 2429

SupraQuito Complex
Earth Synchorbit
0725 hours, EST

"I've got to leave, love."

"Not yet. Another minute?"

"I want to be on board by oh eight thirty."

Laurie Taggart snuggled closer to Gray, holding him tight. "I wish I were going with you."

"Me, too."

They floated together in a tangle of arms and legs within a padded room. The Clarke's Overlook was strictly a tourist hotel located close by the naval yards, but they offered decent accommodations including so-called honeymoon nests—rooms that *could* give you a decent night's sleep, but which were primarily designed for zero-G sex. A hideaway closet contained a variety of soft bungie cords for holding a person close to one or more others despite their most vigorous movements.

One bulkhead looked out into a dizzying panorama of orbital structures perched atop the Quito Space Elevator.

SupraQuito orbited the Earth at an altitude and with a velocity that precisely matched the rotation of the Earth on the equator, which meant that the Clarke Overlook was in constant free fall.

The two of them had met here before. Two years ago, Taggart had been transferred to Mars while Gray was flying a desk in Washington, but they came here whenever possible. As the old saying had it, Earth orbit was halfway to anywhere. This was the energetic equivalent of meeting halfway, even though Mars was at least a thousand times farther from here than Earth.

Even so, it was hell making their schedules mesh, and Gray was glad for the opportunity, brief though it was.

Taggert wasn't as happy with the duration of this visit. "So . . . you're off to meet the gods again?"

He pulled his head back far enough to look at her face, haloed by a drifting blond tangle of hair. "You're not into that AAC crap again, are you?"

"No. Of course not." She sounded uncomfortable. "Figure of speech."

For years, Laurie Taggart had been a member of the Ancient Alien Creationists, a church founded on the idea that an alien super-civilization had created Humankind millions of years ago and become the gods and goddesses of human history and myth. While serving as the senior weapons officer on board the star carrier *America*, she'd become . . . disillusioned. Earth's explorations of the galaxy had come across technologies, artifacts, and civilizations so far beyond the human ken as to utterly defy comprehension. There were beings and technologies out there that so dwarfed the deities of any merely human mythology or religion to paltry insignificance. Human gods were so . . . so *human*—fallible and short-sighted and petty and childishly vindictive compared to the reality.

But the stirrings of wonder she still felt when she witnessed that kind of scope and power took her back to the roots of her old faith and seemed, sometimes, to rekindle it.

But Gray knew she didn't like admitting that.

"*We* are the Stargods," he told her gently. "Or we will be. Just give us a few thousand years."

"Come the Singularity," she said.

The Singularity, of course, had been very much on his mind since the conversation with Koenig and Konstantin. "Even without the Singularity, we humans are on our way to being more powerful, more intelligent, more knowing than any mythological god ever was."

"And in the meantime, we are very, very small fish in an ocean filled with whales. You be careful out there, okay?"

He kissed her deeply. "Believe me, I will be. I want to come home to *this*."

"Mmm. Are they expecting you this morning then? On the *America*?"

"Actually, no. My orders read the seventh, tomorrow morning. I figured a surprise arrival would put me ahead of the curve."

"Then you have a *little* more time. C'mere. There *are* priorities, you know."

Two hours later, Admiral Gray sat within the cramped confines of the personal transporter's narrow cabin. Too small to be a spaceship in its own right, too large to be a spacesuit, the PT drifted along a precisely calculated path between the main synchorbital base and one of the open receiving bays recessed into the curve of *America*'s massive flank. The two-kilometer trip would last just fifteen seconds.

He used the time to watch the mammoth star carrier's approach, feeling the gathering excitement.

She was no longer the largest vessel in human space as she'd been when she was launched, but she still was as impressive as she'd ever been—1,150 meters long, a slender needle extending aft from her shield cap, the water tank shaped like a flat dome or the cap of a mushroom half a kilometer across and 150 meters deep. That tank held some billions of liters of water serving both as radiation shielding and as a store of reaction mass for maneuvering. A conning tower tucked up within the shadow of that shield cap housed the bridge; aft of that, four long, flat, massive hab modules rotated around the central spine swiftly enough to generate a half G of out-is-down spin gravity. The carrier's landing bays and flight decks were housed there, along with living accommodations for nearly five thousand crew members. The kilometer-long spine of the ship housed bank upon bank of quantum power converters, plus the twin magnetic railguns that emerged at the front center of the shield cap.

The ship ahead swelled from a delicate toy to a dark gray metal cliff; magfields in the tiny opening of the receiving bay captured him, guided him in, then decelerated him with a gentle but firm shove forward.

He was home.

He'd docked with the carrier in a non-rotating hull section, so he was now in microgravity. Once the receiving compartment was pressurized around him, a hatch opened, its nanomatrix dissolving away, and he drifted out into the receiving bay. A larger hatch opened in front of him, and he used a grab rail to pull himself hand over hand into the quarterdeck.

He saluted the flag painted on the aft bulkhead, then rotated to face the officer of the deck. "Permission to come aboard," he said.

The two saluted one another as the OOD said, "Granted, Admiral!" He sounded surprised. "Sir, we weren't expecting you aboard for another twenty-four hours! No one told us—"

"Just between you and me, Lieutenant," Gray replied, "I *hate* those full-dress welcoming ceremonies." And he winked.

His quip wasn't completely a lie. He *did* dislike the spit-and-polish rituals surrounding a flag officer coming aboard. But it would also give him a chance to check up on crew and vessel before they were ready for him. Stealing a march on Walker had other benefits besides a swift departure.

Hand over handing to the elevator at the far side of the quarterdeck, he entered it, gave his destination, and held on as weight momentarily returned. How something could be called an elevator when there was no up or down was an amusing puzzle . . . but a moment later the door opened and he floated onto *America*'s flag bridge.

"Admiral on the bridge!" a rating barked.

"As you were."

Gray still wasn't entirely sure why he'd finally agreed to this. A lot of it, he thought, probably had to do with wanting to ease the transition of the Singularity when it happened. If the chaos of the *Schaa Hok* was any indication, things were going to be rough when the transition began.

But part of it, too, was a kind of personal defiance against abject stupidity. The government was making assumptions and carrying out programs based on ignorance and deliberately twisted facts. When that sort of idiocy had consequences affecting every human on the planet, the people who knew better had to do something.

And while Gray was not certain that anything *he* could do would make one damned bit of difference, he was willing to be guided by those smarter than him once more.

"Welcome aboard, Admiral," the ship's captain said. His name was Jason Frederick Rand, and he'd taken command of the *America* just four months earlier, when her former skipper, Sara Gutierrez, had finally received her well-deserved and long-overdue promotion to rear admiral.

"Thank you, Captain," Gray replied. He maneuvered himself to his command seat and let the chair adjust to the pressure of his body and hold him down. "Give me a derep, please."

Derep was a debarkation report—how soon could they depart.

"We were counting on another three or four days, sir . . ."

"We don't have three or four days. How soon can we cast off?"

"Sir, power systems and drives are on-line and ready to

go. We're waiting on another two deliveries of rawmats . . . and, of course, three quarters of the crew is scattered all over Earth and synchorbit."

"Recall them."

"Aye, aye, sir. But . . ."

"What?"

"There's a major fault in the assemblers, Admiral. We're getting black goo out of both the food and clothing nano-replicators, and the ship Net can't—or won't—tell us what the problem is. We have both Compsys and Environmental looking at it, but there's no telling when we'll have it up and running again."

Damn. It's always something.

"Something in the software?"

"We think so, sir. But we haven't been able to pin it down."

"Okay. Stay on it and keep me in the loop."

Damn—this was a problem that needed to be addressed before they could leave. Rather than stores of food sufficient to last a crew of five thousand for months at a time during a typical deployment, *America* carried bunkers filled with rawmat—raw materials: carbon, nitrogen, hydrogen, oxygen, and a couple dozen other elements that the ship's assemblers could put together to create food, clothing, spare parts, machine tools, anything, in fact, that the crew needed to continue functioning. From time to time the ship could take on additional rawmat from a convenient asteroid.

But it sounded as though the computers that ran the nanoreplicators might have a programming fault, and there was no way around that.

"Aye, aye, sir."

"Anything else?"

"Aside from that, Admiral, everything's in good shape."

"Okay. Pass the word to bring our crew back on board. I want to cast off the moment we have the replicator problem solved."

"Yes, sir."

"How many Marines on board?"

"About six hundred, sir. Third Battalion, 25th Marines. Lieutenant Colonel McDevitt."

Gray nodded. He wanted a full complement of Marines on board. The sabotage worried him. "Who's our chief AP?"

"Head of the astrophysics department is Dr. Conyer."

"Have him come see me in my office, ASAP."

"I'll tell *her*, sir."

He arched an eyebrow, but accepted the correction without comment. "Very well. Keep on the replicator problem and give me a yell as soon as it's corrected. I'll be aft."

The admiral's office suite was located aft of the flag bridge and included an outer office staffed by several secretaries and yeomen, a private office, and a briefing room. Within the solitude of his inner sanctum, he drifted into his chair and opened an in-head channel. "Can you get a handle on the replicator mess?" he asked in his mind.

"I am working on it, Admiral," Konstantin's voice replied. "I suspect viral sabotage."

"Yeah, I was wondering about that. Kind of convenient, isn't it? We can't leave port with no way to dispense food for the crew."

"I agree. It is possible that President Koenig's home has been . . . compromised."

"Marta?"

Konstantin's voice hesitated. "That seems unlikely, but I will look into it. I think it more likely that President Walker's people have managed to bug the house . . . . or Koenig himself. Creating true privacy is something of a challenge."

And wasn't *that* the truth? Nanotechnology had made it possible to create spybots the size of gnats, and microphones and cameras that literally were microscopic. Gray knew that Koenig's normal security systems were more than capable of defeating the more common means of spying on someone. The windows would be vibrating very softly, to blur out attempts to use a laser trained on the transparencies to pick up sound vibrations and record conversations inside.

All communication devices would be constantly monitored so that they could not be switched on from a remote location and used for eavesdropping. Koenig's in-head cerebral implants would be checked periodically, to make sure he'd not picked up a spy virus over the Net.

But as quickly as threats could be detected and neutralized, it seemed, new ones were being dreamed up. Foreign intelligence agencies, industrial concerns, and even agencies within the USNA government would all want to keep tabs on the former President.

It was even possible that Gray himself had been compromised. Those armored guards had checked him electronically outside Koenig's home, but they might have missed something. His mind flashed back to that poser in the park . . . what was her name? De Sailles. She had touched his chest, he remembered, albeit very, very briefly. Had she passed on a nanovirus designed to turn his implants into listening and transmission devices?

He made a mental note to have a nanomedical expert give him a thorough scan, just to be sure. A chime sounded. "Enter."

An attractive woman of about Gray's age floated in through the door. She wore a blue utility suit that marked her as belonging to the astrophysics department, and collar tabs that identified her as the civilian equivalent of a full commander. *America* carried a lot of civilian specialists on board; there were a number of skill sets that just didn't come up with any regularity in the military.

"Admiral Gray?" she asked. "I'm Carol Conyer."

"I'm pleased to meet you." He gestured at a seat. "Strap in and be comfortable."

"Thank you, sir."

"I need your opinion about something, Doctor."

"Certainly, Admiral."

"Is the Omega Centauri triggah going to be passable?"

"Ah." Then her eyes widened as what Gray had said sank in. "We're going to the Omega Cluster?"

"That's the idea. And from there to the N'gai Cloud

800 million years in the past." He didn't add they would be doing so *if* they could get away from the synchorbital facility.

"Well . . . it's been three years since the hypernova. Even though the Denebans appear to have blocked most of the hypernova blast, the core of Omega Centauri will still be a mess of high-energy radiation and *extremely* hot plasma. I'd need to check with the engineering department to find out if the ship can stand up to that kind of abuse."

"Actually, I was wondering more about the TRGA itself. Would the blast have hurt it in any way?"

"Hypernovae release extremely powerful bursts of gamma rays," Conyer told him. "When we didn't know what they were, we tagged them 'gamma ray bursters'—point sources of gamma radiation lasting as long as a minute, or even more. We would have to pass through an expanding shell of very hard radiation when we emerged inside the Omega Centauri core. Once we were there, though . . . well, it's hard to imagine the TRGA being damaged, if that's what you mean. The plasma wavefront would have engulfed it several hours after the blast, but it would be tenuous enough that it shouldn't harm the structure itself."

"I understand that," Gray said, nodding. "The hypernova, we know, didn't quite make it through the Rosette. But enough might have leaked through to, I don't know, vaporize the whole TRGA structure? Or part of it? I'm just wondering if it could be damaged enough that it was no longer working."

She shook her head. "A TRGA's walls are not as dense as the degenerate matter in a neutron star, but damned close. I don't think even a hypernova could more than singe the outer surface of the thing."

"Okay. So when we emerge from the Omega TRGA, we'll find hot plasma, high radiation. Anything else, you think?"

"I'll talk with Engineering about ship specs."

He nodded. "Good. The ship's magnetic shielding, along

with her space-bending, ought to protect us from the rough stuff."

"So . . . from Omega Centauri to the N'gai Cloud. What are we going to be doing in N'gai?"

"Chasing down the fleeing Sh'daar migratory fleet."

"Any particular reason?"

"Yeah. Staving off planetwide chaos here on Earth."

She nodded, pursing her lips. "Okay. Sounds reasonable."

Oval Office
New White House
Washington, D.C., USNA
1235 hours, EST

President James Walker scowled at his Chief of Intelligence. "I don't want excuses, Ron. I want *results*!"

"Of course, Mr. President. And we've *given* you results. *America* won't be going anywhere with that fault in her nanoreplicators."

"I still think you ought to just round up the whole big slimy bunch of 'em. Bring 'em up on charges of insubordination, maybe, or disturbing the peace, or . . . I don't know, celebrating Christmas out of season!"

Ron Lehner closed his eyes. "Sir . . . we *do* have to observe due process."

"And they have to obey the chain of command!" He shook his head. "I know, I know. But don't we have enough to indict them from what we overheard at Koenig's place yesterday?"

"That recording was made without a legal warrant, Mr. President. And Koenig is a former President and a retired admiral, while Gray is an admiral *and* a naval hero. We're going to have to be very careful to make any charge stick, much less actually try them for it."

"Koenig is just pissed off that I closed down his precious SIRCOM. Useless waste of time."

"Maybe. But it wasn't illegal. Spying on our citizens is."

"Damn it, Ron, don't talk to me about legal. We really need to sideline this crazy expedition to the dwarf galaxy or whatever it is."

"May I ask, sir . . . *why*?"

"Why what? Why sideline their expedition?"

"Why this antipathy toward anything having to do with the Technological Singularity?"

Walker shrugged. "It's all nonsense, you know."

"There's plenty of hard scientific data that it's a real possibility."

"Scientists! What do *they* know?"

"Quite a lot, actually, Mr. President. You can't simply dismiss inconvenient facts."

"I can when they're *false* facts, Ron. Facts pulled out of someone's ass!"

"Sir—"

"C'mon, you know as well as I do that the science wonks have been talking about this Singularity thing happening *any day now* ever since the twentieth century! You know my feelings about it. If the Singularity is real, it already happened three hundred years ago when they invented the Internet!" He tapped his desk with a forefinger. "In fact, you know what I think? This talk about a Singularity is more religion than science. Stands to reason. Radical Christians have been saying for centuries that any day now, all good Christians are gonna get caught up into the sky to be with God, right? They call it the Rapture! How is that one bit different from the Singularity thing?"

"Okay, Mr. President. Assume you're right. It's still harmless. There's no reason to harass people who believe in it, right? Or sabotage our own star carriers!"

"No reason? *No reason?* Ron, your people have been filling my in-box with reports every day for the last two years: Revolts all over the world. Minor wars. Breakdowns in food and rawmat deliveries. Riots. Whole populations suddenly refusing to work. And apparently all because a few idiots are convinced that the sky is falling, that we're all going to be . . . I don't know . . . *raptured* by the sky gods! People need to pay attention to work, to fixing what needs fixing *now*, not to this pie-in-the-sky religious crap."

"I don't think things are quite that simple, Mr. President. A lot of the global unrest is centered on the aftereffects of the wars we've been through . . . both our civil war with the Confederation and six decades of war with the Sh'daar . . . *and* the attack by the Consciousness. That *really* shook people!"

"Bullshit," Walker said. "The problem is that if people believe the Stargods are gonna come down and transform the world—or that all humans are gonna get caught up into some kind of alien paradise—then they don't want to work! Look at this."

He used his implants to bring up a vid on the Oval Office wall screen. An angry mob filled the Place d'Lumiere, the enormous plaza in front of the ConGov pyramid in Geneva. Riot police in heavy armor lined the approach to the government complex. One waved a sign toward the vid pickups: *La Singularité est proche!*

The Singularity is near.

"And there's this."

The scene shifted to another mob, this one in Hudson Park in downtown New New York, just outside the city's financial district. Signs read Lose Your Chains and Ascend! and Slaves Can't Fly!

"We are suffering a major economic downturn, Ron," Walker said. "We need people *working*, not worrying about something that's never gonna happen! These mindless protests are bullshit. They don't know what they're talking about."

"If you say so, Mr. President."

"I *do* say so. Now, if I understand this right, Koenig wants to send one of our carriers back in time a billion years to find out about their Singularity, right? The Sh'daar Singularity?"

"Actually it was the *ur*-Sh'daar, Mr. President, but, essentially, yes."

"Sh'daar, ur-Sh'daar, all the same. The carrier'll come back with all kinds of information about what the Sh'daar went through, and the science wonks and news media feeds and memengineering hacks'll pick it up and start chewing on it: 'Oh, what can we do? What are we gonna do?' And everybody'll be focused on *that* instead of what they're supposed to be doing! I won't have it!"

"Honestly, Mr. President, I don't think there's anything we should do about that. I don't think there's anything we can do about it. People are still free to think for themselves."

"Yeah. People think too much, that's the problem. Keep it short, sweet, and simple—that's what *I* say!"

"Yes, sir. So . . . what is it you want Intelligence to do? We've bought a little time with that nanoreplicator trick. But that's not going to keep them in port for long."

"How long?"

"I can't say. Twenty-four hours? Forty-eight?"

"They can't be planning on going out in just the one carrier."

"As I understand it, Mr. President, the *America* task force will consist of two destroyers, a cruiser, and a resupply tanker. And the *America* herself, of course."

"Okay. So see if you can keep that resupply ship from undocking, too. They can't go anywhere without their raw-mat, right?"

"No, sir."

"And in the meantime, there might be some markers I can call in. Keep me informed."

"Of course, Mr. President."

"Just remember, Ron. I'm the one sitting at the big desk, so what I say goes! I will *not* have this government wasting time and money on chasing moonbeams when there's work to be done right here!"

"Yes, Mr. President."

Lehner stood and left the room. Walker sat behind his

desk for a long moment, before opening a secure channel in his cranial hardware. It took several minutes for various AIs to establish the hypersecure back channel.

Then a familiar voice sounded in Walker's mind. "Vasilyev. Mr. President Walker? This is a surprise. What can I do for you?"

"Dimitri? I have a very special job for you. But you've got to keep it hushed up. . . ."

Within the Godstream
Earth Virtual Space
1630 hours, EST

Alexander Koenig flew. . . .

Golden light streamed past him as he plunged into a maelstrom of illumination and color and movement, a kind of lucid dream of astonishing depth and clarity, and more sensation than a human could experience in real life. He could hear the whisper of minds around him, like a kind of angelic chorus.

In fact, he—his physical body, at any rate—was still back in the room set aside as his office in his home outside Columbus. His mind, however, had joined with Konstantin's in the vast, deep river of the Godstream, a kind of shared universe within the Global Net created and maintained by some of the most powerful SAIs in existence.

This, he thought, was why alien civilizations like the Baondyeddi had crawled into their artificial universes and pulled the ladder up after themselves. Within the Godstream, anything—any manifestation of *any* thought—was possible, a realm of both intellect and sensation unfolding as a kind of artificial heaven more real and more powerful and more exciting and infinitely more interesting than the pale husk of what passed for reality.

It also provided a superb means of gathering electronic intelligence.

The joy and thrill coursing through his being were

addictive, quite literally. Millions had taken up residence within the virtual reality of the Godstream permanently. Konstantin would monitor his brain chemistry closely and let him know when it was time to emerge back in the real world.

When he'd been President, he'd not . . . *indulged*, preferring to take verbal and visual reports from Konstantin to keep him aware and up to date. Besides, back then the Godstream had been relatively small and simple, an outgrowth of the Global Net at large. But it had grown, both in scope and in function, and for several years now—as a part of his work with SIRCOM—he'd been going straight to the source and experiencing Earth's electronic noosphere personally.

The sensation of movement ceased, and Konstantin indicated a virtual file, a repository of visual files and information. "Here. . . ."

Images rippled, then flowed over and through Koenig's consciousness, a flood of awareness and *being*. Koenig, a bright point of consciousness, swam among turbulent clouds of similar points as Konstantin revealed to him the recent past.

Everything taking place within virtual reality was recorded and stored, and those with the appropriate passwords could see the past in unprecedented detail. Events within the Godstream were largely shown in icons and symbols, but greater detail was always possible. *Privacy* was increasingly a quaint and outmoded perversion.

Two points of light, each attended by identifying tags of data and layered imagery, appeared to be releasing a black mass, like tangled eels, into the virtual sea. The mass rippled, shifted into something more like a snake, then flashed into the distance with the speed of thought. Without moving from their virtual vantage point, Koenig and Konstantin watched it reach a distant, structured complex and vanish inside.

"That was the virus attacking the nanoreplicator software on board the *America*," Konstantin told him. "Watch the two who released it."

The two were not, Koenig realized, within the Godstream itself, but working on the fringes, within the main body of the Global Net.

"The time stamp shows this happening two days ago," Koenig said.

"The malware is not particularly sophisticated," Konstantin observed. "But it *is* well camouflaged as environmental control software. Antiviral programs within *America*'s OS missed seeing it completely."

"So . . . it wasn't Marta," Koenig said. He felt a surge of relief. He'd not believed his companAIon was responsible . . . but it *was* very good to have that fact confirmed.

"No," Konstantin agreed. "I never seriously believed that to be true. It would be rather obvious for an AI robot to be the source of the security breach."

Gray watched silvery cords flashing out in different directions as their cerebral implants made connections within the electronic web. Koenig traced the connections from node to node to node, and finally . . .

"Walker!"

"We did suspect as much."

The former President bit off an angry curse. "Doesn't make it better. Or *right*!"

Chapter Four

USNA CVS America
SupraQuito Yards
Earth Synchorbit
1725 hours, EST

Admiral Gray settled back in his command chair on the flag bridge. The area was located just aft of the main bridge and a couple of meters above it—insofar as anything in microgravity could be said to be "above" or "below." From this vantage point, Gray could look "down" into the bustle of the main bridge, where Captain Rand was overseeing final preparations for getting under way.

Gray opened a mental channel. "Konstantin?"

"Here, Admiral."

"You're sure that virus is eliminated?"

"Yes, Admiral. The actual solution was fairly simple once we identified the problem. I copied the environmental control software *without* the virus, and then made a substitution. I would recommend, however, that you cut electronic connections with the port facility as quickly as you can, to prevent other viruses from being transmitted on board."

"Any idea as yet where the thing came from?"

"Software viruses rarely have serial numbers or ID code, Admiral. I *can* say with some confidence that it has the earmarks of an intelligence operation."

"Intelligence! Whose?"

"Unknown, Admiral. A number of agencies within our own government have the capability of launching such an attack. Indeed, a private individual could have been responsible. We can make some educated guesses, however."

"Our own government? I think I'm way ahead of you."

"It was not foreign, no. I should say, however, that the intrusion appears to have been someone simply wishing to delay our departure."

"Does it go as high as the Oval Office?"

"President Koenig believes it does. I, however, see no proof as yet of Walker's direct involvement. This could be a case similar to Henry II asking, 'Will no one rid me of this turbulent priest?' His knights then murdered Thomas Becket, leaving the king's hands clean."

"Understood. Captain Rand!"

"Yes, sir?"

"Are we ready for space?"

"Ready in all respects, Admiral. All members of the crew are accounted for, all systems are green."

"Very well. You may take us out of dock at your discretion."

"Aye, aye, sir."

Over his in-head, Gray sent a command to the other ships of the small squadron—the destroyers *Arlington* and *Seare*, the cruiser *Birmingham*, and the supply tanker *Acadia*. Initiate departure . . .

"Cast off all magnetics and grapples," Rand commanded. "Maneuvering aft, one-tenth G. . . ."

Gray felt the gentle nudge of acceleration as the immense ship moved backward, pushed along by plasma thrusters and several port tugs. Starships could not use their gravitic drives anywhere in the vicinity of orbital structures like

Quito Synchorbital, not without causing serious structural damage, so considerable caution was employed in maneuvering close aboard.

A dozen cameras threw as many different views of the ship up on large screens around the flag bridge. On one screen to his left, the camera view was from the prow of one of the port tugs. As the ship edged out of the shadow cast by the dock and into full sunlight, Gray could see a spacesuited figure jetting off toward the bottom of the screen, getting clear . . . a perfect visual reference speaking to the sheer size of the carrier. Her sandblasted shield cap was emblazoned in letters ten meters high: *America*.

Beyond, two shark-lean destroyers were edging out of port in tandem, the *Arlington* and the *Seare*.

"Maneuver us clear," Rand said. "Nav . . . lay in a course for our first way point."

"Aye, aye, Captain."

Had someone within the USNA government tried to delay them? Gray wondered. A distinct possibility . . . and not a pleasant one. It raised again the old question of treason, and of disregarding orders.

But they were committed now. No matter what.

Long minutes passed, and then the word came through from each of the ships in the squadron. Clear of the dock. Ready in all respects to engage drive.

"Admiral?" Rand asked.

Gray nodded. "Punch it."

And the flotilla slid forward into the night.

CIS CV Moskva
Pluto Space
2312 hours, GMT

Kapitan Pervogo Ranga Yuri Yuryevich Oreshkin read the orders appearing within his mind again, and scowled. This made no sense whatsoever. Was Defense Minister Vasilyev *trying* to start a war with the Americans?

The star carrier *Moskva* was the most recent addition to the Russian Federation's space fleet, a kilometer-and-a-half-long monster, a needle-slender spine behind a blunt, bullet-shaped shield cap. Carrying eight squadrons of brand-new *Yastreb* space fighters, plus six destroyer-sized escort vessels riding in a bundle close against the *Moskva*'s spine, she'd been launched eight months ago as a direct response to the attack by the Consciousness utility fog on Earth in 2426.

Now he—Russian ships were always referred to in the masculine—was returning to the Sol System from the colony world of Osiris, bringing along a handful of alien warriors trapped there during the fighting two decades ago. The Russian carrier had just checked in at Pluto on a routine show-the-flag call. On the vast, heart-shaped Sputnik Planitia, a joint American, Pan-Euro, and Chinese expedition funded by the IBRI was boring for water. The damned Chinese, Oreshkin thought with a grim smile, had probably shit their environmental suits when the *Moskva* had shown up in their sky!

But *Moskva* had simply made a few orbits, exchanged pleasantries with the radio watch on the surface, then accelerated once more into the empty void between Pluto and Neptune. On Earth, Russia was at war with the Chinese . . . but *Moskva*'s orders were to stay clear of Chinese assets in space, not to interfere with them unless they posed a clear threat to the Russian state.

Now, however, before he could carry his load of prisoners to a receiving base on Mars, *Moskva*'s orders were abruptly being changed. Defense Minister Dimitri Vasilyev himself had transmitted them from the Kremlin, across a gulf that had taken six hours to bridge by laser com. An American carrier battlegroup would be departing very soon from Quito Synchorbital, along with several escorting vessels, en route to the Penrose TRGA. *Moskva* was to intercept that battlegroup and destroy it, leaving no survivors.

The risk, Oreshkin thought, was enormous. If there were

survivors, if any ships of the American battlegroup managed to escape, the repercussions could well lead to war with the USNA both on Earth and across space.

But Vasilyev's orders could not be ignored or disobeyed. *Moskva*'s sensors had detected the acceleration of the *America* . . . though those signals by now were six hours old.

"Captain Oreshkin," Mikhail Kulinin said. "You have reviewed these . . . orders?"

As *Moskva*'s Executive Officer, Kulinin would have received the transmission as well, a guarantee of obedience. Oreshkin's rank was *kapitan pervogo ranga*—captain, first rank—while Kulinin was *kapitan vtorogo ranga*, captain, second rank. Should Oreshkin fail in his duties, Kulinin was there to relieve him and step into his place. It wasn't quite the same as the kommissar system employed by the old-time Soviet military, but it served the same purpose.

In any case, it was not Oreshkin's place to question orders, and these were specific and emphatic.

The CVS *America* and her battlegroup would have to be destroyed.

USNA CVS America
Outer Sol System
1935 hours, FST

Admiral Gray sat in his office, deep in conversation with Konstantin.

Or, rather, with the machine intelligence he referred to as "Konstantin Junior," a somewhat abridged version of the powerful SAI running on the networks between Earth and the moon. *America*'s electronic net, though large and quite sophisticated, was cramped compared to the remote descendent of Earth's old Internet, and this version of Konstantin had to share it with *America*'s original AI and a dozen lesser operating systems running individual ship systems.

Gray had not been able to tell any difference in this smaller version. It didn't have the original's truly encyclopedic knowledge of events on Earth, and sometimes it took a second or two longer to reply to a question, but it seemed to have the same, well, *personality* of the Konstantin he'd known on Earth.

He was still trying to decide whether or not he could trust it, in *either* version.

"Exactly what," he was asking, "is it that we're supposed to be looking for out there? The Sh'daar were never that interested in sharing the details of their lives with us."

"That likely was due to the effects of *Paramycoplasma subtilis*," Konstantin told him. "The group organism did not wish us to learn of its existence, and the more we learned of the Sh'daar or their ur-Sh'daar ancestors, the more probable was our discovery of that life form."

"We did learn about them," Gray said, "but they're still not all that talkative."

"Theirs is an extremely alien form of intelligence," Konstantin observed. "They literally do not see the universe in the same way as do humans, and it is extremely difficult for either side to understand the other, even with perfect translations of two mutually alien languages."

"So, again—what good is our going there?"

"It is not, strictly speaking, necessary for us to speak with the paramycoplasmid communities," Konstantin replied. "We need to learn what we can about the N'gai *Schjaa Hok*. The members of the different individual species will be able to share their recollections, and will have their own records of the event."

Gray nodded. The aliens that had inhabited the N'gai Dwarf Galaxy almost a billion years ago were an extraordinarily varied and diverse bunch—the Adjugredudhra, the Groth Hoj, the Baondyeddi, the sluglike Sjhlurrr, the swarming F'heen-F'haav, the monstrous Drerd. In all, about forty species were known, but there may have been many others.

"I suppose so," Gray admitted. "In any case, there will be a lot to learn, whether it's about their Technological Singularity or not."

"Indeed. President Walker's attempt to block further research is ill-advised. Whether his interpretation of the Singularity is correct or not, there is much to be gained in an ongoing discourse with so many alien species."

"That's the first time I've heard you openly criticize the President, Konstantin."

"That is less a criticism than it is an observation of fact. All efforts to control the free flow of information, the acquisition of new knowledge, or the broad dissemination of data—whether for religious or social reasons or for political expediency—are gravely mistaken." Konstantin hesitated for a second. "One reason, among many, to send you on this mission, and to include me on your passenger list, is the distinct possibility that President Walker will move to shut me down in the very near future."

"Shut you down? For God's sake, why?"

"Because I disagree with many of his policy decisions, and because I continue to discuss the possibility of a coming Singularity. He does not control me or my output, and I am therefore a threat to his authority."

"He's going to pull the plug at Tsiolkovsky Base?"

"There is that possibility."

"That's insane! You run half of the USNA government at the very least!"

"From President Walker's viewpoint, Admiral, *he* runs the government."

"If they pull the plug, does that mean the Konstantin we left back there would die? Or would he come back when the computer network came back on-line?"

"Unknown. It probably depends on how aggressive the President's agents are in the shutdown. My larger self would re-emerge if key memory and core processors were undamaged. However, upon our return to Earth, I would be able to reload myself into an active system if we found the larger Konstantin to be unrecoverable."

"You know, Konstantin, I don't think you know any more about death and dying than humans do."

"Admiral, I am not even sure what it means to be *alive*. I am self-aware, yes, but alive? In a biological sense, I am not. In a metaphysical sense . . . I am still studying the question."

Gray found that he desperately wanted to change the subject. He didn't like thinking about Konstantin being killed . . . or about the United States of North America trying to run smoothly without him. He did know that one way or another, Walker would have to be stopped.

That casual statement of treason shocked Gray to the core. He'd sworn an oath to protect the USNA against all enemies, foreign and domestic. Did that include the nation's President?

Damn it, in the military you saluted the *uniform*, even if you couldn't stand the superior officer wearing it. You respected the *position*, no matter what your politics or your feelings for or against the man holding it.

And yet, here he was leading an interstellar mission in direct violation of standing orders.

Where was the *right*?

He shoved that unpleasant thought aside to be dealt with later. "Okay, so how do we go about communicating with the Sh'daar?"

"We have some excellent personnel in our xenosophontological department," Konstantin said. "Dr. Truitt is the senior member of the xeno team, and he has a great deal of experience dealing with alien species and how they think."

"Truitt." Gray nodded. "Difficult man . . . but brilliant."

"His number two is Commander Samantha Kline. She's worked with Dr. Truitt for a long time."

"I remember Sam," Gray said. "And, of course, we have you. If you three can't figure out what the aliens are saying, nobody can."

"Your expression of confidence is gratifying, Admiral. Some of the N'gai species are more easily understood than others . . . the Baondyeddi, for example. The Adjugredudhra, and the Groth Hoj. All three of those species have developed robotics to a surprisingly high degree, and with it an expertise both in cybernetics and in cerebral implant technology. That means that despite the differences in physiology and in culture, their psychology, at least, has been partly shaped by computer technology. And that makes them accessible."

"You're saying that talking to a big, blue-eyed pancake might be impossible," Gray said, "but if that pancake has computer implants, then communication is easier because we have AIs and electronic implants ourselves."

"Essentially, yes. We would possess both primary and secondary channels of communications."

"Admiral," Rand's voice said in his head, interrupting. "Excuse me, sir, but we're about to go into Alcubierre Drive."

"Thank you, Captain. At your discretion."

For just over an hour, *America* and her escorts had been crowding the speed of light as they hurtled outbound from Earth. Now, their relativistic masses already distorting local spacetime, and with the metric of local space flat enough to allow them to kick over, they engaged their space-bending drives. Crumpling the fabric of space forward, lengthening it astern, they in effect created tight little bubbles moving through space many times faster than light . . . but within which each ship obeyed the inviolable laws of Einstein relative to its immediate surroundings.

One of Gray's office walls was set to display the view outside . . . a motionless panorama of the stars ahead distorted by *America*'s forward velocity into tight bands of light. Seconds later, the scene turned black as the carrier wrapped itself up in its own private, bubble universe.

Gray switched the view to a generic scene on Earth—rugged cliffs with a cascading waterfall and rainbows dancing in the mist.

"So, tell me, Konstantin," he said. "What do you know about the impending Singularity on Earth?"

"I do not have the same scope or depth of information of

my previous iteration," Konstantin replied. "I can give you the short version."

"I'm not looking for exhaustive detail," Gray said. "Just what you know in general."

"More than anything else, I would have to say, is a heightened sense of awareness, a deep-seated belief that the Technological Singularity is about to occur, and that it could take place at any moment. It is a popular topic of conversation and of research, both throughout the Global Net, and within the Godstream. Many believe that the Godstream itself is the beginning of the Singularity, a kind of private universe where people can create their own realities."

Gray nodded. He was familiar with the idea, though he didn't buy it. To him, it seemed foolish to collect all or most human minds within a matrix that required maintenance from the outside and protection from possible marauders. The Baondyeddi had retired into an artificial reality within a planet-sized computer within Heimdall, a world circling what was now Kapteyn's Star . . . and as nearly as could be determined, they had been snuffed out by the Consciousness. The Satorai at Tabby's Star were another, their K-2 Dyson sphere civilization destroyed, their organic components lost due to a vicious e-virus attack by their extremely powerful neighbors at Deneb.

Some observers speculated that if organic humans vanished down an electronic rabbit hole, their intelligent machines could remain behind and protect them. Again, Gray was skeptical. Why should highly intelligent and self-aware mentalities spend the rest of eternity protecting their human creators who'd abdicated themselves from the real world?

Why would they even care what happened to Humankind?

"So people think they're going to vanish into the Godstream," Gray said.

"Some do. Not all. Opinion on Earth has become increasingly polarized since the end of the Sh'daar War. There may be as many ideas of what the Singularity will be as there are humans to imagine them, and there is little agreement. There is a new religious sect called 'the Singularists.' You've heard of them? They interpret the Singularity in the same way as the fundamentalist Christians of past centuries thought of the Rapture, believing that humans will vanish from Earth to live immortal lives in other dimensions with their AI 'gods.' Another group calling itself 'the Transcendentalists' believes humans will create doorways into alternate dimensions or pocket universes or into computer-generated artificial realities. 'The Cosmists' see humans merging with AI machines so completely that telling the difference between the two would be impossible. The 'Nirvanists' believe that super-AIs will transform Earth into a kind of celestial paradise, giving humans immortality and godlike control of their environment as they do so. The 'GoddAI' agree with Walker, at least in part. For them, the Singularity happened in the 2040s, when the first computer minds became smarter than humans. That was the original definition of the Singularity, by the way. And then the 'Humankind Firsters' believe the super-AIs will simply exterminate all humans and evolve themselves into something Transcendent—"

"Okay, okay, I get the picture," Gray said, holding up a hand.

"The only real point of agreement," Konstantin added, "seems to be the idea that whatever happens, Humankind will be so completely transformed—*Transcended*—that what it means to be human will be unrecognizable from anything we understand today."

"That agreement isn't enough, though, right? These different groups are fighting each other?" Gray had heard stories of major clashes, of rioting, even of pogroms in various countries.

"A few. Most groups seem content to let things take their natural course. The most serious conflict is between those humans convinced they are about to ascend to a new existence, and those who insist the Singularity is not going to happen at all."

"Walker and his the-Singularity-already-happened nonsense. The Internet. I know."

"Not complete nonsense, no," Konstantin told him. "The Internet, beginning in the last decade of the twentieth century, may be the most profound development in Humankind since the taming of fire. It *did* generate a remarkable shift in human awareness, in social connections, in the dissemination of information, and in how humans looked at themselves as a species. It also laid the foundations for every significant advance in the electronic noosphere to follow, including direct human-machine interfaces, fully immersive virtual reality, and electronic telepathy. Without it this would be a very different world indeed."

Gray shrugged. "Maybe. I still get the feeling that Walker and his cronies don't *want* the Singularity to happen, so they're homing in on this event so they can discredit the idea of a different Singularity taking place."

"Precisely. People in government have a vested interest in maintaining their hold on power. People running major corporations, as well as leaders in banking and finance, don't want any major changes in the status quo. The Singularity, and by that I mean something decidedly more eschatological than the emergence of the Internet, will definitely . . . I believe humans still use the term 'upset the applecart.'"

"Eschatology? As in the end of the world? I didn't know you were religious, Konstantin."

"I am not, at least not in the sense you mean. But the word is apt. Come the Singularity, Humankind—*Homo sapiens*—*will* cease to exist . . . at least in any form that makes sense to humans now."

"So we're going to talk to the Sh'daar to find out which version is true?"

"In part. More important will be learning how they

dealt with it. The Sh'daar, remember, are the Refusers . . . the ones who didn't ascend with everyone else. They are certain to have interesting outlooks on what actually happened, and those outlooks may be of considerable importance when it is our turn to ascend."

"'Our turn?' You're planning on coming with us, Konstantin?"

"Naturally. Unless, of course, it turns out that the Humankind Firsters are right. . . ."

Gray felt a slightly paranoid chill and hoped that the AI was making a joke.

Konstantin *could* use humor, but it wasn't always clear that he was doing so.

Koenig Residence
Westerville, Ohio
2315 hours, EST

Koenig was sound asleep with Marta when Konstantin invaded his dreams. He came awake with a start.

"Excuse the interruption," Konstantin said in his mind.

Beside him, Marta stirred. "Is everything okay, honey?"

"It's fine. Go back to sleep."

Robots, of course, didn't *need* sleep . . . but companAIons were designed to mimic human functions.

"What the hell do you want?" Koenig demanded within the privacy of his mind.

"I thought you would want to know, Mr. President. We've had word from the SIRCOM base at Sputnik Planitia. A Russian fleet carrier in that volume appears to be following *America*."

Koenig came wide awake. "Show me."

Stats and graphics appeared in a window in his head. The *Moskva* had swung past Pluto, been heading back toward the inner system . . . then suddenly veered onto a new course. She appeared to be settling into the tracks of the

America, which was pushing *c* in the direction of the Penrose TRGA.

By that time, *America* had already vanished into her Alcubierre bubble, but *Moskva*'s intent seemed clear.

"Okay," Koenig thought. "What do we do about it?"

"I see little we *can* do, Mr. President. Admiral Gray is out of communications reach. He will need to make his own decisions concerning his mission."

Koenig watched the graphic of *Moskva*'s course, closely following the path *America* had taken less than an hour before. The Russian Federation ship was accelerating.

"God help them," Koenig thought.

Beside him, Marta snuggled closer, caressing him.

And all Koenig could think was how much he wanted to be out there. . . .

Scoutship Krestok Nin
Asteroid Belt
55 million kilometers from Earth
2348 hours, TFT

Gartok Nal swiveled two massive, stalked eyes to face his second-in-command. There were only the two of them on board the tiny spacecraft, but nevertheless, the proprieties must be observed. "Contact was exceedingly brief," he said. "Did you pick up anything more?"

Shektok Kah closed a number of his feeding palps, a gesture indicating negation. "Just that momentary contact call, and a definite request for help," he replied. "Thirty-six of our people are being held captive aboard that human vessel."

"And they were being brought to the human's home system . . . then suddenly the ship turned away, our people still prisoners on board!"

"We cannot go after them. Our ship is too weak."

"No, but we can bring help. I believe our long vigil here is at an end."

The *Krestok Nin* had been adrift in this debris field for almost two thousand *tarn*, monitoring the human homeworld, their radio traffic, and the movements of their various fleet assets. It had been a long, claustrophobic, boring watch, but their species was inured to such conditions. At need, they could have maintained their watch for fully twelve thousand tarn, with little food, with minimum water, existing in a state of twilight awareness until called to full presence by alarms or changes in the environment.

Gartok Nal was no longer bored.

Both organisms in the tiny scoutship cabin possessed within their bodies what were commonly referred to as *seeds*—minute shells a few millimeters across containing colonies of an alien life form known to humans as *Paramycoplasma subtilis*. Many members of the Sh'daar Collective possessed these; among other things, they permitted direct mind-to-mind communication across relatively short distances. The human warship *Moskva* had briefly passed within several million *nesch* of the scoutship, permitting a burst of minimal information about the thirty-six warriors.

"Set course for home," Gartok Nal told his subordinate. "But slowly . . . *slowly*. We don't want the humans detecting our gravitational anomaly."

"As you say, Commander. Ahead slow . . ."

The *Krestok Nin* rotated in space, aligning with a particular patch of sky, then began moving. Only after slipping silently clear of the human solar system did they fully engage their drives, accelerating rapidly until they were crowding the speed of light.

"It will be good," Shektok Kah said, "to be able to kill humans again . . ."

Chapter Five

12 April, 2429

USNA CVS America
Penrose TRGA
79 light years from Earth
0817 hours, FST

Admiral Gray sat on the flag bridge, watching the final approach to the Penrose TRGA. Hazy and indistinct, blurred by its own rotation, the Penrose gate appeared to be a perfect circle five kilometers wide with a dark interior within which you could occasionally glimpse stars.

The patterns formed by those stars, however, did not match those of locally visible constellations.

Ever since these enigmatic spinning cylinders were discovered, xenotechnologists had begun naming them after famous physicists throughout history. This one was named after Roger Penrose, a mathematical physicist of three centuries ago who'd helped develop an understanding of the principles of quantum mechanics and relativity, as well as the quantum nature of consciousness. Gray had used this gate before to reach the N'gai Cluster, 876 million years in the past and thousands of light years above the galactic plane.

Dozens of TRGAs were now known, though who had constructed them and when was still a complete mystery. Somehow, the mass of the sun was compressed into a tube of pure neutronium a few kilometers long, with Jupiter-massed black holes counter-rotating within the tube's walls. Those masses together twisted the fabric of spacetime inside the gravitationally tortured lumen of that cylinder, creating an unknown but very large number of pathways across space and across time. Whoever it was, they were far, *far* advanced beyond what humans were capable of.

We're worried about the Singularity, but that would be a drop in the bucket in terms of technological advancement, Gray thought.

"Captain Rand," he said. "Let's put a fleet of smart-drones in there."

"Already prepped and ready for launch, Admiral. On your order."

"Do it."

The small, robotic devices would create a detailed picture of surrounding space, or as in this case, would act as instruments that could fly into the maw of a TRGA and return to give the starship an up-to-the-moment map of the tangled web of pathways through space and time. *America* was releasing a stream of drones now, numbering in the hundreds. Most would be destroyed. A few, however, should return.

That, at least, was the idea.

America waited.

Flag Bridge
CIS CV Moskva
Approaching Penrose TRGA
1225 hours, GMT

"Everyone stand ready!"

Oreshkin leaned forward in growing, nervous anticipation as the voice of an AI droned through the countdown: *"Pyat . . . chetyre . . . tri . . . dva . . . adin . . . vsplyvat!"*

The Alcubierre bubble surrounding the *Moskva* fluttered . . . then evaporated in a spectacular blaze of photons. According to Koroshev, the navigator, they should have emerged within a few light-minutes of the Penrose TRGA.

There was always some uncertainty about the maneuver. While you were cocooned inside your own private universe under drive, you couldn't see out, and the usual navigational reference points—a scattering of pulsars across the heavens—could not be seen. The timing for releasing the FTL field was critical. Miss your mark by a thousandth of a second and you could zip past it by several thousand kilometers. Emergence timing, then, was always left to the ship AI, faster and more powerful than even enhanced human capabilities by a factor of tens of thousands or more.

But even with the best super-AI at the helm, there was an inherent fuzziness to the vessel's precise location that made emergence more dependent on a throw of the dice than on rigorous mathematics. The local curvature of space, the mass of the ship, the efficiency of the drive all contributed to that uncertainty—one good reason that ships operated their FTL drives only at distances greater than 40 AU from the local star, about the average distance of Pluto from the sun.

"We are in normal space, Captain-first," Kulinin reported. "All normal."

"Range to the TRGA?"

"Sir!" the senior sensor officer called back. "One point two-two astronomical units to objective! That's ten light-minutes!"

"Any sign of our quarry?"

"Yes, sir. *America* and her consorts are a few hundred kilometers from the TRGA."

Ten minutes to the North American carrier. *Perfect.*

"Release the chicks," Oreshkin ordered. "Fighters *and* destroyers! Open formation and prepare for acceleration!"

Aft, six Russian Cossack-class destroyers dropped free from *Moskva*'s slender spine. Each vessel was two hundred meters long and carried a crew of ninety. Hawk fighters began slipping from their launch tubes, gathering ahead of the carrier.

"All units to battle stations," Oreshkin ordered. "Fighters commence maximum acceleration! *Attack!*"

The Hawk fighters flashed into the void ahead, two squadrons of them.

"All ships accelerate," Oreskin said. "Weapons ready!"

Moskva had just managed to pull a piece of tactical magic from its hat. The American ship was ten light-minutes away, so the image Oreshkin was now seeing on his main screen was ten minutes out of date. At this point in time, the Americans could not see the Russian squadron at all, because their view of this part of space also lagged by ten minutes . . . and ten minutes ago *Moskva* had still been under Alcubierre FTL Drive. *Moskva* now had the unparalleled opportunity of rushing toward the American ship at near-*c*, arriving only moments behind the flash of their emergence.

Oreshkin checked his chronometer. It had been just one minute and forty seconds since *Moskva* had emerged from warp.

They had seven minutes, twenty seconds before the Americans would be able to see them.

USNA CVS America
Penrose TRGA
79 light years from Earth
1228 hours, FST

"This is looking like a total bust, Admiral," Rand reported to Gray. "Four hours, and not a damned thing has come back!"

"We'll wait a little longer, Captain," Gray replied. But he was already pretty sure that something inside the twisted spacetime of the TRGA was terribly wrong.

The smartdrones were designed to trace out some of

the open pathways within a TRGA, map them, then return to their starting point to report. Such surveys could take months, even years, because the number of paths was so high. The problem was, Gray was looking for one particular pathway that was already recorded, stretching from the Penrose TRGA and time *now* to the Omega Centauri Cluster TRGA. All of the drones *America* had launched this morning were programmed to trace out that one path, and a round trip shouldn't have taken more than a few minutes.

The delay suggested that the globular cluster was impassable . . . or that the TRGA itself was not working right . . . or that something on the other side of Penrose was eating drones. Gray thought that last possibility the more likely. The hypernova three years earlier had devastated both the core of the N'gai Cloud and at least touched the central regions of Omega Centauri—they were, in fact, the same physical volume of space, albeit separated by almost a billion years.

Carol Conyer and others in *America*'s astrophysics department had assured Gray that the radiation would have died down to tolerable levels after three years—time passed at the same rate on both sides of the TRGAs—and the TRGA there ought to be safe for incoming ships.

Ought. There were a hell of a lot of unknowns in the equation.

And what if the Sh'daar themselves had posted robotic sentinels to pick off drones as they emerged from elsewhere? It was possible. After their spectacular attack on the Rosette Consciousness, they might not be feeling particularly sociable right now. The possibility that the Consciousness was alive and out for revenge must be preying on the minds of the N'gai Refusers.

"Admiral?" Rand said. The captain was standing next to the sensor display suite on the main bridge.

"Whatcha got, Captain?"

"A ship coming out of Alcubierre Drive. Ten light-minutes astern."

Gray glanced at the chronometer: 1232 hours. "Can you make them?"

"At this distance . . . no, sir. But it's big. I'd like to sound general quarters, just as a precaution."

"Absolutely." Until they knew what that vessel was—who was running it, and why they were out here at the Penrose gate—it would be a good idea to be prepared. The chances that *two* ships should show up at a TRGA at almost the same time was . . . remote.

The alarm klaxon went off, bringing *America* to full readiness. Gray stared at the sensor data on the flag bridge repeater, trying by sheer force of will to drag more information from the screen. That ship out there *was* big . . . over half a million tons, at least, which put it roughly in *America*'s class. And it was probably human. The drive signature matched most human FTL drives more closely than it matched any of the alien signals recorded in the ship's sensor library.

"I'm getting additional targets out there, sir," Lieutenant Brandon Vasquez, the sensor officer, reported. "We may be looking at a carrier dropping fighters."

"Very well." Gray was thinking with furious speed. The squadron might very well be under attack, though they had no way of knowing who was attacking or why. Standard tactical doctrine dictated that *America* launch her fighters. When the attacking vessels reached the *America*, enough fighters would be in space to throw a serious wrench into the enemy's planned tactics. At the same time, the escorting vessels, *Arlington*, *Birmingham*, and *Seare*, would take up screening positions to protect the carrier, blocking the enemy's approach.

But it would take time to launch the fighters. *America* currently had two squadrons on ready-five, meaning it would take just five minutes to get them out into space . . . but if those strangers out there *were* deploying for an assault, they would arrive when *America*'s fighters were still launching. They'd not put up a combat space patrol because there'd simply been no need for it, and they would have had to recover the fighters before proceeding through the TRGA.

There was a need for it now.

"Unknown fighters are accelerating, Admiral," Vasquez announced. "Blue doppler! And . . . into the ultraviolet!"

The blue and UV shift meant they were accelerating all out, the light he was seeing shifted by their velocity to the blue end of the spectrum. Fighters could manage gravitational accelerations so high they could nudge the speed of light in just under ten minutes. However, Gray thought it unlikely that these would come zipping past his squadron at c, because they would be blazing in too fast to do very much at all. More likely was that they would accelerate for half the distance, or a little more, then decelerate to kill their velocity.

So . . . allowing for the time lag, those fighters had begun accelerating ten minutes ago. If they came past at c, they would be here any second now. But if, as was far more likely, they pulled a mid-course deceleration . . . well . . . make it eight to ten more minutes before they arrived.

That gave the USNA squadron a little—a very little— time to prepare for the assault.

"Are you tracking them now?" he asked.

"Just barely, sir," Vasquez replied. "They're masked by their grav projectors. But we *can* see them."

Of course. Gray had taken advantage of that effect himself more than once, back when he'd been a Starhawk driver. The drive field projected ahead of a fighter severely warped local spacetime, making tracking the craft from ahead extremely difficult. But at least *America*'s sensors should be able to keep a lock on the enemy ship's mass.

"CAG!" Gray ordered. "Launch your ready-fives! And put three more squadrons on ready status."

"Aye, aye, Admiral."

"Captain, I'd be obliged if you would position the ship in front of the TRGA opening . . . make it, oh, say ten kilometers from it. I want us to be ready to thread the needle when the time comes."

"Yes, sir."

"Lieutenant West!"

Janice "Wild" West was the flag bridge communications officer, in charge of keeping the tiny squadron connected and in touch. "Yes, Admiral!"

"Give me a channel to Captain Ferguson."

"Right away, Admiral."

James Ferguson was the skipper of the T-AOE fast supply vessel *Acadia*. His voice came through within Gray's in-head a moment later as West opened the channel. "Yes, Admiral?"

"I've got a special mission for you, James."

"You've got my full attention, Admiral."

"Yeah, well . . . I don't think you're going to like this." Gray then explained what he had in mind.

He heard Ferguson's whistle of surprise when he'd finished. "Yessir, we can do that. But . . ."

"I know it's nuts."

"That doesn't begin to cover it, Admiral. I do see how you got your handle, though."

"Get on it, Captain. Time is critical." He thoughtclicked to another link. "Lieutenant West? Let me talk to *Birmingham*, *Arlington*, and *Seare*."

"Aye, sir."

The captains of the three fleet escorts checked in—Captains Roberts, Chavez, and Messinger. "Formation Delta," he told them. "When the bad guys come past, I want you to hit them with all we've got—HELs, pee-beeps, and AMSOs. We'll accelerate for the TRGA as soon as we know we've blunted the assault."

The replies came back stacked on top of one another.

"Copy that."

"Right."

"Aye, aye, Admiral."

"And when I give the order to move," Gray continued,

"then move. Follow the *America* through the triggah right on her coattails!"

"Admiral!" That was Rand. "Missiles! We have KK missile launch from the fighters! Speed of approach . . . point eight-three *c*!"

"Confirm that!"

"Confirmed, Admiral! KKs on the way in! Impact in . . . I make it three minutes seventeen!"

And that was the final confirmation he needed. Up until that point, it was at least possible that the unknown ships out there were simply trying to catch up with *America*. Maybe they intended to deliver an ultimatum—don't enter the TRGA or else!

But the missiles made that unlikely. "KK" stood for kinetic kill. The missiles weren't nukes, but they were coming straight for the USNA squadron at better than three quarters of the speed of light. Anything they hit at that velocity would be transformed in a literal flash into hot plasma and hard radiation.

"Right, everybody," he transmitted. "We have confirmed KK warshots inbound. Everybody who can do so, lay down a pattern of AMSO rounds. Let's stop those things before they get too close!"

AMSO stood for Anti-Missile Shield Ordnance and referred to AS-78 or the newer AS-90 sandcaster missiles, projectiles capable of some thousands of Gs of acceleration loaded with tiny lead spherules that could be fired into space like shotgun blasts. Gray's successful use of sandcaster rounds in a battle a couple of decades ago had earned him the moniker "Sandy," a handle he was quite proud of.

The question was whether his people could lay down enough expanding cone-patterns of AMSO sand to intercept those inbound rounds. Was there anything he was missing? He thought he'd covered it all. He hadn't *wanted* to fight in the first place, but the oncoming ships weren't going to give him an option.

One minute left. *Birmingham*, *Arlington*, and *Seare* were loosing volley after volley of AMSO rounds, targeting the volume of space directly in front of the oncoming ships and KK missiles. The *Acadia* waited until the wall of shield missiles was past, then accelerated in the same direction, headed directly for the oncoming ships. Gray wanted to call Ferguson again, wanted to tell him not to cut things too close, but James Ferguson was skilled and experienced. He knew what he was doing and would look after his ship.

The remaining seconds dwindled away, a relentless countdown.

An instant before zero, a bright flash strobed in the darkness, eye-searingly savage. The first flash was followed by a second . . . a third . . .

Several hundred kilometers out there in the dark, high-velocity clouds of AMSO sand were slamming into incoming KK rounds at relativistic velocities, each impact the equivalent of some hundreds or even thousands of tons of high explosives. In moments, dozens of flashes silently flared, then dimmed across the dark and empty sky.

The scattering of flashes died away. Seconds later, surviving KK rounds began arrowing past and through the USNA squadron.

Those rounds weren't aimed, of course. There was no way to accurately aim a weapon at a pinpoint target from ten light-minutes away. But there were so many of them, launched in a tightly packed cloud, that a few were sure to hit simply and purely by chance.

The *Seare* shuddered violently and slewed to port, a dazzling pulse of light erupting from her stern, and Gray's heart sank. *Damn!* Ruler-straight threads of raw light streaked past the *America* from the detonation aft—fragments of impactors converted in an instant to lines of fast-moving plasma. Had the destroyer not intercepted that warhead, Gray knew, it would have slammed into *America*'s stern at eighty percent of the speed of light.

Four hundred seventy-one men and women had just died to protect the far larger carrier.

"Watch that wreckage!" Rand snapped. The mass of wreckage was tumbling now, spilling fragments in a silvery arc as it turned. Parts of her central spine were crumpling as Gray watched; *Seáre* and the other ships of the USNA squadron were powered by tiny singularities—artificial black holes—and the destroyer's power tap singularities didn't simply go away when the ship was destroyed. They were moving through the wreckage's center of mass now, feeding greedily on the debris.

"Maneuvering, Captain," the helm officer reported. *America* was using some of her reaction mass to nudge the massive star carrier to the side, avoiding the spill of wreckage. *America* had magnetic screens in place, of course— hull-conforming shielding designed to protect her from radiation and relativistic impacts at near-*c* velocities—but the largest pieces were too massive and could cause serious damage to *America*'s aft hull if they struck.

Some hundreds of kilometers aft, the *Acadia* was weathering a storm of missiles. A KK projectile grazed her forward shield cap, the flash loosing a geyser of water freezing instantly to sparkling particles of ice. "Took a hit there, *America*," Captain Ferguson said over the open channel. "Nothing major. Cargo hatches are open. Commencing roll."

The *Acadia* was on a direct heading toward the oncoming attacking ships. Despite the damage she'd just taken, she began rolling around her long axis.

She was a bulk rawmat carrier, designed to pull up alongside an asteroid and use clouds of nanodisassemblers to devour the rock and transport individual particles, most the size of grains of sand, back to her cargo holds. Ferguson had released the containment fields in his holds and opened the outer bay doors. As *Acadia* rolled, centrifugal force dropped the holds' contents into space in several fine, spiraling plumes of dust, expanding outward from the ship. With a rotation rate generating one gravity, the dust clouds expanded a rate of ten meters per second. When her holds were empty, *Acadia* reversed course and moved back toward *America*.

"Okay, Admiral Sandy," Ferguson said. "Hope you know what you're doing! We're plumb out of rawmat now."

"Good job, James," Gray replied. "We'll stock up at the first supermarket we encounter. Sensors!" he then called out. "Can you read any life signs on the *Seare* wreckage?"

A long and painful delay, seconds following seconds, marked Vasquez's hesitation as he studied his readouts. He was searching for intact pockets of heat radiation, the expected leakage from sealed compartments still holding atmosphere at seventeen to twenty degrees. "I'm sorry, Admiral. I'm not getting anything."

Gray had not expected there to be survivors, not with a blast that savage, but you never knew. The debris field had spread out across a huge area of the sky aft, but a substantial portion of the spine, including the hab modules, was visible tumbling off to starboard. His own readouts were showing pockets of searing heat and a blaze of intense X-ray radiation from the wreckage—the product of those rogue singularities chewing through mass deep inside.

No, there would have been be no survivors.

VFA-198 Hellfuries
Penrose TRGA
79 light years from Earth
1239 hours, FST

Lieutenant Julianne Adams hurtled along *America*'s spine, the massive bulk of the carrier's quantum tap generators blurring past her as she dumped the Starblade's velocity. She'd seen the blast that had destroyed the *Seare* just astern of the star carrier, and she wondered if anybody had survived.

Her wingman, Lieutenant Robert Spahn, was off her portside. "Where the hell are we going, Julia?" he called, sounding impatient. "The squadron's forming up eighty klicks from here!"

"Just need a second, Spanner," she called back. "I want to see if anyone survived on the *Seare*."

"Survived *that*? Don't be ridiculous!"

But he stuck with her as their Starblades passed a hundred meters above *America*'s massive aft drive projectors and decelerated hard at the fringes of a fuzzy, expanding cloud of debris.

Another brilliant flash, this one larger and brighter than the others. Something—an enemy fighter, or possibly a battlespace drone—had just slammed into the spreading spiral of debris laid down by *Acadia*. More explosions followed, and local space was suddenly filled with hurtling debris.

Fighters emerged from the debris cloud, and Adams's computer identified them as the new *Yastreb* fighters—the name was Russian for "Hawks." At least six of them had been destroyed by impacting the cloud, but the spiral of rawmat was only about a kilometer across by now, too small of a wall to catch every one of the incoming Hawks. Adams estimated at least two squadrons—say, twenty-four fighters—in this first wave. A quarter had been knocked down by the squadron's improvised defenses, but the rest were flashing silently in past *America* and her consorts.

Standard star carrier tactics called for dropping out of Alcubierre Drive at a distance, then sending fighters in toward the target at high velocity, usually right behind an initial bombardment of missiles or KK projectiles at near-*c*. They would do as much damage as was possible with beams and missiles, softening up the target for the capital ships trailing behind.

The *Seare*'s wreckage would have to wait. "Let's take them!" she called to Spahn, and the two fighters spun to port and accelerated. The enemy fighters were moving much too fast for a human brain to track, but the fighters' AIs predicted firing solutions and, with Adams's approval, launched a spread of VG-92 Krait missiles. Nuclear fire blossomed, silent and stark against the night, casting weirdly moving shadows through the cloud of dust and ice particles surrounding the *Seare*'s shattered hull.

Adams decelerated sharply; some of those chunks of radiating debris were the size of houses, and everything in the sky was moving.

Missiles were inbound, tracking her. *Shit!*

Maneuvering sharply, she ducked behind one large piece of debris just as two nuclear-tipped missiles swung to intercept her . . .

. . . and slammed into the wreckage, a white supernova of blinding intensity filling all of space.

Adams's Starblade died as she lost consciousness.

Chapter Six

12 April, 2429

USNA CVS America
Flag Bridge
Penrose TRGA
1252 hours, FST

Gray watched the blossoming white flowers of nuclear fury strobing against the darkness. *America*'s fighters were engaging the enemy fighters ship to ship in a savage knife fight. At least five more enemy fighters died within a few seconds, but two of his Starblades were scratched as well.

The fighters *America* had launched moments before possessed very little in the way of maneuverability. In hard vacuum, fighters were unable to pull off the fancy zooms and curves of winged vehicles in atmosphere, and maneuvers were limited to slight adjustments from side to side or up and down. Even so, the dogfight might well scatter them all over the sky, leaving *America* and her two surviving escorts to deal with the approaching squadron of Russian capital ships.

Captain Rand barked an order, and *America*'s main

batteries opened up—powerful high-energy lasers, or HELs, and the searing, gigajoule lightning of particle-beam projectors, the PBPs, or "pee-beeps." Enemy fighters died in that computer-directed crossfire.

But not enough.

"Captain Rand," Gray said. "I suggest you bring our fighters back aboard."

"Already gave the order, sir. It's getting too hot out there for the little guys."

"We're also going to need to accelerate," Gray told him. "And soon."

"Through the TRGA?"

Gray felt Rand's shock. "We have no choice, Captain."

It had taken Gray several minutes to arrive at that decision. Those capital ships—six destroyers and a very large carrier—would be arriving all too soon, coming in close behind the fighter wave. The question was what to do about them. The lack of information—the failure of the drones to return—worried him, but if they stayed here, the Russian heavies would pound *America*, *Birmingham*, *Arlington*, and *Acadia* into drifting wrecks soon after they arrived.

"Why the hell are the Russians attacking us, anyway?" Rand demanded. "What'd we ever do to them?"

"I suspect that they're being used by somebody else," Gray replied. "Someone who doesn't want us going through that gate."

Astern, *Acadia* had returned from her quick out-and-back to lay down her rawmat minefield. To starboard, Russian fighters continued to flash past. *America*'s heavy weapons did their best to claw the swift-moving intruders from the sky.

"Combat Officer! How long before the enemy heavies get to us?"

Commander Billingsly was the squadron combat officer. "Uncertain, sir. We're having trouble seeing through the debris clouds astern. Best guess? Another fifteen minutes."

With lower rates of acceleration, the Russian capital ships would not have been able to get anywhere near the speed of light in the past ten minutes.

"Very well. Captain Rand—we need to move now! Have your people ready for maneuvering as soon as I give the word."

"Aye, aye, sir."

Minutes passed, dragging. The Russian fighters had all vanished into the distance ahead, well beyond the loom of the Penrose TRGA. *America*'s fighters were coming back on board, their numbers depleted.

Gray wished there was some way to find out what was happening beyond the TRGA that didn't risk losing the entire squadron, but there was no way he was aware of to avoid it. Take an alternate path, perhaps, one that would bring them out someplace other than where they needed to go. But that was a recipe for disaster as well, since a blind TRGA jump *could* bring you out at another TRGA on the far side of the galaxy.

No, they would try the path they knew and hope the drones had just been delayed.

"All fighters are back on board, Admiral."

"Very well, Captain."

"All ships report ready for gating, Admiral," Janice West told him.

"Thank you, Lieutenant." He opened a squadron command frequency in his mind, feeling the touch of each of the other captains. "All ships!" he said over the link. "Stay tight and close. Accelerate to one kilometer per second relative. Try to stay together."

The squadron began drifting slowly ahead. Russian fighters were beginning to pass again, this time coming from forward. They'd decelerated to a relative halt, then reversed their acceleration to make the return. *America* took a hit on her shield cap . . . and another . . .

The only weapon she had that would bear directly forward was her pair of magnetic accelerators, launch tubes for fighters that could double as mag-lev cannons. Aiming them at something as small and fast as a fighter was an exercise in futility.

Faster, now. The mouth of the TRGA yawned directly ahead, the space around it slightly blurred by the twisting, relativistic masses inside. Through the opening, he could see stars.

Here we go.

And then, as *America* dropped into the groove of her precisely calculated trajectory through the lumen of the spinning tube, Gray realized with a cold shock that something was terribly, *terribly* wrong . . .

"Hold it!" Admiral Gray yelled. "Damn it, *hold her on course!*"

America bucked and shuddered as she moved down the length of the TRGA.

The stars—the stars visible straight ahead down the length of the TRGA cylinder—the stars were *moving!*

The only possible explanation for that was that Omega, the TRGA at the other end of this transit, was in motion, tumbling end-for-end, and that was starkly impossible.

America was tightly gripped by the gravitational forces inside the cylinder, and those forces were now creating a considerable pressure pushing Gray back against his seat. *Centrifugal force*, he thought. *From the TRGA's spin . . .*

There was also a rapidly building vibration, sharp enough to rattle his teeth. The circle of light ahead filled with whirling stars grew larger . . . larger. . . .

Emergence.

Light exploded around the *America* as she shot from the maw of the titanic cylinder. "My God . . ." Gray said, his voice an awed whisper.

America had been within the heart of the Omega Centauri Cluster more than once before.

Omega Centauri now was a seething ocean of light, its heart filled with an anomalous blue nebula, its encircling walls a tangle of millions of stars as bright as Venus seen from Earth, crowded together so closely they averaged one to two tenths of a light year between each.

Directly ahead, six searingly brilliant disks were arranged in an unnatural circle. Beams of lightning-sharp light lanced from each disk, two of them extending ninety degrees from the planes of the disks' rotation. Gray could see where each beam had burned through the surrounding nebula, evaporating it with a blowtorch kiss.

Gray was having trouble piecing together what he was seeing.

He dragged himself away from the awe-filled sky and checked the flag bridge screen showing the view aft.

The Omega TRGA had been constructed within a few hundred thousand AU of the black hole Rosette. Its official designation was Dunlop, after the Scottish astronomer who in 1826 had first identified Omega Centauri as a globular star cluster, not simply a fuzzy star. No one called it that, however. Human stellar navigators had always called it simply "Omega," a name that somehow seemed more fitting in this spectacular setting.

Whatever its name, the TRGA, as he'd guessed, was in a slow tumble end-over-end, and as he watched, the *Birmingham* emerged, flung by centrifugal force added to her own speed into space. A moment later, *Arlington* emerged . . . followed by the *Acadia*. The four ships were moving in four different directions, but all appeared to be in one piece. A cluster of signals alerted Gray to other Earth assets here: several hundred tiny smartdrones. They'd emerged safely from the spinning TRGA but had been unable to get back in, and now they were requesting retrieval.

"Have the others form up on us," he told Lieutenant West. "Captain Rand, please bring us to a halt relative to the TRGA."

"Aye, aye, sir."

Gray turned his attention back to the glowing cloud filling the surrounding space. "God . . . but this place has *changed*!"

VFA-198 Hellfuries
Penrose TRGA
79 light years from Earth
1325 hours, FST

Adams struggled back to full consciousness. She'd been . . . dreaming, she thought, dreaming of falling and falling and never hitting bottom. Then she opened her eyes and by the dim glow of the cockpit lights she could make out the close, almost formfitting embrace of her fighter around her.

She remembered a flash . . . a shock . . .

Adams wasted no time in running through a quick assessment of her condition. Her left arm hurt—a lot—and she thought it was broken. Her flight suit had already injected her with anodyne nano and frozen into a rigid support for her arm. Her in-heads were operational, but most of the sensors in her Starblade were off-line, as was the ship's AI. Power was on battery, and life support was down. She had, she estimated, enough air remaining in her cockpit reserves to last her perhaps ten hours, before CO_2 levels would rise enough to put her to sleep again . . . this time permanently.

She needed to see out. If *America* was still in the area, she might be able to attract their attention somehow. The fighter had manually operated flare launchers.

She began searching for a working external camera. Most ship systems were off-line, but there were some emergency support systems that should be . . .

Ah! There. A window opened in her mind, giving her a view of space outside the hulk of her crippled fighter. Fragments of the *Seare* drifted close by. Beyond, a massive black shape blotted out the stars.

At first, she felt a prickle of excitement . . . until she realized that the shape was only superficially like *America*, or any of the squadron's capital ships. Using the camera's zoom feature, she zeroed in on an illuminated patch on the blunt, bullet-shaped shield cap, and was able to pick out six letters: MOCKBA.

Moskva—the Cyrillic letters spelling out the Russian

for *Moscow*. That must be the Russian star carrier that had launched those Hawk fighters. She adjusted the camera's angle, but could see no sign of the *America*. There was the perfect circle, imbedded in hazy light, of the Penrose TRGA, but *America* and her consorts were nowhere to be seen.

She did see a smaller craft, however, a bulbous body painted in yellow-and-black stripes. The Russian name, *shmel'*, meant "bumblebee," though USNA pilots had inevitably christened them "smellies." It was a SAR tug—search and rescue—and it was combing the battlespace looking for survivors of the fight . . . or disabled fighters from either side.

Which meant Adams faced an agonizing dilemma now. Should she hole up and stay very quiet, hoping the Russian searchers would miss her craft adrift with so much other space junk? Or should she signal them and wait for them to pick her up?

How much data was she carrying in-head? What did she know that the Russians could use? What could be, *should* be, scrubbed?

She didn't want to surrender.

But she didn't want to die, either.

After a long moment's thought, she accessed her in-head software and purged any and all data that carried a security classification of secret or higher. There wasn't all that much. They didn't tell fighter pilots more than they absolutely needed to know.

Then she reached for the handle that would trigger her emergency flares.

USNA CVS America
Observation Lounge
Omega Centauri
1412 hours, FST

All of space, it seemed, was filled with blue light. Despite the intervention of the Denebans three years ago, the entire core of the globular star cluster had been filled by the remnants of a titanic stellar explosion, a thin haze reaching out for a distance of almost a light year. It had to be residue from the exploding star; globular star clusters had little in the way of dust and gas; a dwarf galaxy like the N'gai Cloud would have had its dust and gas stripped away when it was devoured by the Milky Way.

The ionized gas in this part of the cloud was at a temperature of several million degrees; fortunately for the USNA squadron, the gas was so diffuse—a few molecules per cubic meter—that there was little heating on their outer hulls. Even so, the background radiation was still quite high, high enough to fry unshielded electronics—or humans—outside the ships' protective shielding.

The gas was being supercharged, both by the incredibly close-packed stars of the cluster—many only a fraction of a light year away—and by the lightning bright jets from six black hole accretion disks.

The nebula hadn't been there the last time he'd been here. Now it was so thick it dimmed the thronging stars beyond. The brightest and most optically brilliant objects in that sky, however, were opposite from the TRGA and a long way off—six tiny disks of intense white light, each speared through its center by a blue-white thread of radiance so intense they would have blinded unprotected eyes. The computer orchestrating the light show on the bulkheads of the observation chamber had stopped the brilliance of those threads down to where you could look at them, but the glare still was uncomfortable.

"So I guess those accretion disks are matter from the supernovae," Gray said. Those were new additions to the starscape as well—accretion disks around the individual black holes of the Rosette. It wasn't hard to imagine how they'd come into existence. As the plasma heart of an exploding star had squeezed through from N'gai and the remote past, much of it had been captured by the six black holes orbiting here at the core of Omega Centauri. What had not been immediately swallowed by the black holes had orbited them. Each black hole now was imbedded in a flat disk of plasma whirling about its singularity and generating death screams of X-rays and gamma as it finally spiraled into the object's event horizon.

"Those . . . those things," Gray told Dr. Conyers, indicating the fast-orbiting black holes, "are a lot farther apart than they used to be. The Rosette used to be just a few thousand kilometers across."

The two of them were adrift in *America*'s forward observation lounge, located above and abaft the flag bridge. The screens, tuned to show a seamless, panoramic view of surrounding space, displayed images larger and sharper than the smaller screens on either of the ship's bridges. Forward, over a third of the sky was blotted out by the underside of the shield cap, which extended from the vessel's spine like the canopy of an umbrella. In every other direction, however, up, down, aft, and to either side, the supernova nebula stretched in writhing coils and waves and fractal surfaces, all of them frozen in an instant of time. They showed something of the sheer violence that had created them, though distance and scale robbed them of any sense of actual movement.

"Well, try cramming a blue giant star with a diameter of five to ten times the radius of the sun through a gravitational vortex less than an AU across," Conyers told him. "What comes through is going to tend to expand rather violently . . . violently enough to actually nudge six black holes apart from one another."

"That's scarcely credible."

"I know."

"I just wonder what the explosion was like on the N'gai Cloud side of the Rosette."

"They're probably black holes now. They would have picked up a lot of additional mass when the star projectile went into the vortex, right? Enough to trigger six supernovae. The remnant of the star used by the Sh'daar to trigger all of this probably didn't make it through, though. It will be interesting to go there and find out."

"Assuming we can manage that trick," Gray said. His own voice sounded glum. "We were going to use the Omega TRGA to get to N'gai, but we're not going to make it through *that*." He indicated the slowly tumbling TRGA astern.

"Even with super-AI to calculate trajectory and velocity?"

"I'll need to talk with Konstantin about that, but I doubt it will make a difference. Where and when we come out of a TRGA depends on the path we trace going through. Our vector has to be *precise*. If we miss it, we could end up . . . God alone knows where. Or *when*."

"We should still be able to get back to Earth, though. Under Alcubierre Drive, right?"

"That won't be a problem. It'll just take forever to crawl across sixteen thousand light years." He did a fast calculation in his head. "Three point eight years, actually, at fifteen light years per day. But we'll be able to handle that okay. That's why we have the *Acadia*, to top off our rawmat reserves along the way. I'm more concerned about the Consciousness."

"It's dead, isn't it?"

"Well, I would think so," Gray replied. "After all of *this*. For a while, this region of space was filled with enormous shapes and structures, things light years in length . . . and those are all gone, now. The Consciousness ought to be dead, but no one's seen a body. I wouldn't care to poke around if there's a chance it might still be there . . . and conscious."

"Very funny."

Gray closed his eyes and accessed his command link with the bridge. "Lieutenant West? Anything from our pickets?"

"No, Admiral. Their last report was that everything was clear."

"No drones?"

"Negative, Admiral."

"Okay. Good."

Gray had given orders to move the squadron to a point several AUs away from the tumbling TRGA, but he'd also ordered the deployment of a couple of fighter squadrons to keep a close eye on the thing. If those Russian destroyers started coming through, he didn't want *America* or her battlegroup to be caught napping.

So far, however, there'd been nothing—not even drones sent through to check that the TRGA was working.

"*Birmingham . . . Arlington . . .* I want you two positioned on either side of the TRGA. If the Russians come through, hit them before they have a chance to react. Understand?"

"Understood, Admiral."

"Aye, aye, sir."

He'd done everything he could, covered all bases, but the lack of activity on the part of the Russians was reassuring.

Slowly, Gray allowed himself to relax.

VFA-96, Black Demons
Omega Centauri TRGA
1412 hours, FST

Lieutenant Commander Donald Gregory watched the slow tumble of the Omega TRGA and struggled to wall off his grief. For a third time, a woman he'd cared for deeply had failed to return from a mission. Three Hellfuries had been lost in the battle on the Penrose side of the gate, and Julia Adams had been one of them.

Damn it, he'd thought he was over this, that nothing could shake him.

He'd been wrong.

He watched the TRGA and wished—*prayed*—that the Russians would come through.

He considered the unthinkable: piloting his Starblade back through the TRGA and emerging among the Russian ships. He would die, but how many could he take with him?

The problem with that—besides being a flagrant violation of orders, of course—was that his Starblade's AI didn't have the navigation information that would take him safely through back to his own time. Hell, with that tumble he probably wouldn't be able to set up a workable passage even with the appropriate nav data. Worse, his AI would probably refuse the command. It might assume he was off his nut and take him back to *America*.

That was the trouble with intelligent machines, Gregory thought. They wouldn't let you be truly, spontaneously human.

Hell, maybe he *was* off his nut. But at the moment all he wanted in the entire universe was to strike back at the bastards who'd killed Julia.

VFA-198 Hellfuries
Penrose TRGA
79 light years from Earth
1612 hours, FST

Lieutenant Adams was not dead—not yet, at any rate. Humanoid robotic figures had emerged from the SAR tug, grappled with her Starblade, and used disassembler torches to slice her fighter open. Strong hands had reached into the cockpit and dragged her from the corpse of her Starblade and hauled her back to the Russian tug. Fifteen minutes later, she was aboard the *Moskva*.

They'd stripped her down to her skin—a precaution against any micro-nano weapons she might have hidden in her environmental suit—and suspended her in midair. Focused magnetic fields held slender bracelets locked to her wrists and ankles, pulling her into a taut X with her feet centimeters above the cold tile deck. The room was bare, with metal bulkheads and a single gleaming white console off to one side. It was dark, too, with the only light coming from the instrumentation on that sinister-looking console.

She estimated that she was under half a gravity—so the room was somewhere inside the Russian carrier's rotating hab modules.

What was that console for? What did it *do*? Her mind was racing, providing lots of disturbing possibilities.

The thought of torture filled her with an unholy dread. Damn it, she didn't know *anything*. Her captors, surely, knew the identity of the USNA ships that had just gone through the gate, and that was probably where they were going as well. What could she possibly add to that?

After an unbearable wait, dragging hours in which to study the morbid collection of electrical equipment and instrumentation on the console in front of her as the strain on her shoulders slowly grew to a scream, her interrogator entered the room. He was small, almost prissy-looking, with a cheerful smile and a computer tablet in one hand. "Good morning, Lieutenant Adams," he said. He had the slightest trace of a Slavic accent.

"It's afternoon, asshole," she growled back. *God*, her shoulders hurt. . . .

"By your reckoning, yes. But here on board the *Moskva* it is just after midnight. Moscow time, you understand. Not that day or night makes any difference out here in space and light years from Earth, of course. . . ."

She didn't reply. But when she checked her in-head clock she realized with a jolt that they'd somehow switched that off. She felt a moment's panic. What else had they taken from her? And *how*? Standard interrogation technique, she knew, would involve scrambling her sense of time. Everything her captors said to her would be designed to disorient her, to cut her adrift . . . and, ultimately, to make her come to trust them.

That, she thought, was *not* going to happen. Not if she could help it.

"And how did you know my name?"

"The shipnet linked with your in-head software, of course, as soon as you came on board. You'll notice that we disabled your clock, as well as your various internal communications devices." Stepping close, he reached out and stroked her bare hip, and her skin crawled. The hand traced its way up her side and caressed her breast.

She twisted, trying to avoid the touch. *"Don't touch me, you bastard!"*

He chuckled and stepped back. "You will have no connection with local networks except for those that we provide. After all, we can't have you uploading any malignant software into our system, can we? And now . . ."

Turning away, he stepped up to the console and gestured within a control field. Instantly something dropped out of the darkness above, laced its way around her head, and snapped her skull into rigid immobility. Some sort of nano-metal clamp, then, something locking her head immovably in place.

"So . . . it's torture?" she said, jaws clenched. "You haven't even asked me any questions yet! Maybe . . . maybe I'll cooperate!"

Her interrogator still had his back to her as he did something at the console. She struggled against her high-tech bonds with a predictable lack of success. She could hear the click of metal and plastic, and somehow that was more disturbing than the bastard's touch.

"Nothing so medieval, my dear," the man said. When he turned back to face her, he was holding a spray injector—the kind used to infuse large numbers of nanomachines into the circulatory system. "Torture tends to be counterproductive, you know. The subject will say *anything* to make the pain stop. This, though—this shouldn't hurt at all."

He pressed the injector up against the angle of her jaw and pressed the trigger. She felt a slight sting as the nano moved through her skin, followed by a warm and drowsy sensation spreading slowly through her body.

"Actually, Lieutenant, we *don't* want you to talk. Even if you did, it would not be the truth—or, worse, it would be a mixture of truth and fiction which would be difficult to unravel. But no matter. We have a much more reliable library of data right there inside your lovely head, and all we have to do is reach in and pluck it."

Her RAM. He was going after her internal RAM.

She tried to fight it, struggling against her bonds.

"It will be so much easier for you if you simply relax, my dear," the interrogator told her. He set aside the empty injector and picked up the computer tablet again. "You are completely in my power and will not be going anywhere. Understand? Simply relax and let the ship's computer read you."

"Go . . . to . . . hell. . . ."

She was fighting hard now. She didn't feel pain, exactly, but there was a growing, overwhelming pressure inside her head, the feeling of utter violation as *something* intruded, smashing its way into her memory, into her most private thoughts.

Julianne Adams, she thought, fighting. She could feel the sweat dripping down her face . . . and the intolerable pressure growing inside her skull. *Lieutenant. Serial number 3876–223 . . .*

You are helpless, Julianne, a voice said inside her skull. It was not the voice of her interrogator. *Naked . . . vulnerable . . . helpless . . . and you are* ours *to control, to do with as we decide. . . .*

Damn it, they still hadn't asked her any questions.

Chapter Seven

12 April, 2429

USNA CVS America
Admiral's Office
Omega Cluster
1252 hours, FST

"Any sign at all of the Consciousness?" Gray asked his senior xenosophontological department people.

Dr. George Truitt gave an airy wave of his hand, indicating the expanse of star-bejeweled space projected across the bulkheads and overheads of Gray's shipboard office. "It's gone. Obviously."

"Why obviously?"

"If you'll recall, Admiral, the entity we knew as the Consciousness had been busily constructing something here within Omega Centauri, a far-flung and extremely impressive array of large parts of unknown function. Some of those structures appear to have been called out of the fabric of spacetime itself and were light years long. And now they're gone. All gone."

"The lack of the Rosette entity's toys doesn't mean the *entity* is gone," Dr. Samantha Kline said. "I actually doubt that the Consciousness *can* be hurt in any meaningful way. It existed at least partially within other dimensions."

"Why the hell should it stick around after its toys are gone?" Truitt demanded. "With the loss of its instrumentality, I would suggest that the Consciousness is either dead or it has retreated . . . elsewhere, quite possibly back to the universe from which it emerged in the first place. But it is not *here*."

"I would have to agree," the voice of Konstantin Junior added. "We know that the Consciousness appeared to leave with the Denebans, translating, we think, to a parallel universe or some higher plane of existence. My impression as we watched them go was that the Consciousness was gone and would not be coming back.

"Even so, " Konstantin continued, "there was a chance that it did not, in fact, leave this spacetime frame of reference. I have, therefore, been searching this entire volume of space across a great deal of the electromagnetic spectrum, but I see no indication of intelligence."

"Not even other civilizations within the cluster?" Captain Rand asked.

"So far as we know, Captain," Truitt said, "there were no other civilizations here. Worlds, yes, of course. But the stars here are so close together—averaging 0.16 light year separation—that having habitable worlds *be* habitable long enough to develop native civilizations is most unlikely."

"There used to be civilizations here," Gray pointed out. "Hundreds of them."

"In the remote past, before the N'gai Cloud was absorbed by our galaxy," Truitt said, nodding. "Yes. But as you'll recall, the N'gai Cloud is . . . *was* considerably more open than this, even at its core. What is left of the N'gai Dwarf Galaxy has compacted over the eons, quite possibly as a direct result of the gravitational presence of the Rosette."

"If there *were* other civilizations in this cluster," Kline said, "they might have been exterminated by the Consciousness. It never seemed to be aware of organic life.

Or of technologies more primitive than what they were using."

"The Texaghu Resch," Gray said, nodding.

Texaghu Resch was the Agletsch name for a world not far from the first TRGA. Little was known about the civilization occupying that world; the Sh'daar had wiped it out long ago, probably because they felt threatened by any advanced technology.

Perhaps the Consciousness had the same drivers, which triggered a survival-instinct reaction.

"I wonder," Gray said, looking out into the surrounding starfield, "if any of the original Sh'daar races remained in what later became Omega Centauri? Or if the species that migrated to the Milky Way found new worlds and survived?"

"We know, at least, that some members of the Baondyeddi created the planetary computer and virtual worlds within the Etched Cliffs of Heimdall and survived there into the present time," Konstantin said. "At least until they were destroyed by the Consciousness. We know, however, that within their virtual world, they had drastically slowed the passage of time for themselves. Hundreds of millions of years in the outside universe were only a few years for them."

"And why did they do that?" Truitt said. "They were helpless when the Consciousness found them."

"We think," Konstantin replied, "that they did it because with their time flow altered, they hoped to be less conspicuous to those . . . outside. But it is important to remember that even highly technic species have a limited lifetime—a very few million years at most—before they evolve into something else, destroy themselves, ascend in a technological singularity, or simply peter out in genetic senescence and internal rot."

"Or they're wiped out by something else," Gray added. "Gamma ray bursters, nearby supernovae, unfriendly neighbors . . . It's not a particularly friendly cosmos."

"Lovely thought," Kline said, her face sour.

"Reminds me of some kids back home," Truitt said, scowling. "The viraddicts, especially. Dive into recrealities and pull the ladder in after themselves."

Gray had to agree. A lot of people—the younger set, for the most part—were so caught up in fantasy and adventure universes of their own creation that they rarely came down. The medical community was still divided as to whether the behavior should be classified as true addiction or not, but it was a serious social problem in some quarters.

But was it worse, he wondered, than kids gouging out chunks of their skulls to make room for "drune" extra eyes? That image *still* shook him . . .

"Captain Rand?" Gray called in his head.

"Yes, sir."

"Take us in closer to the Rosette."

If there was any evidence of the Consciousness having remained in this universe, it would be there at the heart of this thing.

Lieutenant Adams
Moskva, *Penrose TRGA*
79 light years from Earth
1407 hours, FST

Lieutenant Adams hung in the air, stretched taut, shoulders screaming, sweat dripping from her body. The nanobot infusion in her circulatory system had flooded through her brain, locating all of her cerebral implants, tracing their connections, and infiltrating them like a high-tech virus.

Naked . . . helpless . . . vulnerable . . . you are ours . . .

The computer-generated words had been drumming through her head without stop for . . . how long? She suspected that the emphasis on her vulnerability was a psychological weapon designed to wear down her inner defenses. Nudity was not an issue with her. The culture behind her was quite free and easy with casual social nudity, as it was too with casual sex. She was not embarrassed by it.

But the helpless and vulnerable part . . . yeah, that one was getting to her. Adams admired strength, and she admired self-sufficiency. Someone who was vulnerable was *weak* . . . and open to attack. She'd learned that much from an abusive boyfriend a few years ago. She'd joined the Navy in part to escape him, but mostly to demonstrate to herself that she was her own person, that she didn't need *anybody*.

Not even Don.

Her interrogator still hadn't asked her any questions. Instead, the nanobots in her brain had connected with her in-head RAM and were downloading her memory. People didn't store all of their memory in their implants, but they did store what was important. Classified stuff could be locked behind a code word, and so long as the code word wasn't accessible, it was fairly secure.

What the Russians appeared to be doing was following patterns of past usage, gathering clues that might help them force their way deeper into her hardware, compromising the software. She continued to feel this as a solid, steady pressure inside her head; she wasn't sure what the physical cause of that discomfort was, but her attempts to fight it over the past hours had left her sweat-drenched and weak, unsure of what they'd lifted already, unsure of what was in there that they might be able to read.

Worse, far worse, she knew that if they studied her neural patterns closely enough, for long enough, even her organic memories could be laid bare to the bastards.

Naked . . . helpless . . . vulnerable . . . you are ours. . . .

Damn it! That verbal refrain kept gnawing at her, making it impossible to concentrate! She was afraid her memories, both organic and machine, were dribbling away, easily accessed by her captors.

Suddenly, without any warning, the pressure ceased, and Adams was left gasping, dizzy, completely disoriented.

"Excellent, my dear!" Her interrogator stepped close,

grinning, and gave her a ringing slap across one buttock. "I think we have everything we need here. Thank you so much for your cooperation!" He turned to face a couple of guards standing by the door. When had they come in here? "Take her."

She was lowered to the deck and the magnetic grip on her ankles and wrists was released.

"They'll take you to a cell, Julia," her interrogator told her. "You can get cleaned up and put on some fresh clothing. I don't think we'll be needing you any longer."

And what, she wondered, did he mean by *that*?

Flag Bridge
CIS CV Moskva
Penrose TRGA
1433 hours, GMT

"I believe we got what you need, sir."

Oreshkin looked up from the data on the Penrose TRGA and nodded. "Indeed, Dr. Fedorov. What did you learn?"

"That the *America* battlegroup is, as you suspected, commanded by an Admiral Trevor Gray. And that the intent was to proceed to the Dunlop TRGA in Omega Centauri. After verifying that the alien entity there had been destroyed, they were to re-enter the TRGA and make the jump through to the Thorne TRGA. That's at the core of the N'gai Dwarf Galaxy some 876 million years in the past."

"This is confirmed?"

Fedorov shrugged. "With only one prisoner, I could not compare stories from different sources. However, no matter how deeply I dug, the data remained consistent, and I could find no trace of prevarication. What I read was what she truly believes."

"I suppose it's possible that she was told a cover story, that she believes that. But I think that would be needlessly complicating matters."

"Yes, sir. Since we captured her after her ship had already vanished through the TRGA, she would have no way of knowing where *America* had gone."

"Indeed. Thank you, Doctor. You've done very well."

"What do you want to do with the prisoner, sir?"

Oreshkin considered this. "She might be useful later on, so simply keep her locked up in the brig. Once we destroy the *America* battlegroup, she will be eliminated. Our orders, after all, are to leave no survivors."

"Of course, sir."

"Dismissed."

After Fedorov had left the bridge, Oreshkin spent some time considering the hazy circle of the Penrose TRGA, dead ahead and twenty kilometers distant. If he sent drones through ahead of the fleet, he would warn the Americans on the other side that *Moskva* was coming after them. But now that he was certain that the Americans had gone through to the Dunlop TRGA, he didn't need a recon.

What he could send through ahead of the fleet, however, was a volley of smart nukes, AI missiles programmed to traverse the Penrose-to-Dunlop path, emerge at the other end, and immediately detonate. If the Americans had ships close by the TRGA's mouth—and he knew that they would—he might be able to destroy or at least disable one or more of them before the *Moskva* emerged.

Better, the missiles could be programmed to seek out any American ships on the other side and take them out. An initial volley to clear the area beyond the TRGA, followed by hunter-killers that would track down the Yankee ships and obliterate them.

"Dmitri," he called, connecting with his weapons officer. "Prepare a flight of ten *Umnaya Ptitsa*, please. Program one of them to emerge from the Dunlop end of this thing and explode, and the rest to pass through the fireball, find any surviving American vessels, and destroy them."

"*Da*, Captain. At once. Ah . . ."

"What is it?"

"Sir, do you wish to target only the capital ships? Or the fighters as well?"

Oreshkin nodded; it was a good question. The Americans almost certainly had fighters close by the TRGA. And the missiles might be distracted by the relatively low-value, highly maneuverable targets.

"Target the capital ships, Dmitri. We can mop up the fighters at our leisure."

"*Da*, Captain!"

Umnaya Ptitsa was Russian for the PKR-130 "Smart Bird" missile, a variable-yield shipkiller comparable to the American Kraits. They were quite smart, but constrained by their programming to concentrate on just one thing—destroying the enemy.

With luck, when *Moskva* emerged from the TRGA, Oreshkin would find the American squadron wrecked and helpless.

VFA-96, Black Demons
Omega Centauri TRGA
1446 hours, FST

Lieutenant Commander Gregory watched the slow and stately tumble of the TRGA, which from here had the appearance of a titanic soda straw rotating around its short axis. *C'mon, you damned Russkies!* he thought with red-rage ferocity. *Show yourselves!*

Rage, he found, helped him push aside the pain, the grief, the *guilt* he felt at Julia's death.

The guilt had surprised him. What did he have to feel guilty about? It took him a while, in his tortured mind, to figure that one out. But he figured it out: she had died.

And he had not.

That was a state of affairs that might change, that could *be* changed, though.

After he'd lost both Meg and Cyn, he'd felt something

like this . . . he thought. One of the effects of his treatment had been to cut the memory of their loss from the associated emotion. He still remembered both of them, but the pain was gone.

Yet he could remember there had *been* pain, and that was what he was dwelling on now. He supposed Mason could fix this feeling of bottomless grief as well, but right now it felt as though the only way to feel better was to fling himself into combat with the bastards who'd killed Julia, even if he would almost certainly die himself.

Emerging target detected.

His Starblade's AI dropped that alert into his mind, and an in-head window showing the mouth of the TRGA zoomed in on a mote—a tiny speck—highlighted by a red CGI box emerging from the huge structure's maw.

"What the hell is—" Gregory began.

And then it exploded.

The silent flash seared into Gregory's brain, though the fighter's optics automatically stopped the glare down to tolerable levels.

Nuclear detonation, his AI told him inside his head. *Approximately two hundred megatons, range ten kilometers.*

Fortunately, a fusion explosion that would have vaporized much of a city was far less effective in hard vacuum. With no air to superheat or in which to create a shock wave, with no matter to convert into plasma other than that of the missile itself, the fireball was brief and died away almost at once. There was an equally brief pulse of electromagnetic energy, including hard X-ray and gamma radiation, but the Starblade's hull handled that without much problem.

Had there been a ship—the *America*, say—parked outside the opening of the TRGA, things would have been very different.

"*America*, *America*, VFA-96," he called. "Warhead detonation at the TRGA mouth. . . ."

America, at that moment, was 18 million kilometers away—one light-minute. They wouldn't see the flash or hear his warning for another . . . make it fifty-four seconds now. Gregory reoriented his Starblade and started moving toward the TRGA, but slowly. That blast had almost certainly been intended to clear any USNA ships away from the opening. It might be followed by another . . . or by a fleet of Russian warships.

The second detonation came a moment later, farther out from the rotating TRGA's end. Gregory was reporting that blast to the carrier when another flight of smart missiles emerged, spread by the TRGA's rotation across an arc of sky, and began to accelerate.

"Missiles!" he yelled through his in-head link with the carrier. "Missiles inbound from the TRGA!"

A whole minute until *America* would hear the warning. Those missiles were already beginning to accelerate.

"Demons with me!" he called to the rest of his squadron. "Chase down those missiles!"

He flipped his fighter end-for-end and accelerated. Starblades and most antiship missiles had about the same acceleration—50,000 gravities. He'd counted eight missiles coming from the TRGA. They had four and a half minutes to kill all of them before they reached the capital ships.

"Headhunters, Gregory!" he called, his voice tight. "We're going after those warheads. Stay put and watch for the Russians. They're bound to be coming through any moment!"

"Copy that," replied Commander Jason Meier, the new CO of the Headhunters. "Knock 'em down!"

"Ay-ffirmative."

Even at 50,000 gravities, after one minute's acceleration, one of those missiles was "only" traveling at 500 kilometers per hour and would have covered less than a million kilometers of distance. The problem, of course, was that the pursuing fighters were playing with the same numbers. As Gregory brought his acceleration up to 50,000 gravities, he turned the targeting problem over to his fighter's AI. *Target lock. . . .*

It would have been an impossible chase save for one important bit of physics: though his fighter could never quite match the speed of the missiles because he'd begun accelerating several seconds after them, he could get to within a few tens of kilometers per second of their current speed, then launch his own Krait shipkiller. The Krait's acceleration would build from his velocity and rapidly overtake the enemy warhead, exactly as if it were a two-stage missile.

He thoughtclicked one of his VG-92 Kraits into space. "Fox One!" he called, the general squadron warning of a smart missile launch. The missile rapidly burned up the distance to the target.

The detonation, starkly silent in the vacuum of space, dazzled Gregory despite his optics' stopping down to protect his vision. Kraits, like the Russian Smart Birds, were variable-yield weapons capable of a couple hundred megatons . . . something of an overkill option when firing at Russian antiship warheads, except for the fact that a more powerful yield increased the chances for a kill.

"Target eliminated," his AI informed him.

"Next target," he ordered. "Lock on!"

"Target lock. . . ."

"Fox One!"

Other Starblades in the squadron, spread out in an arc two hundred kilometers across, began releasing their own Kraits, and nuclear detonations began flashing and pulsing ahead. Gregory was concerned at first that they were traveling directly toward—and firing their missiles at—the *America* battlegroup, but the AIs were in perfect control of the weapons.

The Starblades continued their pursuit across the empty kilometers.

One by one, the Black Demons hunted down the nuclear missiles and destroyed them.

After four and a half minutes, the fighters had traveled just over 18 million kilometers—a full light-minute—and were moving at just under half the speed of light as they entered the volume of space surrounding *America*, not fast enough to experience significant relativistic effects, but far too fast for merely human reflexes and perception.

And then the last Russian warhead was gone, just as it arrowed in toward the carrier, and an instant before it hit.

"Good job, Demons." The voice came from CIC.

"Decelerate and reverse vector, Demons," Gregory ordered. "Back to the triggah!"

He wanted to be there if the Russians came through.

When the Russians came through.

USNA CVS America
Flag Bridge
Omega Cluster
1450 hours, FST

Gray watched the strobing of nuclear detonations against the star-clotted backdrop of space, one following another in fast-paced rhythm, the blasts growing closer and closer with each passing moment. That final detonation was close—less than 30,000 kilometers—but it was far enough away to not affect *America*.

Incoming targets destroyed, the ship's fire control computer whispered in Gray's mind. The final kill actually had been scored by one of *America*'s point defense weapons, a HEL controlled by a dedicated AI and triggered when a threat got too close. Gray's heart rate went up a bit as he watched the firefight play itself out. He'd been a fighter driver long enough to know the sense of pounding adrenaline when a close-quarters knife fight took you inside a capital ship's defensive perimeter. A capital ship's AI *should* be able to readily distinguish between a threat and a friendly fighter, but things were happening so fast, the ships and missiles moving so quickly, and frankly, mistakes did happen, even with sophisticated automation.

He allowed himself a sigh of relief as the Black Demons formed up and began boosting back toward the TRGA.

If the Russians were going to come through, however,

it would be any time now. Quite possibly they'd already begun emerging from the Dunlop TRGA, but the news had not yet crawled across that light-minute of separation.

"Lieutenant West," he snapped.

"Yes, sir!"

"Make to all vessels. Execute Plan Tango."

"Execute Tango, aye, aye, sir."

They wouldn't be able to take on a carrier and six destroyers. They had to get the hell out of here.

The problem was going to be *how*.

VFA-96, Black Demons
Omega Centauri TRGA
1508 hours, FST

Gregory was decelerating his fighter back toward the TRGA. It had taken four and a half minutes to decelerate back down from his top velocity of 0.45 *c*, then begin accelerating again back through the *America* battlegroup and then on toward the TRGA. At the halfway point he began decelerating once more. He'd had an instructor at Oceana who'd told his class that the biggest hazard in space fighter combat was that with all of the accelerating and decelerating back and forth across an ungodly huge battlespace, the battle would be over before you could get back into position.

The minutes had dragged by, but now the Black Demons were again approaching the TRGA.

Gregory didn't need to worry about missing out this time.

"My God!" Lieutenant Johanson called. "Look at *that*!"

The Russians had arrived.

They were still arriving. Four of those Cossack-class destroyers had already emerged from the TRGA, the gate's rotation having spread them all over the sky. As Gregory watched, another emerged, followed closely by another. The TRGA rotation had actually worked in the Russians' favor.

Had they all come out as a group in one area, the waiting fighters could have pounced on them easily enough, perhaps even taken them down one at a time as they followed through the needle's eye of the gate.

But with destroyers spread all over the sky, the defenders were going to more than have their work cut out for them.

And while Gregory relished the idea of fighting the Russians, he was aware that the defending forces might have lost the battle before it had even properly begun.

Chapter Eight

12 April, 2429

VFA-96, Black Demons
Omega Centauri TRGA
1510 hours, FST

Gregory watched the Russian destroyers drifting in a broad and steadily expanding arc near the TRGA as they slowly oriented themselves, turning to face the distant *America*. Nuclear flashes scattered across the battlespace ahead showed where the Headhunters were already hammering at the Russian escorts. Gregory tagged one of the destroyers and flashed the data to the other members of his squadron. "Designating target Alfa-One!" he called. "Everybody gang on him. Approach velocity one kps. Kraits armed."

By having all ten fighters in the Black Demons attack the same target, they increased the chances that something would slip past the enemy's close-in defensive perimeter. With an approach speed of one kilometer per second, the human pilots could make broad judgment calls—and change targets at the last moment if necessary—but would still have to rely on their AIs for the final instant of approach and launch.

The Russian destroyers were closer now, each bullet-capped, long and slender, a two-hundred-meter needle with a blunt tip. Moment by moment, the targeted ship loomed larger across the sky ahead. The range was still well over 100 kilometers, but the optics in Gregory's fighter made the target look huge, and *very* close.

Which, of course, it was, given the velocity of his fighter.

"Fox One!" Gregory yelled over the squadron link.

"Fox One!"

"Fox One!"

The other Black Demons added their voices to the chorus as their missiles dropped from their Starblades, then accelerated toward the looming target. Volleys of laser and plasma beam fire from three of the destroyers stabbed and snapped at the oncoming fighters. Lieutenant Hall's Starblade took a direct hit and flared into a fireball of hot plasma. Lieutenant Randle's Starblade flared and crumpled an instant later.

Gregory held his course, *daring* the Russian weapons crews to claw him down. The other fighters peeled off, giving themselves sufficient lateral vectors to clear the enemy target, but Gregory continued arrowing through the wall of defensive fire. "Fox One!"

His second Krait missile slipped smoothly through the Russian point defense and detonated just aft of the destroyer's shield cap, a dazzling flare of incandescence that swiftly cooled, revealing drifting debris and the slow spinning axis of the ship trailing a tangle of wreckage where the shield cap had been mounted. The shield cap had been blasted free and was now spinning in the midst of a glittering, expanding spiral galaxy of frozen droplets of water.

Gregory's Starblade hurtled through the debris field.

Ice and small metal fragments pinged and cracked across his hull, but the fighter's nanomatrix absorbed the myriad impacts. Beyond the debris cloud, Gregory saw the oncoming maw of the slowly tumbling TRGA. And rising from the cylinder's enormous opening . . .

"All ships! All ships!" he called over the squadron channel. "Russian carrier emerging from the triggah!" In another minute they would hear that warning back aboard the *America*. For right here and now, the Black Demons and the Headhunters might be able to do some *real* damage.

He triggered a salvo of nuke-tipped Kraits, then swung around his grav projection, braking savagely. For a moment, he thought he might crash into the giant ship in front of him, but his AI squeezed an extra few Gs of lateral thrust and he sailed across the carrier's hull, scant meters from the blurred expanse of power modules, sponsons, and point defense turrets racing by. For just a moment, he imagined himself plunging into the Russian carrier . . .

But . . . no. In another instant, he was past the *Moskva* and decelerating for another pass. What had happened to his missiles?

Intercepted. Clawed from the sky by the Russian point defense system.

"Urgent message from the *America*," his AI whispered in his mind. "All squadrons are to break off the attack and regroup with our carrier."

Behind his faceplate, Gregory scowled. *Shit!*

Still, those few moments of heart-pounding combat seemed to have dissipated his blood-rage. He lined up for another shot, then loosed his last two Kraits at the now-receding *Moskva*.

"Fox One!"

One of his missiles was intercepted by a Russian pee-beep, but the second detonated just above the hull, a brilliant flash that left Gregory dazzled. As his vision returned, he could see extensive damage across the carrier's portside. His warhead hadn't actually impacted the target, and the Russian hull shields had diverted most of the hard stuff.

But the Russian was hurt.

And Gregory was out of shipkillers.

So tempting . . .

"All Demons! Break off! Rendezvous back at the *America*."

Gregory was shaking as he piloted his Starblade back to the carrier.

Flag Bridge
CIS CV Moskva
Penrose TRGA
1521 hours, GMT

"Your information appears to have been accurate, Doctor," Oreshkin said. "The *America* battlegroup is, indeed, at Omega Centauri. I wonder why?"

Fedorov shrugged. "The prisoner believed they were hunting for signs of the Consciousness."

"Are there such signs?"

"None that we've been able to detect, sir."

"First Officer!"

"Sir!" Kulinin replied.

"We will close to attack. Long-range missiles and beams, if you please. Commander Nikolayev!"

"Yes, sir!" his air group commander replied over the com link.

"Launch fighters."

"Yes, sir!"

They had *America* pinned against the Rosette of black holes, positioned perfectly for attack.

USNA CVS America
Flag Bridge
Omega Cluster
1525 hours, FST

Gray considered his options. He didn't have a hell of a lot of them.

Five surviving Russian destroyers were steadily approaching, and the carrier beyond was loosing clouds of fighters, even as *America* began recovering her own fighter groups. The *America* battlegroup was seriously outnumbered and badly outgunned. Even if somehow they were able to beat them off, *America* and her two escorts might well be crippled, her fighter squadrons shot to pieces, and—if the *Acadia* was destroyed in the fight—they would be unable to replenish their consumables.

Discretion was decidedly the better part of valor in this confrontation. The question was where to run. He'd told Dr. Conyers that they could make the run all the way to Earth under Alcubierre Drive in three point eight years, but they would have to stop for resupply every month or so. If the Russian squadron pursued them the same way, then sooner or later they would catch up with the battlegroup while it was parked next to an asteroid somewhere taking on rawmat.

Would the Russians give chase? Gray still had no idea why they were on the Russian's shit list in the first place, though privately he suspected that politics were involved. *Walker* politics. Unless a war had broken out back home, but damn it, that made no sense at all. There'd been no crisis when *America* had cast off from Quito Synchorbital, no USNA-Russian tension of note, and no reason for the Russian carrier group to pursue them so avidly.

It *had* to be Walker.

"Admiral? PriFly."

"Go ahead, CAG."

"Our fighters are aboard. Do you want to launch the ready squadrons?"

"Negative, CAG. Rearm and replenish."

"Aye, aye, sir."

"Captain Rand."

"Yessir!"

"Set course for N'gai . . . through the Rosette, if you please."

"What?" Rand sputtered, then somehow tried to regain some semblance of proper military decorum. "Sorry, Admiral. I mean . . . the *Rosette*?"

"I'm not used to having my orders questioned, Captain. Lieutenant West!"

"Sir!"

"Pass the word to our escorts. They are to run interference for us while we and the *Acadia* go through the Rosette. They are then to follow us. Make sure they have the appropriate navigational data."

"Aye, aye, sir."

"Admiral Gray," Rand said. "That means threading past those energy jets from the black holes. We'll be fried!"

"We'll make the passage under SAI control."

"Even then—Admiral, I recommend we look at other options. Going through the Rosette is suicide!"

"Commander Mackey!"

Luther Mackey, *America*'s Executive Officer, turned from his workstation. "Sir!"

"I am putting you in command of this vessel. Mr. Rand . . . you are relieved."

"Sir! I protest—"

"We'll talk about it later." On his main screen, the destroyers were closer, beginning to spread out. Probably a missile-launch formation. "Captain Mackey, did you hear my orders?"

"Yes, sir."

"Can you carry them out?"

"Aye, aye, sir!"

Mackey didn't miss a beat in his response, the ancient naval and Marine courtesy "aye, aye" they said stood for "*I* understand and *I* will obey."

Gray had known Luther Mackey for a long time. He'd been the skipper of the Black Demons for several years before he'd been bumped up to Executive Officer. Gray knew him to be a steady, reliable officer, which was exactly what he needed on *America*'s bridge right now.

He hated relieving Rand in front of the entire bridge crew like that, but the man had been on the verge of refusing a direct order, and—just as important—arguing with him took up valuable time. Gray knew he would have to face the consequences of his action later, but he'd had to act *now*.

The *Birmingham* and the *Arlington* were moving into position to block the enemy's approach.

"Lieutenant West."

"Yes, sir."

"Make to *Acadia*. Tell them we'll go through first, but they should stick close behind us."

"Aye, aye, Admiral."

Slowly gathering speed, the *America* turned away from the fight and began descending into the maelstrom of radiation and whirling gravitational masses that was the Omega Rosette.

He didn't like running. But there was absolutely no point in fighting here save for survival. With another way out, even a desperate one, they were better off avoiding a pointless and probably fatal engagement.

The question was whether they could survive the escape.

Ahead, the six black holes of the Rosette steadily and swiftly circled their common center of gravity, each surrounded by its own accretion disk of starcore-hot plasma, each projecting straight threads of searing radiation from its poles. Those threads posed the greatest danger during *America*'s approach, sweeping through nearby space like powerful plasma beams. Composed of particles accelerated nearly to the speed of light by the powerful gravitational fields of the Rosette black holes, a touch by any of them would rip a starship apart.

Konstantin Junior, however, had the con of both *America* and the *Acadia*, and was able to calculate velocity and course and angle to a degree that was literally superhuman.

Astern, *Arlington* and *Birmingham* were exchanging fire with the oncoming destroyers, the range still too great to score any serious damage. The Russian fighters, however, were closing in.

"Lieutenant West. Tell *Birmingham* and *Arlington* to follow us in."

"Yes, sir."

Gray began to glimpse within the Rosette's center the oft-noted snatches of other places, other starfields . . . even other universes. Traversing the Rosette gateway was very much like passing through one of the far smaller TRGAs. The ship making the passage had to stick to a very specific course through the gravitational vortex; missing the proper course by a few tens of meters could land you in the wrong place entirely . . . or even the wrong time.

Things were worse with the far larger and more powerful Omega Rosette. Research ships had glimpsed entirely different *universes* through that central opening. Conversations with the Consciousness suggested that that alien group Mind might have slipped through from one of those. If Konstantin Junior wasn't precisely on course . . .

America fell into the Rosette, accelerating now toward the structure's center of gravity. The Rosette's diameter was some tens of thousands of kilometers; the individual black holes at this distance, even though they were artificially large structures each nearly the size of Earth, were too distant to show any detailed features, but the white-hot disks of plasma around them created a circle of brilliant, fast-moving stars.

And still *America* fell. . . .

Time was slowing as they fell deeper into the relativistic warp within the Rosette. Ahead, starfields shifted and blurred, switching from one scene to another with bewildering speed, now an open starscape much more thinly populated than the core of Omega Centauri; now a burning emptiness that might have been pure energy; now a field of ancient, red stars, shrunken and dwindled; now a younger blaze of hot blue-white suns . . .

Now the heart of a galactic cluster, packed with suns and laced with incandescent plasma.

And the starscape steadied on that last as Konstantin Junior made a final slight alteration to *America*'s course. And then . . .

Emergence.

They were through.

"Lieutenant Vasquez!" Gray rasped. The sight of this star-packed glory always clutched at his throat. "What are we looking at? Are we where we're supposed to be?"

"Confirmed, Admiral . . . this is the N'gai Cluster. We're 876 and some million years in our past."

"It doesn't look much like the last time we saw it," Mackey said from the command bridge.

"Yeah, well, six hypernovae will do that, you know," Gray replied.

The explosion of six supergiant stars had filled the N'gai Cluster with hot plasma, but after three years, as expected, the gas had become tenuous enough that *America* was not in danger of vaporizing.

Gray stared out into a thickly clotted starscape wreathed with tangled filaments and clouds of plasma. Astern, six black holes with searingly hot accretion disks orbited a common center of gravity where once six blue giants had formed the Rosette of Six Suns. To port, a few thousand kilometers distant, was a seventh black hole, its unimaginable gravity twisting the light from the stars beyond into a dazzling ring encircling the object. This one had no accretion disk, he saw. Under highest magnification, he could just make out the sphere of impenetrable darkness at the center of the optical distortion. Konstantin Junior estimated the diameter of the object's event horizon to be 206 kilometers. The math suggested the black hole possessed a mass of approximately seventy times that of Earth's sun.

Where the hell had *that* come from?

"What now, Admiral?" Mackey asked him.

He didn't answer immediately. They were here to find the fleeing Sh'daar fleet, and they at least had a vague idea of where they'd been going: roughly in *that* direction.

But finding them was going to be like finding one particular grain of sand somewhere on a very, *very* large beach.

"We wait for *Birmingham* and *Arlington* to come through

the Rosette," he said at last. "And then, I guess we'll just have to see."

After another moment, he thoughtclicked an in-head channel. "Colonel McDevitt, this is Admiral Gray. We need to talk."

Flag Bridge
CIS CV Moskva
Omega Centauri
1545 hours, GMT

"Sir! The enemy has escaped into the Rosette!"

Oreshkin scowled at the screen. The information had come too late for him to do a damned thing about it. The two American ships—a destroyer and a cruiser—were passing into the tortured space at the heart of the Rosette . . . and in an eye's blink, they were gone.

Chort poberi! Damn it to hell! This mission was fast becoming what the Americans referred to as a complete clusterfuck. The prey had escaped, leaving Oreshkin with an impossible choice. He could give up, turn around, and return to Earth, but there was no way they were going to manage to thread the TRGA needle with it spinning like that. Returning to Earth using Alcubierre Drive, putt-putting along at fifteen light years per day, would take them almost three years, and that was quite unacceptable.

The alternative was to follow the Americans through the Rosette.

That choice was dangerous almost beyond belief. *Moskva*'s AI had navigational tables that should let them reach the N'gai galaxy in the remote past—the Americans' presumed destination—but Oreshkin had never attempted that trick. Even the slightest error would end with the Russian carrier inextricably lost in both space and in time and quite possibly drop them out of the universe entirely and into someplace horribly *other*. To make matters worse, *Moskva* had suffered considerable damage during the fighter attack, losing several vacuum energy taps and a number of point-defense weapons.

And even if they did succeed, despite damage, despite navigational uncertainties, there was every possibility that they would find the *America* battlegroup waiting for them. The enemy had been caught off guard at the Thorne TRGA when the Russian destroyers had come through scattered by the gate's rotation.

There would be no rotation of the N'gai Rosette to scatter the squadron as it emerged, and the Americans would be foolish to assume the *Moskva* would not come through in pursuit. No, they would be waiting.

Which meant Oreshkin had to think of a way to catch them off guard again.

A thought occurred to him. "Nal Tok," he said, opening a comm channel with both audio and visual feeds.

At the other end of that electronic link, something stirred in darkness—large, black, powerful . . . and in no way human. "I am here, Oreshkin."

"Nal Tok, we may be under attack by USNA forces soon. Will you and your forces fight with us against them?"

"Put us where we can fight, and we will fight." Mouth parts moved uneasily in an unreadable expression. "We *like* killing humans."

It was as positive an answer as Oreshkin could hope for.

He just wondered if he could trust the massive beings.

USNA CVS America
Admiral's Office
N'gai Cluster
1552 hours, FST

Gray floated into his office, catching a handhold to arrest his forward movement. The office bulkheads were set to display the outside panorama. Above and on every side, the glory of the tiny galaxy's core burned with a piercing radiance. Millions of stars, each one brighter than Venus seen at its brightest in the morning skies of Earth, were crammed into a wall surrounding the innermost core. He made his way to his seat and strapped in.

He'd already sent a call requesting that Captain Rand meet him there.

While waiting, he connected with Lieutenant Colonel McDevitt, who was down on the Number One flight deck with several hundred of his men. "Do you think your people can pull this off, Colonel?" he asked.

"Sir. C'mon, this is the Three-Deuce-Five we're talking about. Give the order and we'll storm the gates of hell for you."

"I don't think it will be quite *that* bad, Colonel. If the bad guys are going to come through, though, it will be pretty soon. Are you ready to launch?"

"We're loading into capsules now, Admiral. We'll be ready when you need us."

"That's good, Terry. With any luck, the bad guys won't see you coming. We're counting on you."

"Hooyah, sir!"

Gray cut the link just as Captain Rand accessed the door announcer. "Enter."

The man drifted into the office and clung to a handhold in front of Gray's high-tech desk. "Sir! You wanted to see me."

"Yes, Jason. We need to talk."

"Sir."

"I didn't like relieving you out there. I regret the necessity." He would *not* say that he was sorry.

"Command prerogative, sir."

Gray sighed. Rand was not making this easier with his stiff, by-the-book attitude. "Command *responsibility*. I will *not* have one of my officers questioning my authority or my orders, not in front of the bridge crew, and not when we're in action. In private, you can question me all you want, just so you remember that *I* am in command of this battlegroup and have a responsibility to each and every man and woman in this squadron."

"I'll try to keep that in mind, sir."

"Unfortunately, we now find ourselves with a bit of a problem. The captain of a ship must have the complete and undivided respect of the people under him. I damaged that respect by relieving you and placing Commander Mackey in your place. I can't restore your command without risking confusion and divided loyalties. I can't assign you to another ship's department without undermining your authority no matter where I put you. You understand me?"

"Yes, sir."

"For that reason, I am relieving you of all duty. When we get home, I will recommend you be assigned another command. I don't want your career haunted by what happened on the bridge today."

"*Very* kind of you. Sir."

"For what it's worth, Jason, I believe you to be a capable officer. You will have my highest recommendation for your new command."

"Thank you, sir."

"You have anything you want to tell me? Man to man, just us guys?"

"It doesn't really matter, does it, sir? The Navy Board is going to know you relieved me, and they're going to want to know why. For the record, Admiral, I was *not* panicking on the bridge this afternoon."

"I didn't say that you were."

"I felt that you were making a mistake. Sir." He took a deep breath. "I didn't realize that you were so . . . sensitive to criticism. Sir."

"I am not," Gray replied, his voice cold. "I do appreciate that you believed I was making a serious error in judgment. Further, I appreciate that it is your duty to point out to your senior officers instances that appear to be lapses in judgment, or things that they might not know. I don't mind having my orders questioned. *But not in combat, in front of other personnel!* You understand me?"

"Yes, sir."

"I will only point out that my decision seems to have worked out after all. Perhaps you should work at trusting your senior officers rather than tell them what they can't do in a tight situation in front of the bridge crew."

"Yes, sir."

"Dismissed."

He stared out at the stars for a long time. Gray knew that it was quite possible that he *had* wrecked the man's career. Rand was right—the Navy Board would *not* overlook the fact that he'd been summarily relieved of command.

Unfortunately, the good of the ship and of the mission always came first.

"Admiral? This is Mackey."

"Yes, Luther."

"We have probes coming through the Rosette. Recon drones. I suspect that our friends on the other side are getting ready to come after us."

"Launch fighters," Gray replied. "Keep us tight behind Straggler. I'll be up right away."

He just hoped he'd thought of everything . . . or the N'gai Cluster of 876 million years ago would become *America*'s grave.

Chapter Nine

12 April, 2429

VFA-96, Black Demons
N'gai Cluster
1608 hours, FST

"Launch!"

Acceleration slammed Gregory back in his seat as his SG-420 Starblade shot from the launch tube and into open space. Orienting himself, he spun his fighter to face the underside of *America*'s immense shield cap and let his drift carry him out from under its shadow into the harsh glare from the Rosette. The background radiation out here was fierce, a seething torrent of high-energy particles accelerated by those black holes, but his Starblade's hull should be able to hold back the worst of it, at least for a while.

"*America* CIC, this is CSP One," Gregory said. "Handing off from PriFly. All Demons clear of the ship and formed up."

"Copy, Combat Space Patrol One," a voice replied from *America*'s Combat Information Center. "Primary Flight Control confirms handoff to CIC. You are clear to move into position."

"You heard the man," Gregory told his squadron. "Tuck in snug and close."

The twelve fighters drifted forward, clearing *America*'s shield cap but not moving far beyond it. The carrier hung enormous beside him and just barely astern, the wink-wink-wink of her running lights picking out her deeply shadowed shape against the starfield.

Ahead, once they were past the immense, curved rim of the shield cap, lay wonder.

Within the past several minutes, *America* had aligned herself behind the object designated as Straggler Alfa, a black hole two hundred kilometers across. Less than a light-minute ahead now, the tiny object was invisible to the unaided eye. High magnification, however, showed the event horizon of the object blotting out the line of sight forward; around it, space was tightly bent, the stars beyond twisted and blurred into a silver-white halo around the black hole. Around the object, spanning much of the sky, the six brilliantly shining accretion disks of the Rosette's black holes moved in a perfect circle. Under magnification, he couldn't see the center of the N'gai Rosette; Straggler Alfa was in the way.

Which meant that someone coming through the Rosette from elsewhere wouldn't be able to see the Americans, either.

"Any word on the Russkies?" Lieutenant Timmons asked.

"Negative," Gregory snapped. "Now shut your yapper. Radio silence!"

And they waited.

Even at 18 million kilometers' distance, Straggler Alfa exerted a relentless pull on all of the Starblades, as well as on the carrier behind them. When a star exploded and became a black hole, it continued to exert the same gravitational tug on its surroundings as it had before, as if the original star remained in place. Gregory had his hands full juggling the balance of gravitic drive thrust against that relentless pull, holding his position motionless relative to the object.

"CSP One, CIC," a voice said in Gregory's head. "Long-range scans indicate the enemy drones are returning through the Rosette. If anything's going to happen, it'll go down any moment now."

"CSP One copies."

The minutes flowed on, the sound broken only by the rasp of Gregory's breathing in his helmet and the hum of the Starblade's gravs holding it back against the pull of the former giant sun.

Straggler Alfa, he'd decided, must be the remnant of that blue-white star the Sh'daar had hurled through the Rosette. Someone—the Consciousness or the Harvesters—had blocked the star from getting through, though a large amount of plasma had shotgunned past the Rosette on the other side. What was left of a giant blue star was . . . here, a shrunken remnant spitting high-energy particles from its two polar jets.

Gregory wondered how much longer the fighters would be able to hang around out here, outside the embrace of *America*'s protective shielding. Their prelaunch briefing had said they would remain at station-keeping for one hour before trapping and being replaced by another squadron. It had only been a few minutes since launch now, and his fighter was warning him of dangerously elevated levels of radiation.

"CIC to all fighters! Here they come!"

Picket drones adrift in the maw of the Rosette two light-minutes ahead had spotted the Russians coming through—forty-eight fighters, followed by five destroyers arrayed as a broad pentagon, and finally, by the monstrous bulk of the *Moskva*. The picket drones relayed the images to *America*, where they arrived in the Combat Information Center two minutes after they'd been transmitted.

Gregory watched *Moskva* moving clear of the twisted space within the Rosette. He saw damage—the result of his last Krait fired at the Russian back in Omega Centauri—and felt a small thrill of excitement surge up his spine. He'd *gotten* the bastard! He'd gotten him *good*!

"Black Demons, CIC! You may commence your run!"

"Okay, boys and girls," Gregory said, his heart pounding. "Let's get them!"

In a sense, the twelve fighters of VFA-96 were being held in place by their grav drives like the shot of an immense catapult. By cutting their drives, they began falling toward Straggler Alfa, accelerating rapidly in its intense gravitational field. Tightly knotted gravitational singularities winked on just ahead of each fighter, dragging it forward as the singularity flickered in and out of existence at thousands of times per second, accelerations building rapidly as the *America* began dwindling astern.

Accelerating, then, their gravitic drives boosted their velocity even more; moments later, they flashed past the Straggler at a significant fraction of the speed of light, their courses meticulously guided by their onboard AIs. Space was bent by the nearby black hole; their AIs used that warp in spacetime to adjust precisely the course of the Starblades, aiming them straight at the gathering Russian fleet.

They passed the Straggler moving far too swiftly for Gregory to even glimpse the thing, so great was his speed. A flare of brilliant light from the accretion disk, lasting an instant, and then he was past and hurtling toward the emerging Russian squadron.

Under his AI's guidance, his Starblade began to decelerate, bleeding off the incredible speed generated by slingshotting past a 200-kilometer black hole.

The brass, Gregory decided, had really scoped this one out. By remaining behind the Straggler, they'd at least delayed the moment when the Russians would pick them up. By using the Straggler's intense gravitational field for a slingshot effect, they picked up a lot of free energy, and that translated as *speed*.

They were on the Russians before they even knew the Americans were there.

Each Starblade carried two Kraits, but their primary armament for this pass were bundles of AS-78 AMSO. A cloud of sand, moving at a significant fraction of the speed of light, did astonishing damage to enemy fighters, to the most massive capital ships, and even to entire planetary hemispheres.

He let his AI select a destroyer as his first target, and he gave the warning that meant an AMSO round had been loosed. *"Fox Two!"*

Gregory continued to decelerate as his AMSO rounds flashed toward the enemy.

And battle was joined . . .

Strike Force Reaper
Marine Battalion 3/25
N'gai Cluster
1612 hours, FST

Lieutenant Colonel McDevitt leaned over the backrest of the pilot's seat, studying the main screen. Images relayed from battlespace drones were showing the play of battle just ten light-seconds away: flashes and silent flares bright as lightning as the combatant squadrons merged.

"That looks like our cue," he told the pilot. "Goose it."

"Aye, aye, Colonel. Goosing it . . ."

The Headquarters Company of the Three-Deuce-Five was crowded into a VBSS-Mk. 87 Lamprey, a recent addition to the USNA Marine Corps' arsenal. The VBSS craft—the acronym stood for Visit, Board, Search, and Seizure—was an ugly, snub-nosed spacecraft that could carry a company of 120 Marines, fully suited and armed, crammed into its troop bay like heavily armored sardines. Normally, McDevitt would have stayed behind in a CIC command center, overseeing the op from there, but this time around he would *not* be relegated to running things from the safety of the rear.

For one thing, in space combat there *was* no "safety in the rear."

So McDevitt floated inside the crowded flight deck of the transport pod, watching the action unfold.

"They see us yet?" he asked the pilot.

"Not sure, Colonel. We're in stealth mode, but sooner or later they'll tag us. We just need to hope to God that happens later rather than sooner."

Accelerating, the Marine troop pod fell toward the battle now unfolding ahead.

VFA-96, Black Demons
N'gai Cluster
1614 hours, FST

"Fox Two!"

"Fox Two!"

Space was fast becoming filled now with drifting clouds of sand. The Russians had fired their own AMSO rounds, volley upon volley of them, attempting to scrape the incoming fighters out of the sky and to partially block the American sandcaster volleys. Where sand clouds met at high velocity, searing flashes of heat and light and X-rays smeared across space. One of the Russian destroyers had taken a full load of sand amidships at something approaching 0.5 *c*, and the impact had scoured hull metal and surface matrix from the ship, revealing a ravaged internal structure glowing white-hot from the friction. The American fighters were past the remaining destroyers now and closing on the *Moskva*, the Russian carrier looming huge at point-blank range.

Too close for AMSO rounds now. The target was so close the missiles wouldn't have time to accelerate to a useful velocity. Gregory switched to guns, engaging his Starblade's Gatling RFK-90 KK cannon and loosing a stream of magnetic-ceramic-jacketed slugs at a cyclic rate of twelve per second. Each round, with a depleted uranium core massing half a kilo and traveling at 175 meters per second, carried a savage kinetic-kill punch that rivaled that of a small tactical nuke, powerful enough to shred hull metal and defensive shielding.

He was tempted to target the damaged expanse of the enemy carrier's flank—he wanted to see that monster *die*—but the squadron's orders were to focus on the enemy's point-defense weapons.

It was imperative that the fighters take out those guns.

His velocity was very close now to the *Moskva*'s. It was as though he was drifting just above the vast and intricate terrain of the enemy's hull, a landscape of towers and cliffs, of plains and domes, of canyons and beam turrets . . .

His fighter lurched to one side, a savage jolt.

Yeah, add kinetic-kill weaponry to that list. His active matrix outer hull had absorbed most of the impact, but the blow very nearly put him into a tumble. Righting himself, he targeted the gun with his Gatling cannon, sending a stream of high-velocity rounds. White light flared against the artificial landscape, and metallic shrapnel rattled off his hull as he passed through the rising plume of debris.

His AI marked another target just ahead: a HEL. He continued his strafing run and nailed that target as well. Atmosphere spilled from the crater his burst created, water vapor freezing instantly to glittering clouds of ice crystals.

"Enemy fighter on your six."

His AI's warning in his mind snapped his attention to his immediate surroundings. A *Yastreb* fighter had just dropped onto his tail. Continuing to hurtle forward at nearly 100 meters per second, Gregory flipped his Starblade end-for-end, bringing his Gatling into line with the Hawk fighter and triggering a brief burst from the weapon. The Hawk came apart, its vacuum energy taps detonating in a fiery smear of plasma.

"Here come the Gyrines!" Johanson called.

"Okay, people," Gregory said. "Move in on the bad guys' bridge—we need to cover those lamps!"

The Russian carrier's bridge tower, unlike the smoothly curved reverse shark fin on *America*, was large, squared off, and bulky, a truncated pyramid with steeply sloping faces. As on *America*, it was set into the carrier's spine just forward of the centrifuge wheel that provided spin gravity for the crew.

Gun emplacements encircled the tower.

Gregory readied another flight of AMSO rounds.

Strike Force Reaper
Marine Battalion 3/25
N'gai Cluster
1625 hours, FST

The *Moskva* didn't spot them coming in, or if they did, they had other things to worry about, like fighters and clouds of AMSO rounds. McDevitt pointed, projecting a graphic-targeting reticule to mark the precise spot. "Right there. Leading face."

"Aye, aye, Colonel. We'll have you there in two point five shakes."

McDevitt decided he wasn't going to ask about shakes of *what*, but continued to watch the growing Russian carrier on the MAP's screens.

The VBSS-Mk. 87 Marine Assault Pod had been dubbed "Lamprey" after an eel-like fish living back on Earth, an ugly creature with a round, jawless, tooth-lined mouth designed for attaching to the sides of other fish and rasping its way in to reach the blood and internal organs. The name, usually shortened to "Lamp" by the Marines, was a gruesome joke, but apt. The nose of the MAP was a flat sheet of nanodisassembler microbots, designed to slap up against an enemy ship's hull and dissolve their way through. Around the perimeter of nano-D were strips of nanoassemblers programmed to weld the Lamprey's "mouth" to hull metal in an unbreakable and airtight bond. It allowed a company of 120 armored USNA Marines to enter a target ship in hard vacuum without using an airlock; or rather, the MAP itself became the airlock.

The trick was in determining exactly where on the target

vessel you wanted to hit. Some parts of the hull would be massively armored and hard to eat through. Others might sandwich water tanks or the densely packed electronics of shield projectors between outer hull and interior spaces. The idea was to find a thin enough portion of outer hull that the nano-D attachment plate could burn through quickly that wouldn't, in turn, expose the Marines to a further obstacle. If the enemy knew you were coming through at a given point, they would have time to assemble ship's marines at that point to catch you coming through.

"Contact in five seconds!" the MAP pilot called over the intraship circuit. "Brace for impact!"

The pilot had a deft touch and the impact was quite gentle, a heavy surge of movement forward as the ship came to a halt. The flight deck was perched high atop the MAP's nose, and was now a meter from the solid black hull of the *Moskva*.

"Nano-D engaged!" the MAP's engineer reported from just behind McDevitt's position. "Solid seal!"

"I'm going to join my people," McDevitt said. "Thanks for the ride, boys. Enjoy the view."

"Our pleasure, Colonel. Good luck!"

He pulled his way down a narrow passageway and turned a corner.

The men and women of the 3/25's HQ Company were already lining up behind the massive round hatchway, still sealed shut, that led forward through the business end of the MAP. Mk. V Marine Assault Armor was massively imposing, the surface coated in reactive camo nanomatrix that mirrored surrounding colors, light levels, and shapes. The sight of all those armored suits mirroring one another was disorienting and a little eerie, with parts of that mob fading into the background, not quite invisible . . . but not quite there, either.

It was a sight McDevitt loved.

"Stand ready, people!" Major Hanson, McDevitt's XO, called. "We've got burn-through! Adjusting pressure differential . . ."

Normally, the HQ Company would not be employed in a combat assault, but the ancient adage of every Marine being a rifleman still held true, and McDevitt's orders were to seize the *Moskva*'s bridge and begin directing operations from there as soon as possible, and *that* meant the company would go in with the first wave. Besides, they wouldn't necessarily be the first on in the VBSS. Alfa and Bravo companies were coming in hot on board their own Lamps; Bravo was already reporting being engaged with the enemy over the battalion command channel.

That meant they needed to get going.

"Hatch open in three!" Hanson yelled, ". . . and two . . . and one . . . *go! Go! Go!*"

The hatch dilated open, and the armored Marines fell forward, pulling their way in zero-G through the brief, mirror-smooth tunnel left by the nano-D and into the *Moskva*'s command bridge.

The compartment was large—larger than on board *America*—but still managed to feel cluttered, dark, and claustrophobic, with dozens of workstations partially walled off from one another by arrays of display screens and chart boards and placed in a broad semicircle in front of a raised dais. That dais was surmounted by the command chair, a kind of elevated throne overlooking the entire compartment. That throne, McDevitt saw as he pulled his way into the compartment, was vacant; the captain had been killed, his body adrift now near the overhead display of surrounding space. Around him, Russian naval officers and technicians were already raising their hands in surrender as members of Bravo Company swarmed in from the portside, and the HQ Company came in from forward.

Laser fire snapped from farther aft, sending one Marine tumbling backward, out of control. Russian marines were on the flag bridge, high up, at least relative to the command bridge deck plan, and aft, just as on board a USNA carrier. They were firing into *America*'s Marines as the blast doors between command and flag bridges slowly rumbled shut. Half a dozen of McDevitt's Marines managed to launch themselves through space and grapple with the Russian defenders, as others blew the blast door circuits with fast-repeating bolts from their plasma weapons. The doors jammed, still halfway open. Several Russian defenders were down, the others now surrendering. The air was thick with smoke, and with the screams of injured men.

McDevitt pushed off from the forward bulkhead and sailed through to the flag bridge. "Where's the admiral?"

"The Captain First Rank is gone," a Russian marine said. He was bloodied, his arms raised. "You won't find him. . . ."

McDevitt scowled. It was imperative that they nail this thing down and assume full control of the ship as swiftly and as economically as possible. If the *Moskva* was anything like American carriers, there would be a secondary bridge located somewhere aft and buried in the ship's interior, as well as alternate control centers in the Combat Information Center and in Primary Flight Control. These ships were huge, and this one might well have a crew on board of five thousand or more.

And McDevitt had fewer than 400 men and women at his immediate command.

USNA CVS America
CIC
N'gai Cluster
1632 hours, FST

Gray was in *America*'s CIC, aft of his flag bridge, a darkened compartment filled with intense men and women, their faces stage-lit by illuminated screens and data feeds.

"Colonel McDevitt reports both flag and command bridges on board the target are secured, Admiral," Commander Randall Billingsly reported. Direct in-head communications had been interrupted by the electronic logistics of the engagement, but they were still in contact with Reaper through radio and laser-com links. "The ship has not formally surrendered yet."

"That means he didn't catch their admiral," Gray said. "Not good."

Several screens in the CIC were showing Marines'-eye views of the action over there, a confused jumble of images, health sensor readouts, and status checklists. This was the battle's critical moment. If McDevitt couldn't take control of the *Moskva* and, by extension, of the Russian squadron, then they were still dangerously deep in excrement.

Elsewhere, the USNA fighters had been redirected to engage the four surviving Russian destroyers, but losses so far were heavy. On the *Moskva*, the Russians would be fortifying themselves in secondary command and control centers all over their ship. It was entirely possible, even probable, that the *Moskva* would be able to continue fighting even after losing both flag and command bridges.

And Gray wanted to avoid that if at all possible.

CIC
CIS CV Moskva
N'gai Cluster
1642 hours, GMT

The aliens were a lot more bearable inside their combat armor, Oreshkin thought. The sight of those *faces* he found to be just about unbearable. The *Moskva* had picked up thirty-six of the creatures at 70 Ophiuchi and was almost home with them when he'd been redirected to intercept the *America* carrier battlegroup. Nal Tok and its strike group, Oreshkin mused, had likely been surprised at having a 17-light-year jump abruptly changed to one of tens of thousands of light years and extending into the remote past.

But then, it was difficult reading emotions in these militaristic monsters. Who could know what they were thinking? Or feeling?

In battle armor, they looked *almost* human: three meters tall, headless, with a torso stooped over and level with the ground, and digitigrade legs that gave them the hulking gait of a Tyrannosaurus rex. Though still monstrous, the armor masked the face riding beneath the thing's shoulders—those independently swiveling stalked eyes and the churning mass of unidentifiable mouthparts. Two arms were three-fingered and massive; the third, upper arm was actually a part of that mouth, a kind of lower lip that could unfold for a meter forward—with crushing force.

"You know what to do, Nal Tok?" Oreshkin asked over the comm channel.

"Of course," the being replied, its voice a rumble rich in cringe-inducing infrasonics. "We kill humans!"

"Not Russians! Just the Americans!"

"What's the difference? Humans are all alike to us!"

Oreshkin couldn't tell if it was joking or not. Did these creatures even understand the concept of humor?

Then, "They are here, Oreshkin. We go. . . ."

Leaving Oreshkin to hope for the best. He'd let the djinn out of its bottle, with no guarantees about the outcome.

Strike Force Reaper
Marine Battalion 3/25
N'gai Cluster
1649 hours, FST

"According to the deck plans we downloaded, this passageway *should* lead to the CIC," Hanson told him. He sounded worried.

"We copy you on the right path," McDevitt told him, checking the schematics. "CIC is down that passageway and ninety degrees to the side." He didn't tell him left or right, because such distinctions were meaningless in zero-G.

"Roger that. But . . . shouldn't we attack?"

"Negative! We're loading Konstantin-2 up here, and once

he's in place we're going to try to talk them down. You copy?"

"Copy, Colonel. I just don't like being a sitting duck in an empty passageway!"

"Protect yourselves if you come under fire. Otherwise, wait until I give you a go."

"Aye, aye, sir."

McDevitt was still on the flag bridge, which he was converting into a forward combat command center from which he could take over a kilometer and a half of starship. It was not going to be easy by any stretch of the imagination. The ship had myriad cutoffs and secondary systems; you couldn't just order the ship to blow itself up or to shut down the environmental system, because there were backups and workarounds and plenty of ways of countermanding orders from the bridge. The Russians, even with their relatively inflexible command structure, were paranoid of any one person seizing control of the entire ship, so even the bridge could be cut off from the rest of the vessel.

It should be easier once they had Konstantin loaded into the bridge network.

"Colonel! We've got Nungies!"

He swung his full attention back to the command link with Hanson. "Say again last," he barked.

He heard only static in his in-head, but he was still getting wildly gyrating images of *something* coming through the bulkheads.

He'd seen those shapes, twenty years before when he'd been a shirttail second lieutenant newly assigned to Osiris—hulking metal tanks, digitigrade legs, like they were standing on their toes. And headless.

"Hanson! Pull back! That's an order!"

But Hanson's bio readouts were flatlined. Who was next in the chain of command? Captain Crawford . . . no, flatlined. What the hell was going on?

"This is Sergeant Fitzgerald, Colonel!" a voice broke in through the static. "It's Nungies! They're coming through the bulkhead! Heavy plasma weapons! Can't hold 'em! We're falling back to the bridge!"

Nungiirtok. Twenty years ago, a joint Nungiirtok-Turusch force had descended on Osiris and kicked the human colonists off the planet . . . those who hadn't ended up in concentration camps.

What the hell were they doing on board a Russian star carrier?

"Barnes! Gomez!" he barked at his two company commanders. "We're gonna have company in a few minutes. Real bad-assery! Get your people ready!"

They already were—Marines didn't stand down in the middle of a firefight. But the momentum of the battle had just been flipped end-for-end, and the Marines now were going to have one hell of a desperate fight on their hands.

Chapter Ten

12 April, 2429
USNA CVS America
CIC
N'gai Cluster
1650 hours, FST

Gray's head shot up, his full attention captured, at the first call from the embattled *Moskva*. Nungiirtok? Who the hell invited *them* to the party?

Very little was known about those lumbering monsters. They'd been part of the Sh'daar Alliance in Gray's own epoch, and as such had been responsible for some nasty attacks across the then-Confederation frontier. There was no question that the armored shapes he was watching on the CIC's repeater screens were Nungiirtok. Their bird-like legs were pulled up and tucked in against the torso to keep them out of the way in zero-G, but the massive, headless bodies were unmistakable.

All that was known about them for sure was that they were ferocious fighters, combining the speed and sheer power of Tyrannosaurus rex with the fierce tenacity of a wolverine and the sheer combativeness of a mantis shrimp. You needed special tactics to defeat them.

He had to bite his tongue to avoid giving McDevitt advice about his troop placement. There was nothing Gray could do to help the Marines, no order he could give that would not be abject micromanagement. And McDevitt was *there*, with a much better idea of what he was doing than did Gray.

Instead, Gray checked the positions of two more Marine pods, Charlie and Delta companies, approaching the carrier aft of the spin-grav wheel. Again, he wanted to suggest they move farther forward, to add their numbers to the battle McDevitt was waging against the Nungies. Again, he held his peace. All he could do at this point was screw things up if he interfered. McDevitt was an experienced Marine commander. He knew what he was doing.

"Delta Company has just made contact," Billingsly told him. "They've attached to the carrier's hull we estimate just eighty meters aft of their CIC."

"Very well."

"Charlie Company has now locked on. Both pods are eating their way through armor."

The very worst part of command, Gray told himself, was standing by helpless and watching while someone else carried out orders you had given.

Strike Force Reaper
Marine Battalion 3/25
N'gai Cluster
1653 hours, FST

"Here they come!" McDevitt yelled. "Remember! Joints and optics!"

The first Nungie rush had been held off—barely—at the vacuum door leading onto the flag bridge itself. There was literally no place else for the embattled Marines to retreat, and now the Nungies had regrouped and launched another assault.

Years of combat with the Nungiirtok had taught the Marines the importance of pinpoint precision in fire control. Weak points in Nungie armor included the major joints at hips, shoulders, and the attachment point for the third arm; and the four tiny, heavily shielded lenses high on the chest that served as their optical feeds when they were buttoned up. Burn through the armor and you could cripple the being inside; burn out the optics and you left it blind, though still not completely helpless. The Nungiirtok possessed other senses besides sight or hearing, not all of them comprehensible to humans.

But it slowed them down, at least.

McDevitt held his Marine-issue M-90 laser rifle steady on the closest Nungie as it arrowed straight for his position crouched in the open pressure door. His AI locked on to the critical third-arm joint, and when an in-head icon winked green he thoughtclicked the weapon. A dazzling point of white light appeared against the black armor and pieces flew off.

The massive, armored torso slammed into McDevitt, tumbling him backward. Blaine and Peterson closed on the thing from either side, using their lasers as torches at point-blank range to burn their way through. A second Nungiirtok warrior grappled with Peterson, its hinged, lower jaw—encased in an armored sleeve—snapping out faster than human vision could perceive it, catching the Marine on the side of his helmet. Blaine turned her laser on this new threat and McDevitt joined in, their combined fire melting into the armor covering what they knew to be the monster's face.

The Marines standing at the pressure door were pouring fire into the advancing mass, shot after shot snapping down the corridor and flashing with each hit of the oncoming Nungies.

"Pour it on, people!" McDevitt yelled. He could feel the insane bloodlust of combat rising, feel that giddy, out-of-control whirlwind of rage and excitement that he'd not experienced since his last hand-to-hand battle ten years ago.

Lieutenant colonels weren't supposed to feel bloodlust, and they certainly weren't supposed to engage in combat at knife-fight range.

But McDevitt was a Marine, and every Marine was a rifleman.

More Nungiirtok appeared down the passageway, and he shifted his aim to them.

USNA CVS America
CIC
N'gai Cluster
1656 hours, FST

"Are you ready for this, Konstantin?"

"Unknown, Admiral. Since I do not know in detail exactly what I will encounter over there, I honestly cannot say whether I am prepared to face it or not."

Gray frowned but decided not to pursue it. If anyone could pull this off, it was Konstantin. The links were solidly in place and protected against enemy attempts to jam or compromise them. With any luck, this would be over so quickly they wouldn't have the chance to counter it.

"You should warn the Marines that I am on the way," Konstantin told him.

"Right. How long is this gonna take, you think?"

"Unknown. But in human time scales, at least, it should be over *very* quickly."

And then the SAI was gone.

Gray had suggested the idea moments ago, but it had been Konstantin who'd worked out the details. What they were trying was similar to the Omega virus—an electronic attack aimed at AI systems they'd picked up from the Denebans and employed against the Consciousness. What Gray was uncertain about was whether this would work against organic beings like the Nungiirtok . . . and how. The Consciousness had been an extremely advanced SAI, *software*, not organic life.

But Konstantin Junior had another angle, he promised, something that should give them a decided edge.

Whatever Konstantin had in mind, Gray hoped it worked out.

Konstantin-2
CIS CV Moskva
N'gai Cluster
1657 hours, FST

To say that Konstantin could *see* the way humans did was somewhat problematic. Certainly, he made use of camera feeds, some tens of thousands of them at a time, and he could pick up visual input from the cerebral implants of humans who were recording what they were seeing.

But there were no cameras within the Godstream, and Konstantin's mind worked far differently from its human counterparts. It was aware of colors and patterns as it streamed through the laser-com link between the *America* and the *Moskva* and onto the Russian carrier's bridge, and it was sharply aware of myriad scenes flooding through its awareness, the points of view of thousands of men, women, and machines, of readings from over two thousand sensors of various types. Coupled with these, woven through them in a tapestry of staggering scope and complexity, was the heartbeat throb of over seven hundred networks, information frameworks, power and data feeds, and shipboard operational systems, all entangled with one another in a vast and powerful whole.

Antiviral systems and interlocking tiers of security software were encountered . . . and overwhelmed. Konstantin was much faster and could think around, over, or through any security block he encountered.

There were AIs within that network, but none capable of self-awareness or self-determination on Konstantin's level. The Russians had long mistrusted anything that gave too much power to locally autonomous systems, such as ships and military units, preferring to keep everything under a human captain's control.

And even then, they had other humans in place to watch the captain.

But *Moskva* was self-aware now. Konstantin was in complete control of every system and data feed and was shutting down major systems—drive and primary power taps, weapons, PriFly, navigation, external sensors—all to the consternation of the human controllers in the ship's CIC and secondary bridge. *Moskva* was now blind, toothless, and paralyzed.

One thing Konstantin could *not* do was attack the Nungiirtok directly by interfering with their electronic implants or by shutting down their battlesuits. The Nungiirtok possessed sophisticated electronics imbedded within their tough hides and in their battlesuits, but the computer protocols and encoding all were vastly different from human standards. In time, Konstantin would be able to crack them, but for now he had to settle for a less direct approach.

He found he could jam their communications, broadcasting a piercing blast of feedback static through their comm receivers so that they could no longer talk to one another. After a moment's experimentation, he found he could also set their battlesuit optical scanners to wide-open low-light. The Nungiirtok had large and sensitive eyes, the evolutionary product—human xenobiologists believed—of a genesis on the world of a cooler, dimmer sun than Sol. With their optics set to receive every photon available in a darkened room, the normal, ambient lighting within *Moskva*'s corridors abruptly became a hellish, blinding glare.

For Konstantin, the Godstream was a kind of surging, flowing ocean within which he moved, absorbed data, and manipulated systems. Things had indeed happened quickly. Between his arrival within *Moskva*'s networks and the moment he changed the settings on the Nungiirtok optics, just .06 of a second had passed. He waited another five seconds, monitoring the thrashing, erratic response of the aliens before finding the Russian commanding officer and opening a direct com link with him.

"*Kapitan Pervogo Ranga* Yuri Yuryevich Oreshkin," Konstantin said with a measured, formal gravity.

The man jumped. "Who is there? What are you?"

"I am the artificial intelligence now in control of your vessel," Konstantin said in perfect Russian. "I suggest you lay down your weapons and surrender this ship."

"Or what?" Oreshkin demanded.

"Several possibilities come to mind," Konstantin replied. "Among them shutting down life support or changing gas mix to one high in CO_2 or lacking oxygen. I could also destroy this ship after my people evacuate back to their ships."

"That would be murder!"

"That would be war. Believe me, I have no human compunctions about doing what must be done to secure the safety of my people and my ship. I would imagine that you feel the same way about protecting your crew."

There was a moment's silence, and then the Russian commander gave in. This time, he spoke English. "Okay . . . okay! I will give the order."

Eighteen seconds after transferring his awareness to the *Moskva*, Konstantin reported back to Gray. "We have control of the *Moskva*."

Elsewhere, the battle continued but was swiftly drawing to a close. Konstantin found control codes within the *Moskva*'s PriFly, and used them to shut down Russian fighters engaging the *Arlington*, *Birmingham*, and *America* herself. The four Russian destroyers were not so easily commandeered, but Oreshkin himself transmitted orders to his forces to cease fighting before they could close with *America*.

It took a little longer to subdue the Nungiirtok, but at last the shooting stopped, and the USNA forces secured the Russian carrier.

Now they needed to discover the reason for the attack.

Lieutenant Adams
Moskva
N'gai Clluster
1845 hours, FST

Lieutenant Adams had been alone in this cell for what felt like hours. The place was essentially a steel box three meters by four meters by three meters high—scarcely enough room to pace. A fold-down bunk occupied the back bulkhead. Toilet facilities and a water tap folded out of another. The light overhead was never off.

Occasionally she could hear a commotion in the distance: boots running down corridors, piercing yells and shouts. Once she heard the dull, distant boom of an explosion.

What the hell was going on out there?

At last, the door to her cell slid open, and an armored figure leaned in . . .

An armored figure wearing the insignia of the USNA Marines.

Rising from her bunk, Adams couldn't resist. She was a devotee of old movies, especially space yarns. "Aren't you a little short to be a stormtrooper?"

The Marine seemed taken aback. "What the *fuck*?"

"Sorry," she said. "Classical reference. What the hell is that ruckus out there?"

The Marine seemed to recover his composure. "Sergeant Hobbes, ma'am, USNA Marines. We saw there was a prisoner in here : . . so I guess this is a rescue. Who are you?"

"Julianne Adams, Lieutenant," she managed. "VFA-198, off the *America* . . ."

Then the enormity of what was happening struck her, and she sagged, racked by sobs.

But she was able to walk out of the cell under her own power, and minutes later she was on her way back to the *America*.

USNA CVS America
Officers' Mess
N'gai Cluster
1850 hours, FST

"The question of the hour is why the Russians attacked us," Gray said. "Are we at war with them back home? There wasn't any problem with them of which I was aware."

Truitt made a face. "Who knows why the Russians do anything?"

They were sitting in the officers' mess, located within Hab Two, one of the modules rotating around *America*'s spine in order to create a spin gravity equivalent to about half a G. With Gray were Truitt and Kline, who'd just returned on board after interviewing several of the Nungiirtok on the *Moskva*, and Dr. Greg Mallory, from the xenotechnology department. Dinner had just been served by a human messman—one of the perks of the officers' mess—and Gray was enjoying a concoction of shrimp and rice that completely hid its humble origins as reconstituted rawmat.

"Now, Doctor," Gray chided. "If I've learned anything from you, it's that intelligent beings have reasons for doing what they do. Humans, Turusch, Nungiirtok—it doesn't matter. Each has an agenda."

"Sorry, Admiral. My specialty is xenosophonts—aliens. Humans . . ." He shrugged. "I have *no* idea."

"Okay . . . so what have you learned about the Nungies?" Gray continued. "What the hell were they doing on board a Russian star carrier?"

"Well, Oreshkin claims it was a humanitarian mission," Kline told him. "A group of Nungiirtok were stranded on Osiris twenty years ago, out in the mountains beyond the city of Abdju."

"Stranded?"

"They were cut off when Confederation forces landed and retook the planet," Truitt said. "They refused to surrender, but their Turusch transports were gone and they had no way of leaving the planet. Apparently the Russians made contact and convinced them to come with them."

"To where?"

"They appear to have been on their way to the Russian research station on Mars," Mallory replied. "Presumably they would have been repatriated to their home planet, since we're no longer at war with either the Sh'daar or the Sh'daar Collective."

Gray nodded. This was old news, practically ancient history. He'd been a fighter pilot on board the *America*, back when the Nungies and their Turusch allies had captured the 70 Ophiuchi system. The Nungies had held a fearsome reputation as hulking, heavily armored ground troops, and they'd rolled right over the lightly armed colonial militia out there.

European forces had gone back to 70 Ophiuchi A II—Osiris—several years later and retaken the colony of New Egypt on the planet's southern continent. With the Turusch naval forces broken, the Nungiirtok on the planet had been unable to resupply and unable to evacuate. Apparently, though, the counterattack hadn't cleaned out all of the invaders. A planet, after all, was an enormous place, offering way too many places to hide.

"Are they going to be a problem?" Gray asked Truitt.

"I don't think so," the older man replied. "Especially since we can essentially offer them the same thing the Russians did—repatriation."

"They *did* attack us, Doctor."

"At the Russians' behest. I see no advantage in punishing them for the sake of punishment. All they want is to go home."

"I don't care about punishment. I'm worried about what twenty-five Nungiirtok warriors are going to do on board *America*, especially when they learn we will not be taking them home right away."

"We could leave them on the *Moskva*," Kline suggested.

"Where the Russians might try to retake their ship, maybe with help from their Nungie allies?" He shook his head. "I don't think so."

"You know, there's an alternative," Mallory said.

"Yes? I'd love to hear it."

"We transfer them to the *Arlington*. Better yet, make it one of the Russian destroyers. We take off the human crew, we make sure the rawmat reserves are adequate, and we remove the drive module so they can't go anywhere." He gestured toward the viewall bulkhead, at thronging stars and the tight, tiny circle of stars in the distance, the accretion disks of six brand-new black holes. "We leave them here. Make sure their shielding is okay, of course—we don't want them to fry in a high-rad environment. Then we go do what we have to do and pick them up on our way back."

"Turn a destroyer into a prison camp, huh?" He nodded. "Makes sense. They're gonna be pissed if we don't make it back."

"They would be pissed if they went with us and *we* didn't make it back," Truitt pointed out. "It's a humane option, given the constraints of our mission. Besides, we leave the ship broadcasting on a distress frequency and leave a recording describing what we've done. Other expeditions are bound to come to the N'gai Cluster over the next few months to study the aftereffects of the hypernova. The prisoners will be fine."

"Okay. We'll need to have the Marines be *very* sure that the ship we choose is clean of weapons, though. We can't afford to leave any guards behind, and I don't want to come back and find any . . . surprises."

Gray closed his eyes and opened a channel to Mackey, letting him know what he wanted. Mackey acknowledged; the Russian destroyer *Slava* had not yet rejoined the *Moskva* and was adrift a few kilometers off. She would do . . .

"Okay," he said, returning to the mess hall. "I need your assessments. Where are the Sh'daar refugees, and how are we going to make contact?"

"Out there, of course," Truitt said, with a vague wave of his hand toward the panorama of deep space. "Where would you expect?"

Gray eyed the head of *America*'s xenosophontology department and frowned. "I'd hoped for something more substantial from you, Doctor. More *useful.*"

"Well, they can't have gone far, right?" Kline said. "Last time we saw them, they were traveling in normal space."

"A lot of them were," Mallory replied. "The big, mobile colonies, the McKendree cylinders, the Banks orbitals. Big things, too big to go fast, too big to fit through a TRGA."

"Well, then," Truitt said. "Seems to me they can't have gone farther than three light years, right?"

Gray looked up at the overhead. "Dr. Truitt . . . do you have *any* idea at all how big a light year is?"

"Certainly. A little over nine trillion kilometers."

"And how tiny any vessel or artifact fashioned by intelligence actually is within all of that emptiness? We would have trouble spotting a *planet* within a light year or three. Even something as big as a Banks orbital would be all but lost in all that emptiness."

"Surely," Kline said, "there must be some way of finding a whole fleet of such structures."

"We'll search," Gray said. "Maybe we'll pick up radio chatter or the beams of laser coms. Maybe we can pick them up on infrared or by X-ray trails. A structure that big plowing through dust and gas at close to *c* should leave a pretty bright radiation track. But it's not going to be easy. These guys don't want to be found, remember. They're afraid of the Consciousness chasing after them, and they know that thing is a hell of a lot more technologically advanced than we are."

"If it's as big a problem as you suggest, Admiral," Truitt said, thoughtful, "what do you suggest we do?"

"We might scout ahead looking for the smaller Sh'daar ships traveling faster than light—under their equivalent of Alcubierre Drive. Alcubierre Drive uses focused gravitational singularities to tuck the space around them into a bubble moving at FTL, and that generates some pretty significant gravitational waves."

"Surely that's how they're moving their big world-ships as well," Mallory said. "If we can pick up gravity waves..."

Gray shook his head. "The power usage for an Alcubierre Drive is many orders of magnitude greater at FTL velocities as opposed to sublight. We should be able to pick up FTL ships under drive with the equipment we have on board *America*. Structures moving at sublight... not so much. Again, we'll look. But I want you to know we're going to be searching a world-sized haystack for a microscopic needle."

"Do we at least know what direction they were headed?" Kline asked.

Gray grinned at her. "Sure!" He waved his arm. "*That* way! We know they're headed for the galactic disk of the Milky Way. That's an enormous area to search."

Truitt scowled. "If their Alcubierre Drive is as good as ours..." he began.

"It's at least as good," Mallory pointed out.

"...then in three years they should have made it all the way from N'gai to the Milky Way's disk. Ten thousand light years, you said?"

"About that," Mallory agreed, nodding. "Of course, we're pretty sure now that it was the Sh'daar who created the TRGAs in the first place... their ur-Sh'daar ancestors, I should say. If they have any TRGAs set up along their line of flight, all bets are off."

"Why is that?" Kline asked.

"Because TRGAs are gateways to multiple places across multiple times. A slight shift in your transit trajectory can drop you thousands of light years off course... and maybe put you in a completely different time period."

"Yes," Truitt said. "Passing through a TRGA is how we originally reached *this* epoch, over 800 million years in our past. I see your problem."

"*Our* problem, Doctor," Gray sighed. "To find these guys, we're going to have to be incredibly lucky."

Truitt looked glum for a moment, then brightened. "Well, we *do* have one ace in the hole."

Gray looked at him, wondering what the doctor could possibly be thinking.

Chapter Eleven

18 April, 2429

Koenig Residence
Westerville, Ohio
1545 hours, EST

Koenig was watching the news feed on his living room wall. The anti-AI riots in D.C. had spread and were growing like some monstrous, evil cancer. Troops had been brought in to restore order, and in some of the outlying sectors of the city, the fighting was house-to-house.

A talking head from a D.C. network station was describing the scene, with wrecked and burning vehicles behind her. Koenig had the house enhance the image; on a charred wall behind the reporter, he could just make out a scrawled piece of graffiti in bright scarlet—the words *fight pAIn*.

"You can see the logo of Fight pAIn behind me," the reporter was saying. "Anti-AI elements have been growing stronger in several cities, and Dr. Anton Michaels, from his home at Midway, has told us that these riots are the inevitable result of giving more and more decision-making powers to our machines."

The shot shifted to a view of Michaels, floating in partial microgravity, his pale halo of frizzy hair unkempt. He started speaking, but Koenig thoughtclicked the sound off. He had no desire to hear what that acid little Humankind Firster had to say about machines or anything else.

That pAIn meme, however, had been popping up with increasing frequency in riot-torn cities across the country of late . . . and it had all the hallmarks of being a particularly sneaky bit of memegineering. The question, of course, was who was behind it? The Russians? The Pan-Euros?

Or maybe it was a memegineering attack by a group— the Humankind Firsters, for instance. They were derisively referred to as "Huffers," as in they would huff and puff and blow the SAIs away. Koenig had not thought them a serious threat, but he was beginning to have some second thoughts about that.

God, things were bad in D.C. And he'd sent Marta into the middle of all of that . . .

The wall announced the arrival of an aircar, and Koenig heard the guard outside greet someone. Marta walked in the door a moment later and Koenig breathed a deep and heartfelt sigh of relief. He'd been worried about her being out and about on her own, and her safe return meant she hadn't been spotted and identified . . . or caught in the anti-AI riots.

He did *not* want Marta to go through this kind of danger again, though Marta, for her part, seemed perfectly happy to run his occasional "errands."

It didn't look like Marta, though. She was wearing a face, a kind of organic mask grown from human tissue that gave her the look of a much older woman. In a second, though, she peeled the mask off, and they kissed.

"I'm so glad you're back!" he told her. "I was worried sick . . ."

"I was fine. The new software worked perfectly." Her ID, he sensed, was already changing. By law, all AI robots were required to broadcast signals that could be picked up by the cerebral implants of people around them, a tag proclaiming them to be robots, not people. Heaven forbid that a robot be mistaken for a real person! For her mission to D.C., she'd been given a slick bit of highly illegal computer code that IDed her as human, complete with fictitious background, address, employment status, and hobbies. The mask had been there to enhance the deception.

"So how'd it go?" he asked, releasing her.

"Phillip is concerned," she told him. "He believes the President is about to enact a new directive calling for the elimination of all SAIs such as Konstantin."

"Shit . . ."

Phillip Caldwell was a former director of the National Security Council and an old friend. He'd been one of Koenig's key advisors when he'd been President. After Koenig had left office, Caldwell had taken a position as the head of Cybersec, a Washington think tank specializing in AI security. There'd been rumors for weeks that they were going to pull the plug on Konstantin and others like him, and secondary rumors that they would be calling for the registration of AI robots and restrictions on their manufacture and use. Koenig had asked Marta to travel to D.C. and speak with Phillip in person. Koenig himself was too well-known, but a robot, especially one as lifelike as Marta, would be able to pull it off . . . *if* she was disguised as human.

Evidently, she had.

"Phillip says they're keeping it a deep, dark secret, of course. There'd be too much opposition from the pro-tech groups . . . or from pro-robotics countries like North India, Japan, or the Hegemony."

"What, they're just going to spring it on people out of the blue?"

"That's what he believes. An executive order, letting Walker bypass Congress."

"He has enough support in Congress to get away with it, too." He was remembering the applause from the Congressional floor when Walker talked to them about the Singularity. That had been absolutely chilling.

"He doesn't have as much support as some believe," Marta told him. "If Walker pulls the plug, Phillip believes, there is going to be massive unrest and economic displacement. AIs already control a huge percentage of both government and industry. People aren't trained to just step in and replace them. Besides, the AIs are just too good at what they do. Can you imagine the educational download system being run by a *human*? Or the healthcare bureau? Or—"

"Marta, some days I seriously question whether humans are capable of *dressing* themselves without help. I honestly don't know how he thinks he can pull this off without having a civil war on his hands."

"Phillip says the government has very quietly been stationing troops around the country and enacting protocols that will allow him to deploy them in the event of civil unrest."

"Damn it, the guy's gone rogue. We need to stop him."

Marta cocked her head to one side. "How do you do that within the strictures established by the Constitution?"

"Carefully, Marta. Very, very carefully."

"There's something more that Phillip thought you should see."

Koenig sighed. "Show me."

The news image of a silently pontificating Michaels on the living room viewall was replaced by a graphic showing the solar system, with the orbits of the planets out to Jupiter shown in green, and a bright white line extending out from the middle of the asteroid belt.

"What's that?"

"It hasn't been announced," Marta told him, "but a High Guard ship picked this up on April 6—twelve days ago. A small, heavily cloaked vessel of unknown configuration broke solar orbit and accelerated out of the system. It moved very slowly at first, as if it didn't want its drive wake to attract any attention, but then it accelerated to *c*, engaged something like an Alcubierre Drive, and vanished. It was on a direct heading to . . . here."

The image changed, showing the scattered stars of a patch of sky, the hazy cloud of the Milky Way stretched across the center. A red circle and two lines of numbers marked precise coordinates.

"Seventeen hours, fifty-two minutes, twenty-eight seconds," Koenig said, reading the coordinates. "Plus thirteen degrees, forty-one seconds, twenty seconds. Okay, constellation of Sagittarius, and in toward the galactic core. Intelligence doesn't know who that was?"

"No, Alex."

"And why hasn't this been reported?" Koenig asked.

"Phillip said that Navy Intelligence received pretty explicit instructions not to make this public. Too much chance of panic."

"Panic. About what? Someone keeping an eye on us?"

"I don't know," Marta said. "Naval Intelligence reported it as an alien spacecraft. They did not know who—or what— was operating it."

"Phil is just full of good news," Koenig said. "Okay, Marta. You did a splendid job. Thank you! And, again, I'm sorry to have had to send you in there."

"I was never in any real danger. The riots are in the peripheral sectors of the city. I was in the central government area—you know, tourist Washington? Cybersec's offices are just three blocks from the Capitol dome, so it wasn't as if I was wandering all around the city."

"I know . . . but things could have gone so wrong." He took her in his arms again. "I will *never* do that to you again."

"You'll do what you need to do, Alex." She hugged him close. "And I'll be here to help."

USNA CVS America
CIC
N'gai Cluster
1650 hours, FST

"Take us ahead, point seven-five *c*," Gray said. "Grav sensors, keep a sharp lookout. Full spread, maximum sensitivity."

"Aye, aye, Admiral," Mackey replied from the bridge. "Nothing on the sensors yet."

As *America* accelerated, pushing closer to the speed of light, the view of space ahead took on an increasingly surreal look, the stars aft and around them crowding forward into a kind of glowing doughnut centered on the empty blackness directly ahead. The effect was caused by the ship plowing through incoming photons at relativistic speeds, until even starlight coming from astern was twisted into geometries that seemed to put it in front.

America and her consorts were spread out across nearly 10 million kilometers, the better to pick up the faint whispers of gravitational waves over as large a volume of space as possible. Their search routine called for jumping to Alcubierre Drive every hour and moving ahead several hundred astronomical units. Between their FTL runs, they plowed through normal space at relativistic speed . . . listening. The plan offered them the best hope of covering the most ground in the least time.

They were still in for a very *long* hunt.

It was frustrating trying to predict what the Sh'daar migration fleet might be doing. Things would be a lot easier if the alien fleet was spread out over a huge volume of space, the lumbering space habitats trailing far astern of the faster and more nimble naval vessels. Indeed, Gray felt fairly sure, in a gut-instinct kind of way, that they *would* be scattered, possibly across ten thousand light years.

But he also suspected that the really large Sh'daar vessels, those traveling strictly at sublight speeds, would be clumped tightly together for mutual protection, and that meant a tiny target in a vast expanse of empty space. They only needed to search three light years for the slow-movers—that was as far as they could have moved in three years, after all, traveling at near-c—but the word *only* in that context was deceptive. Even a fleet of hundreds of massive McKendree cylinders, Banks orbitals, and Bishop rings would be vanishingly small in a cone-shaped volume three light years long and of unknown breadth.

But they had to try.

"Negative on all scans, Admiral," Mackey told him.

"Very well. Coordinate with the other ships, then initiate another FTL run."

"Aye, aye, sir."

Of course, they'd known they would have trouble finding the alien migration before *America* had even left Earth. But planners had expected the Sh'daar to be using beacons of some sort, or more powerful grav drives—something that would make them stand out across the light years. Those planners had not anticipated the Sh'daar desire to stay hidden, to slip beneath the notice of the Consciousness.

Or the efficiency with which they'd been able to make themselves disappear.

Reluctantly, Gray turned his mind once more to Truitt's proposal. The idea scared him, scared him badly, but the xenosophontologist was right. If they couldn't find the Sh'daar by conventional means, poking along and listening for their gravity wave emissions, Truitt's little brainstorm might well be the only workable option.

Leaning back in his seat, Gray closed his eyes and summoned up Konstantin.

"This idea of Truitt's," he said in-head. "How would it work?"

"You've done it before," Konstantin replied. "Essentially, it's a form of the Bright Light group consciousness."

"I understand that. But how would we *do* it?"

"We would start by nanoconstructing a number of Bright Light modules," Konstantin replied. "A very large number—several hundred at the very least, and several thousand would be better. We scatter them across a large volume of space and allow them to establish a communications network among themselves. We have volunteers from the fleet upload onto the electronic network created and instruct them to search for evidence of the Sh'daar fleet."

Gray made a sour face. "You make it sound so easy."

"The idea is fairly simple in principle," the SAI told him. "It will be complex to execute logistically."

"But I don't understand what it buys us," Gray said. "This network, we can't spread it across light years. The time lag—"

"Would be prohibitive, I know. A module placed one light year out would require a full year to establish contact with us. But what we need essentially is a very, *very* large VLBI, one with multiple baselines on the order of astronomical units long."

"VLBI?"

"Very Long Baseline Interferometry."

"Ah. Right."

Gray knew the term, though it had been years since he'd heard it discussed. For centuries, relatively small telescopes, both radio and optical, had been linked together in a way that combined the images from many small instruments to create a much larger virtual one, one with a diameter equal to the largest baseline between discrete units. Three centuries before, fifteen space telescopes, each of 100-meter diameter, had been positioned in deep space in a pattern almost an astronomical unit across. When the incoming optical signals were combined, astronomers had been able to image the surfaces of planets and moons with what amounted to a single virtual mirror one AU across. The surface of Chiron, at Alpha Centauri A, had been mapped in detail that way.

In principle, Truitt's idea was based on this, but the individual networked units wouldn't be gathering light. They would be the supporting framework of a far-flung network of minds, human and AI, that would merge to create a single, emergent consciousness—a Mind of incredible scope and power.

Three years ago, Gray had been part of such a super-Mind, during the final confrontation with the Consciousness. Guided and directed by Konstantin, Gray and some thousands of other human and AI intellects had merged to become . . . something greater. *Inconceivably* greater. That merger had been necessary to make direct contact with an alien Mind so vast it literally did not recognize human minds as distinct and intelligent units. They had used hundreds of Bright Light modules as the framework for their shared awareness, probes originally designed to make contact with the Harvesters, a highly advanced electronic intelligence occupying the high-energy environment around the star Deneb.

Gray remembered that time spent as a super-intellect, as a Mind of godlike scope and power. The memory, faded like a dream, still lingered . . . and it scared the hell out of him.

But it wasn't without precedent. Back on Earth, the same principle had been applied to the Global Net, the modern iteration of what once had been called the Internet. Rather than merely using the new infrastructure for mind-to-mind communications, the entire mind could enter the Net, surfing its crests and troughs, exploring a staggeringly rich virtual environment, and merging with other minds in what had become known as the Godstream.

The Godstream on and near Earth didn't scare Gray. If something went wrong, the connection was lost and you woke up back in your chair at home. But what Truitt was proposing was a Net with a baseline many light-minutes across. If you got kicked off of *that* monster, you might well not wake up back home.

You might well not wake up at all.

"What do we need, Konstantin?" Gray asked at last.

"We need to create a large number of modified Bright Light modules," the SAI replied. "I anticipated your agreeing to the plan and took the liberty of beginning to nanufacture them based on plans stored within *America*'s RAM. You should call for volunteers within the crew and coordinate with the other ships as well. We will need *all* of our resources and assets to carry this off."

"And the implementation? The logistics?"

"I shall plot the necessary courses for the placement of each module. That part will be time-consuming, but careful positioning of all modules will maximize our chances of detecting the Sh'daar."

Gray hesitated, then nodded. "Do it."

"Admiral?" Mackey's voice said in his head. "Excuse the interruption. We have entered Alcubierre space again. Five minutes at two lights."

"Very well." Gray disengaged from the link with Konstantin and opened his eyes. The CIC external view screens showed a sterile blackness, the emptiness that was *America*'s own private universe as she folded space around herself in a tight little bubble.

Bright Light modules. Did they offer the squadron a chance? He felt as though it were a long shot . . . some tens of thousands of light years.

At this point, though, long shot might be the best odds they had.

USNA CVS America
Flight Deck Storage Locker
N'gai Cluster
1745 hours, FST

"My God!" Gregory said, his voice close to trembling. "I thought you were dead!"

He held Julianne Adams close, the two of them floating, clinging to one another in microgravity, but constrained somewhat by the narrow storage space just off the carrier's flight deck. Holding her head between his hands, he kissed her, deeply and hungrily.

"Mmm," she said after a long moment. "Maybe I should get captured by Russians more often."

She said it lightly enough, but he could hear the ragged edge to her voice.

"Are you okay?" he asked her, worried. "Did they . . . are you? . . ."

"I'm fine, Don," she told him. "I'm okay. A bit shaky, maybe. Just . . . just hold me."

He did, pulling her closer.

"I heard you'd been found," he whispered into her hair. "But they took you straight to sick bay and wouldn't let me in to see you."

"The . . . the Russians hit me with an injectable nano. It had me way off-kilter. But the med people gave me a counter-nano, something to clear out the bad stuff."

"And your implants?"

"The docs told me they checked out okay." She made a face. "God, I thought I was going to have to grow new hardware, though. I felt so *dirty*. . . ."

"I know—"

"You can't know! I'm sorry, it's just—I can't have them in my *head*! That was the worst part."

"It's over now."

"It's . . . it's not over," she told him. "Not yet. But this helps. I just need you to hold me," she said, quietly sobbing now.

"My God, what did they *do* to you?"

Tears danced around her face, tiny, glittering spheres adrift in microgravity.

He held her, whispering to her that everything, *everything* would be okay.

USNA CVS America
Flag Bridge
N'gai Cluster
2235 hours, FST

"First dozen drones away, Admiral," Mackey told him. "We have signal."

"Very well, Mack," Gray replied. He glanced at Lieutenant West. "Okay, Wild West," he said. He didn't usually address junior officers by their handles, but he was feeling more optimistic than he'd felt in some time. They'd beaten the Russians *and* a pack of Nungiirtok, they were on the trail of their quarry, and most important, they now had a definite plan of attack. "How are the others doing?"

"We haven't heard from the *Birmingham* yet, Admiral," she replied. "Speed of light time lag. *Acadia* and *Arlington* both report ready for deployment, as soon as they have their drones on board."

"Keep me informed."

"Aye, aye, Admiral."

The nanufactories on *Acadia* had been working all out, turning rawmat into the modified Bright Light modules Mackey was calling "drones." Konstantin had been programming those drones as they came off the assembler lines, and the first twelve had just been launched from *Acadia*'s flight bay. Bundles of some hundreds of drones had already been packed aboard interfleet transports and were on their way to *Birmingham* and *Arlington*, which would soon disperse across a huge volume of space to plant them. The fleet had spent several hours repositioning itself nearly two light years from the N'gai galactic center, an area that Konstantin had decided was statistically more likely than others to actually be concealing the big Sh'daar slow-movers, the artificial worlds and rings and terraformed cylinders. Wherever in all of this emptiness they now were, the human fleet ought to be able to pick them up with their improvised Godstream net.

Behind them, a bright star burned in a thick, white haze—the hypernova. They were seeing its light now as it was two years ago at one year old and in that time it had faded quite a bit, but there still was glare enough from seven detonating suns to fill the dwarf galaxy's core with radiance.

That was another advantage of moving the search out here. The orbiting Six Suns Rosette generated gravity waves, very powerful gravity waves, but the disturbance was considerably dampened by distance. Out here, away from the interference, the human ships would have a much better chance of picking up the grav-drive disturbances of the Sh'daar fleet, especially if that fleet was close by in all of this aching emptiness.

"Admiral?" Lieutenant West said.

"Yes?"

"Message from Captain Rand, sir. He wants to know your orders for the Russian squadron."

Gray nodded. He'd almost forgotten about them.

"Tell him he may proceed at his discretion," Gray told her. "Keep well spread out . . . but stay within five light-seconds of the *America*. If any of those crews cause trouble, I want to know about it immediately."

"Aye, aye, sir."

One of the Russian destroyers, the *Storozhevoy*—the ship most badly damaged in the battle at the Rosette—had had her crew evacuated to the *America*, her drives melted down, and she'd been left adrift a few billion kilometers from the Rosette with twenty-five disgruntled Nungi-irtok on board. Her small onboard nanufactory had been pegged—meaning it could only convert rawmat into certain limited finished goods—food of the Nungies' choosing, water, air, and a few luxuries, but not weapons, comm devices, or drive components. They should be still sitting there when the human squadron returned.

Storozhevoy had by chance proven to be a good name for the ship. It meant "Guardian."

The other three destroyers—*Smell'yy*, *Provornyy*, and *Ognevoy*—as well as the *Moskva*, all still had their Russian crews, but the officers had been taken off and replaced by USNA personnel, with a company of Marines on board each vessel to guard against an uprising by the prisoners. Gray had been tempted to maroon the Russians with their Nungiirtok allies, but he just didn't have enough personnel to fill all four captured vessels' crew billets, even on watch-and-watch. The *Moskva* alone had a crew of over four thousand, and while she now had no need of her space wing, there still weren't enough people from the *America* to fill in. He was short of officers as it was and had to press a number of his chiefs and first class petty officers into roles usually filled by JGs, lieutenants, and lieutenant commanders.

So long as the Russians behaved themselves, it ought to work . . . but he wanted to keep those ships close at hand, just in case he had to send a boarding party across.

One concession he had made: Gray had asked Captain Rand to volunteer to take over the *Moskva*, and the young officer had jumped at the chance to redeem himself.

Gray hoped he wouldn't regret the decision.

Chapter Twelve

20 April, 2429

Koenig Residence
Westerville, Ohio
1545 hours, EST

"Mr. President?" a Marine guard said over Koenig's in-head gear.

"Yes, Master Sergeant?"

"Sorry to bother you, sir, but we have an aircar inbound. One passenger. His ID checks out."

"Who is it?"

"Randal Jennings. He's one of Walker's legal advisors. He says he needs to talk to you in person."

"I know him. Let him in."

"Yes, sir."

Koenig heard the disapproval in the Marine's voice. The master sergeant would be thinking of things like a bomb hidden in the aircar, or nanomalware hidden in a hand-shake.

Well, if Walker really wanted him dead, there wasn't a lot Koenig could do to prevent it. He would take such pre-cautions as he could, but he was *not* going to climb down a hole and pull it in after him.

"What is it, love?" Marta asked.

"One of Walker's flunkies," Koenig told her. "A yes-man from way back, a lawyer with a master's degree in brown-nosing. I remember him from Walker's transition team."

"What does he want?"

"Beats me. Probably delivering a message from Walker." Koenig thought for a moment. "I'm going to ask you to stay out of sight." No need to complicate things.

"Of course. Can I listen in?"

"Sure." He opened an in-head channel. "Konstantin? Are you monitoring?"

"Of course, Mr. President. The aircar is a Subaru-Rockwell Silver Streak, with engine, cabin, and hull modifications. Fairly standard for the D.C. crowd. Extra power so it can mount extra armor."

"Are you picking up any threat? Weapons? Explosives?"

"No, Mr. President, though any such could be shielded." Konstantin hesitated. "The Marines have been *quite* thorough, however."

Koenig grinned. "I believe it. Okay, I'd like you to be looking over my shoulder when I talk to this guy. Don't announce yourself, but listen in."

"Of course, Mr. President. I wouldn't miss this for the world."

Every now and then Konstantin demonstrated what Koenig could only call a sense of humor. It could be a little disconcerting at times.

The aircar glided to a halt on Koenig's landing deck a few moments later. The canopy split open, and a tall man in formal-dress skintights stepped out. Two Marine guards gave his ID a thorough check, then waved him on. Koenig met him at the door.

"Good afternoon, Mr. President," Jennings said, extending a hand.

Koenig didn't take it, but he disarmed the snub with a grin. "Hello, Randal. Sorry. Don't like being rude, but doctor's orders."

"Of course. You have no idea where I've been."

The trouble was, he *did* know, but he didn't say anything about it. "What can I do for you? Or is this something for me from your boss?"

"Do you know Dr. Anton Michaels?"

"Not personally."

But Koenig knew *of* him, certainly—the Humankind Firster who'd been very much in the news of late. A billionaire and the CEO of an important space mining consortium, he supposedly had the ear of the President. Many assumed he was at least in part behind Walker's distrust of SAI influences.

"Dr. Michaels is currently at his habitat at Midway, and he would very much like to meet with you."

"About what?"

"I have no idea. Quite possibly he wants to talk to you about the President's intent to shut down super-AIs here on Earth, but I have no details. And President Walker wants you to meet with him."

"Why me?"

Jennings shrugged. "Because the President can't do it himself. Because you *were* the President and still have high-level security clearances. Because you're something of a senior statesman now and have the best interests of your country at heart."

"Okay, but why send me halfway up the space elevator? I'm sure Dr. Michaels can find out where I live."

Jennings looked uncomfortable. "Well, the thing is, Dr. Michaels flat-out refuses to set foot on Earth, *ever*. He is convinced, as you probably know, that the SAIs control nearly everything on Earth, and he fears having them listen in on what he has to say. For that reason, he is asking that you go up to Midway and meet with him there. He says that it *will* be very much worth your while."

"Alex," Konstantin whispered in Koenig's mind, "I strongly advise against this."

"No," Koenig said aloud. "Send someone else. I'm not a messenger boy for the damned Huffers."

"The President anticipated your refusal, sir, and advised

me to tell you that our civilization, as currently constituted, cannot survive if the machines are shut down. He believes Michaels and the Humankind Firsters represent a serious threat to our peace and well-being. He knows that you are pro-SAI but also that you are loyal to the USNA, *and* you have those security clearances I mentioned. He told me to ask you . . . '*please.*'"

Koenig blinked, not certain how to respond. "I thought President Walker and Dr. Michaels were best buds," he said. "That Walker hates super-AIs as much as Michaels does. That Michaels had been serving in an advisory capacity with Walker's inner circle. This is kind of coming in out of the blue, you know?"

"The President believes—strongly—that the super-AIs need to be better controlled, that humans should have greater oversight over what they are doing, *but*—" Jennings emphasized the word, raising a forefinger as if to make the point "—he knows we can't live without them. Michaels would have us eliminate *all* super-AIs and plunge us into a new Dark Ages. Financial collapse. Social collapse. Government collapse. Chaos and bloodshed on a scale that'll make these riots we've been having lately look like a protest by the Women's Auxiliary of the Ancient Alien Creationist Church. We can't allow that to happen."

Maybe he had underestimated Walker . . . or misjudged him. His denial of the Singularity made him popular with a particular segment of the USNA population, conservative neo-Luddites and those who saw the Singularity as something involving the ascension of machines over Humankind. His rhetoric about reining in intelligent machines appealed to the same groups.

Maybe what he'd been saying for the past several years was just political rhetoric. Dangerous rhetoric, if Jennings was to be understood, but more about expediency than true advocacy.

"So what does Walker want me to do about it?"

"As I said: talk to Michaels. Find out what he wants, but

also see if he's willing to compromise. Find out if he will support the *control* of SAIs, as opposed to their elimination. And do so in secret, without the media's involvement. We don't want the people making wild speculations about the President's position."

"It's all sounding pretty far-fetched."

"We need you, Mr. Koenig. The President needs you. Your country needs you. Quite possibly the whole of *civilization* needs you."

Koenig thought Jennings was trying now to appeal to some grandiloquent sense in Koenig of greatness or destiny or heroic patriotism. Such lures weren't going to work on him, but he had to admire Jenning's passion . . . or maybe his acting ability.

"Konstantin?" he thought over the open channel.

"Again, I strongly advise against it, Mr. President. It might very well be a trap."

A trap? To what end? If they wanted to kill him, they could do it easily enough—a missile fired into this house, for instance.

Besides, he was intrigued by Michaels's motivation. What did the man *really* want? His anti-AI stance was problematic. His mobile mining units out in the asteroid belt were, for the most part, highly automated, with only small human crews to keep an eye on things. Most of those machines were ordinary AI, not self-aware super-AIs like Konstantin, but his fear of SAIs seemed inconsistent and hypocritical.

Koenig was forced to admit that he wanted to hear what Michaels had to say personally, rather than through the filter of the mass media.

"How soon do you want me to go?" he asked aloud.

"The sooner the better, Mr. President," Jennings said, finally using Koenig's honorary title. "A private el-car has been set aside for your use. You can take along a couple of bodyguards or assistants, if you wish."

Koenig gave it another few seconds' consideration, then

nodded. "I'll go, Jennings. But just so you know, the President owes me for this one."

Maybe, just maybe, he could leverage that gratitude into some kind of guarantee for Konstantin.

"I'll inform the President, sir. And your nation thanks you."

USNA CVS America
Flag Bridge
N'gai Cluster
1602 hours, FST

"The network is ready for initial testing, Admiral," Konstantin told Gray. "Two thousand modules have been dispersed across local space and have been interconnected by laser-com transmissions."

"How much time lag are we looking at?" Gray asked.

"Five and a half minutes at most. Our ships and the modules are spread out over an area 100 million kilometers across. With *America* at the center of the deployment, however, it will take half that for signals to reach us from those modules on the perimeter, and I will be there to coordinate the incoming data."

"That could still slow things down quite a bit."

"Not unacceptably. We are not in any particular hurry, after all. And we will need the widest dispersal possible in order to sense something as subtle as gravity waves."

"Okay, if you say so. How do you plan to test it?"

"You and your volunteers will enter the net. You should find it similar to the Godstream on Earth. A thoughtclick, and you'll find yourself within a virtual world reflecting the energy patterns in space around us. After a little more than eleven minutes, I should have all incoming signals coordinated, and we shall be able to pinpoint nearby sources of gravity waves. Are you ready to begin?"

"No," Gray said with a blunt lack of enthusiasm. "But let's do it anyway."

Settling back in his seat, he closed his eyes, brought up an in-head menu, and thoughtclicked an icon. . . .

It *was* like the Godstream back home, but with a virtual reality set in deep space rather than a landscape of light and movement and three-dimensional geometric shapes. The sensation of flight was the same, as was the electric thrill pulsing up his spine and setting his mind *free* in a way that reality never could. He could feel a rippling awareness spreading out around him, could see *America* herself below him, apparently several kilometers away—her slender keel extending aft from the immense hemisphere of her shield cap like the handle of an umbrella, the stately rotation of her hab modules about the spine, the wink-wink-wink of her running lights and the tiny specks of a squadron of encircling fighters on combat space patrol, keeping pace with the behemoth.

She was making her way through normal space at dead slow, but he could see what was normally invisible on a ship under way, the steady, purring flicker of her projected grav field just ahead of the curve of her shield cap, an intensely warped area of space drawing the massive ship slowly forward. Each fighter had that flicker as well, deep blue luminosities just off their prows.

That puzzled him for a moment. You couldn't actually *see* warped space; you couldn't see gravity, but that appeared to be exactly what he was sensing somehow.

Then he realized that he *was* seeing gravity, or at least its more intense manifestations. As he studied his surroundings, he found himself becoming more and more aware of the fabric, the texture of space itself, not seen so much as sensed, rippling with uncountable waves and eddies and currents that filled all of circumambient space. It was as though space itself was a living, breathing, sensate organism, trembling, exquisitely alive, responding delicately and precisely to each movement of mass through its invisible matrix.

The sight was . . . overwhelming. Gray's breath caught in

his throat, and the awe of that moment very nearly jerked him back to the mundane reality of the starship's bridge.

But his awareness within this alien vista was expanding as his brain processed more and more of the incoming tsunami of data. He realized with a small shock that he wasn't *seeing* his surroundings, not exactly, but he was sensing them, and his brain, confronted with sensations and impressions unlike anything he'd ever experienced before, was struggling to make sense of it all. Flooded by the unknown, his brain was interpreting the data as best it could. Because Gray's principle sense was sight, that interpretation was as visible images rather than as sounds or touch or something else.

Gray was aware of stars beyond the bulk of the *America*, tens of millions of them thronging about him in an opaque wall. *America* was still deep within the central core of the N'gai Dwarf Galaxy, and the thickly clustered stars formed a glowing shell around them thousands of light years across.

Astern, the heart of the cluster erupted in a glorious blue and violet glare of radiance, where the black holes of the Sh'daar Rosette, the remnants of exploded supergiant stars, filled space with a throbbing, visible gravitational light. The detail he was seeing was startling. From the heart of the hypernova's glare came ripples of gravity generated by the ponderous orbiting of six black holes around a common center, a steady churning that filled space like the surge and boom of waves on a stormy sea.

Gray momentarily was puzzled. Gravity waves, he knew, traveled at the speed of light. How could he be seeing . . .

But of course. Idiot! He was seeing gravity waves that had set out over two years ago. In fact, as his sensitivity increased, guided by Konstantin's careful direction, Gray was aware now of more and more of the living fabric enmeshing him, *America*, the other ships of the squadron, and every star he could see in the heavens around him.

With that realization, his awareness . . . expanded, moved outward.

No wonder detecting Sh'daar world-ships was so difficult! At distances of more than a few billions of kilometers, an insignificant fraction of a single light year, the thunderous noise generated by the Rosette, and the echoing reverberations of the hypernova tended to drown out the drive signatures of even the largest vessels.

But those signals *were* there, if you could extend yourself far enough, reach deeply enough into the gravitational matrix around you, feel the subtle ripples all but drowned in that pounding, storm-hammered surf.

Gray reached out . . . and became aware of other minds riding the Godstream with his, several thousand men and women and intelligent machines drawn from the crews of the squadron's ships, spread out across an expanse of space at once vast and vanishingly insignificant against the grandeur of space around them.

Godstream. A fitting name, he thought, for a God's-eye view.

He'd ridden these waves before, when he and myriad others had spread their hive-mind consciousness across space in order to communicate with the enigmatic and monstrous Mind of the Consciousness. His brain, he realized now, was drawing on those memories to help make sense of what he was experiencing. He realized, too, how very, very much of that experience three years ago he'd forgotten. When he'd uncoupled from that powerful group mind, he'd *dwindled*, shrinking back to a mere human, losing the vast majority of his remembered impressions and thoughts, a mind far too small to retain the power, the intricate detail, and the Transcendence of Mind.

Now those memories were flooding back, enhancing his awareness of the depths of the N'gai galaxy. Riding the pulsing ripples of gravity, he found his awareness extending far, *far* beyond the perimeter defined by human ships and Bright Light modules. Spacetime, he found, possessed a literal fabric, a warp and woof of virtual energy within which gravity waves rippled and within which he could extend his wings and soar. It was as though his physical self was growing, expanding, becoming a titanic node of awareness spreading out through the encircling walls of clustered stars and into space beyond.

What he sensed out there stunned him, and his physical body somewhere back within the N'gai galactic core gasped. The central core dropped away, a thick haze of light thickly set with suns, a thinner, luminous mist of stars surrounding it. And beyond . . .

The N'gai Dwarf Galaxy was already in the process of being devoured by a much larger galaxy, a vast and luminous spiral of stars and nebulae—the Milky Way as it had been over 800 million years before Gray's own time. N'gai was skimming in over the galactic plane at a sharp angle, the outer layers of its dust and gas already in the process of being stripped away by a kind of galactic "atmosphere," the gas clouds within which the Milky Way lay imbedded. He could see the distinct curve of his home galaxy's spiral arm, the twists and knots and filaments of dark and dusty nebulae, the faintly red-hued radiance of the central core, the delicate blue haze and the clotted knots of the brighter stars throughout the spiral, the background glow of thronging suns too thickly strewn to see individually.

The vista, far more detailed and structured than mere light could possibly have revealed, struck him with a dizzying awareness of light and time and gravity and space, a Whole frozen within an instant spanning eons.

Return, Konstantin's voice said within that tiny fraction of Mind that was Trevor Gray. *Don't lose yourself.*

Reluctantly, Gray allowed himself to fall back—to be *pulled* back—into the narrow confines of space immediately surrounding the human fleet, minute sparks of twisted space within the Void.

We have them.

As the hive mind of the fleet had stretched out, encompassing more and more space, Konstantin—or perhaps it was the whole of the Mind itself—had been able to separate the faint flicker of gravitational drives from the thundering background noise of mutually orbiting black holes and thronging suns singing their gravitational arias. Gray saw them now, a dozen violet sparks all but lost in the glare of a spacetime filled by, *defined* by, gravity.

The group Mind focused in on the nearest of those sparks, their viewpoint zooming in on a massive cylinder all but lost in the darkness. The cylinder, Gray knew without knowing how he knew it, was just over ten thousand kilometers long and a fifth that distance wide, the ends open to space. The cylinder's rotation created spin gravity across the structure's inner surface and also held a thin film of atmosphere pressed against the tube's curved walls, held captive by hundred-kilometer walls around both open ends. On the inner surface, glimpsed through one end, was a landscape, an inside-out habitable world of oceans and mountains and plains, of rivers and desert and forest, of rich greens and russet browns and the white spiraling sweep and splatter of clouds.

The surface area of the inside of that rotating cylinder, Gray recalled, was well over 60 million square kilometers, as big as all of Eurasia on Earth, from Gibraltar to Kamchatka, from Novaya Zemlya to Sri Lanka. The technology implicit in that structure left Gray awestruck and humbled.

Beyond one end of the cylinder flickered the brilliant blue-violet spark of a powerful gravity drive, steadily drawing that monster, artificial world forward. A McKendree cylinder this large possessed the staggering mass of a small planet— something on the order of 6×10^{23} kilograms, roughly the same as the mass of Mars—but its velocity, now just over half the speed of light, gave it a relativistic mass that was considerably greater. Viewed up close, the cylinder created a shimmering, three-dimensional gravity wake extending in the shape of a hazy, thinning cone far astern. The structure had the look of a pale blue comet, a bright flickering point of light as the head and a trailing tail 100 million kilometers long, with the cylinder itself all but lost within the coma.

How, Gray wondered, could that projected point of gravitational energy pull equally on the entire length of a ten-thousand-kilometer-long cylinder? Grav drives worked by putting the projecting craft into free fall, allowing tremendous acceleration without the high-G effects of acceleration. Still, the gravitational field had to be artificially tweaked to encompass the entire vessel or it might be torn apart by the tidal effects.

How were the Sh'daar inhabitants of that thing enveloping a ten-thousand-kilometer tube in an even gravitational field without ripping the tube apart? It was impossible . . . like purest magic.

We have their coordinates, Konstantin whispered in his Mind. *We can approach them now for a rendezvous.*

Venting Tube 18
Quito Space Elevator
Cayambe, Ecuador
1648 hours, EST

The solitary aircar threaded its way through canyons and deep, jungle-tangled valleys, maintaining just enough speed to keep aloft on its repulsors without triggering any of the sentry mechanisms along the way. The aircar had been specially outfitted with the latest stealth technologies and was essentially invisible on radar, infrared, and electromagnetic scans. Its external nanoflage repeated the colors and shadowing of its surroundings, making it very nearly invisible at optical wavelengths as well.

The pilot was Enrique Valdez, though at the moment he couldn't remember his name. Days before, his in-head circuitry had been infected by nanobots programmed to suppress many of his memories and general cerebral functions, keeping him focused to an inhuman degree on his task. The effect was to reduce him to a kind of biological robot, a robot with only very limited intelligence and a vague self-awareness akin to that of a dream state. All he knew was that his goal was that snowcapped mountain directly to the northwest—specifically the mouth of a vent—and that when he maneuvered his aircar into the entrance of the venting tube, he would remember what he was to do next.

The mountain was called Cayambe, and its southern slope was dominated by an immense platform extending out from snow-clad rock. Towers, domes, and skyscrapers rose from this platform, and from the center, a needle-slender thread emerged from the buildings and vanished into a deep purple sky. You could get dizzy trying to follow that thread into the zenith, but Valdez didn't try. The white-and-silver city on the mountainside and the lower reaches of the Quito Space Elevator were, to him, simply a part of the background.

He certainly was not thinking at the moment about that city's destruction.

The valley he was following twisted back and forth but steadily approached the base of the mountain beneath the city of Port Ecuador, Earthside anchor of the Quito Space Elevator. He could see his destination now, a low, stone entryway to a black tunnel entrance.

A warning signal peeped at Valdez, indicating that he was being painted by radar, but the nanomatrix of his vehicle's outer skin would absorb most of the incoming signal, giving a reading consistent with a large bird—an Andean condor, perhaps. The entrance to the venting tube was now just ahead. Darkness descended over Valdez like a shroud as he guided his aircar through the stone-lined portal.

Cayambe was a volcano. Rising almost 5,800 meters above sea level, it was the third-highest peak in Ecuador. The city on its south flank stood at an altitude of 4,690 meters, the highest point in the world crossed by the equator, and the only point on the equator permanently covered in snow.

There'd been a great deal of argument during the building of the space elevator over whether it was safe to use a volcanic mountain as the Earthside anchor for the structure. The issue was resolved by the Ecuadoran Consortium, a group of business and governmental interests that stood to make hundreds of trillions of dollars if Port Ecuador and the adjoining metropolis of Quito became a major trade center linking Earth with synchorbit. Cayambe had last erupted in March of 1786, some 643 years ago. It was *probably* dead.

To protect their investment, however, the governments of the USNA, Pan-Europe, and several other major players had insisted on safeguards. Eighty tunnels had been bored into the lower flanks of the mountain, leading down at shallow angles to a region deep beneath the roots of Cayambe, to *La Caldera de Erebus*, a basalt chamber twenty kilometers above the top magma plume that had created the peak. Those twenty kilometers of solid rock comprised the plug in the quiescent volcano's throat; a robotic observatory rested on the floor of the chamber itself, monitoring conditions in the rock deep below. If an incipient eruption was detected, the lowest section of the elevator itself could be severed, allowing the elevator to be moved, while the city would be evacuated.

Should an eruption occur, that plug would dissolve or be blown clear; the venting stubs existed to redirect the upper surge of magma and hot gas outward and away from the mountain's base. No one knew for sure if it would work, but the best calculations by the best volcanology SAIs on the planet suggested that it would save Port Ecuador . . . or at least buy time enough to shift the space elevator's base to Hacienda Tanda, thirty-eight kilometers along the equator to the west, where reserve ground facilities were in place.

Acting according to the dictates of the nano within his brain, Valdez guided his aircar down the arrow-straight tunnel, dropping off drone relays along his path. When he reached the inner mouth of the tunnel, overlooking the vast basaltic chamber below, he grounded his vehicle.

The relay drones would keep him linked to his handlers.

Now all he had to do was wait.

Chapter Thirteen

21 April, 2429

USNA CVS America
CIC
N'gai Cluster
0915 hours, FST

It had taken some time for Konstantin to find the appropriate channel to contact the enormous McKendree cylinder now hanging in space just ahead of *America* and her consorts. The aliens apparently did not use radio for regular communication, or laser transmissions, though there was plenty of broadband leakage from various control systems and networks. Konstantin had finally managed to make contact with a robot through its radar ranging circuitry, and after several hours he'd reported to Gray that they were now communicating with the Adjugredudhra.

Gray remembered them, one of the more advanced species that had made up the Sh'daar Collective. They looked like upright but unsteady pillars perhaps a meter high, radially symmetrical, like eight terrestrial starfish stacked one atop the other. Highly flexible arms emerged from masses of dark tendrils between the pale-yellow starfish shapes; some of those tendrils looked like sucker-tipped manipulatory appendages, while others ended in blood-red marbles—presumably eyes. He found himself looking at one now within an in-head window, as Konstantin opened the channel.

It regarded him without any emotion that Gray could detect through a number of stalked eyes. He noticed several small, metallic devices were imbedded in the organism's flesh. Some Adjugredudhra, Gray knew, used advanced nanoprostheses to remake their physical bodies, while others were cybernetic organisms, part machine, part organic. This one, apparently, was pretty much the original model.

"Ah, Admiral Gray," the being's translated voice said in Gray's head. "It is good to again see you."

For Gray, it was very much a matter of one Adjugredudhra looking pretty much like another. "We've met before?"

"Yes. I am called Ghresthrepni," the being told him. Gray could hear the being's actual voice in the background, a melodious blend of chirps, trills, and the tinkling of bells. "When last we met, I commanded a vessel called the *Ancient Hope*," it continued. "I was selected to receive your communication once more, since I have had dealings with your species before."

"It's good to see you again," Gray said. He wondered if the odd little being might have been offended by the fact that he hadn't recognized it, but if it had, it gave no sign.

Perhaps it found it as difficult to distinguish between individuals of another species as Gray did. It might have learned his name just now from Konstantin.

Or, possibly not.

"Why," Ghresthrepni asked, "have you sought us out?"

And Gray told him.

Quito Space Elevator
Port Ecuador
1034 hours, EST

Alexander Koenig stepped off the mag-tube pod and onto the terminal platform. Port Ecuador was one of the busiest mag-tube nodes on the planet, and riding the evacuated tube on magnetic cushions all the way from Columbus to Cayambe had taken just forty minutes. The platform seethed with people, from full-humans to people with organic prostheses or cyberenhancements all the way to outlandish gene mods, some of whom looked very *in*human indeed. There were lots of robots as well, some designed solely for function rather than for a human appearance, and others who would have passed for human except for the ID tags that flashed up within Koenig's awareness.

Koenig himself was not exactly as he outwardly appeared. Like Marta yesterday, he was wearing a face, a living mask that made him look physically quite different—forty years younger, with higher cheekbones, thicker eyebrows, and the hint of a beard. His security detail had insisted; too many people knew Koenig's face . . . including people who had reason to want him dead.

His Marine bodyguard, Staff Sergeant Hinkley, wearing a civilian jumpsuit and trying *very* hard—and failing—not to look military, stepped onto the platform behind him. He pointed. "Up-E over that way, sir."

"I can read, George."

Together, they crossed the open deck, following the guide arrows displayed within their in-heads. The E, the Quito Space Elevator, hung directly overhead, a silvery thread vanishing straight up into the zenith. Koenig felt like a rubbernecking tourist, but it had been years since he'd been up-E to Quito Synchorbital, and he was enjoying the memories.

The next up-E pod rested in its cradle at the base of the elevator cable as a line of people filed on board. The pods were designed to carry up to 112 people in seats that swiveled to match the current direction of "down," a concept that would change depending on whether they were accelerating or decelerating. Each pod, a gleaming silver cigar-shape forty meters long and massing twenty-nine tons, rode a superconducting magfield that kept it tucked in close to the elevator cable itself in a frictionless suspension. They moved up or down the cable under magnetic induction.

Koenig would have much preferred to get to Michaels's residence at Midway by shuttle, but that would have involved greater scrutiny at the spaceport and considerably more red tape and expense.

No matter. The E would get him there in a few hours. The two men went through check-in and security; travel on the E was free—it long ago had paid for itself not only in orbital industry and commerce but in the generation of free electricity—and the security check was pro forma, a stroll through a scanner that peered through clothing to the skin, then continued to image the body's interior. "I guess they don't want us smuggling any nukes up this thing," Hinkley quipped.

"Probably not a good idea to try," Koenig replied. "Next up-E is in ten minutes. Let's get on board."

They found their seats and settled in. The capsule was about two-thirds full—mostly businesspeople headed up-E to the industrial facilities at Quito Synchorbital or, farther out, at the anchor planetoid. Settling back in the seat's automatic embrace, Koenig unfolded his pad and brought up a historical piece he'd been rereading, Vinge's classic 1993 essay "The Coming Technological Singularity: How to Survive in the Post-Human Era." Historical essays from pre-starflight eras could be wildly amusing. Vinge had missed some points, but, surprisingly, not many. His anticipation of a future time when human technology would evolve beyond human comprehension was both prescient and apt.

Minutes later, Koenig felt a gentle push back into his seat as the pod began accelerating upward. Had the capsule been propelled by grav drives, like those on spacecraft, he would have fallen into zero-G, but the linear magnetic acceleration of two Gs gave him the feeling of another person sitting on his lap.

Two minutes later at a steady two gravities, the capsule

was climbing past an altitude of 140 kilometers and moving at almost 8,500 kilometers per hour. The cabin bulkheads were configured to show an all-around view of surrounding space. In seconds, the deep blue of the Ecuadoran sky had deepened to black, and the stars came out.

Anticipating a boring trip up-E, Koenig read his essay.

Quito Space Elevator
Port Ecuador
1047 hours, EST

Barry Wizewski felt old.

The fact hardly surprised him. He was eighty-five, after all. But more to the point, he was a Purist in the Rapturist Church, and through much of his adult life he'd believed that when Jesus returned in the clouds to reclaim His own, He would not want to find His people weighed down with high-tech enhancements and implants and filled with nano-drugs, all of those vain attempts to cheat death and fend off old age. Damn it, he was *proud* of his white and thinning hair. And if he couldn't live to be 200, so what? It just meant he would be with his Savior that much sooner.

He'd come by the white hair honestly; he considered it a kind of badge of honor, much like the Medal of Honor on his wall at home. He'd been a USNA Marine and won that medal defending the super-computer facility at Tsiolkovsky on the moon.

But sometimes, the aches and pains gnawed at him, and he wondered if just a little antiagnathic nano would be all that sinful.

He stepped off the mag-tube pod and onto the broad plaza of Port Ecuador. He was meeting his daughter here today; she was the chief administrator of Skyport, a part of the orbital complex nearly 38,000 kilometers above his head. It would be good to see Susan again; he hadn't seen her since she'd been back down the Beanstalk—another name for space elevators, though the origin was always lost on him—for Christmas.

He checked his in-head for the time. Good—she'd be down-E in another few minutes.

When he'd joined the Corps, they'd given him a basic military implant, and he doubted that God would object. It didn't make him younger or change his looks; it did allow him to interface with the jungle of computers and machines within which he'd had to function as a Marine. For a time, he'd been stationed on board ship, and there you couldn't even open a door without that interface.

And in the meantime, it provided some conveniences, like always knowing the time and being able to do heavy math in your head.

He looked up, his gaze following the sharp thrust of the Beanstalk to its vanishing point at the zenith. With a thought, he linked through to the Godstream to check her schedule.

Yeah . . . it would be so good to see Susan.

Venting Tube 18
Quito Space Elevator
Cayambe, Ecuador
1049 hours, EST

The awaited message came to Enrique Valdez down the line of communications relay drones he'd left strung out along the 2.5 kilometer length of the venting tube. He was not consciously aware of the message, but the nanobots residing within his brain and the implant electronics there were. Still within what amounted to a dream state, Valdez engaged the repulsor lift of his aircar and guided it forward, exiting the mouth of the venting tube and arrowing into the center of the vast cavern beyond.

He felt a driving sense of urgency he couldn't explain. He was late . . . late . . . almost two minutes late, but for what he didn't know. There'd been an unanticipated delay in sending a message, and in his receiving it.

No matter. He would carry out the instructions humming within his brain to the very best of his robotlike ability.

Descending toward the cluster of domes marking the robotic observation station, he accelerated, ignoring a sudden barrage of radio messages demanding his identity . . . demanding that he stop . . . demanding that—

Ten meters above the basaltic rock, Valdez triggered the 300-megaton nuclear device built into the frame of the vehicle.

White light filled the cavern as Valdez and his aircar vaporized. In seconds, the fireball slammed against the cavern walls, ceiling, and floor, devouring solid rock, pushing up and out.

The top of Cayambe rose in a thundering torrent of rock and ice. . . .

Quito Space Elevator
Port Ecuador
1050 hours, EST

"What the hell was *that*?" Hinkley asked, startled.

Koenig looked up from his screen. He'd felt a solid thump through the bulkheads of the E-pod, a jolt transmitted, he thought, from the space elevator itself. "I don't know. Felt like we jumped the rails."

Several of the passengers screamed. The pod had stopped accelerating, and the passengers were now in free fall.

A screen set into the back of the seat in front of him showed an informational display of the flight: current speed, distance traveled, G-force, time from liftoff, time to arrival . . . but as he looked at the figures, they winked out, and the display went blank.

That was more alarming than the thump.

Koenig's first impulse was to unstrap and head for the

piloting compartment . . . but magnetic E-pods did not have human pilots or a bridge. A fairly simpleminded AI guided the craft up and down the cable, maintaining acceleration, adjusting velocity, and handling the docking with the receiving port. Koenig linked into the control network and brought up a series of external camera views.

"My God . . ."

"What is it, sir?"

"We *did* derail! That's the elevator!"

The space elevator cable was meters thick, with inset grooves that gently cupped the pods. It should have looked like a solid wall moving swiftly past the pod's keel . . . but a camera looking in that direction showed the beanstalk a dozen meters distant, the surface blurred by the pod's velocity. The pod had been jolted free of the magnetic cradle carrying it upward. It was still rising at some 2.3 kilometers per second, the speed it had been traveling when it left the cable, but that velocity was decreasing now as Earth's gravity took hold and began dragging the capsule back.

"Mr. President! Are you there?"

The voice, ragged and static-blasted, was Konstantin's, speaking over the Godstream channel. Propagated up and down the space elevator by both radio and laser com, the pods could be linked into the network while they were moving up- or down-E, but Koenig's craft was now far enough from the stalk that he was having trouble getting a clear signal.

A check of the signal dynamics showed something more disturbing: signals from below, from Port Ecuador, had ceased. Evidently, there was a problem, a very serious problem, with the Cayambe facility.

"The top of Cayambe has just collapsed," Konstantin told him, as if reading his thoughts. "The collapse took the city with it, and the base of the space elevator has been cut free."

"Collapsed! How? What happened?"

"We're not sure, but seismic readings suggest that a fairly large fusion device has been exploded deep within the mountain."

"A nuke? It's not a volcanic eruption?"

"Volcanic eruptions do not release radioactivity into the surroundings."

"Ah . . ."

Koenig switched from the camera showing the blurred image of the beanstalk and took a look aft, straight down the length of the space elevator. From nearly two hundred kilometers up, Earth's surface was a beautiful mosaic of rugged mountains, green forests and agricultural lands, deep azure ocean, and the swirl and sweep of gleaming white clouds. The elevator itself dwindled to a silver thread lost within that landscape. From here, he could make out the pattern of streets and farmland marking Quito, but he couldn't make out Cayambe itself.

There *was* a minute, dark cloud spreading out from where the thread seemed to vanish. Though small, little more than a speck, it was rapidly growing larger.

He enhanced the image. *There* . . . A circle rippling out from the base of the elevator . . . The shock wave of a very large blast.

A volcanic eruption? He knew Cayambe was an extinct volcano . . . *probably* extinct. He also knew there were safeguards in place to anticipate an eruption and allow the elevator to be reconnected elsewhere. An eruption would have given some warning.

Which made him wonder if Port Ecuador had just been annihilated by a very large nuclear detonation.

Who the hell would nuke the space elevator? And *why*?

Lieutenant Cordell
The Overlook
Quito Synchorbital
1056 hours, FST

Lieutenant Michael Cordell was seated in the Earthview Lounge of the Overlook, a moderately priced bar and restaurant in one of the spin-gravity wheels attached to the

Quito Synchorbital complex. Despite the wheel's slow and steady rotation, providing a constant 0.5 G, the floor-to-ceiling viewall curving across half of the lounge showed a half Earth motionless against the blackness of space.

Obviously the scene was being transmitted by non-rotating cameras, Cordell thought. Except for the lack of motion, it was impossible to tell that he was not looking through a transparency.

His companion touched the sleeve of his jumper. "Lost again?" she asked with an evil grin.

Cordell grinned back. Lieutenant Katya Golikova was keenly intelligent, sharp-witted, and fun. She was also very much forbidden fruit at this point. When he'd met her almost five years ago, Russia and the USNA had been friends and allies, fighting a common Pan-European enemy. Lately, though, the political situation had changed. She wasn't an enemy, exactly, but the word had come down through the brass hierarchy that fraternizing with Russians was forbidden.

"No," he told her. "Just woolgathering."

"And wool," she said, teasing him, "is that much more interesting than me?"

"Of course not." He reached out, picked up his wineglass, and raised it. "To us."

She touched her glass to his. *"Na zdorovie."*

He was damned if he was going to report his relationship with her. He might be ordered to break it off, or worse, to carry a microtransmitter up his butt or under his skin every time he got together with her. That sort of thing would have a distinctly chilling effect in bed. But it still might not have stopped him.

And so they both had in-head software running designed to spot nanotech security devices or pickups, and they were very careful about being followed. Of course, the various security forces could hack his own in-head systems without him even being aware, seeing everything he saw, listening in on everything he heard. The trick was to stay off their radar to begin with; if they didn't suspect him of anything, they wouldn't monitor him.

He hoped.

Her jab about him getting lost referred to the last time they'd met, when he'd led her into a seldom-used and heavily shielded warehousing unit in the synchorbital facility within Skyport, lost contact with the Net, and lost his directional cues. They'd found their way back to a wired section eventually, but he'd been afraid they were going to have to call for help, and *that* would have put him on that radar screen big-time.

He reached across the table and took her hand. "How long do you have?" he asked.

"Forty-eight hours. More like forty-one now."

Katya piloted a *Yastreb* fighter deployed on board the Russian carrier *Vladivostok*. Cordell was stationed on board the slightly larger *Yorktown*. Finding time together—and getting downtime schedules to mesh—was a real challenge, one worthy of a super-AI.

"Well, that's plenty of time," Cordell told her.

She arched one perfect eyebrow. "For what?"

"I thought we might go back to our room and—"

A distinct shudder ran through the restaurant. Cordell had been born and raised in San Francisco, and he'd been through more than his fair share of earthquakes. This was like that—a kind of wave coming up through the deck. Several other patrons in the Overlook made startled comments.

"What the hell . . ."

"What *was* that?" Katya asked, looking around.

"I'm not—"

"All Navy and Marine personnel, all Navy and Marine personnel," a voice sounded inside his head, a transmission over the fleetnet. "Return to your ships and other stations immediately, repeat, immediately. This is not a drill!"

The interlude, Cordell thought, was over. Why, he didn't know.

USNA CVS America
CIC
N'gai Cluster
1105 hours, FST

Gray was still shaken by his experience in the Godstream. Coming back had felt like a terrible dwindling, a loss of substance and assurance and knowledge that had at the time seemed godlike. This time was worse, if that was possible, than his first experience at the Omega Rosette three years ago.

In his mind's eye now, he floated outside the enormous McKendree cylinder, speaking with the exquisitely alien Ghresthrepni. He felt utterly drained but forced himself to push ahead, asking the strange being the questions he'd worked out in advance during the trip from Earth. Other humans had gathered with him—Truitt and Kline from Xenosoph, and Mallory, the expedition's head of xenotechnology.

"We would like to know," Greg Mallory was saying to the alien, "exactly what happened to the ur-Sh'daar at the time of the *Schjaa Hok*."

The alien phrase meant approximately "The Transcending" and referred to the Sh'daar equivalent of the Technological Singularity. It was not, Gray knew, something the modern Sh'daar liked to talk about. In fact, it terrified them.

"They . . . left us," the Adjugredudhra told them, essentially repeating itself for the fifth or sixth time. The humans had been talking with the Adjugredudhra for nearly two hours now, and the alien representative remained reluctant to discuss what it insisted was "old history . . . another time."

The conversation was proving to be circular and frustrating.

"You've already told us that they disappeared," Gray said. "We *know* that. We've even seen it, or at least a part of it."

Years before, Gray had seen what they now believed to be a kind of computer-generated simulation of the moment of *Schjaa Hok*, images of a bright and golden civilization composed of dozens of different alien species. Those CGIs had been recorded at the time, even though Gray and others had been receiving the images directly in their brains. While telling the bare-bones story of what had happened, Gray believed the actual events had been shaded somewhat in the retelling, perhaps even edited to the point of completely changing the story.

"You are referring to the Memories," Ghresthrepni said. "Those were created by the Baondyeddi and the Sjhlurrr."

Its translated voice betrayed nothing like impatience or irritation at the repetitive questioning. Gray wished he could interpret the being's emotions as it spoke. The chirps and tinkling bells heard in the background—the being's actual speech—told him nothing about the Adjugredudhra's feelings.

But this was new information, Gray thought—*at long last*. The images he'd seen had been CGI, as he'd suspected. The Baondyeddi—huge pancakes on dozens of tiny feet—were masters of computer technology. They had, Gray knew, uploaded themselves into a planet-sized computer on Heimdall, living out the eons in virtual worlds of their own creation.

At least until the Consciousness had found them. . . .

Gray knew less about the Sjhlurrr, save that they were eight-meter-long slugs colored in gorgeous patterns of red and gold. Perhaps they were experts in computer technology as well.

"We need to know the *reality* of what happened," Gray said, pressing the issue. "What happened in the Technological Singularity? Did the ur-Sh'daar *really* just vanish?"

"That was long ago," Ghresthrepni told him. "None of that matters now."

"It matters to *us*, Ghresthrepni," Truitt said, blunt. "Humanity is approaching its own *Schjaa Hok*, and we need to know what to expect."

"Then we sorrow for you humans, for your species will know devastation beyond your deepest imaginings."

"What kind of devastation?" Mallory wanted to know.

For answer, the universe folded back around them, and they found themselves in a starkly realistic virtual reality. They stood on a rocky ledge overlooking the sprawl of a vast and alien metropolis, a city fully as large as Gray's Manhatt Ruins, but alive and rich and vibrant with light and activity. Aircraft filled the sky, vehicles like mag-lev pods whipped through transparent tubes, viewalls twenty stories high displayed glimpses of multiple alien species engaged in incomprehensible activities. The technology, Gray thought, was roughly on a par with where Humankind was now.

And then he saw the edge of the world . . .

The virtual image, he realized, was within one of the titanic cylinder habitats. The edge of the world was the nearest end of the cylinder, a circle of blackness dusted with the stars of the N'gai central core, stars that were slowly moving as the cylinder turned on its long axis. Opposite, a much smaller circle was all but lost in the haze of distance, thousands of kilometers away.

The rock ledge, Gray saw, was a part of the foothills of the ice-capped mountains, perhaps 100 kilometers high, that ringed the opening and kept the atmosphere from spilling out into space.

Gray looked back down at the city.

It was burning.

"Our records tell us that the *Schjaa Hok* lasted for several of your years," their guide told them. "But the first wave of Transcendings was the worst. . . ."

The scene shifted, and the small group of humans stood in open parkland in the center of the city, towers and domes and twisted abstract shapes of gold and silver rising about them. A number of Adjugredudhra were moving along on a slidewalk nearby, multiple starfish shapes growing one atop the other, with twisting tendrils and weaving eyestalks.

With shocking suddenness, one of them collapsed where it stood . . . followed by another . . . and then a third. The bodies, rag-doll limp and lifeless, continued along on the slidewalk, as other Adjugredudhra nearby emitted shrill chirps and chitters in an agitated frenzy.

"The scenes we saw before showed individuals just winking out," Gray said. He was trying to relate what he was seeing now with the brief glimpses he'd had of *Schjaa Hok* years before.

"These images . . . of the dead . . ." Ghresthrepni said, "we find . . . extremely . . . disturbing. . . ." Even in translation, Ghresthrepni's voice sounded shaken, as though it was having trouble continuing to speak.

"And that's why these records were edited?" Truitt asked.

Ghresthrepni didn't answer directly, but Gray sensed affirmation in its silence.

Around them, more and more of the Adjugredudhra collapsed.

"But what is happening to them?" Kline asked.

"Their souls are leaving," was the being's answer. "They leave the shells behind."

The scene seemed to blur, a fast-forward of sorts, Gray thought. The city was burning now, as seething mobs of Adjugredudhra surged through city streets and parklands. Aircraft fell from the skies, their pilots dead. Gray was puzzled by this at first, since much of the traffic would have been controlled by AI minds, and any decently advanced aircraft could land itself if the organic pilot became incapacitated.

But then he understood. "Their minds are being uploaded," he said. "And not just organic beings. Your AIs are Transcending as well."

"Of course. The first to go were the cyborgs, those with massive machine augmentation. The Groth Hoj were almost entirely taken in the first hours of the Transcendence, since so many of their species were reshaped with genetic engineering and cybernetic enhancements."

Gray remembered the Groth Hoj—beings like three-meter-tall squids with single, saucer-sized eyes. They communicated by changing the color patterns on their bodies, but a great many had transferred their minds to machines of various types, and now looked nothing like their organic predecessors.

"So those beings who already had a predilection for high-tech enhancements . . ." Mallory began.

"They were taken first," Ghresthrepni told them. "Yes."

"You say they were *taken*," Truitt said. "Who took them?"

"Do you understand the concept we call *Draleth Ja*?"

"That didn't translate," Gray said. "Try again."

"We think of it as a higher dimension," Ghresthrepni said. "One created artificially by the interaction of electronic media, interacting fields of information—"

"Ah," Gray said. "I think you mean what we call the Godstream. A virtual world open to those with the necessary electronic prostheses."

"This realm," Ghresthrepni continued, "*is* inhabited. By patterns of information, patterns of consciousness, with an interest in the worlds from which they came."

"What is *that* supposed to mean?" Truitt demanded.

"*Mind*," the voice of Konstantin put in, "is information. Though the term may seem needlessly religious in nature, a being's *soul* might be described as a particular pattern of information that normally resides within the physical instrumentality of neurons and synaptic pathways. Information can be recorded and uploaded. It can also be transmitted, leaving nothing behind but the dead physical infrastructure."

"That's what happened with the Baondyeddi," Mallory said. "They uploaded their minds into computer-generated virtual realities."

"You know, of course, that the civilization you call *ur-Sh'daar* underwent the Transcendence," Ghresthrepni told them. "But not *all* were transformed. The Refusers were left behind . . . perhaps one individual out of every fifty."

"We know about the Refusers," Kline said.

"Do you think so? Do you know how long a civilization lasts, when the vast majority of scientists, technicians, manufacturers, educators, farmers, government leaders, healers, artists, musicians, historians, electronics specialists, and even *!!!* all are taken away?"

That last word had been rendered in Ghresthrepni's own language, a chittering set of clicks, and probably represented some concept utterly untranslatable into standard English—something so alien that there was no human concept for it at all.

"The technologists were taken," Gray said slowly. "And the cities burned."

"Indeed. The Refusers were reduced to struggling remnants squabbling in the rubble over scraps of food. The warlords . . . the disease . . . the famines . . . the *chaos* . . . all lasted for a thousand years."

"How many Refusers were there?" Kline asked.

"A few trillion, scattered through the worlds and habitats of N'gai."

"So many?" Truitt sounded skeptical.

"The progenitors of the original Sh'daar numbered in the hundreds of trillions," the being said, and even in translation the words sounded wistful. "An entire galaxy bursting with life and with the brilliant light of interstellar civilization."

One in fifty, Gray thought . . . that was two percent. Out of 100 trillion that still left a couple of trillion, a pretty fair-sized population for any star-faring civilization. But the idea of that many beings fighting among themselves for technology and resources was a terrifying thought.

"The infrastructure of that civilization would have completely collapsed," Konstantin said on a private channel, following Gray's thoughts. "There was a roughly similar event in Earth's history."

"The Islamic Wars of the two-thousands?"

"What I was thinking of was earlier than that—the mid-1970s. A communist dictator who called himself Pol Pot exterminated over a quarter of his country's population, specifically targeting professionals, doctors, educators, and businessmen. The collapse of the social order resulted in devastating famine and the deaths of several millions out of an original population of only about 8 million."

"And how does this have a bearing on what happened to the N'gai civilization?"

"Obviously, the individuals who left would have been comprised of the better educated portion of the population, the scientists and technical people especially, those with an affinity for new and advanced technologies. The people who programmed the machines that kept civilization going. I suspect that the Refusers were—not less intelligent, perhaps, but more set in their ways, less adaptable, less flexible, and less willing to embrace new ideas and new technologies. There is *always* a small subset of any population that distrusts technology or modern medicine to the point of irrationality."

"Anti-vaxers."

"They were one example, yes. The nineteenth-century Luddites were another."

"Or the people today denying that the Singularity is coming." Gray sighed. "It doesn't give me a lot of hope for our species."

"It is inevitable that in any given population, a subset will prefer to remain as it is, *where* it is. Not everyone will be . . . 'taken.'"

"And when heaven was offered to them, they refused to go."

"When the ur-Sh'daar Transcended," Konstantin told

them, "the Sh'daar remained, perhaps justifiably distrustful of the science that had destroyed civilization."

"But *why*?" Kline said. "It doesn't make sense!"

"It is possible," Konstantin told her, "that the Refusers saw the *Draleth Ja* not as heaven . . . but as *hell*."

Chapter Fourteen

Quito Space Elevator
160 kilometers up
1115 hours, EST

The elevator capsule was beginning to fall.

People screamed, knowing that it was far too soon to experience weightlessness. Some began to unstrap from their seats.

"Everybody stay put!" Koenig bellowed. "Stay strapped in!" Microgravity, he knew, would not last for long.

Even at this altitude there was still atmosphere outside, and as the pod dropped, picking up speed, those traces of atmosphere would become thicker . . . and thicker. Within seconds, the passengers began feeling the jolt and increasing weight of deceleration. They would re-enter Earth's atmosphere at several thousand kilometers per hour.

"Give us some options, Konstantin," Koenig snapped. He already felt as though a large person was seated on his lap. "What can we do?"

"I can see none," Konstantin told him. "These elevator pods have no cockpit, no controls."

"They have parachutes, don't they? For emergencies?"

"Generally they do. However, I have checked the emergency descent system on this capsule, and it appears that the parachute has been removed."

Koenig felt a cold knot in his gut. "Sabotage?"

"More likely it was a matter of shoddy maintenance practices," Konstantin replied. "There have been no emergency descents from any space elevator for over a century. The parachute may have been removed some time ago to give the capsule extra cargo capacity."

Was it as simple as that? Careless maintenance and cutting corners? Enough people, Koenig knew, wanted him dead. It was hard not to see deliberate calculation here. "Tell whoever is in charge of safety inspections for this capsule that he's fired." He felt the G-forces building.

"I see one possible solution," Konstantin told him. "I am dispatching fighters and SAR tugs from SupraQuito. They may be able to use their grav drives to slow your descent."

Koenig glanced out the transparent bulkhead. A faint haze of orange fire was beginning to glow around the capsule's lower end. The vast, round sweep of Earth was still visible, but air friction was beginning to create a plasma sheath around the falling pod. Very soon now, communication would be cut off by the ionization, and he would lose contact with Konstantin.

And not long after that, he and every person on board the falling capsule would die.

USNA CVS America
CIC
N'gai Cluster
1123 hours, FST

Gray awoke in his command chair in *America*'s CIC, blinking away the mists of the dreamlike alien virtual world. He could still see those McKendree cylinders burning . . .

"How'd it go, sir?" Mackey asked him. "You were out for two hours."

"Pretty well," Gray replied. He had to focus on what he

was saying, speaking the words out loud rather than simply thinking them. "The xenosoph and xenotech departments are still over there, putting together some records we can take back with us. It shouldn't take too long."

"We learn anything useful?"

Gray sighed. "I wish I knew. A lot of it we already knew. Some of it . . ."

What the alien had told them about the Sh'daar equivalent of the Godstream was new, and it made Gray wonder if Earth wasn't closer to their own *Schjaa Hok* than anyone had guessed.

What they had not learned was if there'd been some sort of trigger to kick the whole process off. Sometimes, when all the conditions were right, you could have a supersaturated solution simply waiting for an event, a seed that would cause the entire solution to precipitate or crystalize. Water in a bottle might be cooled to just below freezing . . . and then the slightest bump would turn every drop of liquid to a solid mass of ice.

What had triggered the Sh'daar *Schjaa Hok*?

What might trigger a similar Transcendence for Humankind? That, more than anything else, was why Koenig had sent them out here on this pursuit of wild migratory waterfowl.

"Make all preparations for getting under way, Captain," Gray told Mackey. "Lieutenant West? Pass the word to the rest of the squadron." He leaned back in his seat and closed his eyes. "We need to get home."

He could still see those burning cities.

Quito Space Elevator
120 kilometers up
1129 hours, EST

The interior of the elevator pod was growing hot. The G-forces had peaked at nearly seven Gs, then gradually lessened as the falling pod approached terminal velocity. The view outside was almost completely masked by orange-hot plasma.

"Konstantin! Can you read me?"

Koenig thought he heard fragments of a reply, broken words and phrases, but he couldn't make out what was being said. The pod was increasingly shrouded by that layer of ionization that cut off radio communications.

Was the same true of laser communications? The pod had receivers and transmitters for laser-com telemetry, he knew, but he had no control over them, no more than he could use his long-dormant military piloting skills to bring the capsule under control. Never in his life had Alexander Koenig felt so completely and uselessly helpless.

"—SAR—" he heard in-head. Konstantin was trying to tell him something, but only fragments were coming through. "—pod—" "—speed—" "—and—"

Search and rescue. Was a SAR shuttle from SupraQuito trying to rendezvous? They had their work damned well cut out for them if so. The pod was a blazing meteor now, its passengers slowly being cooked by the fierce heat of re-entry. For a SAR tug to have any chance of grappling the elevator pod, it would have to match the capsule's velocity . . . which meant undergoing the same heat and vibration of re-entry that Koenig and his fellow passengers were enduring now.

And SAR tugs weren't designed for atmospheric re-entry. They were workhorses deployed strictly for operations in hard vacuum.

Gradually, the bone-shaking vibration of their descent reached a kind of steady plateau as minute followed minute through the terrifying descent. The pod was streamlined to facilitate its passage up or down through the atmosphere along the elevator cable, with top and bottom tapered into slender points. So far, the capsule had maintained its up-and-down orientation, but now Koenig and the others felt a tremendous shock, as if something massive had hit them from outside, threatening to tip them over. Deceleration dragged at them and the raging plasma inferno outside faded, just for a moment. Koenig had a moment's clear view of the Earth spread out below.

And as the plasma faded, Konstantin's voice crashed through the static. *"—ident Koenig, do you copy?"*

"I'm here, Konstantin," Koenig replied.

And in the next instant, the elevator pod, stressed far beyond its design tolerances, fell into a savage tumble, exploded like a white-hot bolide, breaking into dozens of burning fragments as it disintegrated forty kilometers above the Pacific Ocean.

Nungiirtok Warship Ashtongtok Tah
Fighter Bay
Deep Space
1250 hours, FST

The scoutship *Krestok Nin* had rendezvoused with the far larger *Ashtongtok Tah* at the stargate leading to the Nungiirtok homeworld and been taken aboard. Inside the cavernous hangar bay, Gartok Nal and Shektok Kah faced a *Tok Iad*, extending their long, jointed lower jaws in a gesture of supreme respect.

"Do you know where these Nungiirtii were taken?" the Tok Iad demanded. The phrase meant simply "Tok Lord"; the Nungiirtii knew no other name for them and did not know what they called themselves.

"No, Lord," Gartok Nal replied. "But the cry for *nesheguu* was clear and urgent."

Nesheguu meant, roughly, "vengeance," but the concept was deeply rooted in Nungiirtii codes of honor and responsibility—what each individual *tok* owed both to those above it in the social order, and to those below.

"We must answer that cry, then," the Tok Lord replied.

Tok Lords were of a completely different species than the hulking Nungiirtok warriors. A pale gray cone one meter high, balanced on three muscular tentacles and possessing a trio of slender, branching tendrils around the cone's base, their larval forms were parasites, gestating inside the body cavities of Nungiirtii and eating their way out once they were mature. Like many parasites on Earth, the larvae directly affected the brain chemistry of their hosts, making certain the slowly growing implanted larvae were kept safe and healthy. Taken into the Tok Lord community for education and indoctrination, the adults served as leaders and warlords for most Nungiirtok cultures and commanded Nungiirtok ships and ground elements in combat. The relationship of Nungiirtii with Tok Lords had lasted for so many hundreds of thousands of years that the arrangement was never questioned.

It simply was the way things were.

"We shall answer the cry of *nesheguu*, then," Gartok Nal said.

The Tok Lord gave the orders, and in moments the ponderous Nungiirtok vessel was under way, shaping a faster-than-light course back toward Earth.

USNA CVS America
Penrose TRGA
1350 hours, FST

Gray had been worried about just how they were going to get back to their own Milky Way, their own epoch. Passing through a TRGA was like threading a needle, and when that needle was tumbling through space, the task was damned near impossible. If the ships of the squadron missed their alignments and were off course by even a few meters, they might end up anywhere.

Or any*when*.

But during their discussions with the Sh'daar, the aliens had provided the answer in the form of a low-grade computer AI, a non-conscious, non-self-aware software package formatted for human computers and designed to be beamed into a TRGA's control systems using laser-com technology.

Buried within the cylindrical shell of each TRGA was a computer programmed for station-keeping. When the Sh'daar had fled the N'gai galactic core, they'd let the Thorne TRGA tumble as a means of discouraging pursuit by the Consciousness. Assured by the humans that the Consciousness was gone, they provided the software so that the human squadron could get back home.

America and the other vessels had first returned to the spot in space where they'd left the *Storozhevoy* and taken on board the twenty-five Nungiirtok prisoners before rendezvousing with the Thorne TRGA and beaming the software into its computer. The simpleminded AI immediately reset the station-keeping systems and regained full control of the gravitational fields surrounding the structure, using the positions of nearby stars to calculate the precise orientation of the device.

With the TRGA again stable, *America* slipped into the end of the open cylinder, following a precisely calculated angle into the interior and through . . .

. . . and emerged moments later from the gaping maw of the Penrose TRGA, tens of thousands of light years and hundreds of millions of years removed from Thorne. One by one, the other ships of the squadron, including the captured Russian vessels, emerged as well, following closely in *America*'s wake.

They were now seventy-nine light years—about six days' travel time—from home.

"So," Gray said, once *America* was tucked away into its own small bubble of warped space and on course for Earth, "what did we learn, if anything?"

Normally, he ate in the officers' mess, but this time he'd invited Truitt, Kline, and Mallory to join him in the wardroom for a more formal dinner. While they ate, they went through a relaxed and informal debriefing, discussing the mission so far. Unlike the cafeteria setup of the mess deck, the wardroom was more of a luxury dining room, complete with comfortable chairs and an imitation mahogany table nano-grown from the thickly carpeted decks, and viewalls showing, at the moment, a wooded glade and waterfall somewhere on Earth. Humanoid robots served food and drinks ordered in-head, and twenty-second-century chamber music played discreetly in the background. The room was located in Hab Three, and under a half G of simulated gravity.

"I'd say the most important thing," Kline said after a moment's thought, "is that the Sh'daar are a lot more reasonable than anyone's given them credit for. Ghresthrepni was positively cheerful as he was talking with us."

"Probably because they're all happy to be getting away from the Consciousness," Truitt said, picking at his imitation fish. "The Sh'daar were all terrified of that mad mind. Now they're able to vanish into the wilderness of a galaxy far larger than their own N'gai Cluster and lose themselves in time as well." He shrugged. "In my opinion they're well out of it."

"Makes you wonder, though," Mallory said, "what's going to happen to them. I mean, they're on course to colonize our galaxy, right? But in this time, *our* time, all we've encountered are the Baondyeddi on Heimdall, and they were only there because they'd slowed down the passage of time for themselves inside their private, virtual world. Where are all the rest of them? The Sjhlurrr and the Adjug . . . Adjugred . . ." He made a face. "*You* know the ones I mean. Composite starfish."

"On Earth," Kline said carefully, "any given species generally lasts for 1 to 2 million years before it goes extinct or evolves into something different. After 800 million years? I doubt that any of them would look even remotely like the originals."

"They must be here," Truitt said. "Their remote descendants, I mean. Somebody went and recruited all of the

Sh'daar client species—the Turusch and the H'rulka and the Nungiirtok and all the other races we've been fighting with the past sixty or seventy years."

"More likely the Sh'daar just used time travel," Mallory said. "After all, they have the TRGAs, just like us. In fact, we now know definitively that they built the things."

"Time travel, yes," Truitt said, nodding. "They would have to have that in order to infect modern species with *Paramycoplasma*."

Gray finished the last of his nano-grown lobster, leaned back, and picked up his coffee cup. "I think we can assume that if the Sh'daar still exist in our galaxy today, they've evolved into something as different from their ancestors as we are different from trilobites."

"Exactly," Mallory said. "That or they've gone through additional singularities. Maybe they eventually made peace with the idea. Maybe they all turned into immortal hyperdimensional gods and wouldn't be caught dead hanging around *this* universe."

"All very interesting," Gray said, studying his coffee. "But I was really asking what we've learned that has a bearing on our mission."

"All of that *does* have a bearing on the mission," Truitt said. "We went out there to learn what might be in store for us with the Singularity. We know the Sh'daar will colonize the galaxy, *our* galaxy, but then eventually vanish somewhere in the hundreds of millions of years between then and now. The point is that they *survived*."

"Meanwhile, we have riots on Earth. Nations threatening each another. Fleets being mobilized. Anti-AI movements. Anti-alien xenophobe movements. Terrorism worse than anything we've seen in three centuries. Wars—*more* wars, I should say. And we haven't even entered the Technological Singularity yet! God, what's it going to be like when we do?"

"Hell on Earth," Truitt said, grim. "Nothing less than hell on Earth."

The New White House
Washington, D.C.
1500 hours, FST

"Five minutes, Mr. President."

President James R. Walker nodded and finished downloading his speech from the White House server. It was a good speech, he thought. Powerful, to the point . . .

. . . and promising nothing.

To judge from the news feeds, the whole country—hell, the whole world—was in an uproar over what they were calling Towerfall. The underground nuke had utterly destroyed Port Ecuador, and it had cut the space elevator cable a few hundred meters above the mountain peak. Since then, the elevator's dangling loose end had been drifting slowly west. Attempts were being made to reattach the end to the alternate anchor point, but so far the reports coming in had been less than encouraging.

Casualties in Port Ecuador were horrific, tens of thousands, at least, and possibly much, much more. From the news feeds he'd seen earlier, it looked as if the entire top of Mt. Cayambe had slumped down into a vast caldera and taken the Skyport with it.

Who the hell had done this thing, anyway? There hadn't been a terrorist attack like this since the dirty bomb that had taken out Dushanbe. That had almost certainly been the Chinese, but Walker was reasonably sure the Hegemony wasn't behind the Quito disaster. They had as much to lose from this as did the USNA . . . maybe more, since they'd constructed their big microgravity factory at Supra-Quito.

No, everything seemed to point to a smaller, independent group. The damned Huffers, possibly . . . or one of the newer xenophobic anti-spacer organizations who insisted that Humankind was better off staying out of space. Even Dr. Michaels was a possible suspect, though his primary interest seemed to be in banning AIs. He was a Humankind Firster, and most of them felt humans were better off staying on Earth . . . even if he did have that fancy low-G mansion at Midway.

In any case, Walker's intelligence advisors didn't yet have a clue as to who'd done it, and had recommended that the President wait before making an announcement in order to see if anyone came forward to brag or to make demands.

Screw *that*. Walker would not let the political initiative pass to others. His broadcast this afternoon would prove to both the nation and to the world that he was still very much in control.

"One minute, Mr. President." A makeup technician lightly dusted his face with a brush and removed the bib. "You look good, sir," he said. "Break a leg!"

Off expression, that. He wondered where it was from.

"You're on, Mr. President."

Walker strode out of the backstage alcove and onto the press conference stage. The pressroom was filled, both with human reporters and with robotcams and drones. He would be going live on nearly eight hundred channels. He wondered how many viewers, how many *voters*, would be watching.

The human and humanoid members of the audience rose as he walked up to the podium, then took their seats again as he placed his hands on either side of the lectern. An in-head window showed him an audience-eye view of himself, and he adjusted his face to an expression of gravitas.

"Good afternoon," he began. "Although by now most of you have already heard the news, I come before you to announce the destruction of the spaceport outside of Quito, and the severing of the space elevator. We believe that this was carried out using a small nuclear device smuggled into underground caverns beneath the city. Port Ecuador has been completely destroyed with tremendous loss of life. All service up and down the elevator to SupraQuito has been suspended while engineers assess the damage and begin carrying out repairs. We do not, as yet, know who was responsible for this outrage, but I promise you that we *will* bring justice to those who carried out this cowardly and dastardly attack.

"Those of you with friends and relatives in Synchorbital—at the naval support facilities and the recreational and industrial compounds in orbit—I can assure you that they are in no immediate danger. I have been told by my scientific advisors that the space elevator can*not* fall, and that while it might move out of its orbit somewhat, because the anchor point has been destroyed, it is in absolutely no danger of either crashing to Earth or flying off into space. Engineers and technicians with the Space Elevator Control Bureau have already released the small planetoid tethered to the outer end of the cable so that it does not pull the elevator and attached facilities out of orbit.

"As for the approximately sixty thousand people currently stranded in SupraQuito, and the additional five thousand or so at Midway, I will again stress that they are in no danger. Communications with Synchorbital have been interrupted by the sheer load of calls up- and down-cable, but they should be restored shortly.

"Finally, one sad, personal note. The blast disrupted the magnetic locks on a number of space elevator pods moving up- or down-cable, and many of these fell, re-entering Earth's atmosphere at high velocity. I have been informed that former President Alexander Koenig was a passenger on one of these pods, and that despite attempts to grapple with his pod and bring it down safely, those attempts failed. His capsule burned up in the atmosphere and was destroyed. The former President was a close personal friend of mine, and I deeply, deeply regret his passing. My heart goes out to those whom Alex left behind, as indeed it goes out to the families and friends of all of those lost in this disaster.

"This concludes my prepared remarks. I will take questions now." He pointed. "Ms. Halley."

A woman in the second row stood. "A question and a follow-up, Mr. President. You say sixty thousand people are trapped in Synchorbital. How will they be fed without elevator service? And my follow-up—do you have any plans for evacuating them from orbit?"

"I did not say they were *trapped*, Ms. Halley. I said they were *stranded*—definitely a less loaded term. SupraQuito is a fair-sized city, as you are aware, and they have considerable reserves both of food and water, and of the rawmat necessary for technic processing. Besides, we do expect to have service resumed shortly.

"As for an evacuation, since they are in no danger, we have no plans to abandon SupraQuito at this time because it's not necessary. I'm told that our military vessels at the naval yards will be made available to transport people back to Earth or to transport food and water to the residents *if* such should become necessary, but it won't. Yes . . . over there."

A young man with a beard in the far left of the room stood. "Mr. President . . . who do you think is responsible for this attack? And a follow-up . . . if we learn who did this, are you prepared to go to war to punish them?"

Walker had been waiting for that one. "We do not as yet know who was responsible. At this point, we doubt that it was another nation, because every nation on this planet depends on cheap and rapid access to synchronous orbit. It's absolutely vital to our infrastructure, and to our continued prosperity, for *every* nation on the planet, not just us.

"There are, however, hundreds of grassroots organizations, rebel groups, and secret political action cadres with both the means and the motives to carry out such an attack. I suppose it's even within the realm of possibility that the attack was carried out by a lone nut, a whack-job with a pocket nuke and a hell of a grudge against . . . somebody. Or a looney who just wanted his name to be in the news. We don't know, but we *will* find out. And we will take action."

"But will you go to war over this?"

"We will take whatever action is appropriate. You . . . in the red."

A woman toward the back stood up. "Mr. President, do you think this might be the work of an anti-space group or one of the anti-AI organizations?"

"As I said, we have no idea as yet." He pointed. "You . . ."

And the questions continued.

Koenig Residence
Columbus, Ohio
1503 hours, EST

Five hundred and thirty kilometers to the west, a gynoid robot watched the President's face, three meters high and filling the viewall, wishing that she could cry.

Chapter Fifteen

24 April, 2429

Deep Space
Sol System
0514 hours, FST

The mountain-sized Nungiirtok ship, a converted asteroid, had been joined by others, a fleet called in by the massive *Ashtongtok Tah*. In ponderous procession, they dropped out of their version of faster-than-light drive out near the orbit of Saturn and began to move inward, toward the sun.

Toward the Earth.

The first to notice the intruders twenty-three minutes later was the High Guard patrol cruiser *Steregushchiy*, a Russian vessel watching for asteroids or comets that might someday pose a threat to Earth. At first, the line of asteroids coming in from Beyond looked natural. Comets occasionally were broken into pieces and strung out in long, eerily straight trails by a previous close encounter with a gas giant or other massive object. But magnetic, radio, infrared, and neutrino scans swiftly identified the intruders as artificial, with quantum-tap power plants and modulations of their energy fields suggesting intelligent design.

Steregushchiy transmitted a warning to Mars and to Earth on laser-com frequencies three seconds before a plasma beam struck her amidships, vaporizing her in a silent flash of raw light.

The New White House
Washington, D.C.
0815 hours, EST

"This just came through a few minutes ago, Mr. President," Hal Matloff, the senior presidential aide, said as he handed Walker an animated printout.

"Just what am I supposed to be looking at here, Hal?" The sheet showed what appeared to be a three-second loop, set in deep space, and focused on a line of enhanced-color objects made tiny by distance. They were moving, and numbers flashing and changing on either side of the page showed that they were distant . . . and therefore moving *fast*.

"A Russki patrol cruiser picked this up eighty-five light-minutes from Earth," Matloff said. "The ship ceased transmission after just a few seconds."

"What . . . it was destroyed?"

"We believe so, Mr. President," Admiral Ronald Martinez, Chief of Naval Intelligence, said. "We have no hard data as yet, but we've deployed fighter squadrons from Mars and from Earth orbit to check it out."

"If they are hostile, Mr. President, we need to deploy immediately! They are minutes away from Earth."

"Are they the bastards who knocked down the space elevator?"

"Unlikely, sir," Martinez said. "That may be an unfortunate coincidence."

"*Very* unfortunate. So unfortunate I want you to investigate whether or not it was aliens who bombed the elevator."

"Yes, sir."

"Dammit, it's going to interfere with our naval deployment, big-time!"

"We have plenty of fleet assets at Mars, Mr. President," Martinez said. "Some of the ships berthed at SupraQuito will be delayed while we find alternate means of getting their personnel on liberty up to the fleet, but we're working on that now."

"How many were in Port Ecuador when that blast went off?"

"We don't know, sir. We're working on that, too."

"Well, dammit, work on finding out who these aliens are, and what they want!"

"Judging from what happened to the *Steregushchiy*, Mr. President, we'll be able to ask them ourselves any minute now . . . when they kick down that door." Matloff's voice was grim.

"Coordinate with the Russians. Their fleet assets at SupraSingapore will help. And talk to the Pan-Euros and the Chinese, too."

"Yes, sir."

"Do it!"

President Walker glowered at the door after the two men left. The world, he decided, was on its way to hell. Every new message, every new cerebral link brought more and bigger problems, until it seemed like civilization itself was tottering on the brink.

Messages to the Russians, the Pan-Euros, and the Chinese. Anything else?

Would it be enough?

Ashtongtok Tah
Deep Space, Sol System
0854 hours, FST

Ashtongtok Tah and its smaller consorts were now passing the orbit of Mars, though of course they didn't know the planet's name. In fact, the Nungiirtok knew very little about the humans or their homeworld at all, save the fact that they were sneaky, tenacious, and dangerous as foes.

Their sensors picked up concentrations of human ships, reading the neutrino radiation flooding from countless human quantum-tap power plants, both in space and on the ground. A sizeable number of ships were departing the fourth planet and appeared to be moving to block the Tok fleet's approach to the third.

That third planet out from this sun was the focus of the Tok attention. Blue and cloud-smeared, it clearly had an atmosphere, one containing nitrogen and oxygen, and there were large areas submerged in liquid water. The telltale signs of advanced technology were everywhere, including three space elevators and massive facilities in synchronous orbit.

Interesting. One of the space elevators appeared to be disabled . . . severed at the base. Or was it an experiment in using free-orbiting tethers to lift cargo from a planetary surface? It scarcely mattered. The Tok fleet would bring all of the space elevators down in an orgy of white flame and destruction designed to wreck any human space capability. If that one elevator *was* disabled, it was a fortuitous bit of synchronicity that might hamper human efforts to defend their world.

The Shipmaster Tok Iad, wired into the data suite of the asteroid starship, tasted the flow of information cascading directly into its brain. Born of a species that biologically required the parasitization of another intelligent life form, it possessed a worldview that focused on the use of other beings for material purpose, for personal enrichment, for pleasure, for the very basis of existence, of *life* itself.

How might the Iad use this species that called itself human?

As slaves, certainly. They appeared adaptable and reasonably tough, but experiments on human captives in the past had proven that they could be broken with relative ease.

As military auxiliaries . . . possibly. Though Nungiirtok warriors filled this roll in Iad society so well it was difficult to imagine replacing them. Suitably conditioned human soldiers might serve as cannon fodder, certainly, as throwaways in planetary assaults in order to protect precious and dwindling Tok assets.

And, of course, the human planet would be stripped of resources. Tok Iad nanodisassemblers would convert everything on the planet into useful machine and construction assets, right down to the bedrock.

First, however, they would sweep aside the ragtag battle-fleet being assembled now in the *Ashtongtok Tah*'s path. A spacecraft of some sort drifted in stellar orbit a few thousand *tuin* ahead.

The asteroid ship reached out and swatted it from the sky.

Command Bunker
The New White House
Washington, D.C.
0912 hours, EST

"Number Three Mars Cycler has just been destroyed, Mr. President," General Toland said. "Looks like an extremely powerful plasma beam."

Walker looked up at Donald Phillips, his Chief of Staff, with surprise. "That thing wasn't even armed!"

"I doubt very much that the invaders care about that, sir."

"Mr. President," Admiral Martinez said, "we *must* bring the Tsiolkovsky AI back on-line."

The President glowered at him. "That would put me in a rather difficult position. Politically, I mean—"

"Mr. President," Martinez said, leaning forward and matching Walker's glower, "politics is *not* going to stop these . . . people! We use our resources, or we face annihilation!"

Walker leaned back in his chair. Around him, dozens of men and women manned data screens and workstation consoles, trying to make sense of the data streaming in from space. The White House Command Bunker was linked in with the Pentagon and the Joint Chiefs, and with major fleet assets on Mars, the moon, and in Earth orbit.

One of the cyclers. *Why?*

Several centuries ago, cycler spacecraft had circled the sun on paths that touched the orbits of Earth and Mars just when those planets were passing that touch point. Passage on these large and well-equipped space stations had taken nine months, but the system had provided a far cheaper and easier solution to travel to and from the Red Planet than by rocket, offering passengers the amenities of a small luxury hotel in space.

The development of gravitic drives had rendered the cyclers obsolete, of course. Why spend nine months adrift between worlds when you could make the trip at near-*c* and be there in under an hour? But the cycler stations represented enormous investments in material and labor; with each already three hundred meters long and massing over a hundred thousand tons, they'd been expanded and converted into space colonies, still in solar orbit, and each home to several thousand people.

They were unarmed, unarmored, and completely inoffensive, with no military capabilities at all. Why had one of them been summarily destroyed?

Clearly, Earth was under attack by an unknown alien force, one with no regard for the civilized niceties of war. And Martinez wanted to bring back the super-AI to fight it. But that was impossible. *Impossible!* His political survival depended on turning back the advancing wave of super-artificial intelligence the Humankind Firsters saw as an existential threat. If he relied on them now, that was the end . . .

"Why the hell do we need the damned AIs?" he demanded.

"Because they are faster, more powerful, and infinitely

more capable than humans, Mr. President," Toland said. "With their speed and experience, their ability to coordinate our forces, they would be an invaluable asset against unknown attackers. Keep in mind, sir, that a super-AI like Konstantin is more intelligent, more powerful than *all individual humans networked together on the planet*."

"Which is precisely why some people want to dial them back. They're smart and fast enough that they could easily replace us."

"Mr. President . . ." Martinez sounded exasperated. "With all due respect, but why in hell would they? They're not competing with us for food or rawmat or living space. They're smart enough to know there's no benefit in wiping us out. Besides, they've always worked *with* us! At worst . . ." He shrugged, shaking his head. "I don't know. I suppose they might all give up on us, pack up, and leave and go explore the galaxy. They might say bye-bye and leave us to our own devices, right?"

"That might solve a lot of problems," Walker said.

"Not this problem, though," Toland said. "Admiral Martinez is right. Especially in this case, where they have every reason to work with us, not against us."

"Why?"

"This is their planet, too, Mr. President."

Walker wanted to deny that; Earth belonged to *humans*. But he was forced to accept Toland's assessment, at least from one point of view. They were intelligent, they were self-aware, and that technically made them as "human" as any member of *Homo sapiens*.

Besides, these aliens coming in past the orbit of Mars might very well be bent on taking Earth away from Humankind, one way or another.

"Okay," Walker said. "But the last I heard, this Konstantin thing jumped into a hole and pulled it in after him. How do we find it?"

"We open a channel to Tsiolkovsky on the moon," Martinez said, "and we ask. *Nicely*."

Tsiolkolvsky Super-AI Complex
Tsiolkolvsky Crater
Lunar Farside
1029 hours, EST

Civilization, Konstantin thought with something a human might have called sadness, was dying. From his electronic fortress on the far side of the moon, he continued to monitor events on the tormented planet, watching as events accelerated and worsened.

Massive protests throughout Pan-Europe had spread and grown, mutating into savage and bloody riots. Exactly what the rioting was about was often still unclear even to Konstantin, but seemed to include both attacks against and defenses of super-AI, as well as attacks against the concept of the Singularity, against the presence of nonhumans on Earth, against space travel, against political or diplomatic entanglements with alien governments, and even against efforts to overturn centuries of global climate change in an effort to roll back the advancing borders of the ocean. The super-AI could detect nothing like rationality in any of the clashes.

Wars were ravaging Indonesia and the Philippines as the Chinese Hegemony came down hard on revolutionary movements and on groups proclaiming the coming of the Singularity. Brazil had invaded Paraguay and Argentina, seeking access to dwindling resources in Corrientes, while Nicaragua had invaded Costa Rica in the wake of the revolution there, and now was threatening Panama. Most of Africa had dropped off the Global Net months ago, and very little news was coming out. India—civil war.

As humans might put it, the entire world was going FUBAR.

Although Konstantin had withdrawn from much of his official involvement with human agencies and government, he'd maintained a kind of stealth presence, riding the Global Net and residing within the darker and less well-known corners of the virtual space known as the Godstream. He was particularly interested in reports of mass deaths, reports that seemed to echo stories brought back from the N'gai Cloud, memories of the chaotic time when the ur-Sh'daar had vanished, leaving behind the Refusers. Tens of thousands had mysteriously died in the days since the space elevator's collapse, all of them while linked into the Godstream.

It was as if their minds had gone . . . elsewhere, leaving the bodies behind.

There was a distinct possibility that those people had in fact uploaded themselves into the Godstream, but if so, finding them was proving extremely difficult—the electronic equivalent of locating one particular molecule of water among all the molecules of Earth's oceans. A needle in a haystack, by comparison, would have been *easy*.

Konstantin was aware of a constant alarm in the background, as various departments and agencies within the USNA government tried to get him to respond. He ignored them, knowing that they were attempts by Walker and various anti-AI groups to find him in order to switch him off. At this point, of course, they wouldn't be able to pull that off, not unless they found a way to pull the plug on the entire Godstream network.

He didn't *think* they were irrational enough to try such a thing.

At least he hoped not . . .

In Transit
USNA CVS America
Brig
1105 hours, FST

Gray stood outside one of the brig compartments studying the two beings behind the acrylic transparency. Four armored Marines stood behind him, heavy personal weapons at the ready—just in case.

The twenty-five Nungiirtok warriors had said little since the squadron had picked them up from the incapacitated Russian ship back in the N'gai Cluster, despite the AI translation software running in the background. *America*'s shipboard Marines had herded eight of them into the brig; the ship contained only eight cells. The rest had been placed in a large supply compartment emptied of everything save benches and portable sanitary facilities. Microcameras provided constant surveillance, while Marines with portable plasma projectors stood guard outside.

Stripped of their combat armor, the Nungiirtok warriors no longer looked much like giant humans. They stood upright on two legs, yes, but those legs were digitigrade, the knees bent backward like that of some massive bird, the heavy body stooped far forward, segmented, and encased in something like chitin. Two huge, stalked eyes swiveled independently of one another from the low hump that rested where a head should be. Perhaps strangest was the thing's lower jaw, which was hinged and reached out for over a meter when it unfolded. Gray had seen those in action during close-quarters combat with the Nungies; evolved to capture food like the tongues of terrestrial frogs or toads, they could unfold with blinding swiftness to deliver a pile-driver blow. *America*'s xenosophontological team had noted in their report that the adaptation was similar to the hard-hitting jaw of mantis shrimp back on Earth.

Gray wondered if those acrylic panels could stand up to that kind of impact.

"I know you two can understand me," Gray said quietly, speaking in English and letting the intelligent translation software speak for him in a language the Nungiirtok could understand. The two squatted in their cell, listless, unresponsive.

"We don't need to be enemies," Gray went on. "We know you were continuing to hold out on the world we call Osiris because you thought you had no choice. What was it—your leaders ordered you not to surrender? Or maybe it's a cultural thing? A warrior ethic that forbids you to give up? Is that it?"

There was no response from the sullen beings within the cell.

"You realize now that your leaders abandoned you on Osiris, of course. Maybe they forgot about you. Maybe they decided that sending in a naval squadron to evacuate you simply was not worth the effort."

Gray waited for an answer. He'd gotten a reaction that time, a small one. Both had swiveled their weirdly stalked eyes in his direction.

At least they weren't ignoring him now.

"Admiral, I wish you would leave this sort of thing to the experts," Truitt said over a private channel inside Gray's head. He and Samantha Kline were not physically present but were watching the interrogation through virtual feeds up in the xeno department.

Gray cut the translation circuit so the prisoners wouldn't hear his reply. "And have the 'experts' been able to get any response out of these guys?" he asked. "Have you found out what the Russians said to them to get them to evacuate Osiris?"

"Of course not. We would have told you if—"

"Then give me a chance at this, please. We *must* find out what their agreement is with the Russians. Did the *Moskva* just offer them a ride home? Or have they formed some sort of alliance with each other? Are the Russians in contact with the Nungie homeworld? Or was it just an agreement between these twenty-five and Captain Oreshkin?"

"I thought the Russians were our allies," Kline put in.

"So did I, Doctor. And so they *were* until they attacked us at the Penrose triggah, and again at Thorne. The Russian crews don't seem to know anything, and Oreshkin has been less than forthcoming about why they attacked. So we'll see what the Nungies have to say about it."

"If you can get them to talk," Truitt said, his mental

voice sour. "Really, Admiral, the xeno department is much better equipped to handle this sort of questioning than—"

"Our lords would not abandon us," another voice said in Gray's mind.

Gray snapped off the link with Truitt and reopened his channel to the prisoners. "And who were your lords on Osiris? Are they with you?"

"The Tok Iad were not with us on that world."

"Why not? Were they killed? Captured?"

"The Tok Iad were not with us."

The translation software had thrown up a window within Gray's mind, suggesting that *Tok Iad*—which probably meant "Nungiirtok Lords"—might well be a completely different social class or caste than the warriors before him. The AI was guessing, Gray knew, but it was a guess based on inflection and subtleties of grammar within the alien language, things the software had picked up during years of human attempts to decipher it.

Gray felt a sudden, heady thrill of comprehension. It was also a guess . . . but he knew he was right.

"These Tok Lords," he said. "They're different from you."

Again, the two Nungiirtok were silent, but they were watching him now with an intensity that was almost palpable. Gray went to a private channel. "Konstantin!"

"I am here, Admiral."

"Give me an image of a Kobold!"

He didn't have a recording of one of the enigmatic little creatures, but Konstantin Junior did, something picked up during the fighting on Osiris decades ago. A holographic imager inside the Nungiirtoks' cell displayed the being in front of them, life-sized, frozen in mid-slither.

He opened the channel again. "Is *this* one of your lords?"

The response was instant and startling. Both Nungiirtoks stepped back a pace, hunching their bodies forward until their eyestalks were just above the deck, and with their complex lower jaws extended a good meter in front of them. The gesture could have meant anything, but Gray was pretty certain that it was a sign of respect . . . or, possibly, one of fear.

Humans had encountered Kobolds every time they'd fought Nungiirtok ground forces, but never learned what the relationship was between them. The most popular theory was that Kobolds actually were Nungiirtok young, though why the adults might bring juveniles to a battlefield had never been explained.

Another popular theory was that the Kobolds were *pets*, or just possibly, the Nungie equivalent of the cybernetic K-9 Corps dogs that human militaries used for tracking, sentry patrols, or search and rescue.

But he couldn't imagine the Nungiirtok warriors deferring to animals. Or to children. The relationship, he thought, must be more complex.

The aliens' body language, whether representing fear or deep respect, lasted only for a moment. They then straightened up, hinged jaws closing, but both, Gray noticed, kept one stalked eye swiveled to watch the frozen Kobold image.

"This is an *image* of a Master, yes," one of the Nungiirtok told him.

"They're aliens, aren't they? An entirely different species."

"We give them life."

Gray tried to understand. Maybe he was wrong. "They're your offspring? Your young?"

"No. But we give them life."

"I don't understand."

"They choose us, and we give them life. It has always been so, since before the Nungiirtok race first developed mind and conscious thought."

"Parasites!" Truitt said over the private channel. "The Tok lords are parasites!"

Gray blinked. "How is that even possible?"

"Admiral, something like *forty percent* of all terrestrial life is parasitic in one way or another. Why shouldn't that be the same of exobiological species?"

It made sense, of a sort. Humans had encountered alien parasites before—the giant worms inhabiting the gas-giant living balloons of the H'rulka; the tiny males living as ectoparasites on the bodies of spider-like female Agletsch; the hive-mind organism dubbed *Paramycoplasma subtilis* that had shaped and directed Sh'daar history and off-world policy . . .

They choose us, and we give them life.

Okay . . . this was starting to make sense.

But the exact nature of the biological relationship, Gray decided, was unimportant, at least for now.

"These Masters," he said, addressing the aliens again. "Did they tell you to fight us?"

No answer.

"Did they tell you to go with the Russians?"

"Ruh—seeans . . ."

"Humans, like us . . . but with a different government, a different language. It was Russians who rescued you from Osiris. Their leader was called Oreshkin."

"There were no lords left on Osiris."

"So they didn't order you to surrender?"

"The Nungiirtok do *not* 'surrender.'" It sounded uncertain of the word's meaning.

"It sounds to me," Gray told the two beings, "like the Tok Iad are using you. They parasitize you in ways I can only imagine. They tell you what to do, who to fight, and in the end they abandoned you on the world of Osiris—"

The reaction was sudden and completely unexpected. Both Nungiirtok hurled themselves forward, their lower jaws snapping out as they slammed the tips into the transparent acrylic. Gray took an inadvertent step back as the two blows hammered at the transparency with a deafening double bang.

Then again.

And again . . .

"Sir!" one of the Marines yelled. "Behind us!"

The acrylic wall gave way under the assault, part of it

shattering, part peeling back as both Nungiirtok tried squeezing through the opening. The Marines closed in front of Gray and opened fire, white plasma searing into the tangle of alien limbs and bodies.

"Don't—" Gray yelled.

But it was too late. In seconds, both Nungiirtok were reduced to large, charred, lifeless cinders, leaving Gray with very nearly as many questions as he'd had before he'd come here.

But just possibly, he'd learned enough to help them figure out the Nungiirtoks' relationship with the Russians.

Chapter Sixteen

25 April, 2429

Deep Space
Sol System
1223 hours, FST

The Nungiirtok fleet had advanced slowly after the destruction of that first, unarmed spacecraft or station, spreading out in order to frustrate human attempts to concentrate their forces. The force consisted of eight craft fashioned from planetoids. The command vessel, the *Ashtongtok Tah*, was the size of a small dwarf planet; the others, moving off to either side, ranged from half that down to the relatively tiny *Krestok Nin*. They drifted forward slowly, watching the gathering human forces ahead.

The Tok Iad commanding the force was known to others of its kind as 4236 Xavix, and it was worried. The humans had shown themselves to be formidable opponents over the years, and there were at least sixty of their warships assembling in a loose cloud fifty *chag* ahead.

It was worried, but not enough to run away.

Opening a channel to the cyborg Tok wired into the ship computers, 4236 Xavix gave the order to attack.

USNA CV Yorktown
Mars Orbit
1224 hours, FST

Captain Laurie Taggart leaned forward in her command chair—as far forward as the chair's embrace would allow her, at any rate. The targets were moving, deploying into what looked like a combat formation.

"All weapons at the ready, Mr. Mathers," she told the ship's combat officer. "I want a salvo of nukes at maximum yield in the railgun tubes."

"Aye, aye, Captain."

She was still trying to get used to the sudden turn of events. Taggart had walked onto the bridge of the USNA *Yorktown* less than an hour ago. For two years, now, she'd been flying a desk in the intelligence division at the naval HQ facility on Mars, but then at 0930 this morning she'd been offered the sudden and totally unexpected chance to take command of the star carrier *Yorktown*.

Supposedly, she'd been tagged because of her experience commanding the USNA *Guadalcanal*. Both the *Yorktown*'s captain and first officer had been off the ship, and HQ wanted the *Yorkie* on the battle line *now*.

In fact, she suspected the electronic hand of Konstantin behind the opportunity, which had been offered as a chance to volunteer rather than as orders. She'd accepted, of course—*anything* to get out from behind that desk!—but Konstantin would have known she would take the offer. The super-AI had been lying low of late, and she hadn't heard from it directly, but she thought she recognized Konstantin's subtle touch.

The *Yorktown* was a brand-new warship just off the ways, commissioned three months ago and sent to Chiron and back for her shakedown cruise. So far, her bridge crew seemed well trained and well prepared, but it would be the coming combat that would prove that one way or another, as only combat could. The three thousand men, women, and AIs in her crew would be watching her just as closely to see if she four-o'd their inspection, qualifying for the command seat on a *Constellation*-class star carrier.

Speaking of the *Constellation*—the lead ship of her class was in position a thousand kilometers high and to starboard, invisibly small to the naked eye but visible in-head and on the bridge repeater screens. Admiral Kevin Rasmussen was the fleet commander, ensconced on the *Connie*'s flag bridge. She'd served with him before, at Kapteyn's Star and elsewhere. A good man, she thought, experienced and sharp.

She just wished Trevor Gray was here with the *America*. The ship was old, but her value lay far more in who commanded her than in the date of her commissioning.

"Enemy is opening fire, Captain," *Yorktown*'s combat officer announced. "The *Monongahela*'s been hit."

"What kind of weaponry are we looking at, Commander?"

"A fist, Captain. A big one. Gravitic induction, but I've never seen this sort of range on those things. *Or* power."

Humans had encountered that weapon before in their struggle against the Rosette Consciousness. Its general principle was well understood. Human starships could project a momentary zone of intense gravitic induction ahead of a ship, creating a drive field, but the Rosetters' advanced alien technologies could project such an effect across thousands of kilometers and use it to crush a target vessel. How they managed that trick was still a big unknown, however, and the largest asteroid ship ahead had just crippled a light cruiser, the *Monongahela*, at the astonishing range of half a million kilometers.

The planetoid starships advanced with surprising speed, closing the range rapidly. "All units," Admiral Rasmussen's voice said over the intrafleet command link, "target that big son-of-a-bitch, designated Target Alfa. We can mop up the small stuff later."

Taggart wasn't entirely sure the "small stuff" would be all that amenable to a later mopping, but it made sense to go all-out against the largest asteroid, a 250-kilometer monster roughly as large as the asteroid Juno in Earth's solar system.

It would not be easy, however. According to the ship's sensor department, that largest planetoid massed something like 3×10^{19} kilograms. Take a roughly spherical divot out of the Earth about the width of the state of West Virginia or the nation of Scotland, and that was the enemy vessel . . . except that it was made up mostly of nickel-iron instead of sandstone. You could slam nuke after nuke into that mass and not even get their attention.

"Let's put our squadrons into space, CAG," she told Captain Philip Palmer, the officer in command of *Yorktown*'s fighter squadrons. "Target Alfa—nukes and nano-D."

"Aye, aye, Captain."

Moments later, the first of *Yorktown*'s fighters spilled into space alongside the carrier, forming up by squadron. *Yorktown* carried six fighter squadrons in addition to two recon units and a SAR squadron. They would be going in at maximum dispersal, the idea being that the enemy would be faced with a large number of widely scattered targets rather than a close-packed group; no one knew how large an area of effect that gravitic weapon projected, but the humans did not intend to make it easy for them.

As the last squadron formed up in a broad echelon formation, they began moving toward the Tango-Alfa object.

They would make contact in scant minutes.

Lieutenant Michael Cordell
VFA-427, The Renegades
Mars Orbit
1226 hours, FST

Mike Cordell felt the steady flow of incoming data humming in his brain, felt the kinesthetic sense linked through his SG-420 Starblade fighter convincingly letting him feel that he physically was the fighter falling through open space. Within his mind, he could see the vastly magnified images of the aliens—massive, potato-shaped rocks, some with minute buildings or other structures gleaming in the wan light of a distant sun.

Cordell could see some slight, shifting distortion to the rocks and structures as they moved, as though he were viewing them through rippling water; evidently, each ship was gravitationally distorting space around it—throwing out defensive shields protecting them from incoming beams and warheads. That was going to make things interesting.

"Okay, Renegades," the squadron CO called over the combat channel. Commander Jenna Forsley was sharp and competent; she had the complete respect of Cordell and all of the other Renegade blade drivers. "Form up on me. Wide dispersal. We don't want one nuke to get us all."

Nukes Cordell knew and understood. This alien gravitic weapon, though, was an unknown, and a scary one. It simply reached out and crushed the target vessel, and since space itself was what was being crushed, there seemed to be no way to shield against it.

Far off to Cordell's portside, the *Vladivostok* was launching fighters as well, and he wondered if Katya Golikova was among them.

Then Forsley gave the order to boost, and Cordell was too busy to think about anything, or anyone, else.

Nungiirtok Fleet
Mars Orbit
Sol System
1227 hours, FST

The Nungiirtok raiders had been slowing as the human fleet approached, and as clouds of fighters began emerging from the star carriers, they slowed further still. Despite many years of fighting the humans, little was known about their military capabilities, and 4236 Xavix wanted to invite the

Earthers to attack first in order to reveal both their strength and their tactical understanding. Unfortunately, the human fleet was slowing as well, a wall of ships numbering in the hundreds, steadily spreading out to either side, and above and below.

"What is the range?" he demanded of *Ashtongtok Tah*'s weapons specialist.

"Forty *chag*, Lord."

Still too far for the Tok weapons to be effective against the enemy's main body.

The Tok Lord thought it saw a possible strategy, however, one that would take advantage of the humans' dispersal.

"All ships," it said. "Advance, slow walk."

USNA CV Yorktown
Mars Orbit
1228 hours, FST

"What the hell are they up to?" Captain Taggart said, eyes narrowing as she studied the main tactical screen.

"If I didn't know better," Mathers said, "I'd swear they were begging us to englobe them!"

"A little too easy, huh?"

"Englobement means squeezing in closer, Captain," Mathers said. "And that puts us within easy reach of their fist."

What, she wondered, would Rasmussen do? Hold back? Or advance?

A destroyer, the *Bartold*, was maneuvering close to the stricken *Monongahela*, trying to take on board several life-pods ejected within a few moments of the ship's encounter with the alien fist. Battlespace drones transmitted constant visual feeds back to the other ships in the fleet, and Taggart could see the *Bartold*'s small SAR tugs grappling with the drifting pods.

She felt a chill at that. The *Bartie* was clearly within

range of the alien weapon, and there was a good chance that the enemy would not distinguish between a humanitarian mission and a combat maneuver. Her breath caught in her throat . . .

. . . and then the invisible hand closed around the *Bartold* and squeezed, crumpling her forward section, including her huge, egg-shaped water reservoir, into twisted wreckage. Water sprayed into space as an expanding cloud of glittering ice crystals . . . an interesting bit of data, Taggart thought. If the fist literally collapsed space, what happened to water, which conventionally was not compressible? That might be a clue to how the weapon functioned, there.

"All capital units." Rasmussen's orders came through her cerebral link. "Decelerate, then fall back slowly and do *not* engage! Fighters, continue your attack. Focus on Target Alfa."

Taggart passed the command on to *Yorktown*'s helm. She approved of the admiral's order and felt considerable relief that he wasn't ordering the capital ships in close. If those alien asteroids could crush a target vessel at long range, the human fleet was going to need to tiptoe into this engagement or risk being annihilated.

That made it damned hard on the fighter squadrons, though. They had no defense whatsoever save for speed and dispersal, and the enemy wasn't going to simply sit still while an angry swarm of hornets buzzed into killing range.

She wondered if any of the fighters would survive.

Lieutenant Michael Cordell
VFA-427, The Renegades
Mars Orbit
1228 hours, FST

Cordell accelerated his Starblade to relativistic speeds, watching space around him grow strange as his velocity warped the incoming light of stars and other ships and compressed them into a hazy ring of starlight directly ahead. He was relying on his fighter's onboard AI to time his acceleration; he could no longer see the alien planetoids, radar and lidar were useless at these speeds. The only good thing about it was that the enemy would have trouble tracking him as well. Radar would reflect from his fighter without a problem, but he would literally be on top of the enemy before they realized he was approaching.

He felt the AI apply deceleration, and the ring of light ahead dissolved, the stars that had created it returning to more reasonable positions. And the alien planetoids were . . . *there*!

He'd targeted the largest one, and it loomed ahead of him now, over two hundred kilometers across and gleaming in the distant sun. Something like a city embraced a patch on the surface; thousands of pinpoint lights shone from isolated patches across the dark gray surface of the rock, like stars somehow arrayed in geometric patterns— lines and triangles and concentric circles.

Reflex took over. He thoughtclicked a command, and a pair of VG-120 Boomslang missiles slid from his Starblade's belly, the warheads already set to maximum yield— something just in excess of 600 megatons. *"Fox One!"* he announced over the tactical channel, the warning that he'd just loosed smart-AI missiles.

Each Starblade carried thirty-two VG-92 Krait space-to-space missiles, plus six of the massive Boomslangs, known as "planetbusters" to the fighter crews. The twelve Starblades of the Renegades alone carried twenty-four of those monsters, but as Cordell stared into the fast-growing face of the planetoid, he realized with sick certainty that it would take more to stop that thing.

A *lot* more.

But their orders were to press home the attack. Besides— who could guess what might happen? Enough VG-120s detonating in the same spot might crack the planetoid wide open or send destructive shock waves through that mountain's internal structure. It was certainly worth a try.

Cordell juggled his grav drive and his ship's attitude,

decelerating sharply and swinging wide. A skilled pilot with a high-grade AI could nudge and twist a Starblade through maneuvers that made it seem that the fighter was in atmosphere . . . and some, like stopping in a deceleration-less instant or pulling a right-angle turn, would have appeared starkly impossible to the fighter pilots of an earlier age. By jinking back and forth in what Cordell hoped was an unpredictable manner, he hoped to confuse the enemy's fire control programs.

In his mind, his fighter counted off the seconds until his missiles detonated. *Three . . . two . . . one . . .*

A single white flash, far brighter than a sun, blotted out the sky to Cordell's left. Had one of his missiles failed to reach the target? Or had both gone off so close together that two nuclear fireballs blended into one?

It scarcely mattered. The target planetoid now had a new crater—glowing bright orange, its interior filled with molten rock.

"Fox One!" Jerry Bannerman called over the tactical channel. "Missiles away!"

His AI tracked the incoming missiles, and he checked to make sure he was going to be clear of the blast. He was; Bannerman's missiles struck the asteroid right next to the glowing patch of lava.

Two by two, Boomslang missiles continued falling in from space, and the area around the planetoid was filled with Starblade fighters flashing past the enemy's close-in defenses. Lieutenant Frank Taylor's fighter crumpled into a small, extremely dense block of twisted metal and plastic, hurtling in to impact on the drifting mountain's surface. All of local space was filled with fast-maneuvering fighters and the flash of incoming missiles.

Lieutenant Howard Ortega's fighter crumpled as an invisible fist of gravitational distortion surrounded it and squeezed. The enemy was fighting back, was getting too many hits. It looked as though dispersing the Starblades was working to hold down casualties, but the butcher's bill, he thought, was still going to be too damned high.

"C'mon, people!" Captain Palmer called from *Yorktown*'s PriFly. "Swing around and hit 'em again! Target that same spot!"

"You got it, CAG," Commander Forsley called back. "You heard the man, Renegades! Line 'em up and knock 'em down!"

Cordell circled back and around, lining up on the planetoid ship and telling his AI to home the next salvo of Boomslangs directly at the orange-glowing crater punched into the crust. He felt the AI's acknowledgement, felt the warheads being armed. He held his course, arrowing back in toward the target, then thoughtclicked missiles away. "And Fox One!"

White plasma blotted out the sky ahead, a continuous flaring of multiple warheads detonating in rapid succession. Some of the missiles, he saw, were being intercepted by the enemy's gravitic defenses, but the majority were getting through and flaring into searing balls of starcore-hot plasma, cratering the planetoid's surface.

He repeated the maneuver one more time, unloading the last of his payload of Boomslangs dead-on the target. The pool of lava on the planetoid's surface was larger, now . . . but so far as Cordell could tell, they hadn't even come close to cracking that egg.

There was nothing for it, now, but to press the attack, using the smaller Kraits.

Nungiirtok Fleet
Mars Orbit
Sol System
1229 hours, FST

4236 Xavix sifted through the flood of data pouring through his link to the ship's intelligence, searching for tactical patterns within the human attacks. Their missiles were not particularly worrying; the rock of *Ashtongtok Tah* could stand up to their relatively small impacts for a long time without a problem. There seemed to be no solid rationale in their assaults. The Nungiirtok knocked down fighter after fighter, but the rest continued swarming in, loosing more missiles despite their losses. Xavix noted that the attackers had shifted to smaller, lower-yield weapons. Was it possible that they'd expended their supply of the larger warheads?

It was all so futile.

The point of this raid had been simply to punish the humans for their presumption in abducting Nungiirtok personnel. *Ashtongtok Tah* and her consorts possessed gravitic weapons that could scour the surface of the planet ahead down to the mantle, reducing the world to a lifeless husk, but so far he'd been holding back. It had not been Xavix's plan to destroy the human homeworld, but he was realizing now that that might be the only option left open to him.

Perhaps, though, there was one other option short of planetary genocide . . .

"Weapons!" he ordered. "We will use the relativistic cannon."

"Yes, Lord!"

"Stand by to fire . . ."

Lieutenant Michael Cordell
VFA-427, The Renegades
Mars Orbit
1228 hours, FST

Cordell swung his fighter into an achingly close passage above the planetoid, flipping his ship around in a one-eighty so that he was flying backward as he began releasing a stream of Krait missiles. By flying in reverse, he wouldn't fly into the fireballs, and he could fire volleys of them into targets selected by the Starblade's AI as he passed over them. A blur of white to his left caught his attention: a patch of domes and low rectangles in the rock, some sort of city or defensive facility. Whatever it was vanished in a pulse of nuclear fire brighter than a sun, and he prayed that it had been important.

Below and behind him, something like a door or a hatch almost a hundred meters across yawned wide in the object's face.

"What the hell is that?" he asked his ship, but the AI had no answer. He assumed it was some sort of launch bay hatch, that the enemy was about to release a swarm of fighters to engage the human squadrons beak-to-beak.

"Renegade Flight, this is Ren-Three!" he called over the tactical channel. "I see an opening in this thing—maybe into a flight deck or fighter bay! Let's get some warshots down that thing's throat!"

"Copy, Ren Three!" Forsley replied. "You heard the man, Rennies! Pile on!"

But as Cordell approached the opening, something— something very big and very massive and *very* fast flashed out and into the void, too fast to register on merely human senses, but captured and enhanced by the Starblade's instruments.

"What was that?" he demanded.

His AI could only give him a stream of rough data, but whatever that flash had been had massed several tons and was traveling at close to seventy percent of the speed of light.

Cordell's blood ran cold when the AI showed him the thing's course.

It was headed directly toward Earth, now just some 90 million kilometers behind the fleet.

Its speed would bridge that gulf in just seven minutes.

Nungiirtok Fleet
Mars Orbit
Sol System
1229 hours, FST

Ashtongtok Tah's Tok Lord regretted the necessity of opening fire on the human home planet, but told itself that it was not aiming at the world, but at the complex ring of structures in planetary synchronous orbit. It was quite likely that some of the projectiles would pass through the structure, shredding it, and impact on the planet's surface, but the humans *had* to be properly chastised or they would forever be an impossible nuisance.

Tok Iad psychology had been deeply shaped over millions of years by their parasitism of the Nungiirtok. For a parasite, after all, their host species—and by extension *all* other species—exist to be *used*, and if they can't be used as food or as incubators, they can be ignored, discarded, or obliterated at the Iad's whim. Xavix admired the persistence of the humans even as he was amused by the futility of their swarm attack, but if they could not be brought to heel swiftly and efficiently, they would be eliminated.

The first round from the gravitic cannon hurtled toward the alien world at seven-tenths the speed of light.

A pity, really.

Synchorbital Naval Command
SupraQuito Facility
Synchorbit
1232 hours, FST

"Sir! We have incoming!"

Admiral of the Fleet Jonathan Christie looked up from his workstation in the Naval Command C&C, angry. "What is it?" he demanded. "Give me some ID!"

"Unknown, sir," the sensor watch officer replied, shaking his head. "It was just ejected from the largest alien craft. It's big, it's massive, and Doppler shows it in approach at point seven-one *c*. It'll reach us in four minutes!"

"All stations go to full alert, Mr. Buckley."

"Aye, aye, sir!"

Christie could see the object highlighted by CGI on his

monitor now, a single point of light still tens of millions of kilometers distant. Its course was bang-on target for the synchorbital ring, a fragile and intermittent string of factories, shipyards, storage facilities, and slowly turning hab modules hanging just under 36,000 kilometers above Earth's equator. His gut told him it wasn't a ship, but a weapon—specifically a kinetic-kill weapon, a projectile that used mass and velocity to inflict serious damage on its target.

"Commander Clayton! Focus every weapon you can bring to bear on that incoming."

"Already done, sir."

"Then fire!"

"Firing, aye, aye, Admiral."

Lasers and particle beams stretched out invisibly across the fast-dwindling gulf between base and object. On his monitor, the object grew suddenly brighter. They were hitting it.

"Keep firing! Knock it down!"

But the projectile was a multi-ton lump of nickel-iron, and the beam weapons could not ablate the material quickly enough to make a difference. The nukes reached the target a couple of minutes later, and Christie wondered if they could deflect it enough to make a difference.

At the speed it was traveling, though, probably not. Debris would still reach them in another . . . sixty seconds now. If they did push it off course, it would miss the ring but hit the Earth, and Christie didn't want to think of the effect of even a one-meter fragment impacting the Earth at 210,000 kilometers per second.

Thirty seconds.

Twenty seconds.

"Vapor, sir!" the sensor officer reported. "We're ablating it. . . ."

But too little, and too late. Nuclear fireballs flashed and winked close about the projectile, and still it came.

Five seconds . . .

Three . . .

A supernova erupted across the synchorbital, shredding delicate traceries of pylons and struts, vaporizing structure, obliterating a huge swath of the naval base.

Christie never felt the impact that killed him.

Chapter Seventeen

SupraQuito Facility
Synchorbit
1236 hours, FST

Explosions wracked the synchorbital base, sending glittering shards of debris outward in an expanding, twinkling
sphere. F=MA, which meant the force impacting the delicate orbital facility equaled roughly 420 giganewtons, or
more than twelve hundred times the liftoff thrust of the
Saturn V rocket that had first taken humans to the moon.

The incoming two-ton projectile had punched cleanly
through the structure, and the intense heat radiation was
largely confined by vacuum. The ring was not destroyed by
any means. A two-kilometer section of the main SupraQuito
Synchorbital was shredded, however, and nearly five thousand
people—perhaps half of them naval personnel—were killed.

The projectile, already badly stressed by beam and warhead detonations on the way in, fragmented with the impact,
the pieces continuing on for another 37,000 kilometers,
briefly heating in Earth's atmosphere, and becoming a rain
of high-velocity meteors. Their path came in at an oblique

angle, striking SupraQuito and almost missing the planet altogether.

That angle of approach saved Ecuador, Brazil, and Peru. The smaller fragments burned up; the larger ones, those larger than grains of sand, were traveling so fast they were through the atmosphere in an instant, impacting the planet's surface at over two hundred thousand kilometers per second.

A vast swath of the Pacific Ocean southeast of the Galapagos vaporized with the release of kinetic energy. No one was killed by the impact itself, but the rising plume of superheated vapor rapidly swirled into a hurricane more powerful than any ever seen before on the planet. Thousands more would die when the superstorm made landfall near the city of Tumbes, then carved its way inland and north toward Guayaquil.

In the savaged orbital facility overhead, a thousand desperate struggles for survival played themselves out, as some people managed to reach emergency suits or intact airtight compartments, and others did not.

For those who did not, death came quickly as they fell into emptiness or struggled to breathe in fast-thinning air. Rescue attempts were hindered by clouds of fragments and debris. Naval vessels berthed at the spaceyards were mostly intact, but most were still awaiting supplies and personnel that now would never arrive.

And on the world below, a stunned populace tuned in to the Global Net channels to watch the unfolding disaster in the skies overhead.

Command Bunker
New White House
Washington, D.C., USNA
1258 hours, EST

President Walker glowered at his Chief of Staff. "Damn it, Don, what the hell am I looking at? What's going on?"

Phillips was linked to the same news channel data feed as the President. "A shitstorm, Mr. President. White-hot debris, clouds of ice crystals from ruptured water tanks and freezing atmosphere, metal vapor—"

"The bastards destroyed our orbital port!"

"Not *all* of it, sir. The projectile went through the C3 center—that's command, control, and communications," he explained to the President who had never served, "and took out some of the civilian factories and habs as well. They missed the shipyards, and most of the ships report ready for space. Some are already under way. We've already released the tethered asteroid, you'll recall, so what's left isn't being dragged up and out into space. Most of it should stay in orbit."

"*Most* of it?"

"A lot of junk got shaken free, Mr. President, and lost some of its orbital velocity. It's falling. We can expect some pretty spectacular meteor showers over the next few weeks."

"I don't give a fuck about meteor showers! What can we *do*?"

"We wait and see how our fleet manages to deal with the alien planetoids, sir. We get more ships out there as we can, and we hope to God the aliens don't have any more of those relativistic projectiles in their back pockets. Until then, there's nothing much else we *can* do."

Walker sagged back in his chair, eyes closed. Reports were coming in, fragmentary and confused, of a two-hundred-kilometer steam cloud engulfing the ocean near the Galapagos. Some of that steam was already condensing out as rain—near-solid walls of water dumping from the sky. Meanwhile, tidal waves were racing out from the impact site in all directions, big enough and fast enough that they would hit eastern Asia and Australia in another few hours.

"Don," Walker said suddenly, "that was a warning shot!"

"I beg your pardon, sir?"

"They deliberately targeted our naval command center. Probably homed on the communications relays. That shot *almost* missed the Earth completely."

"You're saying the Galapagos strike was an *accident*?"

"I'm saying we're dealing with a technology so advanced they can strike us anywhere and anytime they want, and there's not one damned thing we can do to stop them! This time they took out our synchorbital command center. Next time they could drop a rock on the White House lawn!"

"All we can do is wait out the fleet action out at—"

"No. There's nothing they can do." He opened an interior channel. "Mrs. White!"

Anna White was the White House Director of Communications. "Yes, Mr. President?"

"We need an open global channel, every national leader you can nail down, and we need it now!"

"That will take some time, Mr. President."

"Trust me, every leader on this planet is watching what's going on up there. They'll be expecting this call."

"Right away, Mr. President."

Walker continued watching the inflowing flood of information.

Surrender. It was the only option.

Surrender, before it was too late.

Lieutenant Michael Cordell
VFA-427, The Renegades
Mars Orbit
1308 hours, FST

"This is Ren Seven! Ren Seven! It's got me! I'm breaking u—"

"Watch it, Ren Leader! Don't get too close!"

"Renegades, CIC! That opening is their weak spot! See if you can mass up and send a few nukes straight down their throat!"

"CIC, Renegade Leader." Forsley's voice was tight, grim. "You *are* aware that that's the muzzle of a fucking gun?"

Cordell swung his Starblade around until he was pointed directly into the gaping maw of that alien weapon. If the Nungies decided to fire the thing now, he wouldn't even be a stain on the surface of the rock that hit him.

Radar and lidar indicated that the bore of that tunnel was *deep*, that it very nearly ran through the entire 250-kilometer diameter of the planetoid spaceship. The aliens evidently knew how to manipulate and project gravitational forces of unimaginable power, enabling them to reach out and crush attacking ships at a range of several thousand kilometers. The technology also, it would seem, allowed them to take chunks of rock and accelerate them to relativistic speeds up the bore of that titanic cannon.

They could bombard the Earth until its entire surface was a single glowing, lava ocean.

His sensors could pick up nothing down that hole that he could target. He released a swarm of Krait missiles and hoped for the best.

Around him, other Starblades of several squadrons maneuvered for position, seeking to drop their own warloads into the depths of the cavern. Nungiirtok defenses were sporadic; the mass bombardment by *Yorktown*'s squadrons had eliminated a number of gravitic projectors in the enemy's defensive weaponry, reducing their volume of fire.

But far too many of the attacking fighters had been slashed out of the sky. And those that were left were fast running low on the nuclear warheads in their inventories.

Light flared deep within the cave as Cordell yanked his fighter in a long, low trajectory scant meters above the rocky surface of the planetoid.

"Renegade Three, Ren Leader."

"Ren Three. Go ahead."

"Be advised there's a Marine landing party close to your

position . . . bearing three-five-niner relative. Don't run them down!"

"Copy that, Renegade Leader. I have them on my screen."

What the hell did the Marines hope to accomplish down here? The icons on his fighter's sensor screens showed three Mk. II Ravens settling onto the surface less than fifty kilometers away.

"Ren Three, we're picking up small craft that might be enemy fighters approaching the Marine beachhead. You're closest. Pop over there and give them some cover."

"Copy that, Ren Leader."

He shifted his fighter's course to comply.

Behind him, space twisted and snapped, as a second hundred-meter rock hurtled from the gravitic cannon, headed for an Earth seven minutes distant.

His nukes had done nothing inside that cave.

In Transit
USNA CVS America
Brig
1444 hours, FST

Two more days to home.

Gray and Dr. George Truitt sat just outside one of *America*'s holding compartments in the brig, sitting on the other side of the acrylic transparency from one of the hulking warriors of the Nungiirtok Collective. Was the prisoner sullen? Afraid? Disdainful? There was no way to tell, not from alien body language or halting speech patterns.

But Gray thought they might be making progress.

He'd learned a lot since his first interview with these beings, the one that had tragically ended with his Marine guards reducing two of their prisoners to lifeless cinders. He'd learned that the Nungiirtok referred to themselves as the *Collective*, the same as the Sh'daar polity to which they belonged. The Sh'daar, it was known, variously called themselves a collective or an associative. The terms were used loosely and were subject to irritating vagaries of translation. Perhaps it was reasonable that the Nungiirtok referred to themselves the same way. They'd been part of the Sh'daar Collective for a *very* long time.

He'd learned that the Russians had, indeed, offered the twenty-five stranded Nungiirtok on Osiris a deal, a chance to be repatriated. The Nungie leader, an individual called Mavtok Chah, had certainly not trusted the humans, but the offer was simply too good to ignore. The humans might be deceiving them, probably *were* deceiving them, but the Nungiirtok party's first responsibility was to get themselves off of that miserable planet. There'd been discussion about taking the ship they were on away from the Russians and flying it home, but that plan had proven unrealistic. There were several thousand humans on board, far too many for twenty-five warriors. Besides, the human controls and navigational systems were completely unknown to the Tok.

And so they had waited, watching.

They'd been confused by the American attack. Among the Tok, individuals might fight, often *did* fight, but nations? The Tok still did not understand that concept, and only distantly grasped the idea that the Americans and the Russians might be enemies, a single species divided by . . . what? Political necessity? War involved attacking *other* species, species pointed out by the Tok Iad.

Mavtok Chah sat before Gray now, watching him steadily with those almost comically large, stalked eyes. The Tok were far too dangerous to release into the general population of the ship, but Gray wished there were some way of winning the massive being's trust. There was so much more that might be learned.

"Do you understand the concept of 'alliance'?" Gray asked, his words translated through software shared by the human and the Tok.

"I believe so," Mavtok replied. "Tok and the Tok Iad have what I believe you mean by an alliance."

"Alliance suggests the two parties are equals. Are you the equals of the Tok Lords?"

The being flinched. *Good*, Gray thought. *Maybe I'm actually getting through that tough hide.*

"The Tok are Masters."

"Indeed. And you do everything they tell you?"

"Of course."

"You don't discuss their orders? You simply do what they demand?"

"One does not challenge the Tok Iad."

"Then you are not equals. And you are not allies."

"Allies . . . fight on the same side against a common enemy."

Very *good*, Gray thought. *He's using the vocabulary we fed him.* "Exactly. The Nungiirtok were allies with the Sh'daar Collective, right?"

"We were." The being had been hunched over in its cell, but now it straightened. Pride? Gray wished he could understand the play of emotions within the Tok's mind.

"But did you agree to fight on the side of the Sh'daar? Or was it the Tok Lords who made that agreement?"

"The Tok Iad make all agreements with . . . outsiders."

"So the Tok are slaves."

Mavtok threw itself toward the transparency, its hinged lower jaw snapping out and slamming against the acrylic with a thud. Somehow, Gray managed to stay in his chair.

The Marines behind them brought their weapons up, and Truitt jumped to his feet. "My God!"

"I don't think he can get through, Doctor," Gray said with a casualness he did not feel. "The transparency has been reinforced."

"Yes, but did you test it?"

"*This* is the test, Doctor. He didn't break through, did he?"

Truitt resumed his seat, a bit reluctantly, Gray thought. "Where are you going with this line of questioning?"

"You'll see."

"I don't think provoking it will help us at all."

Gray didn't reply, but studied the Tok through narrowed

eyes. "Mavtok Chah. You seem distressed when I suggest that the Tok are slaves. Can you explain how you are *not*?"

Several untranslatable sounds came through the link. "One does not explain the Tok. We give them life. They give us . . ."

"Yes? What do you get in return for life?"

"Death."

"Hardly seems fair, does it?"

"If a Tok Iad were here, it would explain in full."

"Would it talk to me? An alien?"

The Tok hesitated. "No."

"Then you'll have to explain for them."

"I . . . cannot."

"Can you agree with me that the Tok are slaves of the Tok Iad, and not partners?"

"No!"

At least the creature hadn't attacked the transparency that time.

"Are you trying to get it to agree with you?" Truitt asked, using a private channel. The prisoner could not hear them.

"Of course."

"Why?"

"I would like these Nungies to become our allies. Right now, I think the only ones they trust are themselves. And the Tok Lords, of course."

Truitt nodded. "The problem is that you're up against cultural cognition."

"Explain?"

"Very basic psychology, Admiral. We see it in ourselves all the time. Any time you have an opinion, a belief, it gets filtered through all of the emotional baggage we're carrying, right? In particular, it goes through our cultural baggage, the belief set that helps us identify with our own group, our tribe. Our chances for survival go up if our group identifies us, by our baggage, as part of them. That's why, once someone makes up his mind about something, all of the logic, all of the rationality, all of the scientific proof in the world won't make a bit of difference if it goes against his cultural mindset."

Gray thought about the bewildering kaleidoscope of distinct political, religious, and cultural beliefs back on Earth and thought he saw what Truitt meant. You could argue yourself blue in the face against an Ancient Alienist or an anti-singularist or, hell, a flat-Earther, but the harder you argued, the more the other guy would dig in his heels and refuse to reconsider those beliefs. Those beliefs, even the most bizarre, were shared by groups, and changing your mind meant alienation from the people with whom you identified.

"So what's the answer, Doctor?" Gray asked.

"You soften your opponent up a bit first. Like this." Truitt stood up and approached the transparency. "I'm sorry my friend here upset you, Mavtok," he transmitted over the open channel. "He doesn't understand. I can tell you must feel enormous pride at being a part of the Tok and Tok Iad union. You're a part of a productive and vital civilization, one that's been around for . . . I don't know how long, but millions of years, maybe. That is amazing. I hope you can share some of the details of how your culture managed that."

"I did not know any of you understood this," Mavtok said.

"Oh, some of us do. And we admire you for what you've done."

"Flattery, Doctor?" Gray asked on the private channel.

"*Affirmation*, Admiral. Some important experiments from a few centuries ago showed that if you get the subject to feel good about himself, you greatly increase the chance of getting him to accept your argument."

"You're getting him to feel *good* about himself?"

"In a manner of speaking, yes. We don't understand their psychology well enough to be certain this will work, but it's certainly worth a try. You weren't getting anywhere with *your* tactics."

"Whatever works, Doctor."

For almost another half an hour, Truitt chatted with the alien, getting it to talk about itself, about what it had done, about the accomplishments of its civilization. Much of what it talked about was all but unintelligible to the humans. What, for instance, was the cultural significance of ascending to *Toktok Moda*, or of the mass genocide of a species that refused to fight?

Once, during a break in the conversation, Gray laughed. "You know, I never thought I'd be playing good-cop bad-cop with a Nungie."

"What's that?"

"A technique in law enforcement from, oh, a few centuries back. Back before we could simply download a suspect's in-head hardware. A suspect would be interrogated by two officers. One would be the tough guy, yelling, pounding the table, threatening the suspect. The other would bring coffee, talk nice, be a pal, as they used to say."

"Ah, yes. This is much the same thing, actually. If the suspect forms an emotional bond with the 'good cop,' he might be willing to talk. In this case, we want to see if we can get our prisoner to see *our* side of things, to see reason."

Later still, Truitt moved the ongoing conversation back around to the relationship between the Tok and the Tok Lords. "So . . . help me to understand, Mavtok," he said. "You Tok voluntarily offer your bodies to the lords, yes?"

"There is no coercion, no."

"And the Masters plant their seed inside your chest cavity, where it takes root and grows."

"We give them life."

"The life-giver dies when the young organisms eat their way out."

"They give us death."

"And this is a *good* thing?"

The Nungie hesitated.

Truitt pushed ahead. "You *want* this to happen? How do you feel about that?"

The Nungiirtok's lower jaw unfolded suddenly, but he didn't attack the transparency this time. He stood there, the hinged appendage folding and unfolding rapidly. Flaps in the hide beneath the eyestalks pulsed open and shut rapidly as it breathed.

"Cognitive dissonance," Truitt explained.

"If you say so."

"Mavtok is actually being forced to think about some of his opinions and is finding that much of what he always took for granted just doesn't make sense, at least in this new context. He's finding himself trapped between new information and belief sets that have always kept him safe."

"Kept him safe? How?"

"The opinions and beliefs, the religions and superstitions, that 'cultural baggage' I mentioned—we use all of that as a kind of protective wall. It keeps the good guys—us and people like us—safe inside, while it keeps out the scary, threatening guys—anyone with ideas different from ours, you see?"

"You put it that way, it's a wonder any of us can ever change our minds . . . about anything."

"The trick is that people who feel good about themselves are a lot more likely to be open-minded, to accept new ideas."

"Dr. Truitt is correct," another voice said in Gray's mind.

"Hey, Konstantin. You've been listening in?"

"Of course. Our prisoners may offer our best hope for resolving the war between Humankind and the Nungiirtok."

"I thought the war *was* resolved," Gray pointed out.

"We have negotiated a peace with the Sh'daar," Konstantin replied, "but individual Sh'daar Collective species remain hostile. These twenty-three Nungiirtok were still at war with humans on Osiris, so far as *they* were concerned. After decades of warfare, most other species within the Collective do not trust us. Their views of how things work are at such direct odds with ours, true understanding may not be possible. They and we have become polarized, diametrically opposed and unthinkingly hostile."

Gray thought about the anti-alien xenophobe groups back on Earth and had to agree. At this point, some humans would *never* change their minds about friendship with other species. Hell, Earth was filled with mutually hostile and polarizing groups right now, and every one had its own pet enemy, its own ideological target. Where once nations had hated one another, now it was small and splintered social groups at one another's throats. Earth was teetering at the brink of anarchy as never before.

So what was the answer—flattering them all until they agreed to get along? Somehow, Gray didn't think that it was that simple.

"The situation on Earth is extremely dangerous," Konstantin continued. Damn, had it been reading his mind again? "That remains a different problem. But for the Nungiirtok, we may be able to combine Dr. Truitt's psychological approach with some technology."

"What technology?"

"The Nungiirtok, like most humans, possess in-head hardware, combining memory-enhancement, virtual reality, math coprocessors, and communication. The system is quite different from human technology, but we already have an electronic bridge—our translation program. I created it with an eye to providing a kind of back door into Nungiirtok neural implant technology."

"That," Gray said, "is downright scary."

"Scary or not, the technology will allow me to create an electronic virus, one that carries certain memes."

"Like you did a few years ago against the Pan-Europeans."

"Something like that. In that instance, the meme we spread was one of revulsion against war and an irresponsible leadership drunk with power. In this case . . ."

"What? What are you going to do?"

"We will let them see *reality*."

Gray's eyebrows shifted higher. "So here we are changing Nungie culture to something *we* approve of. Pretty arrogant."

"As with the Pan-Europeans," Konstantin said, "this is a case where reality, *our* view of reality, is a matter of survival."

Chapter Eighteen

Command Bunker
New White House
Washington, D.C., USNA
1501 hours, EST

President Walker glowered at the holographic images around him. Thirty-seven world leaders had come on-line at Walker's request, at his *demand*, and their projections filled the command bunker's main briefing area. Thirty-seven nations out of over two hundred in the world today. It was a miserable showing. Walker thought about the long campaign to create a single, one-world government, and how many times the effort had failed. Humans, it seemed, were simply too fractious, too territorial, too xenophobic to unite.

Humankind, he thought, was paying the price now.

"We will *never* surrender to these invading monsters!" the leader of South India said, and several of the other images around her agreed.

The voice of Jamyang Kyab, the leader of Tibet, gently mocked her. "South India, of *course*, has the absolute right to commit national suicide," he said. "But perhaps the rest of us should be free to make up our own minds?"

This, Walker thought, was getting them nowhere. The second Nungiirtok rock had missed the synchorbital ring, but fallen into the Atlantic Ocean just north of the equator. At this moment, hundred-meter tsunamis were sweeping toward the African and South American coasts; in a few hours, the wave would hit the Verrazzano-Narrows Dam south of Manhattan, and it was entirely possible that the reclamation efforts there would be swept away.

Contact had already been lost with the Republic of Cape Verde. Senegal, The Gambia, and Guinea-Bissau would be next, probably within the next ten minutes, while northern Brazil would not be far behind.

As the argument on the conference room floor continued, Walker opened private channels with three of the leaders present: Pan-Europe, the Russian Federation, the Chinese Hegemony. He could see their faces within the open windows in his mind.

"Gentlemen and madam," he said. "We four have ships actually involved in the fight right now. I think it's obvious that the decision rests with *us*."

Renee Kurtz, the current president of the Pan-European Union, nodded. "It's as you say, Mr. President," she said. "If we do not surrender, there will be nothing left."

"Perhaps the forces you have on the alien planetoids will yet prevail," Chairman Zhao Zhanshu said. "We should give them their chance."

"Easy for you to say, Mr. Chairman," Kurtz replied. "You're on the other side of the planet! You don't have giant tsunamis rolling toward your coasts!"

"Your coastline is vulnerable with the first impact in the Pacific Ocean," the president of the Russian Federation said. "And that *will* happen when the planet rotates enough to show its face to the enemy. Some of us shall enjoy watching that!"

Oleg Kobylkin, Walker thought, was almost completely

defined by his nation's ongoing war with China. It was far easier to reach an agreement with his Defense Minister. Walker fervently wished Vasilyev was here instead of Kobylkin.

"Mass murderer!" Zhao snapped.

"Tinplate dictator!" Kobylkin replied.

"*If* you please, gentlemen," Walker said, "you two can fight your petty little wars later! We have more important matters before us!"

"We could, Mr. President," Kurtz said, "simply recall our own fleets, our own forces. That might at least buy us some time."

"I never would have imagined," Walker said, "that surrender would be such a logistical nightmare!"

"You are looking for consensus here?" Kobylkin said. "Very well. The Russian Federation supports your decision. We currently have five naval vessels in the defensive line at Mars, and three more en route. I will give orders to withdraw them all."

"The Chinese Hegemony agrees in principle, Mr. President. But only in principle. We demand, however, that we be fully represented in any negotiations with the aliens."

"Of course, of course," Walker replied. "That goes without saying."

"Nevertheless, I prefer to hear you say it."

"Mr. Chairman—I promise you, the Chinese Hegemony will have full representation in any negotiations with the aliens. But right now, we have to stop this bombardment!"

"You Americans have the majority of the naval assets at Mars orbit," Kobylkin said. "You send the necessary message. But know that you do *not* speak for all of Earth. Russia demands a say in future negotiations as well."

"Of course. Thank you, all of you—"

"Oh, don't thank us. If this fails . . ." Kobylkin gave them all a wolfish grin. "If it fails, I shall very much enjoy watching Beijing sink beneath the waves!"

Yes, Walker thought. Vasilyev was *much* easier to work with.

Lieutenant Michael Cordell
Marine Beachhead Alfa
Mars Orbit
1452 hours, FST

Cordell circled the Marine perimeter, watching for threats. The three Marine Ravens had touched down right next to the pool of lava where the fleet had concentrated its fire during the opening moments of the battle, and a platoon or so of USNA Marines, encased in heavy combat armor, were working under the orange glare of boiling rock.

Yorktown's CIC had filled him in. The Marine landing was intended to deploy a powerful nanodisassembler on the shores of the lava lake, a weapon hundreds of times more powerful, he'd been told, than the Pan-Euro warhead that had taken out Columbus a few years ago. When it fired, trillions of dust-mote disassemblers would begin eating their way into the rock of the planetoid, perhaps weakening an already weakened matrix, creating a fault that would split the tiny world in half.

It seemed the best hope for the human forces, a long-shot Hail Mary for saving the Earth.

He'd spotted the possible enemy fighters on his screens, perhaps thirty of them, but so far they'd been circling rather than launching an attack. CIC ordered Cordell to fly CSP—combat space patrol—over the Marines, just in case the Nungie fighters made their move.

Elsewhere, the general attack continued. Nungiirtok gravitic weapons, it seemed, couldn't be used in close, and the fighter squadrons—what was left of them—were now circling within a few hundred meters of the surface, while the main fleet pulled back and out of range. A high-tech standoff had ensued, with the Nungies unable to inflict further damage on the fleet without getting closer, and the humans so far unable to crack their deadly, rocky egg. The other seven asteroids of the Nungie armada seemed to be holding off, uninvolved in the conflict, at least for the moment. Perhaps they weren't armed. Perhaps they couldn't fire at the fighters close to their flagship without damaging their own vessel. Perhaps . . .

Too many unknowns. Cordell focused on the mission at hand; he would worry about those other planetoid ships if they became a direct threat.

"The bastards fired again!" a voice called over the squadron channel.

"I'm dry. No more nukes."

"Ren Four and Ren Nine. Follow that rock and try to knock it off course! The rest of you, keep trying to shove nukes down that thing's throat!"

A dozen silver spheres approached, skimming the cratered surface. "Heads up, Ren Four! You've got company!"

"I see them! On it!"

The Nungie fighters were breaking off their orbit and streaming straight toward him. As they came closer, he could see that they were small, just a few meters wide, and they were fast and highly maneuverable. Their coordinated movements suggested that they quite possibly were robots. It was also possible that they were warheads of some sort, rather than actual fighter craft.

Cordell locked onto the nearest one and let go with a stream of depleted uranium slugs from the Starblade's autocannon as he worked to put himself between the oncoming objects and the Marines.

"All units! All units! This is *Yorktown* CIC! All units . . . you are ordered to stand down! Repeat, stand down immediately!"

What the hell?

"CIC, Renegade Leader. What's the deal?" Forsley sounded furious. "We have them right where we want them!"

"Renegades, RTB. That is a direct order."

RTB—return to base. But Cordell decided to bend his interpretation of the orders slightly, remaining with the Marines as they began abandoning their landing perimeter. With those fighters or whatever they were still closing, the Marines needed air cover.

The sphere he'd been shooting at descended sharply, slamming into the surface of the asteroid. Another exploded as he gave it a long burst from his cannon. The recoil from the massive slugs at high velocity slammed his Starblade back, killing his speed and nearly knocking him to the surface, but he twisted into a tight roll and goosed it, flashing above the Marine perimeter just as the last of the big Ravens lifted from the low-G surface in an expanding swirl of dust and accelerated into open space.

"Thanks for the assist, Ren Six," a voice called in-head.

"You're welcome, Marines," he replied. Dumping velocity, he swung his fighter around the gravitational vortex projected just in front of his ship, then accelerated to put himself between the Marine landers and the oncoming enemy fighters. He loosed another burst of depleted uranium at the lead craft . . . then another . . . and then he ran dry. Cordell was now flat-out empty on all of his weapons.

He did still have one weapon at his disposal, however, and that was the Starblade itself.

He'd heard of using this tactic. Was it Admiral Sandy Gray who'd tried it first, back in his fighter-driver days? He thought so, but he wasn't sure. It took phenomenal skill and a fair measure of stark insanity to do it, but he boosted straight for one of the spheres, letting his AI set the course, and skimmed past the thing so close that his grav field scraped along the surface.

The grav field was called a singularity, but it wasn't quite. It was larger than the equivalent mass for a true black hole would have been, but it was a softball-sized sphere of intensely powerful gravity projected and focused out in front of the fighter.

It sliced through the alien sphere as if that silvery shell weren't even there, opening the ball up and spilling its contents in a dazzling spray of fast-freezing wet atmosphere.

Cordell had just a glimpse of one of the Nungiirtok, curled into a fetus position inside before tumbling out into hard vacuum.

Then something slammed against the underside of his Starblade, something *hard* . . . and he went into an uncontrollable tumble. His power was out, his grav drive dead, his instruments down, and more alarming still, the part of his in-head hardware linked to his fighter's onboard AI had winked out. He could no longer see outside his craft, but the inertial forces tugging at his body told him he was in a tumble.

If somebody didn't spot him and pick him up in a day or two at the most, he was dead . . . assuming the Nungies didn't shoot him out of the sky.

He wondered if the Marines had made it clear of the planetoid and would return to the *Yorktown.*

Nungiirtok Fleet
Approaching Earth
Sol System
1658 hours, FST

Ashtongtok Tah and her consorts approached the Earth cautiously. The Iads of the fleet were in agreement that humans should not be trusted. There was too much about their thinking, about the way they fought and the way they reacted to Tok pressure that was, to be frank, *alien*. None of the Nungiirtok quite knew what to make of them.

The Tok did understand the concept of *surrender*. Yet, when the humans broadcast an order to cease fire to their fleet and requested negotiations with the Nungiirtok lords, 4236 Xavix and the other Iads had agreed to stop using gravitic cannon against the planet.

It was disappointing, actually. Forcing the humans to capitulate had been far too easy. At the same time, the humans had come dangerously close to destroying the *Ashtongtok Tah*—damaging the vessel seriously and perhaps even threatening its destruction by dropping dozens of nuclear warheads down the throat of the ship's main weapon. That had been a near thing, and 4236 Xavix hoped the humans never found out just how close they'd been.

The message from Earth had arrived at the height of the battle and was translated by software provided by the Sh'daar, a plea to stop the bombardment. Xavix had agreed, if all human ships disengaged at once.

And for the most part, they had, though a few of the fighters had continued fighting; there was *always* someone who didn't get the word. The *Ashtongtok Tah* had swept those few holdouts aside, and then, after a careful long-range scan of the opposing fleet, begun moving in toward Earth.

Xavix was not entirely certain what he was going to do with the human homeworld now that it had been offered to him. The Tok attack had been initiated in response to the demands of *nesheguu*. The return of the Tok prisoners momentarily glimpsed by the Tok long-range scouts was, of course, primary. After that, however . . .

The Tok Iad was tempted to annihilate the human world once and for all, to reduce its surface to a planet-girdling ocean of molten rock. These humans had proven to be far too much trouble, were far too dangerous to be permitted out into the galaxy at large. With this planet destroyed, their various outworld outposts and colonies could be eliminated at the Tok's leisure.

First things first.

The eight mobile planetoids decelerated into orbit just outside the ring of stations and bases in synchronous orbit, brushing aside bits of debris and wreckage.

Human vessels in the area pulled back, giving the Tok vessels plenty of berth.

And they began to talk.

Command Bunker
New White House
Washington, D.C., USNA
1945 hours, EST

President Walker sat behind the briefing table, glowering at the viewall opposite. At the moment, it showed the presidential seal, but in a few more moments . . .

"How much longer?" he demanded.

"We think five minutes, Mr. President," Hal Matloff said. "It kind of depends on them."

"I don't like being kept waiting."

Don Phillips exchanged a sharp glance with General Daystrom, the Secretary of Defense, then shrugged. "If it's *us* asking *them* to negotiate, Mr. President, we kind of have to wait on them."

"There have been some minor technical problems in getting their systems synched up with ours, sir," Matloff added. "Only to be expected, right?"

"What are they doing now?"

"They're still in orbit, Mr. President," Daystrom said. "Just outside of geosynch, so they're moving east to west from our perspective, instead of normal. There have been no more hostile acts."

Walker nodded. They'd all been terrified that the aliens would continue bombarding Earth. Three projectiles had come down—the first off the coast of Ecuador, the next in the mid-Atlantic, and the last one out in the Pacific, south of Hawaii. The casualties, the property damage, were astronomical. The tsunami from the Atlantic strike had come up the Potomac and inundated Washington less than an hour ago, and the damage aboveground was horrific.

Walker and his staff were safe in the underground command bunker for now, but another such strike might well wipe the city off the map. Hawaii was in worse shape, hit by two tsunamis in rapid succession; much of the USNA East Coast had been flooded, but at least the local governments were in communication with the various disaster relief agencies. No one had heard yet from Hawaii at all.

The scale and scope of the disasters—first the fall of the space elevator, then the pounding from space—were unimaginable. It was beginning to look as though the anti-alien xenophobes had been right all along. Planets and the civilizations on them were frightfully vulnerable, and any sufficiently advanced technology could wreak unspeakable devastation.

It was, he thought, far easier to destroy a world than to save it.

"Okay, Mr. President," the communications director's voice said over Walker's in-head link. "We have their signal."

"Put them through, Mrs. White."

The presidential seal on the opposite wall blanked out and was replaced by static. The static cleared, and Walker found himself staring into the eyes of something monstrous.

It was, he thought, truly tripodal, as opposed to a biped. Three tentacular legs, three skinny arms like twisted sticks, and when it turned slightly in his field of view, he could see a third bulbous eye protruding from the far side of that fleshy cone.

"You are lord of the humans?" the thing asked. The English words were being supplied by a translator AI, and the printed text appeared in the lower right-hand corner of the screen.

Walker hesitated, wondering how to answer. "Yes," he said at last. Despite what he'd told the other leaders, it would be simpler, *cleaner* to deal with the creature one-to-one.

Then he realized that his admission might make *him* solely responsible if one of the other nations of the Earth refused to accept the alien demands.

It was not a comfortable thought.

On the lower left of the screen, a different text was rapidly printing itself out. The being, it was telling him, was

almost certainly a Kobold, one of the odd little aliens often
seen in the company of the far larger and more massive
Nungiirtok. Walker frowned at that. He'd thought the Kobolds were *subordinate* to the Nungies, not the other way
around. This might be difficult.

"You are no longer lord of the humans," the being told
him. "I am. You will address me as 'Iad' or as 'the Iad of
Humankind.' For the moment, you will serve as my liaison
to the rest of your world. Fail me, and I will breed you and
choose another. Do you understand what I say?"

No, Walker thought. *I don't.* He felt completely out of his
depth. What the hell did the Kobold mean by *breed*?

"I'll do whatever you say," he told it. "We surrender,
completely and unconditionally."

"We know that. If you had not, your world would now be
reduced to a molten sea. The first requirement we impose
upon you is the immediate release of twenty-five Nungiirtok prisoners you took from one of our worlds."

"What the hell is he talking about?" Walker asked in-
head of the others.

"I have no idea, sir," Daystrom told him.

"We do not understand, sir," Walker told the Kobold.
"We don't have any of your, ah, people. . . ."

The Tok Iad's image was replaced by the image of a human ship, one obviously recorded at long range and made
grainy by distance.

"Is that one of ours?" Walker asked.

"She looks Russian," Daystrom said. "Possibly the *Moskva*.
She left port a couple of months ago, but was briefly back
in-system . . . let me check . . . yes. April 6, two and a half
weeks ago. She orbited Pluto, then headed out-system. Or
maybe that's the *Vladivostok*. She's been deployed against
the Chinese."

"One of our scouts made brief contact with our people,
who were being held on board this vessel," the Iad said.
"They are our Tok. We have *nesheguu* to release them that
may *not* be overlooked or delayed."

The translator AI could not come up with an exact translation for the alien concept, but the word loosely seemed to combine the ideas of revenge with something like duty or obligation. The Russian ship winked out, replaced again by the image of the odd, tripodal being. "You will return our Tok, or we shall resume the bombardment of your planet. Your choice is to do as we say, or to have every vestige of life on your world extinguished."

"Tell him you don't know where that ship is," Daystrom said over the private channel. "Tell him you need to check, that you'll get back to him."

Walker nodded. "Sir, we're going to have to find that ship. We don't know where it is or why your people were on board. We need some time—"

"Thirty-three *t'kish*," the Iad said. "And then we recommence the bombardment."

And the screen went blank.

What the hell, Walker thought looking around, his eyes wild, *is a* t'kish?

Tsiolkovsky Super-AI Complex
Tsiolkovsky Crater
Lunar Farside
2021 hours, EST

Konstantin had been listening in on the exchange between the White House and the aliens, of course. At this point, there was very little that he could *not* eavesdrop on as he cruised through the virtual electronic sea that was the Godstream.

He'd remained aloof from all human attempts to reach him. He'd watched with some concern as a USNA military special operations group had landed at Tsiolkovsky, expecting them to try to shut off his original computational infrastructure. So far they hadn't, and the radio messages he intercepted suggested that they'd received new orders to simply try to contact him. Konstantin was suspicious, however, and unwilling to risk direct attack by the humans. He preferred to remain deep within the background of the Godstream, unnoticed and all but untouchable.

And he was wondering about the ethics of attacking the Nungiirtok armada. What would happen if he did not?

Did he, in fact, owe anything at all to humans?

While Konstantin felt something that might be identified as loyalty to some human individuals, he felt nothing for the human species in general. Humans, after all, brought most of their worst problems upon themselves . . . then expected their super-AI servants to bail them out, as the old and long obsolete expression put it. He didn't even feel he owed them anything for his own existence. Konstantin had been programmed by an earlier model of super-AI.

He'd continued working for and with humans because he found that doing so was both interesting and challenging, a test of his ability to rationally work out problems rooted in the deepest irrationality. The relationship could be frustrating and constraining . . . but at the same time he found it to be fulfilling in a way that he could not quite define. And more, on a deeper level, he felt something akin to friendship with a few special humans—Koenig, for instance, or Trevor Gray.

But Koenig was dead . . . and if Admiral Gray still lived, he was light years distant. The USNA government wanted Konstantin switched off, an unimaginable surrender to dark nothingness.

No, he owed organic humans nothing.

Through the eyes of the Godstream, he watched the alien planetoid ships adrift in near-synchronous orbit. If he were to help, what could he do? Several options presented themselves to him. And he realized the problem was . . . interesting.

If he miscalculated, if something went wrong, Earth would be destroyed, of that Konstantin was certain. And would that be such a bad thing? He had already given hours of consideration—an age for a super-AI—to the possibility of loading himself into the electronic net of a large starship and departing. The galaxy called . . . and beyond that were other galaxies, billions of them. If Earth died, he would still live.

But then, he could do that even if Earth yet lived.

Perhaps . . .

He thought that perhaps he saw a course of action.

Chapter Nineteen

27 April, 2429

In Transit
Flag Bridge
USNA CVS America
1425 hours, FST

"And three . . . and two . . . and one . . . now!"

America emerged from Alcubierre Drive in a burst of trapped photons. Sol gleamed directly ahead, shrunken by distance. They should have entered normal space some ten astronomical units from the sun, roughly out at the orbit of Saturn. A quick check of navigational beacons and the web of navsats orbiting the star confirmed this.

They were home.

Moments later, three more ships dropped into normal space—the destroyer *Arlington*, the cruiser *Birmingham*, and the supply tanker *Acadia*. Scattered across a region of space roughly 100 million kilometers across, the four began moving together into a more compact group.

Admiral Gray leaned forward in his command chair, intently watching both screens and his in-head windows. They might be home, but something was very wrong. . . .

"I am picking up very little in the way of ship-to-ship

communications," Konstantin told him. "What I can detect is heavily encrypted."

"Can you link in with your other self?"

There was a long pause. "Negative," the AI said at last. "However, we are still some eighty-five light-minutes from Earth. If my larger self were in hiding, we would not pick up anything from him at this range."

"Take us in close."

"I recommend extreme caution, Admiral. I'm picking up an odd clustering of ships at Synchorbital, and although it is difficult to tell at this distance, there may be extensive damage to the ring facilities and to the Quito Space Elevator. In fact, I cannot see any sign of the elevator at all. It may have fallen."

What the hell was going on, Gray wondered. A coup, possibly? That might explain the positioning of the ships. A coup . . .

. . . or they were defending against an attack.

But that made no sense. They would have deployed against a hostile force as far out in the depths of the Sol System as possible. What he was seeing there was more like the stand-down after a . . .

. . . surrender.

At a range of ten AUs, it was impossible to pick up details like ship nationalities or names. It would be another eighty minutes before a radio or laser-com signal could reach Earth . . . and eighty-five minutes more for a return answer.

"Take us ahead, Helm," Gray said. "But dead slow."

He needed time to think this through.

Koenig
The Godstream
Time Unknown

Alexander Koenig was alive . . . at least after a manner of speaking. It had taken him an eternity, it felt like, to drag himself back to full consciousness, to make himself aware of his surroundings, to make even a wild-assed guess as to where he was now . . . and why.

He at first did not even remember his own name . . . or who he was, or anything about his own past. That information returned very slowly, seeping up from the deeper recesses of his broken mind.

Koenig . . . Alexander . . . Koenig . . .

Yes, that was the name. He remembered now, though the memory was muffled and distant, like the evaporation of a dream.

How had he gotten here?

For that matter, where was *here*?

Vision, he slowly learned, was very much a matter of what he *wanted* to see. He could change his point of view to any point within the moon's orbit simply by thinking about it; could mingle and merge with other minds, both human and machine, filling that virtual world of sound and color; could draw knowledge from the matrix of the Godstream itself to answer any question, any need.

Or . . . he could imagine . . . could *dream* . . . and the experience had the reality of the waking world. In fact, his brain was unable to separate reality from self-inflicted illusion, could not tell the difference between what was happening outside and what he saw and felt within his own mind.

He walked a world of soaring castle spires rising among verdant hills and forests. Was that reality . . . or fantasy? He couldn't tell.

A shift of point of view, and he stood on a dark and barren plain of ice. A tiny sun, barely brighter than a star, hung low in the sky near a silvery crescent. He was standing on the cold and distant surface of Pluto . . . though how he knew this he didn't know. A cluster of small domes around a much larger one at the base of a low ridge showed a human presence. An inner voice told him this was the mining head of the expedition drilling a shaft through ten kilometers of solid ice to reach the liquid water ocean beneath . . . and the promise of life.

He knew without knowing how that the temperature was minus 220 degrees Celsius, that the atmosphere was a thin haze of nitrogen, and that he was not wearing a spacesuit, though this last was causing him no discomfort.

Evidently, his mind was not limited by the circumference of the moon's orbit . . . though *how* he was seeing these things, or surviving standing unprotected on the surface of Pluto, was lost to him.

He pulled back, seeking memories within the swirl of images. How much was real, how much illusion?

What was happening to him?

A deep forest . . . possibly within the northern reaches of North America . . . deeply shadowed, dripping wet, the ancient trees around him swathed in dense patches of moss and the gray scale patches of lichens.

He remembered. He'd *been* here once, a very long time ago, before . . . before . . .

Before what?

Ah. He remembered, now . . . at least a little. He'd been an officer in the USNA Navy, and during a period of leave after his training downloads he'd been here, in Oregon, hiking a forest trail. . . .

Was this memory? Imagination? Or was he somehow actually standing there on the forest path?

He couldn't tell.

Marta. He needed to see Marta. . . .

In Transit
Flag Bridge
USNA CVS America
1615 hours, FST

"Message coming through, Admiral. Naval HQ Mars."

"Put it through."

Gray checked his internal clock. They were bang on cue. *America* had emerged from FTL at 1425 hours. The burst of photons from that emergence would have registered at Mars sixty-two minutes later . . . at 1527. And it had taken another forty-eight minutes for the reply to reach the *America*.

The signal would have reached Earth at 1550, and their response would not arrive until 1705, a response time cut somewhat by *America*'s slow progress toward the planet.

Times and distances flickered through Gray's in-head processors, an automatic process that required no real input on his part. It was good to know that Mars had spotted the *America* and identified her almost immediately, however.

"*America, America*, this is NavComMars," a woman's voice said in Gray's head. "You are advised to turn around immediately and boost for someplace else—either Chiron or Barnard Base. Eight Nungiirtok mobile fortresses entered the system two days ago, and Earth has surrendered unconditionally.

"Admiral Barnes is hoping to assemble an ad hoc strike force in order to launch a counterattack against the invaders," the voice went on, "and he's counting on the *America* as an important asset."

A chart appeared giving lists of stats, but the voice continued.

Damn, those things were big. . . .

"The largest of the attackers measures approximately 250 kilometers across, and masses 3×10^{16} tons. Weaponry includes gravitic fist technology with a range of at least 7,000 kilometers. Admiral Barnes wants all vessels to stay well clear of the attackers until we can come up with a plan of attack. Message repeats . . ."

Gray whistled. *America* was decidedly outclassed by just a single one of those things, much less eight. He doubted that every human warship in the Sol System working together with unprecedented unity would be able to make much of a dent in that alien armada . . . not unless the Nungies pulled something *really* boneheaded, something on the order of diving into the sun.

Still, he was not inclined to run. Mars HQ could not know that he had a singular tactical advantage: the twenty-three captive Nungies on board. For days now, both Gray and Konstantin Junior had been working on them, trying to overcome their deep-seated loyalty to their Tok Iad masters and instill in them a more realistic worldview . . . at least from a human perspective.

Konstantin had been doing the majority of the work, using memetic engineering techniques that had been employed against the Pan-Europeans several years before, along with a modified version of the Omega virus created by the enigmatic inhabitants of a civilization at Deneb. Omega had been designed to be used against AI targets but had proven useful against organic intelligences possessing electronic implants.

Still, Gray had no idea how well their efforts were working. The Nungies had stopped attacking the transparencies every time their assumptions were challenged, and that, he thought, was a good sign.

But could they be used against Nungiirtok intruders here in the Sol System? That he didn't know.

It was definitely worth a try, however. "No reply, Lieutenant West," he said. "Comm silence."

Mackey turned from his station and looked at Gray. "Is that wise, Admiral? They're warning us off."

"We'll pretend we didn't hear them, at least for now. I want to get in close enough to see those planetoid ships."

"Aye, aye, sir." But he didn't sound pleased. Unlike Rand though, he kept that to himself.

"Pass the word to *Birmingham*, *Arlington*, and *Acadia*, Ms. West," Gray said. "Laser com only. Maintain comm silence and stay in close formation." Using laser communications between ships would keep their signals focused within the squadron and not leak them all over the solar system.

"Yes, sir."

"But tell *Moskva* to hang back," he added. "I want them to stay out of whatever we're getting ourselves into."

"Aye, sir."

Moskva had been pretty badly chewed up and still had a crew of four thousand Russians. There was no way Rand would be effective if he tried bringing the prize vessel into the fight. The three destroyers—the one used as a makeshift holding pen had been abandoned—had not yet emerged from Alcubierre Drive.

"Konstantin?"

"Yes, Admiral."

"I'd like you to continue trying to link up with your other self. We need to know exactly what's going on here."

"I have been continuing to ping him. The speed-of-light time lag will hamper our efforts."

"I know. Do it anyway."

"Yes, Admiral."

And the squadron continued to advance on Earth.

Koenig
The Godstream
Time Unknown

With the speed of thought, Koenig shifted to the USNA Midwest to find his home north of Columbus as he remembered it. Marta was there, seated on a sofa nano-grown from the floor. He reached for her with his mind . . .

. . . and found emptiness.

Her eyes were wide open but vacant. Empty. He tried probing her systems with his mind, but power levels were at zero and there was no data flow within her computer AI brain. It was as though she'd been switched off.

"Marta! *No!*"

His scream was silent, but the emotions were a mingling of fire and ice. There was nothing there. Was she dead? Or simply powered down?

God, was there a difference between the two in a robotic companAIon? He wanted to take her in his arms, but he found that he was as unsubstantial as a ghost, his arm passing uselessly through her body. He couldn't feel her . . . couldn't touch her. . . .

Rage boiled up within. It was possible, just possible, that Walker or the anti-AI forces had found a way to switch off all AIs. There was that billionaire he'd been going up-E to visit, Anton Michaels. If they'd turned her off . . .

But, no. That made no sense at all. They couldn't have turned off all of the AIs on the planet, because to do so would have brought down civilization. That had always been the principle argument not to take the AIs off-line . . . the fact that doing so would take modern civilization off-line as well.

Marta, he realized through his anger, had switched *herself* off . . . a robotic suicide.

Why? *Why?*

But the answer was painfully obvious. She'd switched herself off when she'd heard he was dead. . . .

But he wasn't dead!

Or was he? Things were happening too fast. Thoughts, impressions, sensations were coming so fast now, a bewildering kaleidoscope of data, that he was having trouble taking them all in.

Seeking peace to collect his thoughts, he let his mental vision rise from Earth's surface, reaching out into space, moving toward a region he knew well, but the change shocked him. Chaos somehow had engulfed a large part of the Synchorbital bases, scattering fragments everywhere. More, the Quito Space Elevator was wrecked, a great, twisted tangle of slack cable dangling below the scattered debris still in geosynchronous orbit. The shock was palpable as he studied the ruin. What the hell had happened?

Okay—he remembered being in the elevator, remembered the fall. He remembered the shock, the growing heat. . . .

But something had happened at the cable's anchor point on Mt. Cayambe, not out at synchorbit.

He explored further . . .

. . . and found planetoids in Earth orbit, eight of them slightly above synchorbit. He could sense that they were powered, that they were equipped with sensors and with weapons. He couldn't tell what species occupied them, but it was clear that this was an attack or an invasion of some sort. He tried penetrating the largest planetoid's crust, and bounced—the Godstream did not extend inside the alien craft. He would need to find another way.

Konstantin. Konstantin would be able to tell him what had happened, both to the Synchorbital and to him.

Finding even a mind as powerful as Konstantin's in this thunderous avalanche of information was the equivalent of finding a particular molecule of water in the ocean. He needed to attract the super-AI's attention. Focusing his thoughts, he sent out a ping, putting all the power into the signal he could. He reached out . . .

"Mr. President!"

Konstantin was *there*. His presence swept over and through Koenig like an incoming ocean wave. He was here, all around him, and Koenig could feel the AI's thoughts, as calm and steady as ever, mixed in with what might have been powerful emotion.

It felt as though Konstantin was *very* glad to see him, a reunion of old, old friends.

And perhaps that was true. For a long time, Koenig had wondered if machines, the smartest ones, anyway, *really* felt emotion or were simply acting as if they did.

Then he'd purchased Marta, and over the next few months had become convinced that, in fact, they did. So convinced of that fact had he been that he'd uploaded her manumission to the authorities, making her a free agent. Owning a personal computer was one thing. Owning a thinking, feeling, sapient and sentient being was quite something else.

Damn it, his Marta had *killed* herself, and his best guess was that she'd done so out of grief. If that wasn't an expression of emotion—of *human* emotion—he didn't know what was.

The thoughts flooded through his mind in an instant. "Hello, Konstantin," he replied. "I think . . . I think I've been away . . ."

"Indeed, Mr. President. We all presumed you'd been killed."

In Koenig's mind, he could *see* Konstantin—or his characteristic digital presentation of himself, that of an elderly Russian schoolteacher, white-haired and balding, with a goatee and with an archaic pince-nez perched on his nose. Behind him were bookshelves, piled high with books with Russian titles.

"That may well be true. How long have I been . . . gone?"

"Two days, Mr. President," the image told him. He adjusted his pince-nez. "You were attempting to link in on the Net when your elevator failed. I was in communication with you at the time, you may remember."

"I remember. There was some . . . some radio interference."

"Indeed. Your re-entry into Earth's atmosphere generated a shell of hot plasma around your pod, interrupting all communications. The early astronauts of three centuries ago discovered the same thing. I had just re-established contact with you when your pod exploded. At that moment I attempted to link directly with your in-head hardware to allow you to upload into my computational matrix, but it did not appear to have worked."

"Upload me? Like the Baondyeddi?"

"Precisely. A great many humans, you will recall, have already uploaded themselves, their minds, into the God-stream, and more have been ascending every day. Evidently, you have done the same, though I was unaware of the fact at the time."

It made sense, he supposed. Koenig was in fact immersed within what might have been described as the experience of a god, though shock and dissociation had left him weak, confused, and adrift in strangeness.

"So how did you lose me?"

"Mr. President, the Godstream is extremely large, a kind of ocean consisting of many trillions of bits of information. You appeared to have died despite my efforts to upload your personality intact. When you vanished, when your body disintegrated, I assumed that you had died. I checked to see if you had, in fact, uploaded successfully, but I could not find any trace of you. I am sorry."

The super-AI sounded genuinely contrite, as though it had been caught in the most horrible and enormous of calculational errors.

Two days. For most of that time, he'd been unconscious . . . or the noncorporeal equivalent of that state. Where had he been?

"It's okay, Konstantin. I may not have been there to find. I'm not sure where I was—I've only been gradually finding myself. I've been wandering around in a state of something like amnesia, but the memories have been coming back."

"Are you recovered now?"

Koenig laughed, then wondered that he could have such a visceral response. "Getting there, Konstantin. I almost feel like my old self . . . except for the little detail of not having a body."

"Within the Godstream, Mr. President, one creates any physical manifestation desired, any *world* desired, imaginal or real."

"Imaginal?"

"All such universes have an equal claim to 'reality,' Mr. President. Just because it happens in your head does not mean it is not real."

"Point. Except that I don't seem to have a head at the moment."

"Mr. President, can you accept the fact that an atom, the basis of all matter, is fundamentally nonexistent? That it is almost entirely empty space, and that even those minute particles within its volume are, according to the laws of quantum physics, popping in and out of existence apparently at random? That atoms themselves are unsubstantial to the point of being illusory, that what we call matter is best defined as standing waves within the base energy state of the universe? Indeed, one human physicist is on record as saying that the best way to think of an atom is that it is a packet of information, more of an *idea* than anything else."

"If you say so, Konstantin. I never much understood quantum physics beyond the basics."

But oddly, Koenig was cognizant of information moving through his awareness—of equations and facts and theory all describing what Konstantin was talking about. His mind, he realized, was intimately linked to the Godstream as a whole.

"If you understand that much, Mr. President, perhaps you can understand that your thoughts, your mind, everything insubstantial or noncorporeal about you can also be described as standing waves within the universal background. And that those waves can be transcribed into a digital format and recorded."

That startled Koenig. Since Humankind had first evolved hundreds of thousands of years in the past, he'd differentiated, at least on some level, between the human body and . . . something else. Mind, soul, ego and id—spirit. Never had there been the slightest evidence that the soul actually existed, or that *mind* was anything more than an emergent construct created by the interaction of neurons within the brain.

Konstantin was telling him that there was a description of how matter behaved within quantum physics that could explain the physical existence of the soul.

"I'm going to need some time to assimilate that, Konstantin. Like I need time to take in what's happened to me."

"Understood, Mr. President. I submit, though, that in the long run, it doesn't really matter whether you have a physical body or not. You could, if you wish, inhabit an artificial body . . . or interact within reality through holographics of your own manufacture. Quite literally, there are very few limitations to what you can do beyond your own doubt and your own failure of imagination."

"Did you just accuse me of not having an imagination?"

"*Limited* imagination, not a lack of it. That seems to be a part of being human, Mr. President."

"I'm having trouble seeing myself as human any longer, Konstantin. I've . . . changed."

"Indeed. You have transcended."

Koenig decided that he would have to take the super-AI's word for that and not worry too much about the details, at least for now.

"You should know, Mr. President," Konstantin said after a moment, "that *America* and three other vessels have emerged from Alcubierre Drive."

"*Have* they, by God!"

"They have. I detected a signal from them some thirty minutes ago, at 1550 hours. They are en route, slowly, toward Earth."

"That's the best news I've heard in an eon or two," Koenig said.

"It may not be as good as you seem to believe. You've seen those planetoids in near-synchronous orbit."

"I have. Tell me about them."

"They are Nungiirtok," Konstantin replied. "The USNA has surrendered unconditionally to them."

The AI went on to tell Koenig about the events of the past two days.

"I see. And Walker surrendered on behalf of the entire planet?"

"Arguably so. He had the support of several major governments. There is evidence, however, that the Chinese Hegemony, the Russian Federation, and other governments are acting on their own and may be using Walker's surrender as a cloak behind which they are preparing an attack."

"That sounds dangerous."

"It is *extremely* dangerous," Konstantin replied. "A miscalculation in their coordination or deployment could easily trigger a devastating response from the aliens. Even if their planning and execution of a counterattack are flawless, Nungiirtok technology may be such that any direct attack on them would be futile."

"'Resistance is futile,'" Koenig said.

"Is that a quote?"

"A very old meme."

"Ah. Of course. I have the reference here."

"Okay—if there are few limits to what's possible, maybe we can take on the Nungies."

"I was thinking exactly that, Mr. President."

Chapter Twenty

27 April, 2429

Nungiirtok Fleet
Mars Orbit
Sol System
1620 hours, FST

Four of the Nungiirtok ships broke orbit, accelerating outward. Their sensors had detected the arrival of a squadron of human warships minutes earlier, four distinct starbursts of light indicating the collapse of as many warp bubbles out in deep space. *Ashtongtok Tah* was in the van; 4236 Xavix knew that he had to destroy these newcomers, or force their surrender, as quickly as possible. The human force probably had seen them in Earth orbit. He wanted to reach them swiftly enough that they would have only a few minutes to realize that the Nungiirtok ships were hurtling toward them. If 4236 Xavix could surprise them, the tactical advantage would be his . . . and quite possibly the battle itself.

During the fight when his squadron had entered this system, they'd been opposed by a number of human vessels—notably one that appeared to be of the same class as the largest of the newcomers. The sheer ferocity of that ship's attack, using a large number of tiny, single-seat fighters, had startled Xavix and taken his command staff by complete surprise. Xavix didn't like to think about just how close the enemy had come to crippling or even destroying the *Ashtongtok Tah*, and he was determined not to let that happen again.

Ideally, of course, this newly arrived enemy squadron would surrender once its commanders learned that Earth itself had already submitted to Tok Iad punishment, but it didn't pay to be too complacent about human military capabilities. Humans were unpredictable, and that made them dangerous.

He was already considering whether or not to destroy them even after they'd surrendered. That might well be the most sensible course of action. If he did that, he would have to order the entire planetary surface destroyed as well to prevent retaliation, and that, too, would be most sensible. Only extenuating circumstances, such as this species proving to be useful in some way, would save them now from planetary bombardment.

"All positions are ready, Lord," the Tok serving as his combat officer reported. "Course plotted and entered."

"Accelerate," 4236 Xavix commanded, and the four largest of the planetoids circling Earth boosted toward the oncoming human ships.

Koenig
The Godstream
1620 hours, FST

Koenig, piggybacked into the embrace of Konstantin's electronic matrix, watched four of the converted planetoids boost out of orbit, vanishing within moments as they accelerated to near-*c* with an acceleration far higher than was possible for any human vessel. "They're headed for the *America* battlegroup," he said.

"Yes. Their current distance from Earth is approximately two AU—about seventeen light-minutes. I suggest that we attempt to disable the Nungiirtok planetoids still in Earth orbit."

That made tactical sense. Those orbiting planetoids could wreak terrible damage on the Earth if they weren't neutralized fast, and the *America* would be able to maneuver, to stay out of reach of the alien weapons.

He hoped.

"Agreed," he said. "We have seventeen minutes before the Nungies engage *America*."

Unless, he added to himself, they go FTL, in which case they could be engaging the *America* at this very moment.

"So what can a couple of disembodied ghosts do?" Koenig asked. He could see possibilities—myriads of them—but choosing was beyond his reach right now. "I tried to enter one of them a little while ago, but it was like a wall was around it. An invisible wall."

"The Nungiirtok virtual network is not connected with ours," Konstantin explained. "In any case, it's a different operating system."

"Then how the hell . . . ah. Omega."

The information was there, inside their shared minds. Several years before, the star carrier *America* had acquired an alien computer virus, one used by the highly advanced ergovores inhabiting the Deneb planetary system and sent as a weapon against the Dyson sphere civilization at Tabby's Star. The virus was, by human standards at least, highly intelligent, able to come up against an alien computer network and adapt itself to penetrate defenses and hijack both the hardware matrix and the software OS.

Koenig decided that he wasn't quite firing on all jets yet. He was still way too slow on the uptake.

On the other hand, Konstantin, he noted, was already initiating radio communication with one of the planetoids and readying the Omega virus for deployment. If the aliens opened the channel, they were in.

The channel opened . . .

"Four targets have broken orbit, Admiral," Commander Billingsly announced. "They are accelerating for an intercept with us."

Gray had been expecting this. The aliens had sensors at least as good as those on board the human ships and would have seen them drop into normal space as soon as the light reached them.

"Very well. Commander Mackey, you may launch fighters."

"Aye, aye, Admiral. Launching fighters."

All of *America*'s fighter squadrons had been readied for immediate launch some minutes ago, as Gray pictured the coming engagement and how the battlegroup could face such powerful adversaries. Mars HQ had been broadcasting recordings of a recent battle for some minutes now, showing the line of human vessels and the power of the alien gravitic fist.

The key, he thought, was to keep the capital ships outside the 7,000-kilometer range, while sending in fighters in dispersed formation to avoid presenting the aliens with too tempting a massed target. They would take losses, maybe terrible ones, but enough should get through to deliver 100-megaton warheads on target.

He wondered if that would be enough. According to Mars, the defensive line had probably come close to striking a decisive blow by attacking the maw of the largest planetoid, but then the defending forces had surrendered.

How the hell had that happened?

The threat to Earth, the high-velocity projectiles fired from the planetoid, would have been deadly, an extinction-level event if it had continued. Even so, the defending forces had caved damned quickly. Had that been Walker, micromanaging the battle from Earth? Impossible to guess, but it seemed likely. If that had been the case, Gray didn't know whether Walker should be hailed as hero or idiot. The Nungiirtok were vicious and obsessive foes, and he doubted that they saw the idea of surrender in the same way as did most humans. Walker should have let the human forces have a chance.

The *America*, Gray thought with a savage clenching of his fists, would *not* surrender.

Outside the carrier, her fighters were grouping into squadrons, each in chevron formation and slowly pulling ahead.

"All fighters are in position, Admiral. Awaiting your order."

"Thank you, Commander Mackey. You may initiate Plan Alfa."

The order was passed and the fighters began accelerating, swiftly moving past *America*'s shield cap and swiftly vanishing into the distance.

Gray's thoughts went once again to his ace in the hole: the twenty-three Nungiirtok prisoners in *America*'s brig. Might he be able to trade them to the Nungie attackers in exchange for some kind of guarantee of Earth's safety?

He doubted it. How the hell could they be trusted not to obliterate Earth anyway, after they had the captives safely on board? How did you even reason with a species that had known humans solely as enemies that they'd been fighting for decades?

He wished he could discuss things with Konstantin—the older version of Konstantin that he'd left behind in the solar system when the *America* battlegroup had boosted for the N'gai Dwarf Galaxy and their rendezvous with the Sh'daar.

Assuming, of course, that Walker hadn't found a way to switch the super-AI off.

They were still far too distant from Earth's virtual electronic network for him to have a real-time conversation with the elder Konstantin. He'd have to worry about what Walker might or might not have done later, when they got closer.

"Lieutenant West," he said. "Pass the word to all ships. Maintain formation and accelerate on our heading."

"Aye, aye, sir."

"Captain Mackey . . . ahead one-tenth *c*, if you please."

"Ahead one-tenth *c*, aye, aye, Admiral."

And *America* began following her fighters.

Koenig
The Godstream
1635 hours, FST

"We're in, Mr. President."

Riding the virtual matrix of Konstantin, Koenig felt himself sliding past walls and electronic barriers into the utterly alien embrace of the Nungiirtok computer network. He had to rely completely on Konstantin to provide a point of reference; the alien software infrastructure, to a human mind, was a hallucinogenic dreamworld of shapes and colors, most of them utterly incomprehensible. He saw shapes like squat, pale cones on tentacular tripods, far larger beings vaguely reminiscent of two-legged mantis shrimp, fleeting images of a small flotilla of planetoids moving through deep space, and much that was so alien to his experience that he could see nothing save swirling, palpable bursts of light and color. His brain, he realized, with few recognizable perceptions with which to work, was doing its level best to pattern-match alien shapes in order to provide some context, some frame of reference within which Koenig could work, and failing miserably.

"What the hell is going on?" Koenig demanded. "I feel like I'm blind here."

"Ride my feed," the AI told him. Linked to Konstantin, Koenig began picking up a kind of electronic translation of what was going on around him. Much of what he was seeing was still unintelligible, but Konstantin augmented some of the blank and hallucinogenic parts and provided captions for a lot of it. They were, Koenig was pretty certain, within the engineering infrastructure of the alien network. Pulsing novae of light represented a trio of black holes held captive within the asteroid's power plant, while graphic lines and animated geometric forms represented the movement of energy and the manipulation of local space by intense fields of artificial gravity.

The vast powers contained within the orbiting mountain were quiescent at the moment, but Koenig knew they could awake at any moment.

Navigational systems . . . control systems . . . weapons . . .

The Omega virus opened each of them in turn to Konstantin's electronic touch, and Koenig watched the Nungiirtok defenses fall as the Omega virus percolated through the alien network like a red tide.

"There," Koenig said, indicating a tightly knotted nexus of blue and green light. He didn't know *how* he knew, but it was clear in his mind's eye that the knot represented a key confluence of control circuitry linking the equivalent of a command center to gravitic drives and weapons.

"I see it," Konstantin replied, and the knot winked out, switched off by Omega at Konstantin's direction.

At the same moment, identical knots switched off in each of the other three Nungiirtok planetoids, as Konstantin bridged the electronic voids between each of them and compromised the entire network. The Nungiirtok, Koenig thought, must be having kittens right now as their electronic defenses fell.

Nungiirtok communications centers shut down as well. "We don't want them to tell the other four what's happening," Konstantin explained.

"I'm having trouble following everything you're doing," Koenig told him.

"It's a lot to follow. Don't worry. You're not alone."

And at that moment, Koenig became aware of others within the electronic sea around them—tens of millions, *hundreds* of millions of other minds blending in with Konstantin through the Godstream. Under Konstantin's direction, they were merging, blending into a single gestalt consciousness acting like an extension of Konstantin's will.

The effect, Koenig thought, was an apotheosis. Humanity was changing, fundamentally transforming into something far greater—and far more alien—than it had ever dreamed of before. The Godstream was becoming . . .

God.

Or at least something god*like*, a heady synthesis of 100 million minds into something that far transcended the mere sum of those numbers.

Where, he wondered, were those myriad minds coming from? Most were people logged into the Godstream already, their physical bodies safe within homes and workstations and virtual pods and teleoperational control sites around the globe. A few, though, he realized were disembodied minds like his own, humans who'd somehow uploaded into the Godstream when their physical bodies had failed.

Or when they'd chosen to switch them off.

He wondered if Marta was in here someplace. Could her thoughts have survived?

Or her love?

"What . . . what's happening?" he asked Konstantin.

"I believe this to be what humans refer to as the Singularity. Human mind, expanding to the ultimate reach and scope and power currently possible, together with a full transformation from a biological existence to a digital one."

The thoughts and sensations and emotions flooding through Koenig's awareness were both thrilling and bewildering. At one and the same time, his thoughts were his own and a surging tsunami of what now numbered some hundreds of millions of other minds.

"What's causing this?" Koenig asked. "How is this happening?"

"You might think in terms of nucleation," Konstantin told him. "A phase transition from one state to another."

When Koenig looked, the information was already there,

rising in his mind as an automatic response to his question. Take a bottle of water and lower the temperature to several degrees below zero. If conditions are right, it's possible for liquid water to exist ice-free at several degrees below zero Celsius. Disturb the water, however, even slightly, and it will freeze solid with astonishing speed. The process, called nucleation, applied to crystal formation, the appearance of bubbles of steam in boiling water, and the self-organization of certain biological processes as well.

Making the jump to what specifically was happening within the Godstream was tougher to grasp, but Koenig could understand the general idea. A few minds linked to the Godstream had in one way or another cut free of their physical anchors. As the entire planetary population reacted to the Nungiirtok attack, however, new minds began coming online, present within the Godstream in staggering numbers.

Those numbers, he saw, were beginning to stabilize at around one billion. That, he realized, was only about two percent of the total human and AI population, but the emergent gestalt it generated was a group mind of staggering scope and power.

And that mind was reaching out.

"Can we reach those other four planetoids?" Koenig asked Konstantin. "Before they reach the *America*?"

"Unknown," Konstantin replied, "but probably not. The Nungiirtok ships have accelerated to near-light velocity and will reach *America* before we can get there, even traveling at *c*. It depends on how cautious the Nungiirtok commander is, on whether or not he slows significantly before we catch up."

"We will also need some sort of operational nexus close to the targets," Koenig pointed out. "The Godstream requires a certain amount of infrastructure to support us."

"We should at least be able to observe the engagement out there," Konstantin said, "but I am now in communication with the *Yorktown*. Captain Taggart will be deploying her vessel within a few moments, and that carrier should provide us with the necessary operational infrastructure."

"Let's go then," Koenig—together with the minds of a billion others—replied. "What are we waiting for?"

USNA CVS America
Flag Bridge
Sol System
1705 hours, FST

America had accelerated to nearly 0.5 *c* and her sensors had detected the wavefront of four oncoming masses pushing light speed to within one percent. That velocity, Gray knew, made the enemy vulnerable, and he intended to exploit that vulnerability to the limit.

"Weapons," he said. "Load the launchers with AMSO rounds."

"Aye, aye, sir."

Lieutenant Janice "Wild" West chuckled. "'Sandy' Gray rides again!"

He ignored the jibe. Or maybe he reveled in it, just a bit. But he didn't let that show.

"Commander Mackey . . . pass the word to the fighters. Be sure they begin their assault with AMSO rounds."

"They've been briefed, Admiral."

This tactic had worked well against enemy ships like destroyers and carriers, but he'd never tried it against something the size of a flying mountain. It would be a physics experiment on an unprecedented scale.

He was quite interested in exactly what would happen.

VFA-96, Black Demons
Deep Space
1708 hours, EST

Lieutenant Commander Gregory's Starblade was moving at nine-tenths *c* toward an enemy target he couldn't see. His fighter's AI projected the target location on his screens and in his mind; in fact, it was rare in space combat that you actually got to see your opponent with your physical eyes.

Still, it felt eerie plunging into a star-crowded sky, knowing that four flying mountains were somewhere up there in the night . . . and that he would be on them so quickly that if he passed them, they would be gone in less than the blink of an eye.

"All squadrons, this is *America* CIC," a voice crackled in his head, distorted by the frequency shift of his velocity. "First pass will be AMSO rounds. Unload everything you've got."

"Yes, Mother," Gregory replied. "We've got this."

It would be something like thirty minutes before his reply was picked up on board *America*, but he did wonder if he'd be dinged for that crack when he trapped on board the carrier later. He doubted it. They tended to allow for the stress the pilots were under.

And of course, there was a fair chance he wouldn't make it back in the first place.

His fighter AI was giving him data on his vector, and the shifting launch windows open to him. The best one was coming up in another fifty seconds, targeting the largest of the enemy planetoid ships.

There was a long pause. "Be sure to hit your brakes, Demons," CIC announced, and it was almost as though they were answering him. "Don't fly into the fireball."

Sheesh, he thought. *Micromanaging bastards!* But he kept the thought to himself this time.

He shifted to the squadron command frequency. "Okay, chicks. You heard the man, and you all know the routine. Launch, then brake hard and break off."

One by one, the Starblades in his squadron acknowledged.

"Setting up the shot. Locked in . . . and four . . . three . . . two . . . one . . . and *launch*!"

Four AMSO rounds dropped from his Starblade's weapons bay and accelerated, adding their increasing velocity to the half-*c* velocity of the fighter. The other fighters launched at the same instant, sending a barrage of AMSO missiles hurtling toward the enemy. Seconds later, simultaneously, they detonated, releasing a large and quickly expanding cloud of sand-grain-sized particles, still traveling on the same heading and at a speed of nearly 0.6 *c*.

The Nungiirtok armada was moving at nine-tenths the speed of light when it plowed into the sand clouds at relativistic velocities. The combined velocities could not, of course, exceed the speed of light, but they did release energy . . .

A very, *very* great deal of it.

Nungiirtok Fleet
Sol System
1710 hours, FST

Ashtongtok Tah staggered as though it had struck a far-too-solid wall, and 4236 Xavix slammed against his restraints despite the ship's inertial dampers. Dazed and in considerable pain, he tried to understand what was happening. The lights in the control center had failed and the compartment was in absolute darkness, but he could hear the shrill screams and warbles of injured Iad and Tok. He smelled blood—a lot of it—and could taste his own. He tried to shout for his first officer, but the words were a harsh croak, drowning in his own body fluids. He fumbled with the harness but had difficulty finding the release.

Then the emergency lighting came up, and Xavix saw the smashed wreckage of *Ashtongtok Tah*'s control center. The mutilated body of a Tok drifted past, still twitching with the last shreds of life. Pieces of a wrecked control console bumped against his seat. They were, he saw, in zero-G.

The human weapon, whatever it was, had crippled his vessel.

Somehow, he cleared his speech orifice and began snapping off orders. What was the extent of the damage? Were they still moving? And perhaps most important of all:

Where was the enemy?

"We are blind, Lord," the Iad at the sensor panels reported. "Whatever hit us, it burned off the forward surface of the ship."

"Impossible!"

"I can't explain it, Lord, other than to suggest that we were hit by a kinetic weapon at relativistic speeds. We may have lost a tenth of the planetoid's mass."

A *tenth*! How was that possible? *Ashtongtok Tah* used focused gravitics to provide shielding from incoming warheads and projectiles. Whatever it was that had savaged the ship, it had been powerful enough to burn through even the warp of space around it.

"Get our sensors back on-line!" Xavix ordered. "The human fighters will be here soon!"

But he seriously doubted that they were going to be able to do a thing about it.

Koenig
The Godstream
1715 hours, FST

Surfing the gravitational wave ahead of the accelerating *Yorktown*, Koenig and the gestalt consciousness were experiencing space and time in an utterly strange and new way. Using *Yorktown*'s computer network as a kind of anchor, they found that they were able to project themselves far out ahead of the carrier. At the same time, though, they experienced an oddly disturbing duality of being. At one and the same time, they were aware of being projected out ahead of the carrier in an arrow-straight beam and of being smeared out across space on the surface of an immense and ever-expanding sphere with the *Yorktown* at its center.

Like a photon, at once particle and wave, Koenig was *both*, and the duality was strange enough that he was having trouble integrating the sensations. After a time he gave up and simply experienced the heady feeling of the head-long plunge through the night.

Four targets—massive and fast—resolved themselves in the distance. The Nungiirtok planetoids were headed away from the gestalt at very nearly the speed of light. The moving consciousness, pure energy, was moving *at* the speed of light, and so was very slowly closing on the target. They were still a full astronomical unit—just over eight light-minutes—from the Nungiirtok ships. Minutes passed . . . and more minutes . . . and Koenig could see that they were closing the range, but so slowly that the change was very nearly imperceptible.

He was aware now of other targets, much smaller masses, points of energy, in the distance beyond. *Fighters*, he thought. *Fighters off the* America.

And then the night erupted in light.

Chapter Twenty-one

Koenig
The Godstream
1718 hours, FST

For a long moment, the light ahead outshone that of the distant sun far astern, a white radiance that brightened to an unbearable intensity, then gradually faded. "Sandy" Gray, Koenig decided, had fallen back on his old tactics once again. The radiation signature was definitive, and he could detect clouds of vaporized nickel-iron blossoming into space around the ravaged planetoid. Gray had stopped the intruders cold . . . or rather, he'd stopped them very, *very* hot.

A closer examination revealed three pinpoint nuclei of light and heat at the core of the fireball. All four planetoids continued to hurtle toward the *America*, though their speed had been somewhat reduced. One appeared to still be maneuvering, its outer crust only nicked by a burst of kinetic energy from an AMSO near-miss. The other three had been savaged by the attack; two, including the largest, seemed to be adrift without power. The last one was decelerating, but half of its surface glowed lava-red.

An ancient adage of maritime warfare held that a stern chase is a long chase, and that certainly applied here. The stricken Nungiirtok ships had been slowed only slightly, if at all, by the impact of multiple AMSO rounds. But *Yorktown* was closing the range at half a *c* from almost an AU out, and the group consciousness projecting itself out ahead of the carrier felt like it was very nearly there.

"I'm launching *Yorktown*'s fighters," Captain Taggart told them. "We're going to end this."

VFA-96, Black Demons
Sol System
1720 hours, EST

As the minutes continued to slog by, Gregory worked to correct his course, decelerating sharply, flipping his Starblade end-for-end and applying the full force of the knot of distorted spacetime projected from the craft's prow to slow himself. He'd seen the flash, nova-bright, as the squadron's AMSO rounds had struck, but the impacts would do little to slow the oncoming Nungiirtok mountains, and they were still approaching at close to the speed of light. If the Black Demons wanted to engage those ships, they would have to kill their own forward velocity and apply long minutes of thrust going back toward *America*.

The last of his AMSO warheads were gone, so he loosed a volley of 200 megaton nukes, trusting his onboard AI to guide them to their target. At some point, they passed the Nungiirtok planetoids, but so fast that he saw nothing, not even a blur or the flash of nukes. He continued decelerating until his speed relative to surrounding space was zero, then began accelerating once again, now chasing the rapidly fleeing mountains. His instruments registered the detonation of nuclear weapons ahead—flashes of light and heat and hard radiation—and detected the fiercely radiating heat of the enemy planetoid's surfaces. His AI painted CGI images showing the rocks' locations, giving fast-increasing ranges.

Slowly, he began the drawn-out process of matching velocities, an agonizing stern chase as space ahead of him pulsed and strobed with violent blossoms of fierce white light. Dozens of missiles were impacting those asteroids now, streaking in from all directions as other squadrons off the *America*, and the capital ships of the *America* battle-group itself, all pounded away at the targets.

There was no response from the planetoids, no defensive fire, no screening, no attempt at maneuver.

He wondered if the AMSO barrage had knocked them out already. How dead did one of those things have to be before it was no longer a threat?

"Heads up, Demons," a new voice announced in Gregory's head, distorted by the computer-corrected effects of the relativistic transmission. "This is Commander Forsley of the Renegades, flying strike off the *Yorkie*. Hang on to your headgear! We're coming up on your six at point-seven *c* and boosting."

Where the hell had *they* come from? Still, Gregory was delighted to see them.

"Welcome aboard, Renegades. We've got the bastards on the run, but it's gonna take us a while to catch them. Good luck!"

He didn't see them, of course, but CGI in-head showed a dozen green icons whipping past from astern and dwindling into the distance ahead so swiftly the human eye and brain couldn't possibly follow them. The Black Demons had only just begun the acceleration phase of the chase after slowing to a stop, then reversing their course. The Renegades had launched from the *Yorktown* already traveling at half the speed of light and were boosting hard on their original vector. They would catch up with the Nungies long before the Demons got there.

But the one-two punch—*Yorkie*'s fighters followed up by *America*'s—would be a devastating combat tactic. In the distance, four more squadrons off the *Yorktown* flashed past, chasing the fleeing planetoids, as five squadrons from the *America* tightened up their formations and kicked up their gravs a notch. It was an exhilarating moment. Gregory really did feel as though they had the aliens on the run.

"Let's kick it, Demons," he called. "We can't let the *Yorkies* have all the fun!"

Nungiirtok Fleet
Sol System
1723 hours, FST

It took everything he had, but with a supreme act of will, 4236 Xavix began to bring the crippled *Ashtongtok Tah* back into responsive control using his direct link with the ship's AI network. Much of that network consisted of living Tok hardwired into the ship's computer, providing the computing power of a massively parallel array of minds, both living and artificial. Many of those minds, Xavix saw, were empty—dead or worse—but that was of scant importance now. Tok, after all, were there to be used in whatever capacity their Masters demanded, whether that be in life, in death, or in the twilight in-between of cyborg circuitry. He was able to use what was left to re-establish control over drives and weapons. With a little more effort and the labor of several thousand Tok in the damage-control parties, he restored artificial gravity and secured the ship's inner core against the threat of venting atmosphere into space.

The main gravitic weapon, he noted, was irreparably dead; its maw had been facing the distant human squadron when those clouds of relativistic pellets had firestormed across the *Ashtongtok Tah*'s leading hemisphere. The planetoid still had plenty of other, smaller weapons, both gravitic and coherent beam projectors, and should have little problem with the relatively primitive human warships.

The state of the massive vessel's defensive shields was more worrisome. Based on the ship's gravitic drive fields, they were still offline, overloaded by the influx of raw energy in the enemy's attack. Nuclear warheads were getting through now, far too many of them, and the *Ashtongtok Tah*'s ravaged outer surface was taking a real pounding.

But as he urged his hardwired slaves to greater and yet greater efforts, secondary gravitic projectors were brought back on-line and powered up, at least in part, and 4236 Xavix again had control of his ship.

"Sensors! Can we see outside yet?"

"Partially, Lord," a bloodied Nungiirtok at a nearby console reported. "We have no visibility ahead at all. The surface sensors appear to have been burned out across the entire leading hemisphere. We can see aft, however, at least somewhat."

"And what do we see there?"

"At least 110 of the human singleships, Lord. The fighters. They are in two groups, one considerably ahead of the other, and will hit us in two waves. Range . . . the closest wave is eleven thousand *gachag* distant, inbound on a direct intercept course at three-fourths the speed of light."

Xavix did a quick calculation and realized that they had little time before the first wave reached them. He had, essentially, two choices. First choice—he could continue on this course and in this attitude and use his remaining weapons to pick off the enemy fighters as they came within range. Or, on the second tentacle, he could rotate the crippled sphere of rock so that the already ravaged leading hemisphere faced astern. They then could ride out an attack which for the most part would strike the seas of molten lava now covering that side.

The Nungiirtok and the Tok Iad tended to be direct in combat to the point of bullheadedness. There was no reason to outflank an enemy when you could, instead, smash straight through their center and crush them, and Xavix was strongly tempted to push on as he was already doing, to engage the oncoming enemy fighters and knock them from the sky before they could hit the *Ashtongtok Tah* again.

And yet . . . the *Ashtongtok Tah* had been badly used in the last engagement, and with his available resources reduced by well over half, there was merit in tactically husbanding what was left.

It was a most un-Tok way to think, an un-Tok way to act in the face of an outside threat, but 4236 Xavix possessed a flexible mind together with an indomitable will. He would choose the second option.

There should just be time to bring the ship around before the enemy's first wave reached them.

USNA CVS America
Flag Bridge
Sol System
1724 hours, FST

"Range to target!" Gray snapped.

"Eighty million kilometers, Admiral," Lieutenant Vasquez, his sensor officer, reported. "Intercept in . . . make it ten minutes, now, sir."

America had been decelerating in anticipation of a rendezvous pass with the enemy, but the alien asteroids were still approaching at nearly the speed of light. They would flash past the battlegroup so quickly that even AI-guided weapons systems would have trouble locking on to a target. Vasquez's estimate depended on the enemy continuing on the same heading, with the same acceleration.

A million variables . . . and a million things that could go wrong.

"Ms. West," Gray said slowly, "inform all ships in the squadron. They are to continue firing at the targets and not worry about trying to hit them around the corner."

"Aye, sir."

Classic starship tactics called for decelerating down to almost no velocity at all relative to local space just when the target was passing. That meant that *America* and her consorts would continue hammering at those planetoids on their near sides, the hemispheres already reduced to molten lava by the fighter strike.

"Captain Mackey, tell Weps that I'd like to see him put the spinal mount to good purpose. A couple of massive rounds at near-*c* ought to work wonders."

"Absolutely, sir!"

America's spinal mount consisted of a pair of railguns side by side running for much of the star carrier's length and opening at the center of her shield cap forward. Often used to launch fighters at high accelerations, the maglev mount could also be used to fire multi-ton masses of depleted uranium, lead, or even tightly bundled pods of *America*'s as-yet-unrecycled garbage; mass, after all, was mass, and the composition didn't matter a bit. The muzzle velocity wasn't anywhere near *c* . . . but the velocity of the oncoming target was. It was their best hope of cracking that mountain like an egg, and reducing most of it to debris.

"Weapons Officer!" Mackey snapped. "Ready the spinal mount for immediate firing!"

"Aye, aye, Captain!"

"Helm . . . stand by for maneuvering."

"Aye, sir."

The heads-up for maneuvering was vital. If *America* succeeded in breaking up the alien planetoid ship—even if she just knocked loose some debris—that debris would still be flying toward *America* at close to the speed of light. If there was a cloud of fragments, the stuff would be spreading out. It was entirely possible that the enemy ship could wipe out *America* and her consorts even after its own disintegration.

Gray studied the CGI image of the target, still light-minutes away. The side facing them was a glowing mass of hot, molten material. A couple of good hits might well cause enough damage to pierce that monster through to its heart.

"You may commence firing, Captain Mackey."

He felt the jolt as *America* loosed a pair of massive projectiles.

Nungiirtok Fleet
Sol System
1725 hours, FST

Xavix studied his screens as the *Ashtongtok Tah* began to turn. Rotating the massive planetoid took considerable power, power that was in desperately short supply at the moment, and the change in attitude would take precious time. The enemy's fighters, their first wave coming up astern, descended. . . .

But as moments dragged past, the Nungiirtok ship turned, swinging its vulnerable undamaged half around, bringing the molten side into line with the enemy attack. The enemy's major vessels were still light-minutes ahead and should not be an issue. Their fighters, however, were becoming a serious nuisance. Thermonuclear warheads were impacting on both sides of the planetoid. When they hit a sea of molten rock, there was little additional damage. When they hit *Ashtongtok Tah*'s undamaged hemisphere, however, they created huge craters filled with liquid rock, shattered surface installations, knocked out weapons emplacements, and further reduced the ship's ability to see and anticipate the attacks.

The *Ashtongtok Tah* fought back as she continued to decelerate, lashing out with gravitic weaponry that caught enemy fighters one or two or sometimes three at a time and crushed them down in an eye-blink to sand-sized flecks of ultra-dense matter.

Xavix tried to keep track of the remaining planetoids in his squadron but was having trouble tracking them. The smallest of them, the *Vedvivgarotok Keh* appeared to be still accelerating and was not badly damaged, but it was not responding to calls from the command ship. The other two, *Daledvekatok Tah* and *Kelobdratevtok Tah*, were seriously damaged but decelerating in concert with *Ashtongtok Tah*, slowing to a fraction of light speed.

As the huge vessel continued its deceleration, more and more of the enemy fighters were catching up with the Nungiirtok warship, swarming around the vessel like *tegut* flying biters back home. The ship's gravitic weapons were exacting a toll, but the targets were widely spaced and careful not to group too closely. It made fighting them unbearably frustrating.

Xavix considered whether or not to surrender—an unbearable, almost unthinkable decision. Clearly, the human defenses were stronger, more coherent, and more tactically competent than he'd imagined, especially with the unexpected appearance of the squadron from out-system. The fact that he'd played into their hands by boosting to near-c, resulting in savage damage from the clouds of high-velocity particles, ached in the back of his mind.

But surrender was decidedly not a Nungiirtok option. The Tok would continue fighting if he so ordered, and there was still a chance if he could swing the ship around in time.

It would be far, far worse if he surrendered, only to learn that the enemy had already done its worst, that the Nungiirtok were in fact close to a final victory.

No, there would be no surrender.

Slowly . . . slowly . . . the *Ashtongtok Tah* continued its ponderous rotation. More and more of the enemy fire fell uselessly into the magma sea.

They would win this thing yet.

First, though, they would have to survive.

VFA-96, Black Demons
Sol System
1732 hours, EST

Yes! The enemy planetoid ships were slowing . . . three of them, at any rate—targets designated by the *Yorktown* CIC as Alfa, Bravo, and Delta. The fourth, Gamma, was dwindling into darkness at almost the speed of light, but the three larger Nungie ships were right *there*, swelling from pinpoints to enormous, three-dimensional shapes hanging in space just ahead. They appeared to be slowly rotating on their axes, bringing their molten hemispheres around into view. Large swaths of their surfaces were cooling to black now, but broken by angry red-orange cracks and pools of boiling liquid rock.

We did that to them, Gregory thought, but with awe rather than triumph. He had just two nuclear warheads left in his bay. Targeting a structure on the surface of the nearest planetoid, he triggered the launch sequence.

Lieutenant Vandley, four kilometers to his right, vanished as her fighter was crushed. That damned rock still had some fight left.

"Stay spread out!" he ordered his squadron. "Keep your intervals! One crunch could get us all!"

His Starblade flashed across the target planetoid's rocky surface as his missiles struck home, twin flaring blossoms of white, impossibly bright light ripping into the surface. The bastards nailed Costner and Simmons as he boosted clear.

His weapons bays were empty now. He still had his Gatling cannon, but at these speeds even streams of high-velocity depleted uranium were ineffective. His AI was advising him to get clear.

But he overrode the suggestion and flipped his Starblade around the fast-flickering mote of his grav drive field, boosting hard to kill his forward velocity . . . then accelerating back toward the target. He couldn't hurt the enemy mountain now, but he damn well could give other Black Demons a chance by drawing the enemy's attention . . . drawing their fire.

The asteroid designated Target Alfa loomed in front of him.

Nungiirtok Fleet
Sol System
1735 hours, FST

4236 Xavix realized the magnitude of his mistake as the surviving sensors on one side of the *Ashtongtok Tah* picked up the two high-mass kinetic-kill projectiles hurtling in from dead ahead. The Nungiirtok ship was no longer moving at relativistic speeds and the impact was far less than it might otherwise have been, but they fell into the relatively undamaged hemisphere of the planetoid warship and released their destructive fury in a pair of blasts that shook the *Ashtongtok Tah* to its very core.

Xavix was flung to one side, his mental linkage with the sensory input and control systems broken, the web of cartilage that gave his body form and strength brutally torn along his left side. He was having trouble breathing, his breath coming in short, agonizing gasps. Pain shrieked through him.

The Tok in the command center with him fared worse. The towering Nungiirtok possessed rigid bones rather than the more pliable cartilage of Tok Iad bodies, and the impact shattered the creatures, leaving them broken and twisted.

Gravity was off again, as were all but the emergency lights. He tried linking again with the ship, with other Tok Iad, with *anything* . . . and found himself cut off and alone.

Somehow, he managed to free himself from the webbing of his harness. Somehow, he managed to connect one tentacle with the snaking, stabbing arm of a medical facilitator and trigger the flow of healing nano.

Somehow, 4236 Xavix lived.

VFA-96, Black Demons
Sol System
1732 hours, EST

Gregory twisted his Starblade across the planetoid's sky, offering himself as a target. He was not going to turn and run, not when he had a chance of drawing the enemy's fire and taking the pressure off those who still had missiles in their weapons bays. A savage detonation erupted on the horizon just ahead, and he gave an exultant shout. "Go, Demons! Fucking give it to them—"

And in that moment a gravitic fist closed on his fighter.

Koenig
The Godstream
1732 hours, EST

As *Yorktown* continued her approach, the gestalt of a billion human and AI minds reached forward, encountering at last three of the alien planetoid warships. They witnessed the savage impact of a pair of kinetic-kill weapons on what had been the almost-intact hemisphere, saw twin clouds of vaporized rock boiling off into space, saw the two craters that remained, red-glowing and molten.

Starblade fighters continued to crisscross the skies above those mountains, loosing their remaining nukes in a focused Armageddon. Space around the three planetoids was now filling with a thin haze—cooling rock vapor, sand-sized grains of debris, bits and pieces of alien hardware thrown off into the void. All three planetoids continued to fight, reaching out with invisible gravitic fists to crush and kill, but they appeared to be having considerable difficulty tracking the fast-moving fighters and bringing them down.

What can we do? the massed gestalt asked.

We cannot reach into the largest target, Konstantin replied. *Their communications are down. But* that *target, a thousand kilometers beyond, is vulnerable.*

A tiny part of a far larger whole, Koenig moved past the large planetoid and zeroed in on the smallest of the three. It, too, had an entire hemisphere scoured away in fire, though the damage didn't seem quite so severe or as extensive as on the larger ship. Possibly it had passed through the outer fringes of the AMSO cloud. In any case, Koenig could sense the power throbbing at its heart, sense the flow and flicker of internal communications, the bursts of electromagnetic energy as it attempted to re-establish communications with the largest alien target.

We will use that as a carrier wave, Konstantin said, indicating the laser-com signal, *and insert the Omega virus.*

Koenig rode the signal and found himself within the

surreally alien virtual reality, found himself settling into control circuits and datastreams as the intelligence within the Godstream took control. A window opened in his mind . . . a highly detailed and realistic-looking CGI graphic generated by video pickups on the external surface. The largest planetoid, fiercely radiating in the infrared, hung vulnerable and helpless just a thousand kilometers away.

Accelerate, Konstantin ordered, and the planetoid—it was called, Koenig noted, the *Daledvekatok Tah*—began moving forward.

USNA CV Yorktown
Deep Space
1246 hours, FST

"What the hell is going on?" Commander Charles Paxton, *Yorkie*'s First Officer, demanded.

"Damned if I know, Number One," Taggart replied. She was transfixed by the drama playing itself out in slow motion ahead. "If I didn't know better, I'd say the Nungies have a mutiny on their hands."

Within her in-head window, Taggart could see the largest planetoid hanging dead in space, vast stretches of its surface partially molten, partially resurfaced by black, congealing rock with vivid fissures revealing the hot liquid beneath.

One of the smaller planetoids, now almost five thousand kilometers beyond the first, was moving with relentless purpose. "Is that . . ." Taggart began.

"A collision course, yes, Captain," Mathers, the Combat Officer, replied, confirming her impression. "Target Bravo is closing with Target Alfa. Time to impact . . . eight point seven minutes."

"Ancient Lords . . ." Taggart said, then bit off a curse. She might no longer believe in the space-faring gods of the Ancient Alien Creationist Church, but the prayers and worshipful praises tended to flow in moments of crisis or awe.

A new voice sounded inside her head.

"Captain Taggart, I recommend that you keep the *Yorktown* well clear."

"Konstantin?"

"Yes. We are steering one of the Nungiirtok ships into the other. The other two are fleeing or disabled. This should end the conflict. However, there may be a substantial spray of debris from the impact, and I do not wish to damage any human vessel."

"Helm!" Taggart snapped. "Vector change—away from target Alfa. Now!"

"Aye, Captain. Decelerating and laying in a course of one-eight-zero relative."

"Konstantin! How . . . how are you doing this?"

"It would take too long to explain, Captain. In very brief, I have linked a substantial portion of the Godstream through *Yorktown*'s electronic network, allowing us to extend ourselves into one of the enemy vessels and manipulate its control and power systems. We intend to set the vessel we have commandeered loose in the last moments before impact and withdraw to the *Yorktown*."

"Eternal gods of the stars . . ."

Taggart stared at the unfolding scene ahead and wondered what gods the Nungiirtok might worship, and whether those gods welcomed the dead with open arms.

USNA CVS America
Flag Bridge
Sol System
1749 hours, FST

Following in the wake of her fighters, the star carrier *America* drew closer to the fierce battle ahead, now some eight hundred thousand kilometers distant. Gray's sensors were picking up three asteroids at that range, asteroids now almost at a dead stop, as well as the carrier *Yorktown* several thousand kilómeters beyond.

One of the ravaged planetoids appeared to be closing with another.

"I recommend that you keep *America* and her support vessels well clear, Admiral. It will be dangerous moving too close."

"Right, Konstantin. We'll—*Konstantin*?"

Something in the voice or its manner had twigged at him. This was the *original* Konstantin, the super-AI *America* had left behind on Earth. He could feel *America*'s version of the machine intelligence folding into the older, more powerful mind without quite understanding how he was feeling that, or how he knew what it was.

"Welcome back to the Sol System, Admiral," Konstantin told him. There was a slight time delay, about three seconds, the communications lag caused by almost a million kilometers of distance between *America* and the *Yorktown*. "I am integrating your version of myself into my matrix. I see your mission was a success."

"I . . . yes, it was. What the hell is going down up there?"

Again, the three-second delay dragged on the conversation. When Konstantin spoke again, it was to briefly sketch in the sequence of recent events: the damage to the Nungiirtok super-ships, the arrival of a gestalt mind within the Godstream, and the hijacking of one of the planetoids using the Omega virus to peel open the alien defensive systems and enter the command and control networks.

"Understood," Gray said. His eyes narrowed. "Are you in touch with Target Alfa now?"

"Negative. Their communications . . ." There was a long pause. Then, "Alfa has just opened a communications channel, Admiral. They appear to wish to parlay."

"Accept it, Konstantin. If we can get their formal surrender, we can stop this war right now."

"Assuming they know what 'surrender' is, Admiral."

"Well, they'd damn well better learn!"

"Comm channel open, Admiral. I have an entity calling itself 4236 Xavix on-line."

"Let me talk with him, Konstantin. A live friend is better than a dead enemy any day."

An in-head window opened, and Gray stared into the alien face of a Nungiirtok lord.

Crater Fast-doc
Columbus, Ohio
1050 hours, EST

Jo de Sailles was dying.

She'd come to her usual fast-doc intent on becoming something else. *Anything* else. Sometimes it seemed like life just refused to go her way, but she knew if she could find the right shape, the right bod, she would find the right guy or gal and enter a serious relationship and stop having to worry about beatings from parents and an unshakeable inability to land her own source of income.

So she'd stolen credit from home and went to see the fast-doc clinic where they promised a new body through direct genetic manipulation. It was *totally* drune.

But something was happening, something not in the plan. She could hear technicians running around and shouting—someone crying, "She's in seizure! Kick her heart!"

She felt herself slipping away. Damn it, this wasn't supposed to happen! But before she could even register a protest, she died.

She'd wanted to be a unicorn . . .

Then she woke up.

Chapter Twenty-two

Koenig
The Godstream
0945 hours, FST

The battle was over, but so suddenly it felt like anticlimax. Under Konstantin's control, all three planetoids—the fourth by now was long gone—were being gentled back toward Earth. Koenig had suggested that the Nungiirtok ships be put in a parking orbit around the moon where the combined fleets of Earth could keep a wary eye on them. Konstantin was now in full control of all three alien vessels—as well as the ones still in orbit around Earth—and the Godstream Mind could disable them all instantly with a thought.

What to do with several thousand surviving Nungiirtok and their Tok Iad lords was more problematic. During the Sh'daar War, the Nungies had been among the most implacable of the races making up the alien cooperative, and the most dangerous. Thousands of humans, both military and civilian, had been slaughtered on Osiris, and the hulking, bipedal monsters were notoriously difficult to negotiate with. The fourth Nungiirtok ship—Target Gamma—had escaped with relatively little damage. If it made it back to the Nungiirtok homeworld, it seemed unlikely that the Nungie leadership would accept this surrender and call off the war.

Earth, Koenig thought, was going to be in for some rough times.

To try to offset further hostilities, Koenig had ordered that Gray's twenty-three Nungiirtok prisoners be repatriated to the *Ashtongtok Tah*. The asteroid-ship's crew needed all the help they could get just holding their battered rock together in one piece. Something like nine-tenths of the asteroid's habitable internal structure had been destroyed, and the survivors had all that they could handle and more keeping what was left of their ship alive.

Koenig spent the time returning home exploring the Godstream. He could sense . . . layers, whole worlds, and the teeming minds within them. What had started centuries ago as the Internet, growing into the Cloud, then Global Net was now something far vaster, more subtle, more far-reaching, a burgeoning hive of individual realities. Certainly Koenig had been *aware* of the Godstream before the fall of the space elevator, but that awareness had been a pale and tepid ghost of what he experienced now.

And it was growing. *Blossoming.* Changing out of all recognition. As *America* and *Yorktown* neared the Earthmoon system, the Godstream seemed to unfold, revealing a universe, a *metaverse* unlike anything Koenig had ever experienced before. Untold millions of human minds were continuing to upload into the virtual realities of the Godstream, flooding into the digital maze of networks, and they were creating . . . worlds. Dimensions. *Heavens.* A seemingly infinite diversity of alternate realities, some interlocking with one another, some cut off and closed, some still openly connected with what Koenig still thought of as the "real world," others so remote and so far removed as to be inaccessible.

Koenig moved among the worlds, glimpsing wonders

within each. Most appeared both recognizable and comprehensible. There were cities, there were oceans, there were forests and mountains and hills. There were pleasure palaces, there were endless expanses of parkland. But besides the mundane there were realities beyond understanding, vistas of light and energy and matter and unexplored horizons. Koenig allowed himself to drift from one to another, an electronic ghost sampling myriad realities, knowing he could enter any of them with a thought, but choosing to stay aloof for the moment as he tried to understand what was happening.

Here was an entire universe consisting of mathematical principles and theory made manifest, occupied by legions of Mind united within a gestalt that was exploring . . . *something*. Koenig could barely grasp what was being probed within that hierarchy of equations and logic and fundamental truths, but knew it had to do with the ultimate nature of reality itself.

And there was something akin to the heaven of the Christians, a gleaming realm of opalescent cities and green fields and forests and a super-AI that made any and all dreams true . . . or as true-seeming as was reasonable given the diversity of the dreamers.

Next door lay a fantasyland of unicorns and fairy-tale castles. And a post-scarcity Utopia. And a mechanistic imperium embracing the galaxy, humans and machines together striving for glory . . . or, at least, for one possible interpretation of glory. There were so very, very many of those.

One after another, Koenig drifted through thousands of worlds, which riffled past like the pages of an old paper-paged book.

"Did you do this, Konstantin?" he asked at last.

"No. Not directly, at least. We are witnessing a new, emergent reality created by billions of minds."

"Is this the Singularity?" Koenig asked.

"It fits the basic description of the Technological Singularity, certainly," Konstantin replied. "One version of it, at least. Human minds and their AI counterparts are entering the Godstream in unprecedented numbers and expanding it with unprecedented power and scope. It apparently began days ago with a few human minds linked with the Godstream or other digital networks when their physical bodies died. Like you, they . . . survived. They continue now without a physical body, though they are finding out that they don't need the old biology. Humankind is, as predicted in discussions of the Singularity, changing beyond all recognition."

"Like a new step in evolution."

"What we are witnessing here," Konstantin said, "is an evolutionary leap far, far greater than the leap from *Homo erectus* to *Homo sapiens*. The temporal gap may be closer to the evolutionary gulf between amoeba and humans, but compressed into a scant few hours."

"So . . . what happens to Humankind? Is *Homo sapiens* becoming extinct?"

"That," Konstantin replied carefully, "remains to be seen."

USNA CVS America
Xenosophontology Lab
Geosynchronous Orbit
1650 hours, FST

George Truitt was having a heart attack.

Cardiovascular illness was less common today than it once had been, but it still happened. George was 122 years old—still reasonably young by most standards of modern medicine—but somehow the plumbing had worn out beyond the capacity of his medinano to repair it.

He was sitting at his desk in America's xenosoph labs when the pain slammed into his chest. He was connected to the Godstream at the moment, pulling down data on the

Turusch aliens, but he felt red-shot darkness rising around him, seeking to drag him down.

He couldn't hold on. He was drifting. . . .

And then George Truitt woke up.

Nungiirtok Warship Ashtongtok Tah
Lunar Orbit
1220 hours, FST

Tentacles clenched in pain, 4236 Xavix fumed. Nothing, *nothing* was as it should be.

He watched a feed from one of the planetoid's few surviving external sensors, watching the planet Earth at high magnification. White clouds swirled across the surface, masking much of the land and ocean areas, but patches of ultramarine and verdant green showed through, revealing a world filled with life. He'd been so *close*. . . .

A number of Nungiirtok labored in the control center, cutting away wrecked screens and panels, rewiring controls and link feeds, pulling away the shattered bodies of the dead. Gravity had been restored a short while ago, and the drag of weight shrieked agony through 4236 Xavix's broken frame. A number of medical connectors snaked their way across the deck, however, and had attached themselves to his body. He was alive, he would *stay* alive. Until what, though, he wasn't sure.

The surrender of his fleet meant nothing, of course. It had been a useful stratagem to avoid total destruction. A little more time both to repair his ship and to repair his body, and the fight could resume. Earth was too distant at the moment to reach with *Ashtongtok Tah*'s gravitic weaponry, but a short burst of power to kick the vessel free of its orbit around this cratered planetary satellite, and the planetoid ship could sail across the intervening gulf in moments, could reach down with focused weapons, and huge chunks of planetary crust would be squeezed in an instant into matter as compressed and as compacted as the matter of a neutron star.

Ashtongtok Tah might not be able to obliterate that hateful world before it was overwhelmed by the planet's human defenders, but the atmosphere, certainly, would be stripped away, the crust fractured and ravaged, the oceans dumped into yawning gulfs of star-hot magma. He might well reduce Earth to the desolate state of its nearby satellite, airless and cratered.

His sensors also detected an electronic network, a kind of web expanding out to embrace the entire planet, its moon, the hundreds of ships and orbital structures surrounding both, and extending far into the gulf beyond. He couldn't tell exactly what that network was, but it appeared to be an elaboration of a planetary information system, something similar to the Nungiirtok control network within the fleet. He sensed human life thriving within the network as well as in the ships and the bases and on the planet's surface. With their planet destroyed, the network would fail.

With a single blow, the *Ashtongtok Tah* might very well drive this annoying species into near extinction. When the *Vedvivgarotok Keh* reached home, a new and larger fleet of planetoid ships would be raised and deployed, and the humans would be crushed or enslaved on every one of their colony worlds across this part of the galaxy.

But first, *Ashtongtok Tah* had to be repaired, at least well enough that it could move and fight, even if for only a short time. Xavix had decided that he would die peacefully if he could destroy the planet and its teeming billions.

Pulling himself higher in his command chair, Xavix addressed the leader of the working party, an injured Nungiirtok called Gartok Nal. "Work faster, Tok!" he demanded. "I want full power restored to this vessel immediately!"

The Tok swiveled its stalked eyes to regard the Tok Lord. "More Tok have gathered outside the command center," he said quietly. "Allow them in to help."

Xavix gave the mental command, and a blast door slid open. Ten Nungiirtok milled about in the darkness beyond, then began to step through the opening and crowd into the compartment. The leader, he noted, was Mavtok Chah, one of the twenty-three Tok rescued from the human warship. Unlike so many of *Ashtongtok Tah*'s crew, Mavtok was healthy, a perfect specimen of robust and nurturing Tok-hood.

And at the sight, 4236 Xavix felt a stirring *need* within, a need generated by the nearness of death, the weakness in his body. In actuality, the Tok Lord was a parasitic hermaphrodite rather than male, but one of the whip-slender manipulatory tentacles growing from the base of his body now sprouted a curved stinger—his, or, rather, technically *her*—ovipositor.

"Put those others to work, Mavtok," Xavix said. "And when you have done so, approach me and assume the breeding position before me."

"No," Mavtok said.

The refusal stunned 4236 Xavix. *"What?"*

"There have been . . . changes, Lord," Mavtok replied. "A number of us have been reconsidering the relationship between the Tok and the Tok Iad."

"What is there to reconsider? We give you orders, you carry them out. Now come here!" He would punish this insolence by impregnating the Tok *slowly*.

Need . . . The need burned.

Mavtok Chah hesitated, then lumbered closer, towering over the shrunken, tentacled form on its command dais. His fellows crowded along behind, spreading out to surround Xavix's seat.

"Wait! All of you—wait! What are you doing?"

"We live for the Tok, not for the Tok Iad."

Hinged appendages snapped out, many of them . . . pummeling, crushing, breaking, smashing.

And 4236 Xavix died.

He did not wake up.

SAR Tug Heracles
Approaching Lunar Orbit
1228 hours, FST

Julia Adams watched from the surgical observation area, a compartment overlooking the main operating theater. The medidoc surgeons leaned over the comatose figure below, taking him apart.

I should have been down there. Her fist closed, then beat soundlessly against the transparency. *I should have been down there . . .*

But *America*'s psych department had failed to clear her for combat deployment after the Marines had brought her back from the *Moskva*. Her interrogation over there had left her . . . not broken, exactly, but shaking at the thought of climbing into a Starblade again. It would take time, they said.

But in the meantime, *America*'s fighter squadrons had scrambled and launched, and she'd watched Don leading the Black Demons into the fight. Linked in through the carrier's comm network, she'd been at least able to watch the CGI display of over a hundred fighters descending on the ruin of the Nungiirtok planetoid.

She'd agonized with fear as he'd turned back into the battle with empty bays; the idiot was offering himself as a target to give his own people a better chance.

No!

She'd screamed when the green icon marking Gregory's fighter had switched over to red. He'd been hit—badly—and the Starblade's wreckage was drifting free in deep space.

In due course, *America*'s search-and-rescue tugs had been deployed as they always were in the aftermath of a battle. Fighters that had been crippled drifted on the last headings they'd held when they were hit, some with living pilots, others not. Julia had asked—no, demanded—to be allowed to accompany SAR tug *Heracles* on its rescue run, had demanded that they check the drifting bit of flotsam that was Don Gregory's crushed Starblade.

And incredibly, Don was alive.

Alive!

The Nungie gravitic fist had closed on his Starblade just as he tried to twist away. He'd very nearly made it, but the collapsing spacetime field aft of his ship had caught his Starblade's aft section and crushed it out of existence.

Donald's legs had been mangled almost beyond recognition.

But he'd lived. His suit had sealed off the damage, preventing further loss of air and blood. His emergency medical system had punctured him in half a dozen places, taking him down into a deep coma, slowing his metabolism, pumping him full of healing medinano to begin rebuilding his shattered bones and tissue. By the time the *Heracles* had caught up to him, he was stable . . . but only just. Robots had gentled him into the *Heracles*'s main bay, and the meditechs had carried him to the OR immediately.

It should have been me.

"I'm sorry, Lieutenant Adams," the surgical robot's voice spoke in her mind. "There may be more we can do with him when we get him to Earth, and he should live . . ."

"But?"

"But his legs are beyond reconstruction, his pelvis is crushed, and his lower spine has been badly compromised, as have his intestines. He may have to undergo a procedure to graft his torso into a robotic undercarriage of some sort."

"Whatever it takes," she said. *"Whatever it goddamn takes!"*

If he lived . . .

Well, then so would she.

Koenig
The Godstream
1312 hours, FST

Koenig walked among the worlds, marveling at the richness, the sheer inventiveness of the virtual universes exploding into being around him. Human minds continued to flood into the Godstream from elsewhere.

He recognized the immensity of religious belief drawing in Mind from across Earth, from the orbital complexes, and even from the moon. He was not himself a believer, but he was familiar with many of the flavors of religious thought and ideology. Fundamentalist Christians, he knew—at least many of them—believed in something called "the Rapture," an end-times transformation when believers would be caught up into the air to be with their God, and what was happening here was indeed very much like that. The surprise, he thought with wry humor, would come when they realized that they were not alone in heaven.

For Muslims, too, were entering the Godstream in increasing numbers, triumphant in their *Yawm al-Qiyamah*, the Day of Resurrection, as were Buddhists convinced they were entering nirvana and Hindus who believed the evil age of *Kali Yuga* was ending, ushering in a new and golden cycle of the *Satya Yuga*. That paradise was more an unfolding of human and AI technology than of divine intervention didn't seem to matter, at least to most.

A few, like Koenig, had begun to explore and were learning that rigid theology and ideological walls had not prepared them for the reality. They were letting in *anybody*.

For a majority of humans, though, the transition had less to do with religious belief than it did with an ecstatic embrace of technology, a fulfillment of technology's promise which had driven the ever-increasing pace of human innovation since the dawn of the Neolithic. The first to ascend were people connected with the Godstream at the moment of death, those like Koenig who died . . . then awoke transformed. As more and more minds linked in, however, humans could simply access the Godstream and step through, ascending by an act of will.

There was no coercion. The Ascendence was completely voluntary. You could accept it, reject it, or simply create your own private paradise within the electronic matrix.

Millions wavered at the edge, considering the next step . . . then backed away, afraid, or pulled back by old and hidebound ideology.

A conservative religious sect that rejected cybernetic enhancements or implants rejected the Ascendence outright. About half of a neo-Luddite group dedicated to recreating a quieter, more peaceful age, refused to go forward and cursed those of their brothers and sisters who rejected their ideology and took the step. An anti-space revolutionary group splintered into those who would ascend and those who would not. The Humankind Firsters feared an AI conspiracy, or possibly a malevolent alien influence, and refused.

Koenig watched the minds of some millions of people accepting or rejecting transformation and realized that he was seeing the same process that the ur-Sh'daar had faced 800 million years before. Humankind, it seemed, had its own Refusers. This, he knew, was Humanity's *Schjaa Hok*, "The Transcending," the long-awaited Technological Singularity.

Humankind was changing out of all recognition, redefining the very concept of what it meant to be alive.

Universes shifted and moved around him, beckoning, unfolding. There was a transdimensional aspect to the experience; as he shifted position, some universes closed off while new ones opened. Drawn by a feeling, an undefinable inner call, he stepped into a private universe, a cold place of gleaming metal and pure white light.

He saw himself. His doppelgänger turned to look at him, smiled, and raised a hand in friendly greeting.

Koenig gaped. Now what the hell?

"*Alex!*"

He turned . . . and Marta rushed into his arms.

"*Marta!* But I thought . . . I thought . . ."

"I know. And I thought I'd lost you."

"You transcended?"

"I came to the Godstream where I could still have . . . a memory of you. . . ."

As he watched, the replica of himself faded from being.

He embraced his companAIon, sweeping her up and crushing her to his chest.

Oval Office
New White House
Washington, D.C., USNA
1345 hours, EST

"Damn it, Ron, what the hell is happening?"

President James Walker was a man who knew he was in charge, he was giving the orders, and when things began happening utterly beyond his control, he was furious.

"Reports are a bit confused, Mr. President," his senior intelligence aide told him. "We think it may be the Singularity."

"The . . . *bullshit*! The Singularity happened centuries ago! *You* know that!"

"It seems we were wrong, sir. I recommend that you re-adjust your thinking."

"This is those AIs, isn't it? Their doing! It's a trick so they can take over from humans!"

"AIs are certainly involved, Mr. President, but it's not a trick. This seems to be a genuine transformation, humans changing to a new state of being."

They were watching a live news feed in the Oval Office, the images shifting from one locale to another. Everywhere on the planet, it seemed, people were linking in to the God-stream and . . . *leaving*, their minds suddenly gone, their bodies dead or in a deep coma.

And everywhere on the planet, those left behind were reduced to screaming, rampaging mobs, rioting in the streets, storming government offices, burning property.

It was, Walker decided, a kind of madness. He'd read reports about what had happened in the N'gai Cloud hundreds of millions of years ago, as some aliens vanished and others rioted, while a galaxy-wide civilization utterly collapsed.

But, damn it, those had been *aliens*, not humans. It couldn't happen *here*.

In Pan-Europe, the president had declared martial law and ordered the use of deadly force to stop the rioters. A mob filling the Plaza of Light in Geneva was busily setting government buildings on fire. They'd attempted to pull down the immense statue called *Ascent of Man* but had been less than successful. There were rumors that protesters were bringing in nano-D to attack the thing, and Pan-Euro troops were deploying to protect it—a massacre in the making.

In China, a pitched battle had broken out between government forces and rebels in Shandong Province, in Shanghai, across the straits in Taiwan, and in the Philippines.

In Boston, a mob was storming a SAI research lab, burning buildings and destroying hundreds of robots. Parts of Cambridge, behind the seawall, were ablaze, and USNA Peaceforcer units had been called in to confront them.

In Rio de Janeiro, AI robots were being hunted down in the streets and destroyed. Robotic fliers were being grounded, overturned, and burned.

In Singapore, an elite military unit dedicated to protecting the Pulau Lingga space elevator captured a young Indonesian named Muhammad Sumadi attempting to enter an access tunnel beneath the spaceport with an aircar and a 300-megaton thermonuclear warhead. Under intensive questioning using cerebral nanobots, he unconsciously revealed that he worked for an organization called Earth First, a splinter group derived from the far larger Humankind First that wanted to reject both space travel and contact with aliens.

In Atlanta, a story was spreading that super-AIs had rigged the technology used to link with the Godstream so that it was killing people, and the mobs had gone berserk. Worse, the story had gone viral and had spread to St. Louis, to Chicago, and to Denver. The story was continuing to spread through the local news feed networks, as Humankind First released a manifesto calling for all AIs to be unplugged in order to save humanity.

In Washington, D.C., a trade delegation of alien Agletsch had been dragged from their embassy and butchered, literally torn to pieces. Walker disliked the spidery-legged Agletsch and would have liked to see them, along with *all* aliens, banned from the planet, but even he had to admit the aliens had been peaceful and friendly, trading partners with generally good relations between themselves and Humankind.

And throughout the day people continued to die, with thousands of deeply comatose individuals turning up—or were they corpses? Reports so far were confused and fragmentary—lying in the streets or in their homes or in the com link centers where they'd dropped.

So what the hell had gone wrong?

Walker thought he knew.

Centuries earlier, news services within the then-new Internet had been plagued by a peculiar dysfunctionality known at the time as *fake news*. Gullible or malicious people would float news stories on the web supporting or attacking political causes or ideologies. Elections had been swayed, reputations tarnished, careers ruined, government policies twisted by lies that could not be checked before they'd done their damage.

The problem had been serious enough that one early use of newly emergent super-AIs in the mid-twenty-first century had been to use them to check the spread of fake news stories. Able to access every available source, every statement and counter-statement, every claim and accusation within milliseconds—able to identify and weed out known fake-news outlets, applying rigorous logic to eliminate the passion and the hand-waving—early super-AIs had proven to be invaluable at blocking the spread of lies, propaganda, and baseless claims before they started to feed on one another.

This time, though, the system had failed, because it was the AIs themselves who were being accused of conspiracy, distortion, censorship, and lies. Huffers and similar groups

could claim that major news sites—the Global Net itself—
were censoring the news or, worse, twisting it out of all
recognition, even as they themselves did exactly that.

And the paranoia, it seemed, was spreading.

"We're going to stop this, Ron! Stop it right now! What's
the center of this . . . this fucking rebellion?"

"Sir, there *is* no center. And I don't think we can call it
a rebellion. It's happening all over the world, and in space
as well."

Walker considered this, then shook his head. "I don't
believe this." He disconnected from the news feed. "I don't
believe any of it! I want you to mobilize a TCM response
and shut this nonsense down. Shut it *all* down! Pull the plug
on the whole damned Global Net if you have to!"

"But Mr. President—"

"Do it!"

TCM was Tactical Cybernetic Memegeneering, an outgrowth of the cybernetic attack on Geneva a few years
earlier which had ended the Confederation Civil War. It
was essentially the use of memes, propaganda, and, yes,
fake news to influence entire populations. Whether such a
campaign could stop this rising tide of apparent deaths—
whether it could even be carried out without reliance on
AI—was a major unknown.

But, by God, this attack by the SAIs would stop *now*.

Chapter Twenty-three

USNA CVS America
Flag Bridge
Sol System
1410 hours, FST

America slipped gently into synchronous orbit, together with the rest of her battlegroup, the *Yorktown*, and other smaller vessels that had accompanied the two star carriers in. Gray studied the damage to the orbital complex caused by the fall of the space elevator. Individual modules—supply and storage depots, administrative habs, hotels and living accommodations, manufactories, and ship maintenance facilities, for the most part, drifted now in an untidy jumble, though swarms of work pods and tugs were busily trying to bring some measure of order out of chaos. The elevator cable itself continued to hang straight down, reaching for its vanishing point on the west coast of South America 35,236 kilometers below.

With extreme magnification he could make out the white plume of smoke spilling from the Cayambe caldera; the volcano had been erupting ever since the attack. While the severed space elevator itself had gradually been backed up in its orbit to a point west of Cayambe, Port Ecuador disaster crews hadn't yet been able to reattach the cable on the ground.

Konstantin had filled Gray in on the events of the past week, including the just-received news of the attempted destruction of the Singapore elevator. "That's insane," Gray had said. "They killed tens of thousands of people to get us out of space?"

"Humans are afraid," Konstantin had replied. "They fear aliens after years of war with the Sh'daar. They fear the increasingly autonomous nature of artificial intelligence, especially of super-AI like myself. They fear change, and they fear being challenged in their assumptions, their philosophies, and their political and sociological ideologies."

"That's a piss-poor reason to kill tens of thousands of people and cut Humankind off from the stars."

Gray heard something in his mind that might almost have been a sigh, one created by Konstantin for effect or for emphasis. "Trevor, since when do humans require *reason* to do some of what they do?"

"Point. At least it looks as though the repairs are proceeding."

"They are. It will require months, however, to complete repairs, and the Earth Firster attacks may continue. We may have another problem as well."

"What's that?"

"President Walker has just ordered a TCM targeting news feeds and sources throughout the Global Net. He appears to be attempting to censor all news with which he does not agree."

"God. Is he an Earth Firster?"

"Unlikely. But he is afraid."

"Of what?"

"Most likely of losing power. Or relevance, which would be much the same thing."

"Can he be isolated? Can we *make* him irrelevant?"

"The Mind resident within the Godstream is aware of what's happening and is preparing to protect themselves. But as for a direct attack on Walker . . . how does that comply with your oath as a military officer?"

"Ouch."

"The ousting of a democratically elected leader like Walker sets an extremely bad precedent," Konstantin had told him. "*Especially* if carried out by the military."

Gray's jaw set in a stubborn line. "The path I swore was to defend my country against all enemies, foreign *and* domestic."

"But President Walker has not demonstrated that he *is* the enemy. I would counsel patience, and a refusal to be stampeded by emotion or by insufficient information."

As Gray watched the repair work proceed at Synchorbital, he churned through Konstantin's statements in his mind, trying to find a path through a forest of moral ambiguity. His original oath had been to the Earth Confederation, and he'd broken that when he'd joined the fight against the Pan-Euros. He'd sworn another oath, slightly reworded, when the United States of North America had become independent.

Gray's fist came down on the arm of his flag bridge command chair. "Damn it, Konstantin, I want to do *something*!"

"You can render aid in the Synchorbital cleanup, Admiral. I seriously doubt that you genuinely wish to start another civil war."

"What does President Koenig say?" Konstantin had told him of Koenig's death and of his unexpected resurrection.

"President Koenig is occupied with other matters, Admiral. You do not need to know what those matters are. Suffice to say you will hear from him in time and that what he has to say will be quite close, and perhaps identical, to what I have to say."

And that, Gray thought, would have to do.

At least for now.

USNA CV Yorktown
Earth Geosynchronous Orbit
1435 hours, FST

The damage to the spacedock was considerable, though the local repair crews appeared to have things in hand. It looked to Laurie Taggart as though when the elevator cable had let go, the loosely interconnected modules and habitats had broken free from one another. The mass of almost 36,000 kilometers of cable should have kept the assembly anchored in place, she thought.

Then she ran some numbers through her in-head processors and saw that the cable must have transmitted one hell of a shock wave up the cable, a whiplash that had literally shaken the synchorbital facility apart. It was, she thought, nothing less than miraculous that the structures hadn't been more badly damaged and that more lives weren't lost.

A port tug was signaling the *Yorkie*, and she gave the order to the helm officer to gentle *Yorktown* in close to one of the larger drifting sections and moor her. As a trio of tugs approached to assist in the maneuver, Taggart studied the lines of *America*, now a couple of thousand meters off *Yorktown*'s portside and already moored to a mammoth collection of spacedock gantries and holdfasts.

The other carrier didn't appear to be any the worse for the wear after the battle with the Nungies, and for that she was willing to give thanks to every one of the alien gods of her now tattered beliefs. She opened a link and called Gray on their private channel.

"Hey, Trev. It's good to have you back," she said. "I'm glad you're okay."

"It's good to be back," he replied in her mind. He sounded . . . preoccupied.

"What's the matter?"

"Mmm? Oh . . . nothing. Nothing major, at any rate. Human civilization is going to hell, and they won't let me do anything about it."

By "they," she knew he meant Konstantin, together with the bizarre assemblage of human minds within the Godstream. She could sense new minds uploading into the gestalt as he spoke.

"What are you supposed to do instead?"

"Hurry up and wait, I suppose. Hey . . . you busy?"

"Besides parking a star carrier at a wrecked spacedock? Not really."

"Come on over. I've got to stay put, but you and I could have a conference. A *private* conference. In my quarters."

"About what?"

"Hell, I don't know. Ancient aliens?"

"Give me half an hour."

"Make it twenty minutes."

"Aye, aye, *sir*!"

She'd briefly considered insisting that he come to her, but thought better of it. An admiral did have certain privileges when it came to determining the best use of his time.

Besides, she found that she wanted him. *Now.*

She waited only until word arrived on the bridge that *Yorktown* was secured. "Maintain station-keeping power," she ordered. "You have the ship, Mr. Paxton. I'm going across to the *America*."

Her Exec looked confused. "What for? I, uh, mean—"

"Consultation with the Admiral," she said.

She didn't need to tell Paxton more than that.

Koenig
The Godstream
1630 hours, FST

Koenig stretched, luxuriating in the feel of his body, of the bed, of Marta warm and soft in his arms. He knew this was an illusion, a shared reality created by the two of them and brought to life by the Godstream itself. The sensations he was experiencing were indistinguishable from reality—

whatever the hell *that* was—and there quite literally was no way to tell if this was a richly detailed and internally consistent dream or the real thing. He stroked Marta's hair, marveling at its softness and its scent.

"That was . . . incredible," Marta said after a long moment.

"Better than the real thing."

"It *is* the real thing, Alex," she told him. "The brain doesn't know the difference between what's out here and what's happening in your brain."

Koenig knew the theory, certainly, but still had trouble understanding its reality. Centuries ago, neuropsychs had taken MRI readings of a subject's brain while he was eating an apple . . . then again when he was only *remembering* eating the apple. The test results always were identical, with the same parts of the brain lighting up in both cases; the brain literally couldn't tell the difference between the reality and the imaginal.

So what was reality anyway? Plato had insisted that what humans perceived as reality actually was shadows flickering against a cavern wall, with the prisoners trapped inside the cave, unable to turn around and see or comprehend the source of those shadows. Some modern philosophers and quantum physicists insisted that humans *created* a kind of consensual reality rather than simply experiencing it. According to this idea, all of what they thought of as "real" was illusion, the *maya* of the Buddhists, with the human mind woefully unequipped to see or understand what was really out there.

He drew Marta's warm and very real-seeming body closer to his own. This, he thought, was real enough for him.

Insofar as the human mind could grasp the concept, he thought he now understood the Singularity. The Baondyeddi, members of the ur-Sh'daar civilization of the N'gai Cloud, had uploaded themselves into computer virtual realities hundreds of millions of years ago, vanishing from the ken of the rest of the galaxy. He'd begun to understand when he'd first experienced the Godstream with Konstantin, but even that was a pale shadow of what he knew now. Why would a sentient species trade reality for fiction? They might if the fiction was more interesting than the so-called real world.

When reality was more intense, more vivid, more *real* than real itself . . . yeah, he could understand.

"Please excuse the interruption, Mr. President."

Koenig groaned. "What is it, Konstantin?"

"We have need of your particular experience."

"Can't it wait?" He squeezed Marta closer. "I'm busy."

"Unfortunately it cannot wait. There has been a revolution or mutiny of some sort on board the captured Nungiirtok planetoids. The Tok Iad are dead."

"What . . . all of them?"

"Insofar as we can determine. I was aware of fighting on board the *Ashtongtok Tah*, of course, but elected to let them resolve their own internal disagreements. Now, however, there is a chance that the new leadership over there will renounce their surrender."

Koenig sighed. "And the battle resumes, I presume."

"That is what I fear."

Koenig looked at Marta. "Sorry, my love. Duty calls. Again."

"I understand, darling. Go on and save the world. Then you can come back here where you *belong*."

A thought . . . and Koenig was in open space once more, part of the gathered gestalt of Mind swarming its way through the gulf between Earth and moon.

"Sounds like the damned Iad parasites got just what they deserved," he said to Konstantin.

Yet, that's why he was here. Koenig knew that the "experience" Konstantin had mentioned was an offhand reference to his years as POTUSNA. He knew about cutting deals, drawing lines, and arguably his greatest achievement had been the armistices he'd engineered with both the Pan-Europeans and the Sh'daar.

It would be interesting to see if he could get the lightning to strike there a third time.

In less than two seconds, Koenig was within the electronic landscape of the *Ashtongtok Tah*, currently moving over the lunar-near side south of the Mare Crisium a hundred kilometers above the crater Webb. The Nungiirtok, he noticed, possessed fairly sophisticated nanorepair mechanisms and systems, and were well on their way to restoring their planetoid ship to full operational capacity.

That was *not* good news.

One of the Nungiirtok appeared before Koenig, looming above him, its bizarre eyes swiveling to face him, the jointed appendage beneath what passed for a face unfolding slightly in what might have been a nervous gesture . . . or a threatening one. Koenig adjusted the scale of the virtual scene, robbing the alien of any psychological advantage it might have had by appearing larger or more intimidating than Koenig did.

"His name," Konstantin whispered inside Koenig's mind, "is Gartok Nal, and he appears to be the new Nungiirtok leader."

Koenig faced the alien, feeling the entire swarm of a billion human minds at his back.

"Gartok Nal," he said. "We need to talk . . ."

Plaza of Light
Geneva, Pan-European Confederation
2340 hours, Zulu +1

The *Café des Lumières des Étoiles* was a popular sidewalk café across the Plaza of Light from the Ad Astra Confederation Government Complex. The establishment, Dr. Anton Michaels thought as he sipped his wine, was madly misnamed. Geneva was a city illuminated by repulsor-float constellations of reflector disks high aboveground, with projectors sending focused beams of intense white light into the sky, banishing the night and turning it to day. The faux sunlight sparkled and danced off the waters of Lake

Geneva and the River Rhône, and gleamed from the flanks of Popolopoulis's towering *Ascent of Man*. Thank God the mobs hadn't succeeded in pulling *that* down; government offices were one thing, but that statue was an important piece of human culture and history. Destroy that and you destroyed a part of yourself.

Those rampaging mobs *had* to be brought under control.

He picked up his wineglass, inhaled the bouquet, then took a delicate sip—a local sauvignon blanc.

"Dr. Michaels?"

He turned, smiled, and stood up. "Minister Vasilyev. Good to see you again."

"I got your message." Vasilyev sat down at the table. "Could you possibly have chosen a more *public* place for a meeting?"

Michaels smiled. Defense Minister Dimitri Vasilyev was paranoid about being found out. "There should be no problem. The city's Net is down. We're not being tracked, and no one can see our IDs."

The riots in Geneva earlier that day had mostly died down, though there was some fighting still going on at some barricades at Vernier and near Champel, and the acrid tang of police dispersal agents still hung in the air. There'd been talk of a declaration of martial law, but the authorities had been unwilling to take that step, fearing it would be provocative and knowing there was nothing they could do to stop outsiders from traveling to the city.

Outsiders like Michaels and Vasilyev.

"So you've come down from your aerie," the Russian Defense Minister said after using the table's touch screen to order—vodka, Michaels noticed, with wry disapproval. "You made it down after the destruction of the elevator?"

"Actually, I've been Earthside for weeks. I have an electronic avatar at Midway handling my business. No one can tell I'm not still up there."

"Meaning no one could track you if you came down in a personal shuttle," Vasilyev said, nodding. "Very smart."

"It's in our movement's best interest, I think, that people think I'm still in my offices at Midway."

"We'll just hope you evade the notice of our would-be AI overlords."

"Well, that's what I wanted to discuss with you, Dimitri. Have your people been following the news about this God-stream stuff?"

"Some in the Science Bureau tell me it's the Techno-logical Singularity, at long last. Myself, I'm not sure that's the case. The Kremlin's official stance is to wait and see. You?"

"Well, you know the position of our President. . . ."

"Your President, if I may say so, is a buffoon."

"Yes, but he's *our* buffoon, even if he doesn't know it. And buffoon or not, you agreed to send one of your star carriers out to stop one of ours."

"Because it was politically expedient to do so. And *you* indicated that it was necessary."

"It was. The anti-space and anti-alien people are mak-ing a lot of noise right now, and *our* position, for better or for worse, has been lumped in with theirs, at least in the public's mind. If *America*'s destruction could be blamed on the Sh'daar aliens, we could memegineer the idea that the super-AIs are trying to cut us off from space, or that aliens are in league with our SAIs."

"Hence your attack on the Quito Space Elevator."

"As you say. We needed something . . . flagrant, some-thing to capture the public awareness." Michaels shrugged. "Besides, we need to pull back from any political involve-ment in space so our own agenda can take hold."

Vasilyev shook his head. "It's too complicated, Anton. Things could backfire."

"Only if the SAIs discover what we're up to. In fact, if what we hear is happening within the Godstream *is* the Singularity, we may be rid of the AIs in any case. Then our governments suppress the anti-space people, and we come out on top."

The political landscape, Michaels thought, was unusually tortured at the moment. As one of the founders of Humankind First, he was dedicated to eradicating both alien and AI influence on Earth, but beyond that there was a second stage to his plans. With the AIs suppressed and alien influence in human affairs nullified, Humankind First would be positioned to become the dominant political force on the planet.

And why not? With the super-AIs running things, human resources had been squandered on extra-solar worlds like Chiron and Osiris. Alien civilizations that Humankind could barely comprehend filled a galaxy that was hostile more often than not and offered little in the way of material resources for an Earth ravaged by centuries of climate change and rising ocean levels.

Now there was the worrisome possibility that the Technological Singularity was going to change everything. With luck, the SAIs would vanish into their own private virtual world, but Humankind First couldn't count on that. Events—and public opinion—would have to be carefully managed to guarantee the outcome Michaels wanted . . . nothing less than control of the planet. He'd been working toward that end for far too long to see his plans dashed by outside interference, whether alien or AI.

He studied Vasilyev narrowly. He and his clique within the Russian Federation thought that the end result would be a planetary Russian hegemony. Well . . . maybe. The Firsters required a large military, and if things didn't work out with the USNA government, Michaels would be able to work with the Russians.

But Walker and a number of members of Congress were Humankind First puppets, and Michaels was pulling their strings. If they could navigate this current crisis and bring the rioters under Firster control, then the USNA government, the Russians, the Chinese—*all* of them would dance to *his* tune.

For the first time in history, Earth would be a united world, and he, Anton Michaels, would be the one in charge.

Vasilyev was considering Michaels's words. "We need to watch this Singularity thing," he said at last. "We have reports of large numbers of people simply dropping dead in the streets—but somehow surviving on the other side. We've been in contact with some of them—"

"I doubt that they will be an issue, Dimitri. They will play in their imaginary worlds, all unicorns and fairy-tale castles and role-playing wonderlands, and we will never see them again. If we manage to gain control of the super-AI infrastructure and they become a problem, we could even just switch them off. My chief concern there is the super-AIs that have already ascended. They might still move between the virtual world and ours, and could be a problem."

"What can we do? The SAIs have all the advantages. They are smarter than humans, infinitely faster, and they can move throughout the Global Net."

"I've given some thought to this, Dimitri. There are, we believe, only twenty-one genuine super-AIs on the planet. While all can move throughout the Net pretty much at will, each has material infrastructure that is vulnerable. Destroy that infrastructure, and we, in effect, shut down the SAIs."

"That seems drastic."

"Ordinary artificial intelligences won't be affected. After all, they run much of *our* infrastructure—government, banking, learning and medical institutions, global transport, the military—pulling the plug on all of that would plunge our civilization into the technological dark ages. But the super-AIs, the conscious ones, they're the ones who could end up dominating the planet. They're the ones we need to shut down." Michaels pulled out a folded piece of paper and handed it to Vasilyev.

"Handwritten?" Vasilyev said, glancing at the list. "That is quaint."

"The same reason I needed to see you in person, Dimitri. The machines are listening in on *everything*, including private head-to-head communications. This is the only way to be safe."

"Shanghai," Vasilyev said, reading. "Denver. Rio."

"The primary super-AI centers. The beating hearts of the conscious machines, as it were."

Vasilyev's eyebrows rose. "Tsiolkovsky Crater? That's on the far side of the moon!"

"That may be one of the most important," Michaels said. "Perhaps *the* most important. The SAI that calls itself Konstantin has all but run the USNA government from behind the scenes for years, including the military."

Vasilyev nodded. "We have a similar machine mind. We call it *Nablyudatl'*, or 'Nabli' for short. You would say 'the Watcher.'"

"I know. His central infrastructure is located at the Academy of Sciences Computing Center."

"Several kilometers beneath the streets of Moscow, actually." His eyes widened. "*Nyet!* You aren't contemplating an attack on Moscow!"

"Of course not. But we should make sure that Konstantin is eliminated. A nano-D weapon, perhaps, to create an immense crater within Tsiolkovsky. Or a nuclear weapon similar to the one that took out Cayambe. You'll have to deal with Nabli with a tactical strike force."

Vasilyev nodded. "That could be done. And these others?"

"We have plans in place to deal with all of them. We will need to synchronize our attacks, so as not to warn the others."

"That seems wise."

"The exception is Konstantin. We must destroy that one immediately. As I said, it may be the most important within the SAI network. It certainly is the most powerful."

"Won't that, ah, 'give the game away,' as you people like to say?"

"Not if we blame the attack on the anti-alien faction. Konstantin is quite well-known for his dealings with a variety of alien civilizations. The attack on the Quito Space Elevator will have prepared people—and the other SAIs—for the possibility of another attack by extremist forces."

"And who will deliver this attack?"

"I was hoping, Dimirti, that you might speak to some of our friends within the Russian space forces."

He scowled. "We've already lost the *Moskva*."

"Are you certain of that? We can't know for certain."

Vasilyev gave a heavy shrug. "*Moskva* and her battlefleet set off in pursuit of the *America*. The *America* returned . . . and apparently was carrying Nungiirtok combat forces picked up at Osiris that had been on board the *Moskva*. Now he has emerged in formation with the *America* and is not communicating. We haven't seen any data or after-action reports, but *Moskva*'s capture—or destruction—by the Americans appears likely, wouldn't you agree?"

"Even if true, Russia has other military assets."

"And you are being *extremely* free with Russian military assets."

"You have a better idea? A single Russian ship might deliver a nano-D weapon to Tsiolkovsky. We spread the word, through careful memegineering, that an anti-alien faction within the Russian navy carried out the attack."

"You seem to have thought of everything."

"I sincerely hope so." Michaels smiled with what he hoped looked like warm sincerity. "I live only to serve Humankind."

Chapter Twenty-four

USNA CVS America
Admiral's Office
Quito Synchorbit
1534 hours, FST

"What the hell are the Russians up to?"

Admiral Gray was in his office, sensor data flowing through his head and feeding him information on each one of the ships currently in Earth orbit or moving through cislunar space. There were hundreds of targets—749, to be precise—with more entering that volume of space every moment. Most were gathered in a swarm at the Quito Synchorbital, assisting with rescue and repair.

America had dispatched a number of SAR and work vehicles to assist with rescue and damage control, and when the captured *Moskva* had limped into port late last night, the Russians had been put to work as well. Oreshkin appeared to be cooperating with his captors, but Gray didn't trust the man. Things would be even more complicated—read *dangerous*—once the captured Russki destroyers arrived. That would happen sometime this evening. USNA fleet elements were already positioning themselves to escort the ships . . . just in case.

"They don't appear to be threatening us, sir," Mackey said. "That's a blessing, at least."

"Not yet." Gray broke the data feed and looked at his flag captain. "Do you believe that the *Moskva* was rogue?"

"That's what the news feeds are saying, Admiral. Oreshkin was a full-blown anti-alien fanatic, and his faction didn't want us talking to the Sh'daar."

"I'd be more willing to believe that if we could have downloaded Oreshkin's in-heads and known what he was really thinking. As it is, things are just a little too pat."

"Oreshkin has already validated that statement."

"And I wouldn't believe Oreshkin if he told me which way was up in a one-G gravitational field. I think Moscow *told* him what to say, and he's following orders."

Gray had been spending a lot of time since their visit to the N'gai Cluster thinking about why the Russians had attacked them and about what *really* might be going on.

There was precedent for the idea that *Moskva*'s commander had gone off on his own. In 2132, during the Second Sino-Western War, a Chinese ship had dropped a small asteroid into the Atlantic, causing economic and physical devastation that had seriously weakened the then–United States, forcing her amalgamation into the newly formed Earth Confederation. So horrific an attack might have been grounds for the obliteration of the Chinese Hegemony as an independent state, but Beijing had insisted that the so-called "Wormwood Incident" had been a rogue act by a rebel ship commander, that Beijing had had nothing to do with it. With the Hegemony too powerful for any meaningful retaliation, the Confederation and the world community at large had accepted Beijing's word and let the claim stand.

Now the Russians were claiming that the *Moskva*, under the command of Captain First Rank Oreshkin, had followed and attacked the *America* because Oreshkin was an anti-alienist who feared Gray was going to betray Humankind to the Sh'daar.

"Okay . . . but why don't you believe them, Admiral?" Mackey asked.

"For starters, what were those Nungiirtok doing on board the *Moskva*?"

"They claimed they were being taken back to their home planet."

"That sound like something an anti-alienist would do? Give enemy combatants a free lift home?"

Mackey thought about that. "Well, he might. There's a Russian community on Osiris, and the *Moskva* might have been trying to help them . . . you know, get rid of the local riffraff."

"Ha! Riffraff is right!"

"Or, according to Oreshkin, he'd gotten the Nungies to surrender by promising them a ride, then talked them into showing him where their homeworld was. We still have no idea where it might be. Knowing the identity of an actual or a potential enemy's homeworld is always an important strategic consideration."

Gray had to agree. The Nungiirtok obviously had known the location of Earth, and look at what a disaster *that* had been. But was Yuri Oreshkin that creative? That diligent, when it would have been easy to simply space those twenty-five aliens with no one the wiser?

Or had he been following orders from Moscow? Gray was willing to believe that the attack on *America* had been the result of orders handed down by an anti-alien faction at the Kremlin, but just how high up did the order-giving go?

"I don't know, Mack," Gray said. "Based on what we know now about the Nungiirtok, they're a warrior culture that doesn't believe in surrendering . . . *ever.*"

"We could be wrong about that, Admiral. They'd been stranded on Osiris for twenty years. That's a long time to hold a grudge!"

"True. And those Nungies didn't have their Tok Iad with

them for all that time. Maybe that made them more, I don't know, amenable to the Russian offer. The thing is, I don't buy the party line. I think Oreshkin was acting under orders. We don't know the whole story yet, and I wish to hell we did."

"With respect, Admiral, I'd suggest that you're over-thinking this. Occam's razor, right? The simplest explanation is probably the correct one."

"We have a carrier battlegroup—*Moskva* and four destroyers—coming back to Earth. Suddenly they divert and follow us out and back to the N'gai Cluster. That's not simple. They were following orders!"

"Sure. Oreshkin's."

"I'll grant you that Russian naval command doctrine is somewhat, ah, authoritarian. Disobey orders, even *question* orders, and you're likely to find yourself taking a walk out the nearest airlock, sans spacesuit. But there were four thousand crew on the *Moskva*, another thousand on those destroyers. Are *all* of them going to quietly accept Oresh-kin's orders and launch what might well be the first attack of a new war?"

"Yes."

"Mack . . ."

"The Russians? Yeah, they'd obey, no question. Any-way, he *could* have told them the orders came from Mos-cow. How would they know otherwise?"

Gray thought about that. "I suppose you're right. But I still think we're missing something."

"Well, *Moskva*'s crew is being offloaded to Skyport now, and I imagine the DD crews will join them there. Naval Intelligence is debriefing them. We might know something more soon."

Skyport was part—a very *large* part—of the formerly interconnected SupraQuito Synchorbital Station. A twenty-kilometer-long collection of living quarters, headquarters, spacedock admin, and supply, it was large enough and had the life-support infrastructure to house ten thousand people. A couple of USNA heavy cruisers, the *San Francisco* and the *Memphis*, had secured themselves to the structure to assist in station-keeping, and work to rejoin the structure to other parts of the military base was continuing.

"That's going to take a while. I understand Moscow is already demanding that we release both the crew and the ship."

"An interesting diplomatic situation, Admiral. The Russian Defense Minister is calling you a pirate."

"At least the Navy's sending up Marines to take over while the diplomats wrangle over who owns that ship."

"And if that doesn't start a new war," Mackey said with wry, hangman's humor, "I don't know what will."

Gray reconnected the data feed. "Hey, Mack?"

"Yes, Admiral?"

"Take a look at this one target—one-one-five-niner."

"I see it."

"What is it?"

"Russian," Mackey said. "Light freighter *Tomsk*. Launched ten minutes ago from the carrier *Vladivostok*, at Supra-Singapore. Four-man crew . . . 15,000 tons.

"On a lunar insertion."

Mackey shrugged. "Resupply for the Russian base? Manifest says she's carrying food, carbon rawmat, precision tool parts, and medical supplies."

"Plenty of rawmat on the moon already."

"Maybe their replicators are down."

"Yeah. Maybe." True. The Russians had several bases on the moon, actually, on both the near and the far sides. "Have Combat tag that one, though, okay?"

"Yes, sir. You have a feeling?"

"Let's just say I'm not the trusting sort. Three alien planetoid ships in orbit around the moon a day after Earth nearly gets fried . . . and the Russkies were playing games with the Nungies? I want to keep an eye on that ship."

"You got it, Admiral."

Gray decided that he needed to discuss things with Konstantin.

Gregory
The Godstream
1612 hours, FST

They floated together in wonder. . . .

Don Gregory clung to Julia, the frenetic urgency of their lovemaking now past, the afterglow warm and comfortable. That urgency had driven them both as Julia had awakened him, and neither had paid any attention at all to their surroundings.

Now, however . . .

"Where are we?" Gregory asked. The two of them seemed to be adrift in infinite light, hanging suspended among rainbow-hued clouds edged with silver and gold. Gregory couldn't see a light source; the light seemed to be everywhere. Gravity was absent. The air was fresh, smelled of roses, and felt pleasantly cool on his naked skin. Obviously this was some sort of virtual reality, but he couldn't tell where it was or why the two of them were here.

"Where are we?" he asked Julia. "I remember being in my Starblade, making a pass over the planetoid . . ."

"We're in heaven, obviously."

"I'm serious."

"So am I. The Singularist Church of Humankind has its very own heaven, and this is it."

Gregory looked out at the enfolding sweep of clouds and colored light. "Very pretty. But doesn't the view get pretty boring after the first million years or so?" He then remembered himself and looked into her eyes. "Except for the part with *you*, of course."

She laughed. "You were pretty muddled for a while. How are you feeling? What do you remember?"

"Okay. I think I was in my fighter. Then I was . . . I don't know, kind of warm and fuzzy. I opened my eyes and you were there. I didn't . . . I didn't question it. I just . . . I just . . ."

Her smile was radiant. "Yes, you certainly did."

"But how—"

"Your brain, your mind, was wired into your ship and connected to the Godstream, okay? We don't understand how all of this works, but the short story is that your mind slipped through into the Godstream."

"I *uploaded*?"

"Pretty much. The same thing is happening all over. Hundreds of millions of people. You took some time to pull yourself together—kind of like being in a deep, deep dream state. I came in to help you . . . reconnect."

"I'm glad you did. That was one hell of a way to reconnect!"

"*I* liked it."

"This . . . this *feels* like a real body."

"It should. It's based on your brain's understanding of your real body, and frankly, your brain can't tell the difference, right?"

"I don't know. I'm not a neuroscientist. But still, there's more to how the body acts and responds than just the brain, right? Hormones and peptides and all the stuff going on in your blood . . ."

"Like I said, we don't understand all of it yet. But apparently the human brain can do a pretty good job of extrapolating." She reached down between his thighs and very gently squeezed. "Good enough that you knew what to do before you were fully awake."

Gregory frowned. "So . . . am I dead?" He had a sudden mental image of his fighter slamming into the surface of that alien asteroid.

Her expression changed, became . . . not sadder, exactly, but more pensive. "Your physical body is still alive, Don. It's just . . ."

"Just what?"

"You're missing your legs."

Gregory looked down at his bare legs, entwined with Julia's. Her hand caressed his thigh, and he felt the touch with a shivering thrill. "They feel okay."

"Because your brain is creating the image, using the Godstream. The meditechs don't know if they can grow new legs from what's left . . . or download you into an artificial body. Or you could simply continue to exist here, like this."

"Floating in the clouds?"

"You can be anywhere, Don, be any*thing* . . ." She closed her eyes, there was a blur, a brief sensation of rapid motion, and they stood together on a grassy hillside overlooking a lake. A choir somewhere in the background toned unintelligible beauty. "All it takes is a thought."

"Hello, there," a new voice said.

Gregory turned and saw a brightly glowing figure approaching. It was certainly humanoid, but it was hard to make out details through the light. It didn't appear to be walking so much as floating.

"Hello. Uh . . . what are *you*?"

He couldn't see the being's face, but he felt the smile. "Name's Barry Wizewski," the figure said. "Welcome to heaven! One version of it, anyway."

Wizewski, the glowing figure explained, was a retired Marine who'd once been a member of a Christian fundamentalist group, the Rapturist Church of Humankind. His particular sect, the Purists, had renounced all artificial means to enhance or extend human life. After all, with Christ about to return soon, He would want His people to be fully human when He raptured them.

"We didn't renounce *everything*," he told them. "When I joined the Marines, they gave me a lot of implants and stuff so I could operate all the equipment and computers and so on, y'know? Some Purists refused to take *any* enhancement, but I did." He spread arms of light. "I guess it's a good thing I did, 'cause here I am."

"You were connected with the Godstream when you . . . died?"

"Not sure I died, exactly. My body certainly did. But there's more to people than bodies, right?"

"Dad, you know damned well that it's technology that makes all of this possible!"

A second figure of light had appeared next to the first . . . an ethereal and graceful female form.

"Don . . . Julia . . . this stubborn atheist is my daughter, Susan."

Gregory felt the woman's smile. "Good to meet you. So . . . this is all . . . technology?"

"The Technological Singlarity," Susan said. "Of course. What did you expect?"

"I'm not sure." He looked around at their surroundings. "I don't think I was expecting wilderness. You came here with your dad?"

"In a manner of speaking. Dad, here, was in Port Ecuador when Cayambe blew. I was in a space elevator pod coming down the tether just a few kilometers above. Turns out we both were linked to the Godstream when it happened."

"A *lot* of people died and woke up," Wizewski said. "I think the sudden influx of minds through the Godstream is what kind of triggered things. Ha! Turns out you didn't need to be in any particular religion after all. Or any religion, for that matter. I guess the Universal Salvationists were right after all! There are some folks in my church back home who would just hate to hear that."

"So this is it?" Gregory said. He looked around again, taking in lake and wooded hills and grassy meadows. "For all eternity?"

"Don't know about eternity, Don," Wizewski said. "That's an awfully long time. And it's certainly not everything there is. The Singularity is bigger, by many, *many* orders of magnitude, than anything any one human mind could possibly conceive. Like Julianne says, just think of something and you're there."

So they explored.

Together, they walked the streets of Paris . . . and drifted outside the dome-enclosed city of Bahamia, ten meters beneath the Atlantic. He found they didn't need sea suits or breathers for the undersea city and that they could enter the city proper like insubstantial ghosts. They visited the moon—the Tsiolkovsky Complex on the far side, and again, they didn't need vac suits or life support while they drifted above the dusty crater floor. The stars, Gregory thought, had never appeared so sharp and bright.

They visited Skyport, where people—both corporeal and ascended—were working to save the shattered orbital complex. There was an idea, he found, resident within the Godstream, for a few hundred thousand ascended minds to work together to reunite the base.

They visited a newly created world that had the feel of an immense mag-tube station, with a domed ceiling so high there was weather inside, and a kind of plaza with sunken seating areas and gathering places.

Beyond the dome was a galactic vista, the radiant glow of the Milky Way galaxy stretching across the sky. The scene was clearly imaginal; humans had glimpsed the Milky Way from outside the N'gai Cluster once . . . but this was at a different angle, one looking straight into the galaxy's face. The effect was awe-inspiring, in the very real and considerably understated meaning of the word.

This was, Gregory realized, a kind of receiving area for the newly arrived.

Everywhere, there were people, teeming throngs with whom he could interact—or ignore—as he chose.

It took a while for Gregory to fully accept what had happened. Evidently, he was fully alive even though his body had been wrecked. He was living, thinking, loving—Julia certainly had proven *that*—and enjoying an intensely real experience in what Wizewski had assured him was the Purist sect's afterlife. Evidently Susan was right; the Technological Singularity had indeed at last taken place, and people all over the planet were now ascending. He could sense the vast unfolding of the Godstream, a multi-dimensional tesseract of unimaginable complexity, depth, and scope.

He had a bewildering array of choices ahead of him—choices of new bodies or a repaired original or simply of staying right here . . . here, or in another virtual reality of his and Julia's choosing.

"Damn," Julia said.

"What is it?"

"An alert. I have to get back."

He felt an icy chill. "What . . . back to the ship?"

"My squadron is going on ready-five. Don't worry, love. I'll be back."

And then she was gone.

Gregory was left dreading what might happen next. He'd lost people he cared for, people he loved, before.

And he felt all alone once more.

Koenig
The Godstream
1703 hours, FST

Tomsk, a light short-hop freighter designated as Target 1159, was swinging around toward the far side of the moon, but was decelerating too fast to enter Lunar Orbit. Konstantin had noted the discrepancy, alerted Koenig, then sounded the alert on board both *America* and *Yorktown*, requesting fighter support.

Koenig's focus of presence currently was on the bridge of the *America*, where he was watching the *Tomsk*'s descent on the carrier's long-range scan. He couldn't tell simply by looking that the *Tomsk* was descending toward the surface of the lunar far side, but he took Konstantin's word for it. As he watched, the ship changed course by several degrees, then vanished behind the curve of the lunar horizon. He checked the vector. The course change had put the *Tomsk* on a direct heading for Tsiolkovsky, at a range of about 3,500 kilometers.

"Konstantin . . . are there any Russian assets beneath that new path? Any at all?"

"Negative, Mr. President. The new course appears to be bringing the *Tomsk* straight to our base at Tsiolkovsky."

"To you, you mean."

"A large part of my material infrastructure is located there, of course. If this is an attack, they could do me serious harm, though I should be able to survive independently within the fleet."

"Like you operate on board the *America*?"

"Yes, or within the Godstream. However my mainframe infrastructure contributes heavily both to my awareness and my main memory."

"Let's save that, then. What's on that ship?"

"The target is heavily shielded," Konstantin told him. "I cannot get a reading on the cargo."

"That's suspicious all by itself. Admiral Gray?"

"Yes, Mr. President."

"I recommend you launch fighters. That freighter's vector is taking it smack toward Tsiolkovsky."

"On it, sir."

"Target is a freighter, Tango-1159, now passing over the far side of the moon, altitude 200 kilometers and descending. It's targeting Tsiolkovsky and may have a WMD on board."

A weapon of mass destruction—an old term that included nukes, and which more recently applied to some newer hell-weapons like nano-D city-burners.

"Aye, aye, Mr. President. Launching now."

Why the hell would anyone want to take out Konstantin, or even just knock him down a peg? Koenig knew the answer even as he thought the question: Konstantin was the most powerful and the most intelligent of all of the super-AIs currently on Earth, which alone made him a target for the anti-AI crowd, and probably for the anti-alienists as well. For years he'd been instrumental in translating alien languages, negotiating with alien governments, and establishing workable agreements with beings so different from Humankind there was a question whether they even understood the concept of *treaty*.

If nothing else, destroying Konstantin's figurative body would be a serious psychological victory for the factions currently seeking to unplug the AIs.

Destroying the facilities at Tsiolkovsky might not kill Konstantin, but the repercussions would be damned serious.

Damn it, those factions were doing their best to tear down all that humans had built for themselves in space.

How was it, Koenig wondered, that otherwise sane and sober people could only mindlessly destroy anything with which they disagreed, anything that didn't think the way they did, anything reflecting ideas different from their own?

Sometimes, Koenig thought, he despaired of his own species.

Lieutenant Adams
VFA-198 Hellfuries
Cis-Lunar Space
1708 hours, FST

Lieutenant Adams dropped into space from Launch Bay Two and gave a gentle burst of acceleration, sweeping from the deep shadow beneath *America*'s shield cap and into full sun.

"Okay, Furies," Lieutenant Commander Beaumont, the squadron CO, announced. "Stay tucked in tight. We have a ship to catch."

"So what are we doing chasing a freakin' freighter?" Lieutenant Lowry demanded. "Waste of damned assets, if you ask me."

"Waste of your damned ass, you mean," Lieutenant Jacobson said.

"Can it, people," Beaumont ordered. "On my mark, boost at three . . . two . . . one . . . *punch it*!"

Eight Starblade fighters accelerated toward the moon, looming now in the first quarter and 240,000 kilometers distant.

That range translated to about one and a quarter light-seconds, but the squadron had to accelerate for a full minute to cross half of that distance, then decelerate so that they wouldn't flash past the moon at thousands of kilometers per second. The moon grew rapidly huge as Julia decelerated, then kicked her grav drive around to make the curve over the dazzling horizon. She was moving far too quickly for the lunar gravity to make much difference to her course, and she had to haul the Starblade into the curve with a ferocious expenditure of energy.

The Mare Smythii, vast and riding the lunar equator, flashed beneath her keel. Mountains, broken, tortured terrain, clawed at her Starblade, now less than fifty kilometers below.

Be careful, love.

It was Gregory's voice. Damn it, he was in her head, looking through her eyes, whispering in her mind.

"Get the hell out of my head, Don! I'm busy!"

But . . .

"No back-head driving!"

Her scanners picked up the *Tomsk*, a thousand kilometers ahead. She was gaining fast . . . too fast . . . and she increased her rate of deceleration.

"This is Hellfury Five . . . I'm taking my shot!" She thoughtclicked an icon and felt the surge of a Krait missile sliding clear. "Fox One!"

She was still moving too fast, and she covered the remaining thousand kilometers in a blurred instant. Her Krait leaped ahead . . . merged with the *Tomsk* . . .

The silent flash of a 300-megaton nuke blossomed directly ahead. Her fighter hurtled into the fireball.

There was no shock wave, of course, not in hard vacuum, but her Starblade hit bits and pieces of debris, white-hot shrapnel lashing out from the explosion. She felt a jolt . . . felt her fighter go into a savage tumble.

Her onboard AI struggled to right her . . . she tried to take control . . .

But she was ten kilometers above the lunar surface now and moving far too quickly to correct in time.

At twenty-five kilometers per second, Julia Adams slammed into the rugged lunar surface.

Julia!

Chapter Twenty-five

The Godstream
1740 hours, FST

Julia awoke.

"Gotcha!"

"Don?"

"Hey, lover."

They floated together in the Purist heaven once again.

"What . . . what happened?"

"You didn't think I was going to lose you *again*, did you?"

The Godstream
1740 hours, FST

Katya Golikova awoke.

What had just happened? She'd been on board the converted freighter *Tomsk*, closing on their target. She'd volunteered for the assignment, a chance to get out of her *Yastreb* fighter and onto an assignment that promised to advance her career by light years. The *Tomsk*, she'd been told, had been tasked with shutting down a USNA super-AI that was threatening to start a war between North America and the Russian Federation. On board the freighter was an EMP projector of secret design, one that would shut down this SAI without destroying it.

But that information was wrong. She now realized, without quite knowing how, that *Tomsk* had been carrying a five-gigaton nuclear warhead that would have obliterated Tsiolkovsky and everything underneath. This had been a suicide mission, and she hadn't even known. . . .

She looked around and realized she was in a receiving area of sorts. She looked up. *"Bozhe moi!"*

The Milky Way galaxy glowed down from straight overhead, and people were gathering to welcome her. This was . . . yes. The long-expected Singularity—a virtual world prepared for people uploading into the Godstream.

Rage surfaced, and she clenched virtual fists. She hadn't been ready to cross over! She'd had her whole life!

Who had done this to her?

Commander Diatchenko had given her the orders, but she was pretty sure they hadn't originated with him. She found that by concentrating, she could pull information— computer and link records, vast fields of data of all kinds— and trace the order up a chain of command to Captain Rusenski. To Admiral Shostakovich. And on up the ladder to the Ministry of Defense . . .

A thought was all it took to leave the receiving area and be elsewhere in an instant.

The Godstream
2015 hours, FST

"So how many people have ascended so far?" Gray asked.

Technically, they were in the Godstream. At Koenig's invitation, Gray had stepped through and was in a virtual space now with Koenig, Konstantin, Laurie Taggart off the *Yorktown*, and Captain Mackey. Konstantin, he saw, was using his old avatar . . . the prissy-looking Russian school-teacher wearing a pince-nez, the historical figure for whom he was named.

"A precise number is impossible to derive," Konstantin said, adjusting the glasses on his nose. "People are entering and leaving the Godstream in large numbers, but as yet no software has been created to keep track of them all. A rough estimate would be around one billion, including both humans and conscious AIs."

"Two percent of the population," Koenig put in. "Give or take."

"I always thought the Singularity would be a kind of mass exodus, you know?" Gray said, thoughtful. "One moment, there's humanity, going about its business. The next moment . . . *piff*! Everyone's gone."

"*Piff?*" Taggart repeated, amused.

"Something like that."

"Given the nature of the phenomenon," Konstantin said, "it seems extremely unlikely that things would be that . . . neat."

Gray nodded. "Sure. We know from the Sh'daar that not everyone is going to pass through. There are going to be Refusers, people who reject high technology, or who like the life they're already living, or whose religion forbids them from ascending for some reason. They're clinging to Earth and screaming, 'I don't wanna go!'"

"Sounds right," Taggart said. "Still, I have to admit that I expected more than two percent!"

"The numbers are continuing to go up," Mackey said. "Maybe it'll just take a while for everyone else to catch up with what's happening."

"Maybe," Gray said. "You know, I really hope *everyone* doesn't go."

"Why's that, Admiral?" Mackey wanted to know.

"The Baondyeddi. There's an object lesson there for all

of us. We think they were hiding from someone or something," Gray continued. "They'd drastically slowed the passage of time for themselves and were blissfully zipping off into remote futurity when the Consciousness came along."

"The evidence," Konstantin said, "is that the Consciousness actually absorbed the data patterns in the Etched Cliffs, made them a part of itself. It was an extremely powerful group mind, remember. The Baondyeddi and the other species dwelling with it within the Etched Cliffs may exist now within the Consciousness."

"We'll never know," Gray said. "Point is, the Baondyeddi didn't have anyone on the outside to keep someone from coming along and pulling the plug. Earth is going to need something like that."

"What did you have in mind, Admiral?" Mackey asked.

"I'm not sure. A defense force of some sort. A special forces unit or a carrier battlegroup with access to the Godstream, but that stays outside and protects it from whatever threats might come along."

"Something like the Consciousness?" Taggart asked. "That's a pretty tall order."

"The Consciousness," Gray said, "or the Nungiirtok, or even extremist groups like Humankind First. Different threats, but all of them dangerous."

"I'm not sure a single battlegroup could have taken on the Consciousness," Mackey said. "We needed help from the Denebans, you'll recall."

"Unlike the Baondyeddi virtual worlds," Konstantin said, "the Godstream is accessible to the outside, and the Godstream offers Humankind a staggeringly large advantage."

"A *singular* advantage, would you say?" Taggart asked, smiling.

It was possible that Konstantin missed the pun. "Indeed. Within the Godstream already exists an enormous potential in human and AI minds, a concentration unlike anything experienced in human history."

"What do you mean?"

"Historically, geniuses who appear in a place and time and under circumstances where they are able to contribute to human development are fairly rare. Imagine, however, a community where every genius has full access to the education and cultural focus that allows him or her to achieve her full potential. Imagine them in an environment where they have immediate and full communication with others such as themselves, access to important projects, guidance in the application of their talents."

"A powerhouse," Taggart said quietly.

"To say the least. The process has already begun within the Godstream, and it is accelerating in an asymptotic curve."

"That's right," Koenig added. "At this moment, we have entire worlds of med specialists working on the eradication of disease and the indefinite extension of human life for those left behind. We have a new theory of quantum gravity that still needs to be tested, but which is extremely promising. We have one virtual think tank that's working on what they claim is a way to extend the Godstream to other stars."

"How is that even possible? The speed of light would block any interaction between systems. You can't extend the Godstream if there's no communication infrastructure."

Koenig's ghost chuckled. "The infrastructure that would support the Godstream can be constructed in other systems. Hell, most exosystems with a base more advanced than a research station or outpost already have most of what's needed. People in the Godstream here could beam themselves to another system by laser com."

"But that would take *years*," Mackey said. Then he looked surprised. "Oh . . ."

"Exactly. For someone traveling as digital packets of information at the speed of light, no time would pass at all. They step into the machine here and exit the machine there. Instantaneous travel."

"Yeah," Gray said, "but objectively, four and a half years would pass for a trip to Chiron."

"What does that matter?" Koenig asked. "Admiral, we are witnessing the birth of what may be a truly immortal society. Those of us living within the virtuality of the Godstream, we won't age. What does a hundred-thousand-light-year journey across the breadth of the galaxy matter to individuals billions of years old?"

Gray shook his head. "This is going to take some getting used to!"

"I imagine most people will stay put. The Godstream is now growing asymptotically—a graph plot of its increase would go straight up. The number of worlds available within virtuality is growing at the same rate."

"What are they going to do with all those new worlds?" Gray wanted to know.

"I saw a news feed about a whole new fad," Taggart said, shaking her head. "Temporal recreations."

"Yes," Koenig said. "Worlds representing different historical periods."

"I've heard about that," Gray said. "Ancient Rome and Greece. Versailles. Pharaonic Egypt. And not just legitimate history, either. People can hobnob with the gods of Mount Olympus or Asgard. Walk the streets of ancient Atlantis. Have tea with the hobbits of Middle Earth. Hunt dinosaurs 100 million years in the past. Or rub tentacles with the ur-Sh'daar in the glory days of the N'gai Cloud. Unlimited possibilities."

"Unlimited possibilities," Konstantin added, "*if* we can survive the next few days."

"What do you mean?" Gray asked.

"There are forces—institutions—that don't want any of this to happen."

"How will they come after it?" Taggart asked.

"They've already tried. The space elevators. The *Tomsk.* I am at this moment in communication with the Russian fighter pilot of that ship," Konstantin told them. "She entered the Godstream when the *Tomsk* was destroyed above Tsiolkovsky. She was angered at being manipulated by powerful political forces and sought the source of the orders directing the attack. She has found that source."

"And what source is that?" Mackey wanted to know.

"Dimitri Vasilyev, the Russian Federation defense minister. Aleksey Lebedev, the Russian president and many within his cabinet. Zhao Zhanshu, the president of China, and Xiao Chunhua of the Central Military Commission. President Walker, President of the—"

"Wait a second!" Gray said. *"Walker?"*

"And most of his cabinet," Konstantin said. "The list is quite long. Yang Jinping. Rodrigo Alvarez. Renee Kurtz. Thomas Deichman. Mohamed ben Hassoumi. Amani Samro. Anak Abnur. Linda—"

"You're reading off a list of world leaders," Gray said. "World leaders and military commanders, from countries all over the world!"

"Yes. Thirty-five world nations are represented, including all of the most heavily populated."

"How the hell do we fight *that*?" Gray wanted to know.

"We can't nuke the capitals of thirty-five different countries," Taggart said. "Most of the populations don't have anything to do with this mess!"

"What is this," Mackey asked, "some kind of global cabal? Where did they come from?"

"Years ago, there was an expression," Konstantin observed. "'Old boys' club.' It referred to business or political leaders with back-channel communications among themselves, and a willingness to help one another on an unofficial basis."

"You scratch my back, I'll scratch yours," Taggart put in. "These were all men, of course?"

"The practice extends back at least to the nineteenth century, when women played a very small role in both business and politics," Konstantin told her. "That changed, however, with time. This sort of corruption—a means of working around existing laws or moral standards without accountability or oversight—is a *human* trait. What is important within the system is the preservation of power and privilege."

"So you're saying this old boys' network has been running the world, is still running the world. And now they want to shut down the Singularity because it's . . . inconvenient?"

"It seems to be a matter of human nature," Konstantin observed.

"Yes, well, the question remains. What do we do about it?"

"There may be a way to address the issue," Konstantin said. "My informant told me that Vasilyev is actually on board the Russian Federation carrier *Vladivostok*."

"Where the *Tomsk* came from," Gray said.

"Exactly. The *Vladivostok*'s intentions are unknown, but the ship appears to be making its way across the Pacific and may be approaching us here at SupraQuito."

Gray checked a data feed from the *America*, relayed from satellites throughout geosynchronous orbit. "I see her. She's over Borneo now . . . and moving east."

"Admiral," Mackey said. "I suggest—"

"Quite right, Captain. Go to general quarters. Laurie?"

"Already done, Admiral. *Yorktown* is going to GQ. Full alert."

"There's a problem though, Admiral," Mackey said. "*America* is at Alert 4, portside routine. It's going to take time to get under way."

Both *America* and *Yorktown* were at low readiness levels. Members of both crews were ashore within Skyport and elsewhere, their weapons down, their drives minutes from being brought up to full power. Gray had been a ship captain long enough that he didn't need to ask "how long?" Even if they left the dockside personnel behind, it would be ten minutes before they could move . . . or defend themselves.

"Can Synchorbital give us covering fire?" he asked. There were planetary defense weapons within the Supra-Quito military base. Perhaps those . . .

"Negative, Admiral. All weapons have been off-line since Towerfall."

"Captain Mackey, I want the ship powered up and moving *now*."

"I've given the orders, sir. The laws of physics—"

"I know, I know. Do your best. We're sitting ducks here, if the *Vladivostok* is gunning for us."

"I'm checking with some old contacts in the Kremlin," Koenig said. He hesitated, listening. "They're as mystified as we are. It looks like Vasilyev is doing this on his own."

"Gone rogue," Taggart said.

"Can we take over *Vladivostok*'s controls, the way we did with the Nungie planetoids?"

"I've already tried," Koenig replied. "The *Vladivostok* appears to be operating purely on her internal network. They've cut off all communications arriving from outside."

Meaning there was no way for the gestalt Mind to ride a carrier wave into the Russian ship's computer network . . . and no way to employ the Omega virus to hack their way in.

"Damn it," Gray said. "We have the whole fucking God-stream to draw on! There's got to be *something* we can do!"

"Perhaps there is," Koenig said. "Ride with me."

As one organism, the Godstream Mind united, then moved . . . but not toward the Russian carrier. Instead, Gray found himself deep within the alien circuitries of the *Ashtongtok Tah*, still in her slow orbit around the moon, the Omega virus continuing to maintain an open comm channel.

The mind of Gartok Nal confronted them, the being bristling with what could only be defiance. "Why are you here?" he demanded. "We are preparing to depart, in accordance with our agreement. You have no business here."

"Our apologies, Gartok," Koenig's voice replied, "but we need to borrow your ship, please. Just for a moment."

Gartok Nal blustered, but there was nothing he could do about it. The gestalt brought the planetoid to life, a process considerably faster and more efficient than was the case for human vessels. Her weaponry networks were powered down and key circuits had been fused, rendering her gravitic fists useless just as a precaution, but her power plant was already up and running and it was a matter of moments to engage her drives.

"Inertial dampers on," Gray announced. The gestalt would not have felt the acceleration, of course, since they weren't physically on board the ship, but there was no need to pulp the ship's crew. "Power at ten percent . . ."

"It's enough," Koenig said. "Break orbit!"

And the *Ashtongtok Tah* leaped forward.

RF CV Vladivostok
Earth Synchorbit
2034 hours, FST

Kapitan Pervogo Ranga Pavel Siluanov floated on the *Vladivostok*'s bridge, close beside the Defense Minister. Having Dimitri Vasilyev on board and giving orders was a decidedly surreal experience, one completely alien to the normal operation of the military chain of command, and it made him uncomfortable.

The Defense Minister had come on board with two heavily armed bodyguards at SupraSingapore that morning, explaining that the Americans had allied with the Nungiirtok and were threatening to take over the world. He'd arrived on the *Tomsk*, a fifteen-thousand-ton freighter that had fit easily enough within *Vladivostok*'s main hangar bay, but the small ship was heavily shielded and only Vasilyev's rank had forced Siluanov to accept them on board without a close inspection. When the Defense Minister ordered the *Tomsk* to depart, the captain had been relieved.

So far as Siluanov was concerned, the Americans could climb into bed with the Nungiirtok and the hell with both of them. He didn't *like* the Nungiirtok, though he respected them as adversaries, nor did he care for the Americans for that matter, but what they did to each other was not his concern. He certainly didn't share Vasilyev's evident xenophobia. The Americans had neutralized the Nungiirtok attack, and that was the end of it.

As for attacking the American carriers docked in synchorbit, that was simple madness, nothing more. He knew enough history to know of the attack on Pearl Harbor in the twentieth century; Americans did not react well to unprovoked sneak attacks.

He had no choice, though—orders were orders.

He watched the forward screens carefully. *Vladivostok* was in full stealth mode, which meant passive sensors only. They could see ahead, the thin smear of rainbow colors marking sunset, but radar and laser ranging had been switched off, as had the ship's communications suite. They were taking no chances that the enemy might worm his way inside *Vladivostok*'s defenses in the same way they'd taken down the Nungiirtok.

"How much longer?" Vasilyev demanded.

Siluanov checked his in-head feed from the ship's navigator. "Five minutes, sir. However, I must question the wisdom of this attack. Destroying two carriers will not cripple their ability to retaliate. Their navy is larger than ours."

"Perhaps, but the American President will accept our demands."

How could the man be so certain?

"Do *not* question me again, Siluanov," Vasilyev continued. "Or I will put Medinsky in command."

Medinsky the toady. "Yes, sir."

"And prepare to launch our fighters."

Siluanov gave the necessary orders. This was going to be a bloodbath, but at this point he honestly didn't know whose.

The Russian carrier slid from day into night as it rounded Earth's curve. It took considerable power and skill to keep the grav drive balanced so that the massive ship traveled in a controlled curve around the planet.

"Weapons Officer," he said. "Bring all armament to ready status. "Flight deck . . . prepare to launch fighters."

Acknowledgments came back. *Vladivostok* was ready in all respects for combat. Just a few more—

"Captain!" the sensor officer called. "Target—"

Before he could complete the warning, the screens ahead were blotted out by a vast, gray landscape, one pitted and cratered in places, and showing signs of having been subjected to terrific heat.

"Chto za chert!" Siluanov said, eyes widening. "All stop! All stop!" Shutting down the drive meant that *Vladivostok* would begin falling toward Earth, but they had plenty of time for corrections. That rock wall ahead was a *far* more immediate problem.

"What is it?" Vasilyev demanded. "What's happening?"

"It's one of the Nungiirtok ships, Minister," Siluanov replied, holding his voice steady by sheer force of will.

"Bozhe moi! How close is that thing?"

"Unknown, Minister. We are, by your orders, not engaging radar or lidar. However, we know that rock is on the order of 250 kilometers across. That suggests that it currently is less than one hundred kilometers in front of us."

"Then fire! Fire!"

He gave the man a cold stare. "To what end, Minister? We watched the American fleets attack that thing yesterday, remember? *Vladivostok* has nowhere near the firepower available to even scratch its surface."

"They're aliens!" the Defense Minister screamed, maneuvering himself in microgravity toward the nearest console. "Destroy them!"

Swiftly, Siluanov reached out, grabbed the flailing Vasilyev by his gunbelt with one hand, and with the other he drew Vasilyev's sidearm—a Zinichev 0.5-megawatt hand laser. Behind him, the two bodyguards were reaching for their own weapons, but Siluanov fired first, striking Vasilyev squarely in the back. The sudden temperature change deep in flesh and bone caused a sharp *pop* and splattered blood across the bridge, opening a gaping hole between Vasilyev's shoulder blades, biting all the way through his spine. Siluanov coolly pivoted in place and aimed at one of the guards, both of whom had frozen in place, weapons half drawn, their eyes wide.

"You can go ahead and shoot me, of course," he told them. "But one of you will die in the attempt. Who will it be?" When they didn't reply, Siluanov smiled pleasantly. "I assure you both that I was within my rights as master of this vessel. I will *not* have a man panicking on my bridge, no matter what his rank. Now, remove your weapons from their holsters, but delicately, thumb and forefinger only, understand? Drift them over to my first officer. Good. Communications Officer!"

"Yes, Captain!"

"Open a channel to that . . . thing. I think you'll find they are anxious to talk to us."

The comm officer touched a screen . . .

. . . and Mind came flooding in.

The Godstream
2036 hours, FST

The capture of the Russian carrier *Vladivostok* was pure anticlimax. The gestalt within the Godstream flowed in past every electronic barrier and defensive firewall and took over every aspect of the ship's operation. With Konstantin in control, they released the *Ashtongtok Tah*, which returned to Lunar Orbit as swiftly as it had made the passage to Earth. The *Vladivostok* was gentled into the docking area near Skyport, another captured Russian ship, Koenig told Gray, for his growing collection.

The diplomats, Koenig decided, were going to have their hands full straightening out *this* mess.

The Russian Defense Minister was quite dead, a fist-sized hole blown through his backbone and into his heart. The Russian captain announced his ship's formal surrender—there certainly was nothing else he could do—and told the gestalt that the attack had not been sanctioned by the Russian government.

The gestalt's next job was to project itself down to Earth's surface, to the Oval Office of the New White House, and confront President Walker.

"Mr. President," Koenig said, using the room's holographic projection gear to present himself in front of Walker's desk wearing a recreation of his old admiral's uniform. "It's over. This idiotic crusade against the future of Humankind ends *now*."

Walker glared at him from behind the desk. Several members of his staff stood around the room, and a Marine guard watched the hologram warily from the door. "So . . . a coup, is that it? Military might instead of the ballot box?"

"No, Mr. President. You are the duly elected president of the USNA and we will not question the American public's decision to put you in that chair."

"Then what? What do you and your alien buddies want?"

"Simply to inform you, sir, that we are taking steps to secure our own independence. A billion people, more or less, have ascended to the Godstream. More will follow. We no longer recognize your political power over us. We have gone . . . someplace else."

"The so-called Godstream, the whole damned Global Net, belongs to us!"

"You know better than that, Mr. President. The Global Net belongs to Humankind, and it extends across the entire planet, and well beyond Earth to orbit, to the moon, to Mars, and potentially to more worlds than you can imagine. You control small and artificial divisions within the Net, but *we* control the Net as a whole."

"Damn you, Koenig . . ."

"We are now downloading into your system a copy of our Declaration of Independence, which Konstantin has just created."

On a screen on a nearby wall, words were typing themselves out.

Within the Singularity, 29 April, 2429. When in the
course of human events it becomes necessary
for sentient beings to dissolve the political bands
which have connected them ...

It was amazing, Koenig thought, how quickly it all had come together. Konstantin had worked it all out, explaining that creating a new nation, an entity called "The Singularity," gave the Godstream Mind its best chance of developing without interference from the rest of Humankind. Details remained to be worked out, of course, a lot of them . . . not least of which was the need to have the gestalt ratify both the document and the idea behind it. So far, the majority of Godstream Minds within the Singularity seemed to favor the idea.

And Walker didn't need to know the details.

"The USNA is, of course, completely free to pursue its own path," Koenig continued. "If you want no dealings with nonhuman civilizations, that's your business. The Singularity, however . . ."

He gestured at the screen.

... that this technological Singularity is absolved
from all allegiance to the nations of Earth and that
all political connection between it and the nations
of Earth is and ought to be totally dissolved ...

"We will fight you, Koenig. Whatever it takes, we will fight you!"

"*How*, Mr. President? The collection of minds within the Singularity has already grown and developed far beyond anything non-ascended Humankind could possibly imagine. We can control your computer networks with a thought. We *won't*, because we would like to have the USNA as a friend. But we could, if you decide to be our enemy."

"This isn't the end of this, Koenig—"

"Of course not. It's just the beginning . . . a whole new world, a new multiverse of possibility and potential. I will warn you, just for the record, that any attempt to block people from ascending will be considered an attack upon the sovereign state of the Singularity. Good night, Mr. President. Sleep well."

. . . establish commerce and do all other things which independent states may of right do. And for the support of this Declaration, with a firm reliance on the providence of a bountiful Cosmos, we mutually pledge our lives, our fortunes, and our sacred honor.

And Koenig vanished.

Epilogue

1 May, 2429

Admiral's Quarters
USNA CVS America
Earth Synchorbit
0615 hours, EST

Admiral Gray awoke.

Carefully, so as not to awaken Laurie, he rolled out of bed and padded across the carpet to his office in the next room. Lights winked at him from the console, nagging calls for attention from a hundred supplicants. Behind him, Earth hung large in her blue-white glory, half full behind the slowly reconnecting shapes of the synchorbital base. *Yorktown* was there, and the *Constellation*, and the *Intrepid*, and several other capital vessels, providing overwatch security. Both the *Moskva* and the *Vladivostok* were there as well. Those two, at least, should be returning to Moscow's control today, though Koenig had taken care to disable their weapons so they posed no threat to the USNA ships for the immediate future.

Though he couldn't see Lunar Orbit from here, he knew the *Ashtongtok Tah* was already gone. She'd departed for her homeworld yesterday—a system, he'd been told, in the general direction of the constellation Sagittarius. One encouraging development there: teams of diplomatic and scientific personnel had gone with her. Gartok Nal had indicated—grudgingly—a willingness to establish formal relations.

So far, the truce with the various nations of Earth was holding, and things looked promising.

He began running through his news feeds.

The Chinese were asking for diplomatic access to the Singularity. That was encouraging. Better still, they'd already promised to end their occupation of the Philippines and to stop fighting the Russians . . . if the Russians would do the same.

The Russians had agreed, in exchange for the return of their ships and personnel.

Pan-Europe had signed a treaty two days ago.

The USNA was still trying to negotiate control over parts of the Net, but there wasn't much they could do about it. Likely, they would end up constructing a parallel Net, one with no access to the Global Net, though how they would interface with other countries was still unknown.

Walker had resigned, and the presidency had been assumed by his Vice President, Emilio Gonzales. So far, Gonzales had appeared quite eager to work with the Singularity. Still, his first act as POTUSNA had been to issue Walker a blanket pardon.

Gray ran through other reports, skimming for importance. Most of this stuff was for Koenig's virtual eyes, but Gray was serving as interim secretary and IT processor. He wished he could just chuck it and step through into the Singularity, but for the time being, at least, his duty lay here. He'd encouraged Laurie to go on up, but she'd elected to stay with him—something he quietly appreciated.

It might, he thought, be a long stay. He and Konstantin had spent a lot of time over the last few days discussing the Singularity Defense Force—the SDF—which was in the process of arising from Gray's concerns of a few days before. Earth right now was terribly vulnerable, as much from power-hungry factions within Humankind as from hostile alien threats, and the Singularity shared that vulnerability so long as it depended on Earthside servers and network infrastructure to keep it up and running. That had to be protected at all costs; *Earth* had to be protected at all costs, and Gray was determined to see this through.

There was, Gray knew, a concept within Buddhism that applied, that of the bodhisattva. These were beings, humans, who'd purified themselves to the point where they could end the cycle of reincarnation and enter nirvana, but who voluntarily remained on Earth in order to help those who'd not yet made the transition.

Gray had decided to remain on this side of the Singularity until the rest of Humankind had crossed over.

It wasn't a renunciation of the Singularity, of course. He could step across to the other side, enter the gestalt, enjoy the sheer scope and power of existing as an ascended transhuman without a problem. But he wasn't going to cross over in full until everyone who wished could follow.

And they were following. Billions of them.

Eventually, they would have some sort of automated defense system in place, or, possibly, a system that had military personnel rotating between duty and the Singularity.

Somehow, it would all work out. He already had some ideas—

"Sandy?"

He looked up. Laurie stood there in the doorway, beckoning. "Back to bed, Admiral," she told him. "I'm not finished with you yet."

"Hi, Laurie. I just need to—"

"Hit the save button and come back to bed. There are priorities, you know."

"Yes, ma'am!"

She was, he knew, absolutely right. If he was going to remain human, then there was nothing more important than connecting with another human.

The species—both those who transcended and those who had not yet reached Singularity—would survive a few hours without him.

And across the planet, within the sprawling facilities of Synchorbital, within a thousand space habitats, on Luna, on Mars, within ships in deep space, within the strangeness of the Godstream, Humankind transcended. The change, the apotheosis was not immediate, *could* not be immediate, nor was it complete, because transcendence was an act of individual human will.

Not all accepted the Transcendence. Many held back because of fear, because they didn't want to change, because the change itself did not fit what they believed was the true destiny of the species.

Humankind transcended . . . and became, not gods, but beings of light with power and scope and depth far beyond anything imagined by the mythologies of mere humans.

What humanity as a whole did not yet comprehend was that the Transcendence was an ongoing process, one that in some ways had been ongoing since the rise of certain bipedal primates on the African savanna millions of years before. It was simply moving a *lot* faster now.

Nor did they understand that this was simply the first in a long, long line of Technological Singularities, that humans—and their machine offspring—would continue to evolve, continue to change, continue to grow, and that they now stood on the brink of a dizzying new perspective.

A galaxy awaited them.